Lord Shallow

Eileen Putman

Lord Shallow

Copyright © 2020 Eileen Putman

Formatting by Wild Seas Formatting
(http://www.WildSeasFormatting.com)

This book grew out of a story published in 1995 as *So Reckless A Love*. It bears no resemblance to that book.

For Abby, who taught us to believe in miracles.

Such is the fate of simple Bard,
on life's rough ocean luckless starr'd!
Unskillful he to note the card
of prudent lore,
till billows rage, and gales blow hard,
and whelm him o'er!

Robert Burns

PROLOGUE

Summer, 1795
Summerlin House, Gloucestershire

From that darkest of days, the day by which he measured all others, it had always been Elizabeth.

"Why are you crying?" A small hand shook his shoulder.

Sebastian buried his face in the clover. He wanted to be alone. He had run far and fast from the faces that tried to comfort him, the solemn words as meaningless as they were brutal.

Doctor did what he could...both gone. Your cousin wishes you to know of his sorrow.

Sebastian knew William wasn't sorry. Feeling did not live in such a man.

Although Sebastian was only a boy, his legs were strong. And so he had run. He ran toward the horizon and the waning light that wouldn't last the hour.

Was that rain on his face? Not tears, surely. Traherne men did not cry.

His mother did, though. Usually her eyes danced with life, copper sparks shimmering amid the silver-green— except at those tedious family gatherings that came with disparaging remarks uttered without heed as to whether a small boy was listening.

Where did Gerald find her? 'Tis fortunate William's got Hubert next in line. With luck, she'll never be duchess.

Sebastian knew Faylinn heard. How else to explain why she fled up the stairs, why his father followed, calling her name in such a stricken voice?

Gone. Both gone.

"Boy," the girl said. "What is wrong?"

He raised his head. Her brown eyes filled with concern. He guessed she was about his age. Taller, but girls his age usually were.

Have patience, his father had said. The time will come when you will tower above them.

Gone. Both gone.

Sebastian batted at her hand. "Go away!"

Now he recognized her. He'd seen her in a carriage with a man he guessed was her father. "You're Elizabeth."

"Yes." A smile swept her features. "Who are you?"

Sebastian looked away.

But she caught his hand, and even though hers was smaller, he allowed her to pull him up. She started to run toward a large house in the distance.

Sebastian ran after her. He didn't want to go home. Home was where his parents lived.

Had lived.

What would happen to him? Where did he belong?

Not with William, surely.

His mother's family? He'd never met them. He didn't even know her family name. Pell, he thought, or some such. Who would take care of him?

Clover-scented air filled his lungs as Sebastian ran faster, relishing the exertion, for it pushed the questions aside.

"Boy!" she shouted as he swept past her.

Finally, she caught up, crashing into him. They went sprawling in a tangle of legs.

"What's this?"

The man he'd seen with her in the carriage stood over them. He had the same brown eyes. "You'll be Gerald's son. Sebastian, is it?"

Sebastian scrambled to his feet. He nodded warily.

The man's eyes filled with compassion. "Sir Bertram Throckmorton, lad. Our property marches with yours. I cannot think why we haven't met. No matter. Supper's ready. Come in, and bring that little hoyden with you."

Elizabeth giggled. Sir Bertram extended an arm to help her up. She grabbed it, and he swung her up and over his head. Her laughter had a joyous sound, like bells.

In short order Sebastian found himself sitting at the table with Elizabeth's family—Sir Bertram, and Lady Throckmorton.

The table was laden with cold gammon and jelly, fresh bread, greenish vegetables, boiled potatoes, a plum pie. Everyone talked at once. He absorbed the chatter without hearing it.

Once or twice, Sebastian saw Sir Bertram and his wife eye him with something that might have been pity. But no one asked him questions.

He was grateful. He had no words.

An incoherent swirl of emotions consumed him. Sebastian felt sick, sicker than he'd ever been—sick unto death, a phrase he'd heard in church without knowing what it meant.

Now, he knew.

Elizabeth said something that must have been funny, for her parents laughed. Her soft brown eyes shifted to him.

She was good, Sebastian decided. A friend.

He wanted her with him, always.

After dinner, Sir Bertram brought the gig around and drove Sebastian home.

To the place that had been home, but never would be again.

Chapter One

Spring, 1816
Anglesey, Wales

The arrow shot swift and true.

Instead of the villain who haunted Gwynna Owens's dreams, the lone elm near her mother's tomb stood as her target. Two dozen yards away, an easy shot. The next would be harder, for the rain had picked up, and with it, the wind.

Night had stolen the light, save for a sliver of moon that peeked from rolling clouds.

Gwynna focused on a tiny, irregular spot on the tree.

Nocking another arrow, she brought the bow up in one fluid motion. She drew the string, savored the pull on her muscles. Despite her size, she could hold full draw longer than most of her countrymen.

Darkness teased the spot in and out of view.

Now.

Relaxing her fingers, Gwynna let the arrow fly.

A precise hit. Had the elm been her nemesis, he'd have been dealt a mortal wound.

Her bow would attract notice on her journey. The dagger must serve in its stead. Gwynna pulled the knife from its leather sheath. The cloak covering her newly shorn hair slid back as she held up the blade, sharpened on the stones of the ancient tomb.

"Eryr digrif afrifid Owain…" Her mother's language. She repeated them in her father's: "Thou delightful eagle Owen—"

Rain pummeled her face, but Gwynna paid no heed. She raised her voice against the wind: "Thou art immortal, a wise and able warrior, and thy onset in the field of battle is terrible."

It was the first time she had uttered the ancient words since childhood. Silence had long been her due.

All the more reason, then, to fling the last lines to the hills: "May due authority, success, and praise attend the Knight of Glyn!"

Thunder boomed, as if Prince Owen himself echoed her battle cry.

Owen was her legacy, but this journey was in the service of a different legacy—one that existed in shadows and secrecy, maddeningly out of sight.

Gwynna turned toward the tomb and slid one finger over the deadly blade. A drop of blood spilled upon the dull, gray stones.

"Megan Glendower Owen," she said softly. "I will find him. I will make him pay for your pain. And I will make him help me rout the evil from this island."

Lightning flashed behind the tomb, as if the ancients urged her onward.

It was time.

Did truth lie at this journey's end?

This new path felt foreign and strange.

But Owen was with her. The ancients, too. Her mother.

All she needed was courage.

***

London

Four seconds and two strides lay between him and freedom.

Sebastian Traherne dodged the purple ostrich feather as its wearer nodded vigorously. Eluding feathery missiles was a skill he'd honed during an oppressive number of nights in the company of matchmaking dowagers like Lady

Hereford-Smythe.

Despite his best efforts, the feather grazed his cheek. Drat. His reflexes must be slowing.

He took the first of those two strides, now nearly beyond range of easy conversation.

Two seconds gone.

"Oh, I quite understand your discomfort, Your Grace," the lady declared, raising her voice to stay within earshot. "Perhaps you think it is too soon to begin thinking about your choice of a bride. I know how devoted you were to *dear* Elizabeth." Her beady eyes narrowed.

A bird of prey in a purple turban. How had she been permitted to leave her home in that garish monstrosity? Ah, but there were so few true stylists, these days. He should know. All of London followed his lead.

If only servants had the wherewithal to face down purple-turbaned ladies *before* they took that first, disastrous step into the evening, and declare, "Madam, that simply won't do."

Or, failing that, to extend a leg and cause my lady to take the slightest tumble—nothing fatal, but sufficient so she must needs retreat and seek a cold wrap around that ankle, sparing the ballroom the sight of that feather.

Three seconds gone.

She closed the distance between them, sending that plume perilously near his eye socket.

A blind duke. That would scare away matchmakers.

"Elizabeth's poor mother had such hopes for a match between you," Lady Hereford-Smythe purred. "But life does go on. And you have obligations, now, *Duke*."

Ah, there was the rub: Blind or no, a duke was a duke. And an unattached one was prime husband material. The devil take William for dying without producing a more willing heir.

Come to think of it, the devil *had* taken him.

It was no use hoping that dark angel would return his

cousin upon discovering him to be a cold, mean-spirited curmudgeon. William would give the devil his due.

Time had expired. Sebastian started the count anew. He'd give himself fifteen seconds and count backward, just to stave off tedium.

The matchmaking creature stared at him, her lips parted in a crocodile grin. She gestured to a young woman hiding behind her skirts.

Sebastian knew what was expected. An introduction, a dance. Flowers the following day, an afternoon call. The parson's noose drifting inexorably toward his neck.

But the new Duke of Claremont had no intention of being outdone by a rapacious mama hen. He pulled out his bejeweled quizzing glass, pausing to brush an imaginary speck from the lapel of his midnight evening coat.

Truly, he couldn't see a damned thing out of the glass. Nevertheless, he was now at twelve seconds.

He allowed an additional moment—two seconds!—for an ostentatious inspection of his coat sleeves and the strip of spotless white muslin at his wrists that echoed the snowy white of his cravat.

Ah, the cravat. The Throne of Love was his own masterful creation. He preferred *trone d'amour,* if for no other reason than to mock the *ton's* absurd envy of all things French—rich irony, since the two nations had been at war for centuries, give or take.

Regrettably, the cursed neck-cloth made it nearly impossible to move his neck. Indeed, he had spent an hour in front of the mirror last night, striving for ever more intricate architecture and height. What he had achieved was wildly inventive, and silly in the extreme.

Ten seconds.

Sebastian returned his attention to Lady Hereford-Smythe. He peered at her through his quizzing glass, having judged it a kindness not to take note of the timid creature behind her.

Favoring the woman with his haughtiest gaze, he did not dignify her speculation about what had transpired between him and Elizabeth.

Yes, he was cruel. No gainsaying that.

Perhaps one day his situation would cease to be of interest to the vultures who masqueraded as polite society. Yet he could hardly blame them, as he himself had planted the story that kept their tongues wagging.

Alas, the death of his obscenely wealthy cousin had but added to his allure by gifting him a title that was a magnet for misses with scheming female relatives.

Burns, ever present when least wanted, niggled at him..

The polish'd jewels' blaze
May draw the wond'ring gaze;
And courtly grandeur bright
The fancy may delight,
But never, never can come near the heart.

Best to keep one's heart locked in the dark dungeon of one's blackened and useless soul.

Ah, but *blackened* and *useless* weren't quite right, were they? Alliteration would better serve. *Beaten? Battered? Bruised? Bullied? Bedeviled?*

Plainly, poetry did not reside in him. Burns, God rest him, had nothing to fear.

Duty, devotion, discipline, denial—*that* was the alliteration by which Sebastian lived. Order above all. Messiness cluttered the mind, obscured the path.

The woman's features remained frozen in an expression of naked greed. If she held it for a moment longer, it might become permanent. Her death mask, perhaps.

Seven seconds! He shouldn't have allowed himself the luxury of Burns, much less his own pitiful poetic meandering.

Sebastian's gaze slid languidly to a spot across the room.

"Egad," he drawled.

"Is something wrong, Your Grace?" Lady Hereford-Smythe asked.

Sebastian pulled out his watch. He flicked open the case, with its entwined leaves in three kinds of gold: rose, yellow, and white. Carefully, he inspected the watch face, where tiny diamonds were embedded at twelve, three, six and nine o'clock.

Three seconds. Damned near a death knell.

From his lofty height Sebastian looked down at the woman. His brow furrowed, as if he couldn't quite recall who she was. "Please excuse me, madam. Lord Sidmouth has arrived."

She granted him an obsequious smile. "You must not let us detain you, Your Grace. I collect that you have important business with the Home Secretary."

"Indeed." Sebastian dismissed her with an idle wave of his quizzing glass. "He has most urgently requested the name of my tailor."

He melted into the crowd. Thus, he did not hear the softly terrified voice of Lady Hereford-Smythe's trembling charge as she ventured into the open at last.

"What is it, Auntie?" she asked.

"His Grace is excessively puffed up with his own consequence," Lady Hereford-Smythe replied acidly. "One would never consider such a prideful fop husband material were he not so very handsome and exceedingly wealthy."

"He is indeed beautiful," her niece whispered. "I wonder why his fiancée cried off."

The ostrich feather bobbed more vigorously. "Perhaps when he is not putting on a show for his admirers he is quite repellant." Her aunt's gaze narrowed. "It would take a strong woman to bring that one to heel, Hyacinth. You are not up to it."

"Certainly not," her niece agreed, aghast.

Lady Hereford-Smythe sighed. "Very well, then. We

must adjust our sights. I see a crop of eligible church mice in the corner. Perhaps *they* will not frighten you. Come."

***

"Unrest is all about, Claremont. Last week there were riots in Suffolk and Norfolk."

Sebastian emitted a bored sigh. Boredom was his endless lot these days. He was so bored, in fact, he might be dead.

Was it possible to check, somehow? If he stood before a mirror, would his reflection deign to look at him? Or would it be entirely too bored to show?

He'd give Sidmouth five minutes. Home Secretary, and all that. Former prime minister, as well, so perhaps six minutes. An eternity.

Already, Sebastian was studying the pattern of the parquet floor, plotting an escape route.

Sidmouth had stopped talking. He seemed to await a response. Sebastian sent his brain back a few seconds and retrieved a memory—riots? Yes, in Suffolk and Norfolk.

Was there a reason he should care?

Words. Sidmouth expected words from him.

Fine. He was a wordsmith *par excellence*. Had he not dazzled Metternich, Nesselrode, Wellington, and countless others with his verbal acrobatics?

Alas, Sidmouth was not one for acrobatics, verbal or intellectual. Simple concepts only.

"There have been riots in the country for years, Henry, courtesy of Ned Ludd," Sebastian said. "I fail to see why I should be concerned about an unruly mob in Norwich."

"I never mentioned Norwich. So you *have* kept up." The other man eyed him accusingly

Truly, being shallow required inordinate work. One ought never read a newspaper.

"These aren't Luddites," Sidmouth continued. "They could care less about machines. Down in Bideford, a kick-up erupted at the quay over a cargo of potatoes. The rioters say prices are too high. They claim people are starving."

Potatoes. Three minutes to extricate himself from a conversation about potatoes.

"Nonsense," Sebastian replied dismissively. "The riots are but cover for those who want to reform Parliament. Universal suffrage, or some such."

Did "suffrage" exist in Sidmouth's vocabulary? he wondered.

"Still, we cannot dismiss the uprisings, and now I am afraid you must deal with these matters directly," the man said. "Have you forgotten your new position?"

Sebastian surveyed the ballroom. He could see Lady Hereford-Smythe's beady eyes searching the crowd. The woman was indefatigable. "What is my cursed title to anything?"

"If you had bothered to respond to my emissaries, you would know the Duke of Claremont is Lord-Lieutenant of Cheshire—responsible for security, magistracy and so forth. Your authority extends to the border of North Wales. Both areas are ripe for unrest. The war depleted our security forces; there's none to send to restore order. You may have to form a militia."

"I have no wish to dirty Weston's best by breaking up potato riots."

Sidmouth scowled. "Inheriting a dukedom has made you too high in the instep."

"On the contrary," Sebastian drawled. He was proud of that drawl. It began in the low register—"on the contrary" must start low or lose its power—and drifted up past baritone before descending again with admirable finality.

"The rarefied *heights*"—Sebastian let the word bloom into full-on condescension—"have always been my milieu. If you must know, a dukedom is deuced inconvenient."

He eyed Sidmouth mournfully. "I've had to give up Wednesday nights at Almack's. The price on my head is too high. Matchmakers assume I'm in urgent need of a wife to spend my money. Before, I could move about at will. But now…"

Hell. That prideful little speech had cost twenty seconds.

Out of the corner of his eye, Sebastian saw Lady Hereford-Smythe marching determinedly through the crowd, dragging her unfortunate relative.

Sidmouth glowered at him. "I suppose what I hear is true—that you haven't lifted a finger to take up your new responsibilities. Shockingly, I've been told you've not met with the late duke's solicitors or taken the reins of your affairs, or been presented at Lords, or—"

"Perhaps you will enlighten me as to how that is your concern."

"Have you not been listening?" Sidmouth demanded. "Things are urgent. The old duke took so little interest that the area is ripe for conflict. There's talk of revolution. You served your country admirably in the effort abroad, but it is time you attend to your obligations here."

Obligations. It was the second time tonight Sebastian had heard the word, so he took a moment to parse it.

Obligation was not one's actual duty, but someone else's opinion of that duty. All of society might think he was obliged to be presented at Lords, but that was merely their view.

In fact, Sebastian was *not* obliged to don a taffeta-lined scarlet and ermine robe, carry a cocked black hat, and prance to the bar to kneel before the Lord Chancellor. Not that he didn't admire Lord Eldon, a tenacious supporter of the war effort, although his politics—like those of all politicians—were mutable.

Responsibility, on the other hand, was different, for it came from within. Responsibility dictated that he create unique neck-cloths and flaunt them. That he breeze through ballrooms in ten minutes or less. That he disregard someone's idea of his obligations.

That sort of thing.

Parsing had taken fifteen seconds, but it had been necessary to clear his head.

Sebastian stifled a yawn. "I cannot drop everything and set off for some godforsaken rustic corner. Why, I would miss the height of the Season."

"England needs you," Sidmouth insisted.

"I think not. As you say, I have already done all my country has asked."

Sidmouth drew himself up to his full height. As he was nearly a foot shorter than Sebastian, that did not have the desired intimidating effect.

"Your country wishes you to visit your estates. And, if it's not terribly inconvenient, to see to the welfare of those who have the very great misfortune of being your responsibility."

If only the man knew.

Time was up.

Lady Hereford-Smythe was in view. But that was not what caused Sebastian to suddenly search urgently for a different escape route than the parquet path he'd chosen.

No, it was another man, whose attention had evidently been caught by Sidmouth's posturing. A set of coal-black eyes fixed on Sebastian from across the room.

Andrew Maitland started toward him.

If there was anyone Sebastian wished to avoid more than that predatory purple feather wearer, it was Drew Maitland. Thus, he edged toward the door that led out to the balcony.

"Come to think of it, London is becoming a shade tedious at the moment," Sebastian allowed. "The countryside might be diverting, though I imagine it has nothing approaching an adequate tailor. Wales, did you say?"

"Cheshire," Sidmouth corrected as Sebastian disappeared through the balcony door. "Claremont, where are you off to?"

"Fresh air."

And, though the balcony was some fifteen feet above the ground, the new Duke of Claremont jumped nimbly down to the courtyard below.

Just in time.

***

Eerie figures marched in the night, silhouetted against the inky horizon by a sliver of moon. Torches flickered, held aloft by faceless members of the outlaw group. An occasional barked command caused the figures to turn abruptly and march in a new direction.

The moor's scrub grasses muffled the sound of their boots, but Gwynna could hear the men's grunts from her position on the slight rise above them.

She hugged her arms around her against the chill. Cold had seeped into her bones, no matter that it was the cusp of summer.

Perhaps it was just the strange spectacle below that caused her to shiver.

Gwynna usually relished the night. At home, she loved to watch the low mountains across the serpentine strait disappear as darkness fell.

But here, in this land beyond the mountains, the night was a sinister place of forbidding moors where strange men drilled in secret, preparing for unknown battles.

Her companion giggled nervously.

"Quiet, Anne," Gwynna whispered. "We don't wish to be discovered."

The brown-haired young woman at her side looked fearful. "Papa says it is dangerous even to speak of these men. What would he do if he knew we were spying on them?"

"They won't discover us. But your frock is light-colored, so best keep to the bushes."

Anne glanced at Gwynna's dark cap, tan breeches, and

brown shirt. "Perhaps I should have dressed as a boy, too."

Gwynna couldn't envision her new friend, endowed with a womanly shape, in breeches and rough-woven shirt. "It's easier for me to travel as a boy."

Anne regarded her sadly. "I wish you would allow me to tell Papa about you. I cannot bear to think of you sleeping in that old abandoned cottage night after night."

"I am grateful for the food you brought," Gywnna said. She had been down to a single piece of bread when Anne found her.

"Papa could help you," Anne said.

"But you say he does not know the duke."

"No one does," Anne replied. "He is said to be quite old, and lately I have heard rumors that he is sick. For years he has been shut up in that drafty castle."

Gwynna's gaze returned to the marchers. "I must see him."

"You will not tell me why?"

"It's a private matter."

Anne shook her head. "I hope you have the sense to give up your disguise before long. In the darkness, you can pass for a boy but during the day…" She trailed off.

Gwynna frowned. "Why not the day?"

"You are small like a boy, but your features are too delicate," Anne said. "You are brave to have traveled so far alone."

Gwynna studied the figures on the moor. They looked to be a rough sort. Instinctively, her hand moved to the hilt of her dagger. "What do you know of these men, Anne?"

"Some fear they mean to seize the crops rather than pay such high prices."

"They are clever to organize in this manner. The government would never countenance such meetings in the open," Gwynna said.

"'Tis said that what they are doing is treasonous," Anne said. "Papa called it sedition."

"Sometimes it is necessary to rebel."

"The way you talk is so strange. It makes me afraid."

Gwynna glanced at her. "Welsh have always had to fight for their rights, especially on Anglesey. The instinct for combat runs deep."

"This island of yours sounds very unusual."

"It's lovely. And yet..." But she wouldn't think about Evans now.

Footsteps crunched behind them. Anne gave a little shriek.

"Eh, Billy!" said a rough, masculine voice. "What have we here?"

The man's face appeared to have been smeared with coal dust.

"Stifle it, 'else you'll have the law on us. Let's have a look." Another blackened face peered from behind him. A slow smile exposed a coarse set of rotting teeth. "Just a scrawny lad and his wench. Pretty thing, too. What yer doing out here?"

"Taking the night air like yourselves, sir," Gwynna said in a gruff voice. "We have no more desire to bring attention to ourselves than you do."

This brought guffaws. "Lad's trying to scare us, Bill. Oughtn't stand for that."

"Watch out, Davey." The second man smirked. "The lad has spunk."

The men were so close Gwynna could smell the sweat and thistledown on their clothing. Her gaze flicked past them to the moor below. Pointless to hope for rescue. No one with good intentions traveled these moors at night.

One of the men held a length of rope. "If yer nice, laddie, you'll save your neck and your lady friend's, too. We'll even let you watch us with the wench here."

Instantly, Gwynna whipped out her dagger. The men stared at it, then laughed.

"Look at that old piece of tin, Bill. The lad's ready to

die for his wench's honor."

"Finish the upstart," his friend said. "I'll have me a bit of sport over here." He crushed Anne against him. She screamed.

Gwynna lashed out with her knife. But the other man grabbed her wrist and twisted it. The dagger sliced harmlessly through air.

With a rough laugh, he kicked her. Gwynna fell to the ground, stifling a groan of pain.

"Two fine manly specimens you are," she taunted, "hiding your faces and bullying people half your size. I give your revolution precious little chance if the rest are the likes of you."

"What do ye know of any revolution, laddie?" her assailant growled. "Don't remember mentioning it myself."

He snapped his rope taut. "This'll make short work of that scrawny neck of yers. Then there'll be no more talk about revolution."

"An utterly boring topic, in any case," drawled a masculine voice.

All eyes shifted toward the sound.

A lone figure on horseback surveyed them with an air of extreme ennui. Under arched brows, his eyes evinced only idle curiosity. Wind ruffled his sandy hair, giving him a rakish appearance at odds with his aristocratic clothing and remote demeanor.

Gleaming brass buttons on his midnight blue coat illuminated its precise fit. A snow-white cravat tied in an elaborate fashion bloomed at his throat. The buff riding breeches and banded dark boots were less showy, yet grander than any Gwynna had seen on Anglesey.

He sat atop a magnificent roan. Silver trim on its richly appointed leather saddle gave the enormous beast a princely air.

The rider himself looked to be well into his third decade. He was tall, for rider and horse together took up a large chunk of landscape.

Gwynna had never seen a London dandy, but he must be the epitome of the breed. He cut a strange figure here on the moor, yet eyed them as if they, not he, were the peculiar sight.

"As I suspected." He sighed. "No one here has the slightest idea how to dress."

The two ruffians stared at the apparition. "Madman," one muttered.

The horseman favored them with a smile. Then, as if noticing their particular circumstances for the first time, he tilted his head in puzzlement.

"Pray, is there some trouble here? I've no wish to ruin my travel clothes by embroiling myself in a local dispute."

Gwynna eyed him with contempt. This man was no rescuer, but a pretentious peacock.

"No trouble at all, yer lordship," one man said with a smirk. "Jest having a little fun."

The horseman's brow cleared. "Some eccentric game, I expect, that requires grown men to gad about with coal dust on their faces and tussle with two young persons in a desolate place."

Shifting uneasily, the men touched their faces. "We keep to our own business in Cheshire, mister," one snarled.

The horseman nodded. "Indeed. I'm afraid you are reputed to be most unfriendly."

The men rolled their eyes at one another.

"Which is why," the horseman added, almost apologetically, "I take precautions against inhospitable dispositions."

A silver pistol appeared in his hand.

His demeanor remained unchanged. He sat atop his great horse, gazing at them benignly, the pistol pointed at the men. Yet something about the way he held the weapon—as if it were a natural appendage of his hand—suggested he was an excellent shot.

Their assailants turned and fled into the night. The horseman eyed them mournfully.

"Such manners." He rubbed the pistol barrel with the tip of one elegantly gloved finger.

Anne nearly collapsed in relief. Gwynna put an arm around her. "All is well, Anne. They are gone. I do not think we have anything to fear from this pretentious prig."

"I am honored at your high opinion of me, boy," the horseman said. "Nevertheless, I appear to be cast in the role of knight-errant. As your mistress appears a trifle indisposed, I suppose I must help you get her home."

When neither of them responded, he arched a brow. "She does have a home, I trust?"

"You need not trouble yourself," Gwynna said gruffly. "It is not above a half mile."

Anne eyed her fearfully. "What if those horrible men return?"

"Precisely." The horseman dismounted. "Hold the horse, boy. You and I will walk."

In short order, he tossed Anne on the big roan and set the horse in the direction she indicated. Gwynna trudged beside him, relieved he hadn't seen through her disguise.

A quarter hour later, the horseman deposited Anne at her father's manor house. He said nothing until Anne was safely inside. Then he turned to Gwynna.

"What sort of groom lets his mistress wander across the moor at night?" he demanded. "Had it not been for the risk to the young lady's reputation, I would have insisted on informing her father of your lapse. I'd have sacked a groom who behaved thus."

Gwynna lifted her chin defiantly. "I am not her groom. 'Tis none of your concern."

"Would that were true. Regrettably, I've learned that everything here is my concern."

"How so?"

"Apparently, the cursed title comes with

19

responsibilities." He gave a bored sigh. "I'm hoping they're merely obligations I can disregard."

She regarded him scornfully. "Pray, are you someone important? To anyone besides your tailor, that is?"

He lifted a brow. "I do not take my tailor's approbation lightly. Indeed, he named his new horse for me. It's a high honor. But then, I am easily flattered."

The horseman's tone was mocking, but Gwynna could not tell if his target was her or himself. "You have not answered my question."

"Such a persistent imp. I am Claremont. Perhaps you can tell me where my castle is."

Gwynna stared at him. "Claremont? The *duke*?"

"You appear to be in awe. I ought to have mentioned it earlier. Might have spared me those barbs of yours."

Panic rose in her throat. "Impossible."

"That is what I've been telling myself these past months. Why it should affect you so, I cannot hazard a guess."

Fear that Gwynna had kept at bay during her long journey suddenly swamped her. She sank to the ground.

"You are too young," she protested.

"This grows tedious," the horseman groused. "Too young for what?"

"Too young to be my father."

The bored expression abruptly fled from Sebastian Traherne's face.

Chapter Two

"**W**hat duke doesn't know the way to his own castle?" the boy muttered as Sebastian hauled him up onto the horse. The imp clutched that rusty dagger but offered no resistance to his decision to take him to Claremont Castle.

"One who isn't obliged to explain himself to whelps like you." He nudged Captain forward. "It is this way, you say?"

"I think so," the boy mumbled.

Perhaps the lad was dropped on his head as a babe, which would explain his nonsensical talk. Regardless, Sebastian meant to get to the bottom of his wild ramblings this very night.

He was more than ready for the comforts of bed, not to mention the castle's other luxuries, starting with a glass of his cousin's finest brandy. *His* brandy, he amended with some satisfaction. Finally, something about this business to look forward to.

They rode in silence. Now and then, Sebastian felt the boy's slight form trembling behind him. Was he cold? Frightened? On the run from the local magistrate?

Wasn't *he* the magistrate? Sebastian had paid little attention to Sidmouth's ramblings, but he recalled nothing about outlaw boys. Still, who knew what went on in this godforsaken place?

Sebastian did know, with certainty, that he had fathered no offspring.

He wouldn't mind having a son and heir one day. But

if he recalled matters correctly, it was necessary to have a wife for the whole thing to work out properly.

Ah, but he already had one of those.

The ceremony in Vienna had been rushed, and not up to the shade of elegance that Elizabeth deserved. Not that she noticed.

Had that really been a year ago?

A year of secrecy, for the *ton* still thought their betrothal had ended. A year of celibacy, not that it bore thinking of. Indeed, he tried mightily not to think of it.

Since then, he had existed in a tedious netherworld made only slightly less so by calibrated moves akin to those of a high-stakes chess game. Otherwise, the endless immersion in superficial muck would make it impossible to rise from his bed each morning.

Sebastian never understood why chess revolved around the fate of the king, when the queen was far more worthy. Worth dying for, really.

Which he was. Boredom killed as surely as any knife.

It was mildly diverting to have a castle—if he could find the blasted thing in the gloom that floated across these moors like a ghost from centuries past.

When they came upon a pair of rotted wooden gates, he halted Captain. Was this the entrance to his castle?

Just his luck: It matched the state of his marriage.

Sebastian dismounted. "Hold Captain," he told the boy.

Controlling a horse this size was likely beyond him. Fortunately, Captain had the manners to hold on his own.

On close inspection, he saw the gate hinges were only tenuously connected to the posts. If William had neglected the gates to his fortress, what else had the man let go?

Sebastian pushed the gates aside. Beyond them, lay more blackness, and no hint of civilization.

"You don't mean to leave me here?" the lad demanded gruffly, his cap pulled down low.

"Of course not. I'll need you to protect me from the ghosts." Sebastian couldn't resist that bit of mischief. Had the boy been less surly, he might have been kinder.

"I don't mind good spirits," the boy replied. "It's the evil spirits one must guard against."

What an odd child.

Evil spirits? Yes, William would have those.

Was this his grand joke on the heir he never thought worthy?

Alas, William had never made a joke in his life. Thus, this was likely the work of the Great Balancer of Scales.

They had tangled before. Sebastian tended to come out on the losing end.

Far past the gates they came to what must have once been a stone courtyard. Beyond it rose a menacing monolith, its details obscured by the dark, save for a few jagged cracks that looked as if the structure was coming apart at the seams.

His castle.

No welcoming torches blazed. No lights shone from within.

Sebastian made out a dark, rectangular shape that appeared to be an enormous door. As he drew closer, the castle's stone turrets condensed from the gloom.

How gothic. Likely there would be gargoyles, with dead stares and fearsome visages.

Centuries of decrepitude and ruin stood before him. Claremont Castle was a rotting pile of stones. A veritable bastion of doom.

"Do you suppose anyone is here?" the boy croaked out.

Sebastian turned to him. "Why did you not tell me my castle was a wreck?"

"Why did you did not know its condition yourself?" the boy retorted.

Prickly child. No one had taught him any manners. Then again, no one needed them here, Cheshire apparently being rife with savages.

Sebastian viewed the prospect of spending the night in this relic with as much enthusiasm as he did lingering in the company of this churlish lad.

If only he hadn't abandoned his carriage when it rolled into the mud in Stoke and broke a wheel. But the urge to flee London was too great. He saddled Captain, leaving his coachman and groom to deal with the repairs.

Such an excellent decision, that.

Normally, he was a patient man. Indeed, patience was at the core of his work, and perhaps his very being. Had he remained true to his nature, he'd be contemplating a featherbed in Stoke, instead of this horror of a castle.

Looping Captain's reins around a rusty iron post, Sebastian moved to the door and lifted the ancient knocker. It sounded with a thunderous thud.

"I'm coming, too." The boy slid off the horse, landed clumsily on his posterior.

Sebastian glanced down at him. "And to think I mistook you for a groom."

The lad scrambled to his feet. "I can handle a horse. This is just a blasted big one."

As they waited at the door, the boy edged closer. "Not sure I want it to open."

"Pray, consider the alternative," Sebastian offered.

"What?" the lad said uneasily.

"The two of us, stranded here in the black of night, as the malevolent creatures that haunt this place devise a fine torture to which we will be condemned for the rest of our days."

Sebastian fixed his gaze on the door, so his expression wouldn't betray him. "They'll fly us up to those turrets, then dash our bodies onto the stones so that our eyeballs pop from their sockets to be feasted on by crows, or wolves, or whatever beast lies in wait."

Silence.

Hell. That was poorly done. He had terrified the lad.

Warily, Sebastian looked over at him. The boy did not look terrified.

Instead, he fixed Sebastian with a hard glare. "You are vile, Englishman."

An odd epithet. Was secession afoot? Sidmouth hadn't mentioned it.

And still no one came to the door. Sebastian knocked again, more insistently.

Finally, a peephole opened.

"Who goes there?" a reedy voice called.

"Sebastian Traherne." He was proud of his surname. It had been good enough for his father, and he had no wish to part with it.

But it brought no response. Alas, everyone wanted to make him someone else now.

"Claremont," Sebastian added. "Your, er, employer."

No response.

The boy gave a rough laugh. "He doesn't believe you either. You'll have to break down the door."

Sebastian gifted him with his haughtiest glare. "And ruin these fine leather gloves? I'll have you know the fit is sublime. They're irreplaceable."

A fulminating look was the lad's only response.

Finally, the door creaked on its hinges. An elderly man in a dressing gown and cap stood huffing alarmingly, apparently from the effort of hoisting the long chain that controlled the door.

Quickly, Sebastian stepped forward to help.

"Thank you, sir, that is—" The man broke off. "You are…?"

"The unfortunate owner of this castle," Sebastian said. "Who are you?"

The man's rheumy eyes widened. "Rowland, Your Grace."

He bowed so deeply Sebastian feared he might topple

and extended a steadying hand.

"We were not expecting you," Rowland said.

"It appears that you rarely expect anyone," Sebastian observed.

"Oh, no, Your Grace. We never do."

Sebastian waited for him to gather himself. Finally, Rowland lifted a brace of candles and led them into a cavernous great hall.

Festooning its walls were medieval implements of death. Mace, club, broadswords, shields, longbow, javelin—at least a hundred.

The room itself was hardly less horrifying. Flickering candlelight revealed cobwebs encasing the furniture. What lay in its darker recesses, he didn't care to imagine.

Inside and out, the castle had been ceded to time without a fight.

Sebastian wondered if Rowland lived here alone, which struck him as precarious, as the man didn't seem altogether steady on his feet.

"Do I have a study, Rowland? A bottle or two of brandy? A bed? Or is that a vain hope?"

"The late duke's chamber has not been used for some time," Rowland said mournfully. "It will be musty. I will ask Mrs. Carson, the housekeeper, to prepare it for you."

"Ah. And the brandy?"

Rowland brightened. "That is easier done. This way, Your Grace."

The boy was studying the weaponry on the wall; his attention seemed particularly fixed on a bow. But when Rowland started down a corridor, he quickly followed.

Halting before a door, he fumbled with some keys.

The door opened into a room deeply ensconced in shadow and dust. A decanter on the desk lifted Sebastian's spirits; the amber color within suggested it might be a fine, aged brandy.

Rowland lit another set of candles before brushing off

a cracked claret leather chair behind the desk. Eyeing the boy, he removed the covers from another chair.

"My, er, page, will require a room as well," Sebastian said. And a good deal more, judging by the lad's ragged clothing and thin form. When had he last eaten?

Rowland bowed and disappeared into the corridor, leaving Sebastian to survey his study.

Gloom infused the room—ideal for morose contemplation, if that's what William had been aiming for. Bookshelves were laden with musty-looking tomes. A nook in the corner might be a fine place to read, were the atmosphere less depressing.

On the wall opposite the desk hung a portrait of William in his younger days. Here, too, dust ruled; one could discern few details beyond his generous nose and pallid complexion.

"A fine homecoming for a duke—*if* you are a duke." The lad plopped into the chair.

For the first time, Sebastian studied the boy closely.

There was something peculiar about him.

His eyes, even in faint candlelight, appeared to be a startling shade of blue. Strands of reddish hair poked out from the tattered cap. His cheekbones were high and fine, almost delicate.

But any impression of fragility was belied by the defiant manner in which the lad was glaring at him, elbows out, his pose tense—as if preparing to launch himself into combat. He clutched that dagger as if it were a lifeline.

"Anne said the duke was old and ill. You might be a pretender, after his wealth and—"

"His castle?" Sebastian offered darkly. "Verily, all the pretenders in England must be plotting to steal this wretched rat trap."

"One man's rat trap is another man's home, Englishman," the boy retorted.

Insolent lad—yet strangely articulate. He was the very

opposite of deferential, as if he had never learned to conduct himself with an employer or other superior.

"The previous duke was my cousin," Sebastian said. "His health failed three months ago, whereupon the title landed on me like a dead weight."

The boy blinked. For the first time, he looked shaken. "Three months ago?"

"No more questions. Let us revisit that paternity nonsense. Who the devil are you?"

Piercing blue eyes held his. "The duke was my father."

"William sired no offspring," Sebastian snapped. Of that he was certain. His cousin had guarded the family bloodline zealously.

"You are wrong."

"No." His voice hardened. "You'll never persuade me his blood runs in you."

Indeed, the boy was all heated passion, if that scene on the moor was any indication—the polar opposite of Sebastian's unfeeling cousin.

The lad regarded him with distaste. "As much as it displeases me to be related to you, Englishman, I know it in my very soul."

"Your soul is no proof. Any connection could only be on the wrong side of the blanket. William never would have—"

The boy leapt to his feet. "My mother was as fine a woman as your own! She would never have lain with him out of wedlock!"

A flurry of blows landed on Sebastian's chest. He caught the boy's wrists. The lad cried out in pain.

The blue eyes brimmed with tears. The eyelashes—extraordinarily long, Sebastian saw at close range—fluttered shut. Candlelight illuminated what he hadn't noticed earlier: a porcelain complexion, graceful jawline, lush lips.

Holy Hell.

Sebastian ripped off the torn cap, exposing a mop of close-cropped red hair. With a low curse, he released his grip. "It's not enough that I have a moldy castle unfit even for vermin. Now I must needs have a girl on my hands."

A sharp gasp. Then: "You know?"

Sebastian grabbed the decanter, poured a large amount of brandy into a dusty glass. "You may have fooled two dim-witted thugs in the black of night, but whatever else I am, Miss…"

"Owen. Gwynna Owen."

"Whatever else I am, *Miss* Owen, 1 hope I am able to identify a girl."

"I am not a girl," she corrected. "I am twenty-five."

Twenty-five. Sebastian stared at the boyish figure, cropped hair, brilliant blue eyes.

A woman's eyes. How had he missed that?

Trouble! Turmoil! Tyranny!

Damn his brain. It had grown intrusive lately, taunting him with alarming hints of insanity. Besides, "tyranny" was wrong. Alliterative, to be sure, but wrong.

Sebastian wrestled his brain into submission and focused on the person who was, quite clearly, not a boy.

She brandished her knife. "If you touch me I will slash you to ribbons."

He eyed her incredulously. "With that rusty thing?"

"You have no idea the blood it has drawn, the lives it has ended, the families it has torn asunder, the—"

"Is that supposed to paralyze me with fear? You barely come up to my shoulder."

She glared at him. "Others have underestimated me. They carry the scars."

The woman possessed courage, if not common sense. After all, she had taken on those ruffians on the moor, though plainly outmatched.

For one horrifying moment, Sebastian found himself riveted.

Then his hand went to the bell pull. Ah, but this was not a place where servants waited to answer bell pulls. He strode to the door, threw it open. "Rowland!"

No response. Sebastian said the man's name again, more loudly.

Some minutes passed, during which he drank in full measure the surprisingly excellent brandy while Miss Owen fingered the blade of her dagger. Her only other possession appeared to be a small pouch she wore at her waist. Perhaps it held other weapons—a slingshot?

He was beginning to feel like a very grumpy Goliath.

At last, Rowland stepped into the room. "Yes, Your Grace?"

"Do I have a secretary?" Sebastian demanded. "A man of business nearby?"

"Horace Busby, sir. He served the late duke for thirty years. We have not seen him since His Grace's lamented passing."

"You will have him on my doorstep before breakfast," Sebastian ordered. "In the meantime, send to London for my solicitors."

Rowland hesitated. "Begging your pardon, Your Grace, but there is no one to send on such errands until Jim Crowley comes to do the marketing for Mrs. Carson."

"Very well, whenever Jim Crowley arrives."

"That is not for another three days," Rowland continued. "Unless I am mistaken, and today is Wednesday. In that case, he will be here tomorrow. No, I am almost certain it is Monday. I seem to recall attending church…yesterday?"

Sebastian stared at the elderly retainer. "So I have no staff, no stable lads, no servants of any sort in my employ other than you and this Mrs. Carson?"

"I am afraid not, Your Grace. In the old days, we had a staff of fifty. I remember—"

"You have my permission to hire a full staff tomorrow.

But first you will find someone—anyone—to fetch this Mr. Busby. Do you understand?"

The man gave a creaky bow and disappeared into the dark corridor.

For a delusional moment, Sebastian allowed himself to hope that the castle, Rowland, and this spitfire of a woman were mere illusions, and that he would awaken in Grosvenor Square tomorrow with no more pressing task than to send to Bond Street for his tailor.

Unfortunately, he was well-acquainted with reality—from a too-early age. This was the hand he'd been dealt. He reached again for the brandy.

"I should like some as well," Miss Owen said.

Eyeing her darkly, he poured her a glass.

She gulped it. He had never seen a woman down brandy with such determination. Most women—Elizabeth, that is—professed a distaste for spirits.

Elizabeth. That brought reality crashing back.

"If you have satisfied your thirst, I want a full explanation." There. He sounded calm—no need for this odd bit of buzzing in his head.

She took a deep breath. Her eyes closed. Stayed that way.

The glass in her hand wobbled.

Sebastian caught it just before it would have fallen. He set it on the desk and regarded her. "My patience is not endless. I've a mind to toss you out into the night, leaving your fate to the ghosts undoubtedly lying in wait in that miserable courtyard—"

"Ghosts do not frighten me. I embrace the dead."

Ah. She'd escaped from Bedlam, found her way to the Cheshire moors with the purpose of driving him insane—beyond the madness this past year had already wrought.

Sebastian took a deep breath. Counted to three.

"You were frightened enough when I spoke of night creatures," he pointed out, though he felt guilty about that now. It was one thing to tease a surly boy, quite another to taunt a helpless female—although this odd creature seemed more mad than helpless.

"Because they were foreign," she said. "I am not frightened by the spirits I know."

Had she been mesmerized by one of the quacks like those at Elizabeth's convalescent home? Did she think herself a witch, or perhaps the reincarnation of some long-dead spirit?

Sebastian didn't believe in witches or spirits, or magic of any kind. But he meant to wait her out.

Because in truth, he *was* possessed of endless patience—despite the aberration of abandoning his carriage in Stoke. He was certain no one in England possessed more.

It is why he'd excelled at diplomacy. Why he'd been married for nearly a year without once sleeping in the same bed as his wife.

Or any woman's bed, for that matter.

And so, he merely arched a brow.

"I will hear your story," he said, "if it takes all night."

***

Gwynna had prepared herself to face an old man who might have lingering feelings for her mother and who might wish to set things right in the twilight of his years.

Instead, she had this aloof aristocrat.

That tousled hair was probably the height of fashion in London, though its deep gold made her think of Parys Mountain at sunset. Candlelight didn't reveal the precise color of his eyes, but they seemed a mix of green and bronze, like the mountain and its copper ore.

She did not wish to see the charms of her island in this conceited coxcomb. But pretentious fop or no, the Duke of Claremont was something else as well.

Beautiful.

As handsome a man as Gwynna had seen.

The classical slope of his brow, the chiseled jaw, the

slight stubble that gave him a dangerous air—made it nigh impossible to look away.

Moreover, he was immense. Measuring him with her Welshwoman's eye, which could judge at a glance whether there was meal in the larder to last the month, Gwynna decided he was nearly half a foot taller than any man she knew.

And strong. That broad chest had been unyielding as she flailed at it, and he needed but one hand to control her. For all that, his figure was lean and elegant, not coarse.

No doubt his tailor did worship him. Ladies must swoon when he entered a room.

Yet his eyes—the color seemed to change with the light—held a cool intelligence. He was no one's fool.

Despair swept her. She might have faced down an old man preparing to meet his Maker, but she'd never persuade this too-perceptive aristocrat—whose features had only hardened since discovering her gender—that she was a member of his family.

"Well?" His resonant baritone held an edge. This was not the man who had tossed off a joke about her slide from the horse.

Still, she was an Owen. He was but an Englishman. Welsh did not give way to English.

"I am the daughter of Megan Glendower Owen of Ynys Môn," Gwynna said.

"Never heard of it—or her."

"Anglesey is the English name. It's an island off North Wales."

He frowned. "At the end of the Dublin Road?"

Gwynna eyed him in surprise.

"I have a passing familiarity with geography, Miss Owen." His clipped tone betrayed not an ounce of humor, his eyes no hint of the teasing gleam she glimpsed when he thought her a boy.

"It's there William and my mother met," Gwynna said.

"They fell in love."

His gaze narrowed. "How the devil do you know that?"

That was the rub. She couldn't know. Everyone involved was dead. But Gwynna had examined the matter from every angle. No other conclusion was possible.

The duke looked down that patrician nose at her. "You Welsh are storytellers, are you not? Doubtless you felt compelled to put a lovely bow on something sordid—"

"It was love," Gwynna insisted.

He set his glass on the desk with a thump. "William was not one to exert himself. He wouldn't have gone to the trouble of crossing those mountains."

"It is not necessary to cross mountains to get to Anglesey, only to sit back like any lazy Englishman and allow the horses to take you around on the coastal route," Gwynna retorted.

The duke took a pocket watch from his waistcoat. He ran his thumb over the case, opened it, glanced at the time.

Was she being dismissed? Ignored?

"I believe they married." Gwynna dared him to ignore *that*. "Secretly."

Instantly, the hard gaze returned to her. "There's no reason to believe a word of your tale, especially since you've been engaged in pretense from the first."

"I pretended to be a boy because I couldn't travel alone as a woman," she protested.

"Those ruffians were on the verge of unmasking you," he pointed out.

"I would have prevailed. Owen was with me."

The duke frowned. "The only person I saw at your side was your terrified friend. Owen, whoever he may be, was nowhere —"

"Owen is Prince of Wales."

He blinked. "If I recall correctly, England already has a Prince of Wales. Just the one, mind you, and his name isn't Owen. Moreover, he would be the last person to rush to any woman's defense."

"You refer to the Regent—English royalty," Gwynna said. "I do not regard him. Owen was the last true Prince of Wales. I am his blood descendant."

"Ah. He would be dead, then?"

Gwynna was not used to verbal jousting. She'd grown up in a house where questions went unanswered and argument wasn't permitted. "His death was never recorded."

He regarded her for a long, unnerving moment. "Perhaps it is the word 'dead' that you have difficulty with. Let's make it less harsh—'deceased,' perhaps. As in: Your *deceased* royal relative Owen was nowhere in evidence on the moor tonight."

She glared at him. "His spirit lives—unencumbered by your simplistic view of death."

"The extent of your delusion is stunning."

"You see only with English eyes," Gwynna said. "*That* is delusion."

Crossing his arms over his chest, the duke leaned back against the desk. The fabric of his coat strained across those broad shoulders. He could have dispatched those men on the moor without a pistol if it had come to fisticuffs, she realized.

Did dukes lower themselves to fisticuffs?

"Why would my cousin and your mother have wed in secret?" he asked.

"Her parents—my grandparents—had no use for English. Perhaps she needed time to accustom them to the marriage. It is the only explanation."

"I can think of others," he said softly. "My cousin would not be the first man to enjoy a woman's charms, then tire of her."

Gwynna felt her face flush. "My mother would not have succumbed to falseness."

"Why is she not here to speak for herself?"

"She was walking at one of the old tombs—in December, so it would have been icy. It was near her time. She fell hit her head. I was born as she breathed her last."

A muscle tensed in his jaw. "You never knew her?"

Gwynna shook her head. A man born into privilege, whose parents had likely coddled him from the cradle, wouldn't understand the depth of that loss.

His thumb slid over his watch. "Who raised you?"

"My grandmother died a year after I was born, so it fell to my grandfather." To Gwynna's dismay, her voice wobbled.

Something flickered in his gaze. "He is deceased?"

"Nearly three months ago."

He reached for the brandy and refilled his glass. To her surprise, he also refilled hers.

"Miss Owen," he said, not unkindly, "you don't know the truth of any of this."

The brandy burned her throat, so she drank it quickly. "I found no marriage documents in my grandfather's house or elsewhere," she conceded. "I had hoped William kept them here."

"Illogical and unlikely."

The man had an answer for everything.

"Perhaps William wasn't ruled by logic," Gwynna persisted. "A man with your lofty self-regard cannot possibly fathom how passion can sweep all else aside."

He stiffened. "You know nothing of me."

His jaw had turned to granite. A frisson of uneasiness swept her. They were all but alone in this dreadful castle. Unbidden, Evans's contorted features came to mind.

Something must have shown on her face, for the duke appeared taken aback. "Do not look at me like that. I will not harm you."

As if to underscore the point, he retreated to the far side of the desk.

"I cannot pretend your presence is welcome," he said.

"Regardless, you are safe here. Unless the castle falls down on us—which, regrettably, seems entirely possible."

Safe? Even her grandfather's home hadn't been safe. She'd never be so foolish as to trust the assurances of this powerful stranger who was so displeased at her presence.

"It's late," he said. "We'll continue this tomorrow."

Relief swept her. She was exhausted from the day's events—the altercation on the moor, the discovery her father no longer lived, the need to reckon with this elegant stranger.

And the brandy. She rose unsteadily.

The duke frowned. "Are you ill?"

Gwynna shook her head.

"I regret there is no maid to attend you." That hard gaze again. "But if you have any intention of turning this to your advantage, think again."

"Advantage?" Her brain felt thick.

He cleared his throat. "You are a young woman sleeping under my roof—such as it is—without benefit of a chaperone. It is not…respectable."

"I am not accustomed to respectable."

Frowning, he eyed her sternly. "If, in order to press a connection to my family, you try to assert that I compromised you, it will not wash. I…cannot be trapped into marriage."

Marriage?

It took Gwynna a moment to find her tongue. "I seek only that to which I am entitled."

A scowl settled over his features. "A claim to the family fortune, I suppose."

"I'll have what I'm due by rights, Englishman, not trickery." Gwynna moved toward the study door. "And while I am certain every woman in England finds you a catch, my tastes are plainer. I have no use for puffed-up peacocks."

Dear Lord. Had she actually spoken those words

aloud? She hadn't eaten in hours, and the brandy had loosened her tongue. She had to leave before disgracing herself further.

Flinging the door open, she stepped into the corridor—only to find it dark and disorienting.

Dizziness swept her. Gwynna reached out for the wall, but it eluded her.

Just as she feared she might fall, a strong hand under her elbow steadied her.

"That was a grand exit," the duke murmured. "But you can have no more notion than I as to where Rowland and the as-yet-unseen Mrs. Carson mean to put us."

Mortified, Gwynna could think of no response. He called for Rowland.

They waited for an eternity—silently, awkwardly—in the musty corridor.

The duke relinquished her arm, but remained close, perhaps to save her if she toppled.

Gwynna tried not to feel grateful.

***

William in love? A laughable notion. The man possessed not an ounce of human emotion. He'd shown no interest in anyone other than himself—least of all family and the only member of it who, by accident of birth and attrition, ended up his heir.

Sebastian entered his bedchamber, steeling himself for whatever lay inside. He would hope for cobwebs, rather than vermin.

It was no overstatement to say his family had contributed its share of vermin—the human kind. Among the three cousins, the youngest—Sebastian's father, Gerald—had been alone in possessing any warmth. All had the misfortune of being related to the iron-willed patriarch, Ambrose, who delighted in others' misfortunes.

Or so it had seemed to Sebastian, barely out of leading strings when Ambrose gifted him a pony for his birthday, then doubled over in laughter when Sebastian failed to get a leg up.

Hell. Hadn't he done something similar by teasing the lad—Miss Owen, rather—after her ungainly descent from Captain? Sebastian shuddered to think Ambrose would have approved.

In William, Ambrose's son, the apple hadn't fallen far from the tree. When Sebastian's parents died, William sent a short note. He did not attend the funeral.

Hubert, the remaining cousin, died a few months later fighting the French, leaving Sebastian the sole heir. William deigned to visit, but seemed stiff and unmoved by the loss of three family members in such a short time.

Sebastian could not comprehend that. More than two decades after his parents' deaths, he still felt their loss to his marrow. Yet memory played them false, for they were forever fixed in the prism of his seven-year-old self.

Gerald had been lively and affectionate, with an infectious smile. Faylinn—the name conjured sylvan glades—remained the deeper, enduring mystery.

Her eyes were a changeable mix of silver and moss—a trace of copper if her emotions were high—and hinted of secrets.

Wholly occupied with one another, Faylinn and Gerald cocooned themselves against the family barbs. Sometimes, Sebastian felt left out.

Wasn't that a thought filled to the brim with self-pity?

Thank God for Angus, who had prevented a seven-year-old orphan from turning into either Ambrose or William. Still, Sebastian had always longed for what lay forever beyond his reach: the chance to once more hear his mother's voice and his father's laugh.

Perhaps it was a trick of this wretched bedchamber—a floor with layers upon layers of dirt, a worm-hole of a bed with tattered hangings, and unknown pests lurking in the shadows—that conjured not Faylinn's voice, but Angus's, floating on the breeze through the windows.

Miss Owen was an orphan, too, that voice reminded him. She had traveled alone from Wales, probably suffered countless indignities on the way. Despite her bravado, she had to be terrified in this moldy castle with a man she didn't know.

Damned Angus for giving him a conscience.

Even so, William was as likely to have fallen in love with a Welsh wench as to walk naked through Parliament. He was consumed with protecting the family bloodline. He would never have carelessly conceived a child.

Nor could he have fathered such an unruly specimen as Miss Owen, whose judgment was so faulty as to make her believe she could pass for a boy, or wield that dagger with any authority.

They differed in another way. William had no skill with words. People only paid attention because the man was a duke. Afterward, one could never remember what he'd said.

Miss Owen possessed a great many words, and they stuck in one's brain, especially that bit about puffed-up peacocks.

Sebastian valued words. They were the essential tools of his chosen field of diplomacy.

Occasionally, other tools were needed. At the Vienna talks, aimed at resizing the Continent after Napoleon's marauding, the parties were prideful men who gave no quarter.

Enter the peacock.

A preening aristocrat with no apparent purpose than to display his feathers was a fine decoy. Learning each man's tipping point was easy when one was seen as inconsequential.

In Wellington's towering presence, the others simply needed burnishing. For Nesselrode, a much-decorated Russian diplomat, Sebastian created a new honor—Vienna

Order of Peace—to add to his ribbons.

For Metternich, skilled at devising peace plans, he created a parchment—every peacock worth his salt knew calligraphy—heralding "The Metternich System."

Finally, agreements were signed.

Playing the peacock had served his country. But his current masquerade was different.

It was destroying him. He spent his time striving to appear superficial. The ordeal was only tolerable if he divided it into finite, manageable units.

Of late, his brain had been rebelling. It gave him alarming snippets of dialogue, foolish urgings he tried to ignore even as they grew more insistent.

Everyone had quirks, of course. Miss Owen, for instance, seemed unnaturally attached to that dagger, almost as if it were her talisman.

That, perhaps, he could understand. His fingers slid over his watch, a flawed timepiece that gained nearly an hour each day. Faylinn's wedding present to Gerald.

Sebastian loved the feel of the case design—the leaves that entwined flirtatiously, the mysterious bold slashes within a circle. The slender band that joined case and cover, the small protruding stem that falsely reassured him of its constancy.

Yes, he was inordinately attached to a watch that didn't keep time. But it was tangible and true in ways that mattered, for it kept his parents near, even as the years faded them.

The watch was *his* talisman.

A child's fancy that lingered still.

Chapter Three

Horace Busby was in his sixth decade, but fit. And so, when Jim Crowley presented himself at the door shortly after dawn with a summons from the new duke, he did not hesitate to set out for Claremont Castle on foot. It was only four miles, and the circumstances in his household were such that any opportunity to be elsewhere appealed.

Such a peremptory summons could only mean a matter of great urgency, so he gathered the papers he had been keeping for just this occasion.

Entering the duke's study, Horace looked around eagerly. He had not been in this room for a dozen years. The late duke preferred to conduct his business from his sitting room upstairs. Perhaps this was a sign the new duke meant to put things in order.

When the door opened, his jaw nearly dropped.

This Duke of Claremont was the most elegant man he had ever seen. His top boots were polished to a fare-thee-well, the leather gleaming like tawny port. Even Horace's untrained eye saw that the fawn-colored coat was stitched to perfection.

But while His Grace had the demeanor of a man accustomed to privilege, there was nothing soft about the eyes or jaw. He possessed considerable height on a lean, muscular frame.

Horace tried to recall what he knew of the man. The late duke had rarely spoken of his heir. He was a diplomat, or some such, he thought.

The duke seated himself at the desk and indicated

Horace should sit as well. He wasted no time on preliminaries. "What do you know about Gwynna Owen of Anglesey?"

Horace wasn't accustomed to such directness. The old duke often drifted off during their meetings. But this one was regarding him sternly, in apparent expectation of a swift answer.

"Er, just before his death, His Grace initiated proceedings to become Miss Owen's..." Horace trailed off, uncertain as to how this information would be received.

The duke frowned. "Her what?"

"Her guardian," Horace finished. "He directed me to research her...history."

This drew a sharp elevation of those aristocratic brows.

Horace took this as command to continue. "The proceedings were never completed, the duke having succumbed to an inflammation of the chest, as Your Grace undoubtedly knows."

"Do you mean to say that William acknowledged a familial connection to Miss Owen?"

Horace cleared his throat. "Not precisely."

"What then? Was someone trying to blackmail him?"

"Oh, no," Horace said quickly. "His Grace was the soul of rectitude. He had done nothing to be ashamed of."

That earned him a dubious look. "My cousin was not the soul of anything. Indeed, I suspect he had no soul whatsoever."

Horace did not know what to say to that.

"Let us not mince words," the duke said. "Miss Owen has arrived here to lay claim to the Traherne name and, presumably, a share of the family fortune."

Horace blinked. "Miss Owen, here?"

"Is there any basis to her claim?" the duke demanded. "Is she William's by-blow?"

To speak thus about his late employer was painful. "I do not know," Horace croaked out.

An ominous silence greeted this response. Then: "Can you rule it out?"

"I never saw any documents that would verify such a claim," Horace said.

"That is not what I asked."

The man could not have been a diplomat, Horace thought, to favor such blunt talk. "I cannot rule it out, Your Grace, but I was not in a position to do so."

"By your own admission, he directed you to research the matter."

"It was not that sort of research."

"What sort was it?"

Horace reached for his handkerchief, the room having grown exceedingly warm. "To be frank, Your Grace, while I was the duke's man of affairs, I am but a simple countryman, not worldly in the least, and—"

"On the contrary, Mr. Busby," the duke said. "You are not being frank."

Horace had never felt so at sea. He had lived his entire life in Cheshire and had no skills to match wits with this man, especially over such unseemly matters.

"What I wish to know," the duke added—and Horace did not miss the warning note in his tone—"is precisely what research you did, and the result."

This interview could not end soon enough. "A few months ago, His Grace asked me to learn whether there were birth records for Miss Owen on Anglesey. Unfortunately, there is no parish church on that island."

"What about parishes near the island?"

"There are many parishes in Wales, Your Grace." Horace mopped his brow.

"But you did not write to those."

"That is, er, accurate."

The duke steepled his fingertips. "To be clear: Your research consisted of essentially doing nothing."

This was God's retribution for missing Sunday's

church service, Horace thought. Perhaps the Heavens could simply strike him dead and spare him this merciless interrogation.

The duke's eyes—ice with a hint of green, like frost on spring barley—impaled him with a most deadly stare. "What did my cousin do to further the process of making him Miss Owen's guardian?"

"He directed his London solicitors to draw up papers. But he died before anything could be finalized." Horace hesitated. "They did not inform you of the matter?"

A flicker in the duke's eyes was the only reaction. "Regardless, Miss Owen is on my doorstep. I must manage without the solicitors—although I suspect that is no loss, since they appear to have been dragging their feet."

Horace was happy to have the duke focus on the solicitors' shortcomings, rather than his.

"Did William have any women in his life? Liaisons?"

"I knew nothing of His Grace's private life," Horace said, flushing. "In his later years, he was a recluse."

"Do you know whether he ever traveled to the island of Anglesey?"

"No, Your Grace."

"What of his documents and papers?"

At last, a question to which he knew the answer! Horace nearly wept in relief. "I have brought the account ledgers. The duke spent little money in the last years. He lost interest in the running of his various estates."

"One imagines they are all in a similar condition." The duke pulled out a pocket watch and set it on the desk.

Horace removed the ledgers from his satchel and pushed them toward His Grace.

He didn't glance at them. "William must have known Miss Owen was too old to need a guardian. Perhaps this was a way to acknowledge her connection to the family."

As he didn't seem to expect an answer, Horace remained silent.

"Do you have a wife, Mr. Busby?" the duke asked.

That took him aback. "Wife? Yes. Yes, indeed."

"Is she much occupied with household duties?"

Horace was confused. "Oh, no. She is not occupied with much. Just the children."

"How many children?"

"Five. Two of them grown."

"I believe we will grant that that she is busy." The duke's focus shifted to the wall opposite the desk where the late duke's portrait hung. "I must engage a temporary companion for Miss Owen. Someone who can accompany us to Wales."

"Wales, Your Grace?"

"I intend to get to the bottom of Miss Owen's parentage. But I need another female to see to the proprieties—a chaperone. Perhaps you or your wife can recommend someone suitable?"

Horace's thoughts instantly shot to the other adult female in his household, one he longed to send packing: his wife's sister, Jeanette.

"I do know someone," he said happily.

"Excellent." The duke pulled the tattered bell cord, only to have it come apart in his hand. Muttering something Horace had not a prayer of catching—his hearing wasn't what it once was—the duke crossed the room to open the door.

"Rowland," he called, "send Miss Owen to me."

The duke began to peruse the ledgers.

At last the door swung open. A petite young woman fairly flew into the room.

Horace rose. The young woman was...unusual. Her short red hair gave her a boyish air. Yet she wore an ornate gown that might have been fashioned during the last century.

Its heavy blue fabric was trimmed in a profusion of lace. The long, bell-shaped sleeves nearly swallowed her.

The neckline gaped, and the tufts of lace at the bodice did nothing to hide the slight roundness of the young lady's bosom. Indeed, there was not quite enough fabric to cover all that should have been covered.

"I shall not wear this monstrosity," she declared.

Neither of them took notice of Horace.

In fact, the duke had undergone a transformation. His features arranged themselves in an expression of extreme hauteur. The keenness about his eyes gave way to abject boredom.

He lifted a quizzing glass. "That frock does you no favors. Blue is not an altogether dreadful color on you, but this is too much fabric." His gaze dropped to her bodice. "And yet, not quite enough."

Before she could reply, the duke gestured toward Horace. "Miss Owen, allow me to present Mr. Busby, my late cousin's secretary. We were discussing you."

She turned toward Horace.

"Mr. Busby says that William took initial steps to become your guardian," the duke said.

Her eyes widened. "When?"

"A few months ago, just before his death."

She frowned. "Does that mean he had the marriage documents?"

Horace gasped. Surely, he would have known if His Grace had wed.

"Thank you for bringing us round to the point," the duke said. "Is there a clergyman to whom your mother—or grandfather—might have confided? If there was a wedding, someone officiated. And duly recorded it."

She looked away. "We have few clergy. I found no records."

"Then I very much fear that we shall have to see this island of yours."

Miss Owen regarded him in amazement. "We?"

"Since the research on the subject is sadly inadequate"—the duke's stern eye fell upon Horace—"I intend to search for myself."

Impulsively, Miss Owen touched the duke's coat sleeve. "You will come? To Anglesey?"

The duke froze. He eyed the feminine hand on his sleeve as if it were a lethal weapon.

"We leave in three days." He eased his arm away from her. "That gives you time to obtain a suitable wardrobe. Please burn this monstrosity. Where the devil did it come from?"

"Mrs. Carson found some trunks in the attic. But everything was old and did not suit me."

"In that we agree." His Grace returned his watch to his waistcoat. "Though we cannot hope for miracles, I will not travel with someone whose attire is unsuitable."

Her face flushed. "You, sir, are a pompous prig."

Horace blanched, but the duke merely nodded.

"My dear Miss Owen," he drawled. "I have never pretended otherwise."

***

Over the years, her grandfather could have filled in the empty spaces of her life. He chose not to.

Instead, he told her fairy tales, legends deeply embedded in Welsh lore. In them, places and people never truly disappeared, but simply moved to a place beyond human ken.

"The land where fairies live cannot be destroyed," he'd say, beginning his favorite story. It comforted him to believe in magical constants, realms that did not vanish with time, beings and spirits that lingered, unseen.

Yet Gwynna yearned for real stories of her mother, before her life was cut short. She understood it was too painful for him to talk about Megan. But his silence left her feeling invisible, even unworthy.

She retreated into solitary pursuits—books and archery—and gained self-reliance, if not confidence.

With her grandfather's passing, the burden of his silence began to lift.

In its place grew a burning need to seize her fate. It had carried her here, to a man whose very presence seemed to disturb the universe.

Gwynna marveled that the duke had listened to her claims. Most in his position wouldn't.

Like many English, he didn't see beyond literal truth. That Owen no longer walked the earth didn't make her irrational. His blood ran in her, both burden and gift.

Her kind was bred to battle, for it would always fall to Owen's kin to fight English usurpers.

But she wasn't the leader her legacy demanded. She didn't blame her grandfather or even Evans for that. She alone had allowed that cloak of invisibility to define her.

At home, she'd seen questioning looks, as if people wondered when she would become who they expected. Entrenched in her culture was the struggle for sovereignty.

Fight was glory; it just wasn't hers. Her quest was to uncover the truth about her parents, learn why William hadn't claimed her, and find her place in this family.

Now, as she watched dawn stalk across the Cheshire moor, the sky wore a haze, as if millions of dust particles hovered in the air. Like those swirling bits, the answers she craved flitted like fairy dust—sensed, but out of sight.

Elusive, like the duke.

Proximity had provided no insight into his character.

Gwynna occupied the chamber next to his, but their paths rarely crossed. He worked long hours in his study, writing or meeting with Mr. Busby, whereas she endured endless fittings for frocks he decreed she must have.

Yet despite the duke's excessive regard for clothing and his irritating mannerisms—that dratted quizzing glass being at the top of the list—he didn't seem unkind.

He had pledged to keep her safe.

The very word made her realize how much of her

journey had been spent in peril—scraping for food, avoiding the rough sort that plied the roads, keeping to the shadows for fear someone might see through her disguise.

Tension had seeped into her bones, knotted her muscles, kept her on edge, ready to defend herself. And while her dagger was more symbolic than serviceable, there was one weapon at which she excelled.

It was why she donned her breeches and slipped out of the castle before dawn. Why, after three days of staring at the wall of weapons in the great hall, she could no longer resist the one that summoned her.

The Welsh longbow. A warrior's bow, meant for close fighting and swift movement. How it came to hang with English broadswords and axes was anyone's guess.

It wasn't smooth and polished like English bows. The wood—Welsh dwarf elm—was rough, as nature intended.

Gwynna nocked an arrow, tested the bowstring. The tension held. The arrow's worn fletchings would spoil precision, so she chose an easy target—a big oak.

As she sighted it down the length of the arrow, she felt the familiar thrill. Anchoring her middle finger on her jaw, Gwynna exhaled a half-breath.

Released.

The arrow struck the oak with a reverberating thwack.

Exhilaration swept her. Warriors of old had used this very bow. She felt the connection to them in her bones.

Her grandfather had begun teaching her archery as soon as she could hold a bow. By her thirteenth year, she was proficient. The lessons stopped, but Gwynna never stopped perfecting her skill.

Her toughest challenge—a night shot—brought a joy like no other.

Night after night, she went to the beach at low tide, when it was wide and empty, stacking pieces of driftwood as targets. All she needed was a sliver of moonlight, but the feckless moon loved to tease, slipping in and out of the clouds, playing havoc with her vision.

The first time she hit a night shot, Gwynna ran to tell her grandfather. But he'd already begun to recede into himself; her achievement barely registered. From then on, she vowed to master the shot as a tribute to what he taught her, and to what was yet possible.

By the time death claimed him, darkness had long been his prison. Whatever secrets he kept died with him.

That's why it shocked Gwynna to find her mother's note tucked at the bottom of an old knapsack he used to take to the lifesaving station for drills.

Send for Claremont, if I am unable.

One sentence, in what she knew to be Megan's hand, dated just weeks before Gwynna's birth. Was it a clue to her father's identity?

In the Beaumaris library, she found Mr. Debrett's peerage book and learned that Edward III created the Claremont dukedom in the fourteenth century to console the Earl of Chester, whose title was abruptly appropriated by the Crown's heir-apparent.

William became Duke of Claremont upon the death of his father Ambrose in 1791.

The very year of her birth.

From some older islanders, Gwynna heard that a high-handed lord visited years ago and quarreled with one of Anglesey's most revered families. No one recalled his name, or the date.

Still, it was enough to send her here.

That William no longer lived crushed her hope of finding, if not a true father, some explanation of why he had abandoned her mother and their child.

Now, her life's story rested with a shallow, preening dandy.

Gwynna shot another round of arrows, then another. Gradually, the familiar rhythm settled in. With that, her thoughts began to rearrange themselves.

A more intriguing picture of the duke began to emerge. She sensed he harbored secrets.

That air of entitled ennui was belied by the sly, seamless efficiency with which he rescued her and Anne on the moor. That bored gaze grew stern when he spoke to Mr. Busby.

Moreover, she now had a better fix on the duke's eyes. That odd color—it ran to green with flecks of ochre and silver—seemed somehow familiar.

Perhaps William, in his younger days, had been like him: handsome, wealthy, polished—appealing, despite the arrogance. Was that what Megan had seen in him?

Shouldering the bow, Gwynna started back toward the castle. Spring's chill had not yet given way to summer. It was the same on Anglesey. Some said the ancients, angered over the Crown's theft of the oat crop, were to blame.

Abruptly, she halted.

A man on horseback loomed fifty yards away. The sun was in her eyes, but by the size of horse and man, it could only be the duke and his enormous beast. His rigid bearing suggested displeasure.

By the time he reached her, those ducal eyebrows had drawn together ominously.

Despite the early hour, he was elegantly turned out in a dark topcoat, buckskin breeches, and brown riding boots banded in black. Did every English aristocrat attire himself thus? Surely, none rivaled this one in magnificence.

Without moving a muscle, he evoked power.

He offered no greeting, but merely pulled out his watch and glanced at it.

Then he shifted his gaze to her. "The new footmen will be disappointed that you took the morning air without summoning one of them."

"I am accustomed to walking by myself," Gwynna said. "It was too early to wake anyone."

"Dangers reside out here, Miss Owen. That night on

the moor surely taught you that. From now on you will take someone with you if you wish to wander."

His imperious air irritated her. "I walk briskly. A footman wouldn't keep pace."

"Knock on my door. I shall do my best to keep pace."

Gwynna eyed him in surprise.

The duke's gaze swept over her, lingered on the bow. "Where did you come by that?"

"It was on your wall." Perhaps she should have asked permission.

"Give it to me."

"You need not bark orders." But she held it out. It was his, after all.

Looping the bow over his shoulder, he extended a gloved hand. Did he want the arrows? She held those out.

He ignored them. Instead, he took her arm and pulled her onto the horse behind him. At her startled protest, he shrugged. "I've other duties. No time to walk you back."

But as he set the horse toward the castle, Gwynna began to slide. His arm shot out to save her.

"Hold onto me," he groused. "And never tell a soul I once mistook you for a groom."

Staring at the duke's broad back, she wasn't sure what to hold. His coat fit snugly, with no excess fabric. Gingerly, she eased her hands around his midsection.

"Press your legs into the horse. I suppose it's fortunate you are wearing…not a skirt."

Gwynna nudged her legs against his. He kept a sedate pace as they rode in silence.

"You're an archer?" He turned slightly, so she could hear his words. "Like Robin Hood?"

"Welsh have no need to borrow English folk heroes. We have our own."

"There's a Welsh counterpart to Robin?"

Gwynna made a disparaging sound. "Our archers are a class by themselves. *Sui generis.*"

He was silent for a beat. Then: "You know Latin."

"Some." How odd to have such a conversation on a horse.

"Girls weren't taught Latin when I was young. Most didn't go to school."

"You went to Eton," she guessed. "Oxford or Cambridge?"

"Oxford. How did you learn Latin?"

He was trying to draw her out, Gwynna realized.

"Girls on Anglesey attended school with the boys, but we couldn't advance to the mainland school. A teacher in Beaumaris offered to tutor me. She runs a subscription library and does Latin translations for scholars."

She hesitated. "Why did you come for me this morning?"

"When you weren't at breakfast, I had Mrs. Carson check your room."

"Why are my comings and goings your concern?"

"You're staying in my castle, such as it is. That makes you my concern."

"How medieval," Gwynna declared. "As if you were a feudal lord controlling everyone on your property."

He stiffened. "Controlling you isn't my aim. Indeed, I suspect that is quite impossible."

"How did you find me?"

"I simply thought of where I least wished you to be—the place where you previously encountered danger, and thus would be inexorably drawn to."

The man had come to fetch her from any harm.

Yes, that was proprietary and feudal. Nevertheless, Gwynna tightened her hold on his midsection, allowed herself the weakness of leaning into his solid strength.

For the first time in a long while, she felt...*safe*.

***

"That color is dreadful."

As Sebastian expected, that got a rise. Miss Owen put

down her spoon and regarded him.

They were seated in the small breakfast room for a light supper of barley soup, bread, and cheese. The formal dining room, like almost every other, was unfit for use.

Sebastian preferred not to spend more time in her company than necessary, but they were leaving tomorrow and he wished to discuss preparations.

He had another motive as well: to restore them to more distant footing after that odd bit of familiarity this morning when he fetched her from the moor.

Bringing her up onto Captain had been an expedient choice. But having her tucked against his back, her legs pressed under his thighs, felt shockingly intimate.

He had a strict rule against touching females—that point underscored now, as he recalled the feel of Miss Owens's arms locked around his middle, her soft front pressed into his back. If only she had remained a boy.

On the return ride, Sebastian had tried counting backward from one hundred, but he kept losing the count with each new revelation about her.

She knew Latin and archery. He revered ancient languages, the foundation of modern civilization. And while he hadn't touched a bow in years, the one she'd taken resembled Faylinn's, which hung in his library at Summerlin.

Thus, alarmingly, he and Miss Owen had commonalities. More distance was required.

"Gray saps the life from your cheeks," Sebastian said, though it was untrue. The gray of her frock went nicely with that red hair. It gave her the look of a fine watercolor; the muted backdrop served to focus attention on the vivid forefront.

Her jaw set—thank God.

"I care this much"—she flicked her hand, as if swatting a fly—"for your fashion sense."

He arched a brow. "Everyone follows my style."

"Fashion is the whimsy of the ruling class," she said disdainfully. "It's utterly without substance."

Sebastian was tempted to pull out his quizzing glass, but doing so at supper would be insulting. He settled for a disdainful look down the length of his nose.

Instead of taking offense, she smiled. "That's meant to put me in my place, but if you think I quail in my boots—"

"You're wearing *boots*?" He tried to look appalled. "Slippers are preferred at dinner."

"Never say you are in the habit of peeking under the table to see ladies' feet." She eyed him in mock horror. "And you dare to lecture *me* on manners?"

How very wicked of her to give him his due.

"I merely point out what is required," he said frostily.

"If it is rude to peek, what does it matter what is required?" she returned.

Oh, she was quick. He tried not to focus on the beguiling curve of her mouth, only the words that came out of it. "About that class nonsense—"

"Mary Wollstonecraft thought fashion aimed to control women The same is true more broadly. The ruling class sets rigid styles to set itself apart and keep others out. But fashion's no true measure of worth."

Dear God. No woman he knew brandished such logic, or talked to him with such spirit.

Or knew Latin.

Something in Sebastian's brain came alive.

Mary Wollstonecraft!

"Even if that's true, I fail to see what problem fashion causes," he said gravely.

"The fashion elite won't acknowledge those below their station, for it risks their own standing. That's selfish. They spend money on clothing that could be better used to help the poor. That's cruel."

The woman meant to preach at him, did she? Not for nothing had Sebastian been first in his debate classes, a skill he honed in diplomacy. Regrettably, since immersing himself in false colors, he hadn't debated anyone.

Oh, he was ready.

"You assume one's outer appearance mirrors the inner being," he said. "That's judging the book by its cover. Thus, you are guilty of what you accuse others."

Her lips pursed, which immediately caused his attention to fix there.

"Perhaps," she conceded. "But sometimes one has only the cover by which to judge."

Sebastian stabbed a piece of cheese. It disturbed him that her mouth—rosy, full, and many other appalling adjectives—had distracted him.

"Sometimes a cover is only a cover," he muttered.

Certainly, *his* cover bore no resemblance to what was inside—he hoped. Then again, how long could one wear a façade before it ceased being a façade? Could pretense become reality?

She folded her hands in her lap. "If someone presents one image to the world, when the truth is otherwise, he has only himself to blame when people draw the wrong conclusions."

Ah. The crux of the matter.

"I don't disagree." He regarded her thoughtfully. "You might have the makings of a diplomat."

"I don't aspire to your class, or share its values."

"Values you deduce from my clothes," he parried.

Her gaze narrowed.

Sebastian didn't know whether she was any good at archery, but one thing was certain: Words were her métier. Matching wits with her was sheer pleasure.

Suddenly, her expression faltered. "These new clothes are not…me." She reached out and pressed his arm.

Egad. The hairs of his arm roused in panic, despite being shielded by his coat fabric.

Carefully, Sebastian eased his distressed limb away.

"My dear Miss Owen. If any woman ever needed new clothes, it's you."

My dear Miss Owen. That sounded improper as hell.

"I would rather travel as a boy," she said.

"Anyone could see through that disguise."

"You did not, at first," she pointed out.

Sebastian cut a piece of bread. "It was dark, and those thugs compelled my attention."

"But afterward, when we arrived at the castle, you still did not suspect," she persisted.

He waved a dismissive hand. "Because I was focused on the sheer horror of possessing England's most dilapidated castle. Once I paid attention, it was obvious."

"How?"

"Men recognize these things." A delicacy about the cheeks, full lips, eyes framed in long, fluttering lashes. Her petite form, without lavish curves but distinctly feminine, nonetheless.

He had no intention of laying out that evidence. "Women ought not wear breeches."

"Breeches are more comfortable than frocks."

"They direct the eye upward. 'Tis unseemly."

A mischievous gleam appeared in those blue eyes. "Upward?"

"Don't be obtuse." His face warmed. Wasn't he past the age of embarrassment? "Women must be covered up. Men ought not be reminded that they have…parts."

Hell. Now he *knew* he was blushing.

"Men's breeches direct the eye upward. Is it acceptable to call attention to *their* parts?"

Sebastian glowered. "You are being provocative."

Abruptly, the light in her eyes vanished. "The truth is, I felt safer as a boy."

The forlorn note in her voice sent his wildly inappropriate meanderings crashing to where they belonged: dead and buried, never to rise again.

"Let us go to my study. I have something important to discuss." His voice sounded gruffer than he intended, but perhaps that was best.

Sebastian put his napkin on the table. He had enjoyed the verbal fencing more than was fitting. Sternness would serve to put distance between them.

And perhaps make him forget that throughout their discourse over supper—and, for that matter, on the return ride this morning—he had been the very opposite of bored.

***

Gwynna was stunned. All manner of words had poured out of her at supper.

In her mind, she was quick with incisive arguments, like Socrates or Plato in the dialogues she had studied with her tutor. But reality was different. Her grandfather had not tolerated such, and she never developed the skill.

With the duke, she had ready responses. Odder still, he seemed to relish them.

His study looked as it had that first night with dusty bookshelves and faded paintings. The duke poured out a brandy and offered it to her. "Miss Owen—"

"Can you not call me Gwynna?"

"Excessively familiar," he said brusquely.

"We are cousins," she pointed out.

"*If* we are related, it is more distant than that. Second cousins at best." He poured his own brandy and fixed her with an austere gaze.

"I do not wish to insult you," he began.

"Then perhaps you might stop doing it." Truly, those words had tumbled out without thought or intent. Gwynna wanted to laugh at the simple pleasure of such speech.

His lips twitched. Almost, a smile. "Are you finding your time here a trifle difficult?"

"On the contrary. Your constant indictment of my appearance has not been the least off-putting."

Then, he did smile—which made him look younger.

How old was he? she wondered. Not as old as those stuffy airs suggested.

Who was the man under that hauteur?

When he smiled, his eyes sparkled. His mouth broadened, making him appear *nearly* human. She took note of other attributes. Strong men often exhibited a thickness of form, but his torso tapered into a trim waist without coarseness or unnecessary flesh.

Below that—well, in truth, breeches *did* call attention to certain areas.

Belatedly, Gwynna realized she had been dissecting him, piece by piece, as if he were an object in a museum dedicated to gentlemen of extraordinary beauty.

Quickly, she returned her gaze to his face.

He was no longer smiling.

That he'd caught her openly cataloguing his physical assets—no use pretending otherwise—mortified her. She never thought of men in *that* way. Evans destroyed any interest she had in the masculine form, no matter how well-proportioned. Or so she'd thought.

"You refused the maid from the village. Why?"

"I am accustomed to doing for myself."

"You must have attendants for our journey. The proprieties will not be satisfied."

Gwynna shrugged. "Won't one of your servants do?"

"My coachman and groom have only just arrived, the latter fighting an inflammation of the lungs from shepherding my coach through a chill rain," the duke said. "Even if both were fit, they are insufficient chaperones."

"No valet?" she asked in surprise.

"My cravats are my own creation—and the rage of London."

"How gratifying for you."

He ignored that. "You must have a maid. I do not wish your reputation to suffer."

"You forget that I am widely thought to be a bastard."

That earned her a severe frown. "I would not have chosen that word, nor should you. If you care nothing for your reputation, think of mine."

Why would a duke—especially this one—care what others thought?

"Unfortunately, I have lately found myself the subject of rather relentless efforts to drape me in the parson's noose," he went on.

"Who would wish to marry an overweening fashion plate freighted with self-regard? That would rob her of such light as is more properly *her* due, would it not?"

Where had those rude, brittle words come from? She ought to apologize. "I—"

"Blast," he growled.

Any apology—any words, for that matter—instantly evaporated. Even in their short acquaintance, Gwynna had not known him to speak intemperately.

"I do care for my reputation, but not for the reasons you think," the duke said. "A scandal would cause pain to someone for whom I care deeply."

The duke cared deeply? That itself was a revelation.

"My situation is…complicated," he said. "I have a wife. That isn't generally known."

Gwynna stared at him. "A wife? *You*?"

He appeared taken aback. "It cannot be that difficult to envision."

But it was. What woman could endure his oppressive airs and artificiality?

A lady from his own world, of course. One who prized his wealth and title and all that came with it, including—it must be said—that handsome exterior.

Still, he seemed so…solitary.

"Where, er, is she?" Gwynna ventured.

"At a convalescent home. She's long been ill." His gaze fixed on the wall behind her.

Had he made her ill? Who knew what lay beneath that

elegant façade? Men could be cruel, as she could attest. "How long have you been married?"

"A year."

"And she's been ill all this time?"

He drained his brandy and set the glass down with a decisive thump. "I do not wish to discuss my marriage. Only to caution you against any marital schemes."

That stung. "Perhaps marital 'schemes' are common in your world, Englishman, but I have no designs on you. Indeed, the notion is repelling."

His gaze lost its remoteness. "Repelling?"

"Utterly." Gwynna pitied the ladies vying for his favor, unaware he was taken. "Besides. Welsh do not marry English."

"Yet you claim your Welsh mother married my oppressively English cousin."

"I know the truth of that in my bones, Englishman."

"'Englishman.' You say the word as if it's a curse. Why?"

She scoffed. "Do you wish a history lesson on how your country has oppressed mine?"

"Nothing so tedious. But I fail to see how your mother would have married my cousin if she felt as you do about the English."

"She fell in love. And I think it strange you keep something so consequential as marriage a secret. Stranger still that you entrust me with it. I do not suffer deceivers, Englishman."

"Says the women who presses a dubious claim to my family name and money."

"I seek only the truth," Gwynna insisted.

"As do I."

Abruptly, she rose. "I'll take you at your word, then. Let us seal our bargain." She pulled out her dagger. "This blade has been sharpened on centuries of traitors."

The duke stared at her in amazement. "Am I to take

that as a threat?"

"If you betray your pledge to seek truth, there will be a reckoning."

He lifted a brow. "And what might that be?"

"Your blood will flow through the streets of Anglesey like the blood of all the foolish English before you."

Yes, perhaps that was a bit much, but Owen's dagger always inspired lurid images. Its pedigree was bloodthirsty to the core.

Something flared in the duke's gaze.

"To the battle joined." He lifted his glass in salute.

Chapter Four

She was avoiding his gaze. Gwynna—her given name had replaced "Miss Owen" in Sebastian's thoughts—had scarcely spoken since seating herself across from him, arranging the skirts of her new traveling dress, and training her brilliant blue eyes on the passing scenery.

If only the *other* woman in the carriage would ignore him as well. Jeanette Kendall, the widowed sister of Horace Busby's wife, was accompanying them to Wales as chaperone. Sebastian suspected Busby offered her up solely to rid his house of the lady's constant chatter.

That mauve-colored dress was as heavy and oppressive as a great aunt's tablecloth. Her hair had a few streaks of gray, but she did not look old, so much as sour.

She'd brought many bandboxes, no matter that Sebastian assured her theirs would not be a lengthy trip. It had taken an hour to load her belongings onto the baggage coach. Sebastian knew he hadn't imagined Busby's look of satisfaction as he bid his relative adieu.

Mrs. Kendall possessed another quality that grated—her "knowledge" of proper behavior and her urgent mission to declare it to all within earshot. Given the responsibility of ensuring Gwynna's respectability, Mrs. Kendall saw fit to correct her at every turn.

"A lady does not cross her legs in such a fashion," she warned, after Gwynna—accustomed to the freedom breeches conferred—stretched her legs across the carriage.

"A lady sits up straight," she instructed. "Imagine a rod of steel, and align yourself with it. All else invites judgment of a wayward disposition."

Sebastian suspected Gwynna was content with her wayward disposition and would not scruple to say so if the woman kept issuing orders. For now, Gwynna ignored her.

Likely, that wouldn't last. By her own admission, she didn't suffer fools, and Mrs. Kendall had thus far revealed herself to be a fine example of one.

Would Gwynna plunge that dagger into the woman's heart? Not implausible, if one still had in one's mind—as one did—last night's conversation.

Sebastian's pulse had kicked up at her pledge that his blood would flow through the streets if he betrayed her. That florid image was wholly at odds with the civilized, boring life he had endured this past year.

Nevertheless, he was sure they were on a fool's errand, seeking proof of a marriage that existed only in Gwynna's fertile imagination. Even William wouldn't have abandoned a wife expecting his heir.

A decent man would have supported an out-of-wedlock child, but William hadn't bestirred himself until the end of his life. Why?

Now the matter fell to him—no small irony, as Sebastian had left London to avoid entanglements, only to slam headlong into this one. Still, he'd see it through. He had Angus to thank for his vexing sense of responsibility.

Unfortunately, Mrs. Kendall's baggage made for a late start. It was nearly dusk.

"The coachman ought to be more careful," Mrs. Kendall complained as they bumped over a deep rut. "He might break a wheel."

Sebastian closed his eyes, striving to convey fatigue. Gradually, her voice intruded less.

His thoughts meandered from Gwynna to Elizabeth and back again.

Gwynna appeared to possess spirit, stamina, and resourcefulness. She'd undertaken an arduous journey alone to find her father. Despite the setback of William's death, she persevered.

Elizabeth was withdrawn and quiet. It hadn't always been so. As a girl, she had a buoyant nature. Her parents' deaths and her own illness sapped the life from her.

Sebastian had made it his mission to bring the light back into her eyes.

He visited her weekly, rearranged her pillows, served her tea, kept up a one-sided conversation about nothing, and waited for her to return to him. He wasn't sure she knew who he was, or that they were married.

That saddened him deeply. Elizabeth was everything to him. She had saved his life when he was mired in grief and sorrow too deep for a boy to understand.

Now she seemed too frail to go about the business of living.

Gwynna, though small and fine-boned, would never be taken for frail. No woman he knew was capable of trekking miles before dawn, as she had yesterday to practice archery.

She wasn't beautiful by the standards of the day. That short, chopped hair looked as if someone had taken a cleaver to it with no effort at symmetry or style.

But its vibrant red brought out the luminous white of her skin, the blue of her eyes, the blush of her mouth.

Gwynna Owen was to the color born.

The inclination to compare the two distressed him. Yet the contrasts were inescapable: Elizabeth was reserved and fragile, Gwynna was rash and possibly barbaric.

Sebastian found her stimulating. Stimulation was an unfamiliar state.

Over this year, as he waited for Elizabeth to heal, winter had seeped into his bones. Ice lodged around his heart. His soul fled to a frigid netherworld.

He had frozen his life. It was a deliberate choice. The cost, he was beginning to understand, had been dear.

Nevertheless, he would wait for Elizabeth as long as it took.

If Gwynna Owen made his blood run, it was only a little. Not enough to worry about.

Sebastian sank deeper into the squabs and prayed for sleep. Blessedly, it came.

***

Sir Bertram had written to William.

Sebastian had learned that fact from Elizabeth's letters after he returned to boarding school following his parents' deaths. It was the second year he attended Michaelmas Half, a courtesy Eton extended to promising students too young for regular enrollment.

He had not especially wished to go away to school the first time, but Gerald had explained it was a great honor to be chosen. Sebastian had found it isolating to be among older boys. Gerald's death but deepened the loneliness.

Each time he looked in the mirror, Sebastian saw a trace of Faylinn, especially about the eyes. Each time, her loss hit him anew, made him crave her more.

He could not imagine why a letter from Sir Bertram would sway William. But Sir Bertram was a man of compassion; perhaps that dented his cousin's implacable armor.

Days and weeks went by with nothing from William himself until the last day of the term, when a note with the ducal seal caused the headmaster to summon him.

"A. MacDuff will fetch you," William's missive read. That was all.

Sebastian knew no such person. That first year, his father had come to fetch him home. He'd felt pride in that, for many students' families sent only servants.

This time, Sebastian waited on a bench outside the school chapel, its soaring arches and spires seemingly designed to make one feel small. His hands nervously twisted the straps of his small case as he waited to see who would appear.

Not a quarter-hour passed before a man of slight build,

reddish hair graying slightly at the temples, and solemn green eyes stood before him.

"Angus MacDuff, my lord. Come with me."

Was he a lord now? His father, second in line to the dukedom, had styled himself simply Gerald Traherne. His father's cousin Hubert was first in line, but he died in a naval battle just weeks after Gerald's death.

Though Sebastian was now heir, a courtesy title seemed wrong. He resolved to follow his father's example.

So he looked at Angus MacDuff and said firmly, "My name is Sebastian Traherne."

The man nodded and picked up the case, leaving him to follow.

The coachman who usually drove his father waited by the carriage, which brought a lump to Sebastian's throat as he climbed in. The stranger sat on the opposite bench.

Was he expected to make idle chit-chat with the man? He couldn't. His father's absence consumed the space around them. The carriage became a suffocating prison of memory and loss.

Sebastian trained his eyes out the window and hoped the man would not speak to him. He tried to focus on the counting strategy his mother devised to help him manage the night episodes.

Half an hour passed in this fashion. Gradually, Sebastian was enveloped by the silence. He disappeared into its emptiness, glad the man had chosen to ignore him.

Yet that made him sadder, somehow.

As he formed that thought, the man leaned forward.

"I was eight—near your age—when my father died. Three decades gone now."

Sebastian stared at him in horror at the unflinching words—*my father died.* They flung the truth at him with blunt, inescapable finality.

"The sorrow doesn't end," the man said. "With time, it gets easier to bear."

A sob that must have been waiting for this single, terrible moment burst from Sebastian. He buried his face against the seat and wept for the loss that would never end.

A handkerchief found its way into his hand.

Finally—he could not have said how long—Sebastian had no more tears.

Only then did the man speak again. "On Sir Bertram's recommendation, His Grace has engaged me to run your household." He hesitated. "I'll do more than that, if you'll allow it."

Sebastian stared at him blankly.

"I will take care of you, lad," Angus MacDuff said. "Would that be acceptable?"

Slowly, Sebastian nodded.

***

"I need money."

Sebastian opened his eyes. He'd been dreaming of Angus, of that terrible time when he'd been at school, newly orphaned, without moorings.

"Your interest is the money, not the name?" he asked as her deep-blue gaze held his.

"I am an Owen. There is no better name in all of Wales. But the money was my mother's right, and mine as William's daughter."

Ah. She would abandon her claim if he paid her off. Disappointing. His foolish meanderings had endowed her with heroic qualities, not mercenary ones.

"You might find it rewarding." She looked away. "I know you don't like me. Perhaps you can set that aside."

Sebastian fixed on the only possible meaning of her words: She was offering herself to him in exchange for money.

And yet, his brain sought a more favorable view: Was she ill? Were there orphaned children for whom she was the only hope and support?

That's it! She's an ill, penniless, auntie trying to save

helpless babes—

No, this was simply greed. Sebastian fixed her with his haughtiest gaze. "I think not."

"You have not heard me out," she protested. "How do you know you will not—"

"Miss Owen," he said sternly, "do not pursue this."

He slanted a gaze at Mrs. Kendall, who appeared lost in sleep. "As I told you last night, I am wed to another. I am not interested in purchasing your favors. Nor do I suffer extortionists, regardless of the lure. We'll go to that island of yours or be damned trying."

"My favors?" She stared at him blankly.

Perhaps he had missed something. Even as the idea formed, the carriage rolled to a stop. Soon his coachman was at the door.

"Beggin' your pardon, Your Grace, but there be a great number of men up ahead blocking the road. Some wagons of corn look to be the cause."

"Corn?" Mrs. Kendall repeated groggily, waking.

"Farmer trying to get his crop to market," the coachman said. "Crowd won't let him pass. We might bluster our way through, but it could get ugly."

Mrs. Kendall's eyes grew wide. "Heavens! Are we to be killed?"

The coachman's gaze briefly met Sebastian's before he disappeared to see to the team.

"Your Grace! Do something!" Mrs. Kendall implored. "What is the point of traveling with a duke if one is to be set upon by peasants?"

For the first time, Gwynna turned to her. "Peasants?"

"They are law-breakers." Mrs. Kendall fanned herself. "That is not to be borne."

"I imagine they think it is the law that is not to be borne," Gwynna said.

Mrs. Kendall gaped at her. "There is no use trying to teach you manners or how to go on because I can see your sympathies lie with those ruffians!"

"They cannot feed their families because the law requires farmers to sell to the Crown and sets the prices high," Gwynna said. "They only seek to buy local corn at a reasonable cost."

"She is a radical—nay, a revolutionary!" Mrs. Kendall cried. "She would have good English folk turn out their pantries to feed the rabble-rousers!"

Sebastian suppressed a sigh. "What would you have me do, Madam?"

"Take me home," she declared. "I refuse to go any farther."

He glanced over at Gwynna, whose flushed features suggested she was but seconds from whipping out that dagger and plunging it into Mrs. Kendall's indignant, heaving breast.

Sebastian left the carriage to talk with his coachman. It would be dark in an hour. They had little choice.

"John recalls an inn a half-mile back," he told the women. "We'll stop there tonight."

Gwynna eyed him disdainfully. "Are you afraid of a mob, Englishman?"

"I should be remiss in my duties were I to march us into the thick of battle. Besides," he could not resist adding, "I have no desire to scuff my new boots."

Mrs. Kendall sat back against the squabs in relief.

"You are useless, Englishman," Gwynna said.

Sebastian was content to draw her fire. It was better than Mrs. Kendall's caterwauling. "Pray, what is the point of leisure if one cannot be useless?"

When they reached the inn, only one room remained. The innkeeper offered to displace servants so Sebastian could have a room. He declined. "I'll bed down in the barn with my coachman."

The man blanched. "Oh, no, Your Grace—"

"The barn is quite acceptable."

Sebastian accompanied the women as the innkeeper led them up two flights of stairs to their room. On the landing, Gwynna turned. "You would sleep in the straw?"

"Do not breathe a word to my tailor."

She tilted her head to study him. "You are full of surprises, Englishman."

From below came the sound of shouts, and something shattering. Sebastian frowned.

"Don't worry," she assured him. "I have my dagger."

As if that would serve. "On the moor—" he began.

"I was caught off-guard. Usually I acquit myself well enough."

Usually? Was the woman often embroiled in combat?

"Your dagger would have been useless against that mob on the road," he pointed out.

"I'd have taken their side," she said. "On Anglesey, we also suffer from the Corn Laws. We, too, cannot buy what our neighbors farm."

"Do not people protest?"

She looked away. "Evil has a way of corroding will."

Sebastian hadn't missed her tiny frown. What evil troubled her? But he didn't ask. It would not do for her to think he had an ounce of depth or compassion.

Did he still? Pretense was a dangerous game. "It would surprise me if evil could dent your will."

"And it would surprise me if anything could dent your sartorial splendor." Her sly, mischievous smile robbed the words of sting.

"You but note the obvious," Sebastian said lightly.

She studied him. "I am beginning to suspect there's little about you that is obvious."

Staring into that intent blue gaze, Sebastian felt his moorings slip. With her short hair and small frame, she might have been a playful pixie who stepped out of a fairy tale to waylay him on the stairs. Those invariably meant trouble, as best he recalled from his mother's stories.

"Twill be noisy," the innkeeper cautioned them. "The hubbub on the road kept people from traveling farther. Tavern's packed."

That changed things. If a drunkard intruded on the women, Sebastian couldn't protect them out in the barn.

The innkeeper was a perceptive man. He led Sebastian to an alcove at the end of the hall. "Isn't much, but better than the barn. There's a pallet, and I hung a cloth, for privacy."

The floor was hard, and the pallet didn't help. But Sebastian fell asleep instantly.

***

Mild weather prevailed that summer, and he and Elizabeth had set up a playhouse of sorts in the gazebo that his mother had loved at the edge of the lake. Vines snaked around the airy wood scrollwork, as if nature sensed Faylinn would come no more and wished to reclaim it.

Sebastian mourned his parents deeply, but he hadn't had another spell like that in the carriage with Angus. That torrent of sorrow had broken, like a wave that peaked and retreated out to sea. Sorrow remained, but as an undercurrent, fed by the unassailable power of loss.

Sometimes he caught Elizabeth looking at him with such kindness it nearly brought tears to his eyes. He fought them, afraid that if he gave in, the tears wouldn't stop.

They spent their days building forts from field rocks, stacking them into uneven walls. They pretended to be soldiers fighting the French, or pioneers forging their way to a new land.

When it rained, they ran to the gazebo and looked out into the mist, pretending to be fairies invisible to the outside world.

One day, Elizabeth met him there, her expression troubled.

"I am to have a governess," she said. "Papa says I should have had one long ago. I am to be *educated*. I already know how to read. What else is there to know?"

"Latin, I suppose," he said. "It's required at my school. I find it interesting."

"No one speaks it. I won't learn it, even if she insists." Elizabeth slumped. "She is to come next week. She'll be old and sour and evil."

But Hannah Miller was none of those things.

Sebastian judged her to be relatively young. She had nice brown eyes and hair that she wore in a tight braid pinned up with black ribbon. Her calm dignity gave her an air of authority, tempered with kindness.

"She will tell me nothing about her husband," Elizabeth complained, days later. "Every time I ask, her features tighten and she talks of something else."

"She prefers to be private," Sebastian said. "Anyone can see that."

"I sense secrets in her. I wish to know them."

"Perhaps she feels she's entitled to keep them."

At her sudden smile, Sebastian felt a quiet peace steal over him. Elizabeth felt like home, the home that had been ripped away with his parents' deaths.

Mrs. Miller proved an amiable teacher. Although Sebastian had tutors, he liked sitting in on her lessons. If the day was fine, she convened class in the gazebo. He was welcome to attend, with the strict warning that the moment he distracted Elizabeth, he would be banished.

When the weather was wet, Mrs. Miller often brought Elizabeth to his house for lessons. She required a full morning's work before allowing play. Then she would visit with the servants, or take tea with the housekeeper Angus hired on the recommendation of Sir Bertram's wife.

Angus himself was a wonder. True to his promise, he had reordered the household, made everything work as it was supposed to.

As time passed, Sebastian found he didn't feel his parents' absence as acutely. His father's leather chair still stood by the fireplace, but with a cheerful blanket thrown over it. The table where Faylinn wrote out her stories now held teacups and a cheerful teapot.

The servants no longer shot him furtive, pitying looks. Angus insisted that they look Sebastian in the eye when they spoke to him. They were not to avoid mentioning his parents, as if they hadn't existed.

Grief, Angus assured him, worked in its own way and time. If he felt sad, it was all right, and if he felt happy, he was not to feel guilty. He was to enjoy the outdoors, and run to the farthest ends of the estate if he wished, or sit all day under a tree and contemplate its leaves.

Sebastian did not do that, for it seemed silly, but it was enough to know that he might, and that no one would think him odd.

Above all, Angus took care of him. As he promised.

But Angus did not coddle. He insisted, for instance, that Sebastian write a note straightaway to Elizabeth's parents each time they had him to dinner. He had to make his bed and keep his room orderly. He had weeding chores in the garden, and a job shoveling out stalls in the stables.

They cooked. Angus taught him how to chop vegetables, to poach an egg—and one very special dish that involved boiling an egg, wrapping it in sausage meat topped with breadcrumbs, and frying it. They made a number of dipping sauces, all delicious.

Angus would pack those special eggs, fruit, and bread in a basket and take Sebastian to a nearby stream or field, where they would eat and inhale the fine air.

And if the rain caught them, there was nothing for it but to shelter under a tree or look up at the heavens and allow the drops to trickle down his face and clothes to the earth where they were bound. There was freedom in accepting the rain and not trying to run from it.

Sebastian still wished for his parents, but understood they were irrevocably lost.

Angus was right: Gradually the loss got easier to bear. Less raw.

The days went by. Summer ended, and he was back for another Michaelmas term until finally, he was old enough to enroll full time.

He made friends there, Drew among them. Andrew Maitland was not rowdy like some of the boys. He was quiet, yet insistent, and his mind always seemed to be working, never idle. One might even call him calculating, if boys could be that.

One holiday, Sebastian brought Drew to Summerlin. It was nice to have his friend to himself, away from the bustle of school.

Then Elizabeth arrived, and balance was upset. Sebastian didn't like the way Drew's eyes lingered on her.

Moreover, she seemed different. She was thirteen, and had lost some of the fullness about her face. Fullness had begun to show in other areas, to noticeable advantage.

The changes made Sebastian uneasy. Drew's attention to her unsettled him further. Elizabeth was *his* friend. Not Drew's.

She smiled at Drew oddly. Fluttered her lashes.

Were they not too young for this?

Finally, wearied by the task of trying to hold back change, Sebastian fled.

Angus found him in the gazebo. "Tis a time for everything, lad. Yours has not yet come."

Sebastian glared at him. "You don't know everything."

"No, I don't. You make your own decisions. My opinion shouldn't matter. Doesn't."

Sebastian put his head in his hands. "It does. It matters so very much."

"It's been you all along, lad. You got yourself through this, found your own solace. You will chart your own course. You're becoming a man, a fine one at that."

Sebastian swallowed hard. "Sometimes I wish

everything back the way it was. But the worst part is that even if both of them were alive, it wouldn't be the same."

"Because you've grown beyond them," Angus said. "But here's the truth, lad: Though they're gone, they're still part of you. You'll never lose that."

Sebastian knew that was true. Still, sometimes it hurt more than he could bear.

***

The face in Gwynna's dreams was a mask of contorted rage and sinister laughter. Bushy eyebrows framed dark eyes that gleamed with feverish intensity.

Even in church, that black gaze had sought her out. Afterward, visiting her grandfather, his message was for her alone. It was as black as his soul.

"Daughter of Sin." The low, insidious whisper. "In sin did thy mother conceive thee. Repent, and be freed from the stain of your conception."

On her grandfather's dying day, Evans darkly proposed marriage. "Open thy heart to the cleansing of God's emissary," he intoned. "Save thy mother's soul."

As he forced her onto her bed, Gwynna kicked out.

"Damn it, woman, come to your senses before you punch a hole in my lungs."

The duke.

Gwynna's eyes opened. She stood on the landing. The duke was on the step below, his hands at her waist, steadying her. The innkeeper was there, too, looking groggily out of sorts. And Mrs. Kendall.

"She's possessed!" Mrs. Kendall cried. "Walking in her sleep. I've never seen the like!"

"Are you ill?" the duke asked quietly.

Gwynna's brain was thick, but she shook her head.

He turned to the innkeeper. "Is there a parlor where Miss Owen can compose herself?"

"Parlor's filled with folks," the man said. "There's yer alcove down the hall, Your Grace. Ye can be private there, with that sheet and all."

The duke scowled. "It's a *sleeping* area. Does that strike you as suitable for a lady?"

The innkeeper blanched. From a floor below came a crashing sound.

"Closet under the stairs," he said quickly. "Has some cleaning supplies and a washtub. Happens, it has no door, so it's respectable but private enough for her to recover."

"A closet." The duke frowned.

Another loud noise sounded below. The innkeeper looked frantic to see to the matter.

Gwynna's brain was still clawing its way through the layers of her dream. Apparently, they were to retreat to a closet with a washtub. Nothing made sense.

The duke's gaze assessed her. He nodded to the innkeeper.

"Wait." Mrs. Kendall returned to their room, then reappeared to slip a shawl over Gwynna's shoulders before retreating—an unexpected kindness.

Their host led them to a dark recess under the stairs, handed the duke a candle, and fled.

Setting the candle on the floor, the duke reached a long arm into the closet and turned the washtub over so it became a makeshift stool. He gestured for her to sit.

"It must be you," Gwynna said. "You'll not fit otherwise." The space followed the stair line, higher on one side, lower on the other. Even at its high point, he wouldn't be able to stand.

He sighed, then folded himself nearly in half to enter. She slipped into a corner.

Perched on the washtub, the duke looked exceedingly uncomfortable. The space was tight for one, never mind two. His knees were bent sharply at an awkward angle.

He wore no waistcoat. The laces of his shirt were open, exposing a swath of skin at his neck. But there was no straw. "They fetched you from the barn?" she asked.

"No. Makeshift arrangement down the hall." He regarded her intently. "Are you well?"

Was she? She didn't often dream about Evans. "It was just a nightmare."

"I had those as a child. Wandered at night. I'd awake at the top of the stairs." His voice was a low rumble in the shadows. "One of my parents would be there to block my path so I couldn't do myself harm."

He'd done the same for her tonight. True to his word, the duke had kept her safe.

"So you see, I don't think you possessed, despite Mrs. Kendall's words," he said. "You were quoting Scripture, or some such. A tussle with your conscience, perhaps?"

"Nothing plagues my conscience."

"Something—or someone—plagues your sleep. Not for the first time."

She eyed him in surprise. "How do you know that?"

"You were fighting someone, and plainly terrified," he said. "From my observation, having known you all of a week, little terrifies you, least of all a dream."

He was wrong. She wasn't fearless. She'd been too afraid to publicly expose Evans.

"Therefore, what you fear is other than imaginary," he went on. "The terror's real, and it persists. Perhaps you're accustomed to hiding it, but tonight fear made a grand escape. Who disturbs your sleep?"

The man was perceptive beyond all measure.

"You're a fine one to talk about hiding things," she parried. "I'm beginning to suspect you wear those magnificent clothes and airs in the service of keeping yourself well hidden."

Gwynna felt, rather than saw, his shock. The air seemed to still.

"I don't know why I didn't see it earlier," she mused. "Blinding the world with your elegance obscures whatever truth lies beneath."

Silence.

But already, Gwynna regretted her words. It was one thing to debate over supper, another to do so in close circumstances and in nightclothes.

The candle in the corridor cast his features in ever-changing light and shadow, and she couldn't discern his expression. What didn't elude was the large outline of the man, the long legs that, even bent, took up the space.

It felt as if there wasn't air to sustain them both.

He shifted his legs. They brushed hers. Instantly, he pulled them back.

"This is deuced awkward," he muttered. His attention shifted to a point over her shoulder. It stayed there as candlelight flitted over his maddeningly opaque features.

Finally, he returned his attention to her. "Sorry. I was counting."

"Counting what?" Gwynna ventured.

"Seconds usually. Sometimes minutes. Something I learned as a child."

That confused her. "Doesn't everyone learn to count as a child?"

"This arose from the sleepwalking. Episodes occurred so often that I feared going to bed. Faylinn—my mother—devised a counting system as a distraction."

He smoothed his palms over his thighs. "Gets me past the rough spots, disciplines unpleasantness into manageable bits. Not working as well tonight."

"Is it the closet that's unpleasant?" Gwynna couldn't resist asking. "Or my presence?"

The duke blew out a breath. "I don't know."

Well, that was honest.

"It's cool for this time of year," he said, abruptly changing the subject. "One hears a volcano is to blame. An eruption halfway across the globe."

Truly? He wished to talk of weather?

At least it would avoid the topic of her nightmare. "On

Anglesey it's said the derwydd—Druid spirits—are to blame. They're angry we can't keep our crops."

"Druid spirits," he murmured. "Do you believe in such things?"

"I believe in the power of spirits. Of good." She hesitated. "And evil."

"It's the latter that dominates your dreams, I gather."

So he'd led her back to that. "There are evil men on Anglesey, as everywhere."

His legs jostled hers. Gwynna put her hand out for balance and found his solid shoulder. Instantly, he stiffened. She withdrew her hand.

"My fault," he muttered. "I fit in this closet about as well as a whale in a fishing pond."

She laughed, glad of something to break the tension.

"Dear God," he murmured. "What have you done with Miss Owen? I'm certain she does not laugh. If I had my quizzing glass, you can be sure I would expose you as an impostor."

"I'm sure I have never heard *you* laugh."

He tilted his head consideringly. "Quite right. I've forgotten mirth—the unadulterated kind, anyway. The sardonic kind is alive and well. I can't think where I'd be without it."

"Perhaps, like me, you've had more pressing concerns."

"My most pressing concern at the moment is leaving this closet," he groused. "I'll ask you again: What or who is the evil that torments your dreams?"

Suddenly, Gwynna wanted to tell him. "January Evans. He calls himself a man of God, but he is far from that." To her dismay, her voice wobbled.

"Pray don't continue if it causes you distress—"

"I can face my demons."

"I will grant that you seem possessed of uncommon strength." He bent forward. "Here's the thing, Miss Owen.

I have found that sometimes we all need a little help."

Candlelight chose that moment to burnish the gold in his hair, the bronze in his eyes—eyes that held hers intently. "Did I misunderstand you earlier?"

"Earlier?"

"In the carriage, before the disturbance on the road, you said giving you money would bring me pleasure. I thought you were offering your favors. Your, er, person."

Gwynna stared at him, aghast.

"Forgive me," he said gruffly. "I fear my ability to trust has gone the way of mirth."

He cleared his throat. "Perhaps, as neither of us seems fated to sleep tonight, you might explain. Why do you need the money, and why would it be my pleasure to give it to you?"

"Because it would help others," she said.

"Ah. The satisfaction of doing good." The duke sat back. "Let us stipulate that some people find reward in good deeds. Why do you think I might be one of them?"

"Tomorrow, I'll show you my country. Perhaps we'll find out."

"Very well. Let us quit this infernal closet while I can still move." He shifted so she could exit, then extricated himself.

When he picked up the candle, Gwynna pulled the shawl around her, suddenly aware she stood in her nightclothes. Tactfully, he kept his gaze elsewhere as he walked her to her room.

At the door, she turned to him. "To see the truth of my country, you must be open to belief."

He frowned. "What sort of belief?"

"Magic lies at the heart of Anglesey—of Wales."

"We are not seeking unicorns, Miss Owen," the duke said sternly. "I require documents and records to prove your case. I won't fall for mirror tricks."

"Not tricks, nor unicorns," Gwynna said. "Belief in

legend and lore, in valor that fights on against certain defeat, even death. Belief that those who are lost live on, until the end of time. I'll ask you to see with those eyes."

He stared at her as if she were speaking in tongues.

"I expect it won't be easy for you, Englishman. Perhaps you'll surprise us both."

With that, Gwynna slipped into her room.

Chapter Five

Angus MacDuff stared at the missive, with its elegant seal and elaborate scrawl. He was accustomed to receiving frequent letters from Sebastian, expressing the heartfelt desire that Angus's health continue to improve.

No matter how often Angus assured him of his excellent health, Sebastian always insisted he take time before returning to his duties—though he had precious few of those anymore.

Angus did not wish to take time. Inactivity did not suit him, for he was not a passive man. Already, he felt like a fossil. Four months of idleness seemed a lifetime.

Sebastian had sent him to this trim little cottage in the Cotswolds, where he was to enjoy the air and take upon himself only those activities that resulted in complete and utter relaxation.

Such a dreary chore.

Every morning Angus walked from one end of Chipping Campden to the other, duly pausing to appreciate the fine gothic architecture of St. James Church, its medieval relics, imposing bell tower, and the folly of wealthy wool merchants who had not thought it absurd to have a staple of wool carved over their tombstones or laid at the feet of their sculpted likenesses.

The traders in Market Hall did not hold his interest; Sebastian had fitted the cottage with everything he could possibly need. The town's tallest hill afforded a splendid view of the valley, but he had explored all the place had to offer and then some.

Angus thought it likely he would die of boredom.

Oh, the business with his health had given him pause. He'd had a fainting spell—a series of them, in honesty—but he felt fine. Had the last episode not occurred in Sebastian's presence, no one would have been the wiser.

Sebastian had summoned a team of doctors and, upon their recommendation, insisted that Angus retire to this far-too-placid village to recover his health.

In truth, there was only one reason to be in the Cotswolds. Otherwise, Angus would have defied Sebastian and all his quacks. He'd have won that battle because his Scot's disposition had a bedrock of stubbornness that, when circumstances warranted, would not be moved.

But come here he had—on a whim, when Sebastian had given him his pick of locales. Unfortunately, while Angus's health had recovered, his melancholy deepened.

He had a growing sense that the mistakes he had made in his life had brought him to this solitary cottage and, perhaps, a turning point.

Yet he had no plausible excuse for seeking out the person he most wished to. Oh, he knew where to find her. He'd kept track of her over the years. She, too, was the beneficiary of Sebastian's generosity. They had that in common, if little else.

Angus hadn't sought her out for many reasons—among them, the knowledge that she would turn him away, for she, too, possessed a fine, impermeable stubbornness.

And so, without the distraction of even such light duties as Sebastian allowed him these days, the melancholy had come upon him.

The past was ever present, it seemed.

Angus broke open the ducal seal with a faint hope that change was in the offing.

Change indeed.

He read with growing alarm Sebastian's account of recent events and what amounted to a plea — no, it must be taken as command. Angus's heart leapt to his throat.

For Sebastian was quite clear as to the other personage whose assistance he also required.

Well, and he had been wishing for an excuse, hadn't he? She would not turn down a ducal request. Rather, she would—just not one from Sebastian.

Emotions Angus had not felt in a very long time threatened to bubble upward, but as he had long since achieved a degree of discipline that might seem to some as excessive, Angus did not worry overmuch about an occasional, uncharacteristic lapse.

Happily, Sebastian's summons was meant to be carried out instantly. With a thrill of anticipation he tried half-heartedly to suppress, Angus began to pack a small bag, which took him all of five minutes.

Then he donned the hat he usually wore to church, a pair of neat, plain gloves, and left his cottage on Calf Lane, driving the carriage Sebastian had left for his use.

Half an hour later—so close, all this time!—he knocked on the bright blue wooden door on Chapel Street in Stow-on-the-Wold.

Angus had not been to this house. He hadn't seen its occupant in several years. As he waited, his brain recited the worn couplet: "Stow-on-the-Wold, where the wind blows cold."

He couldn't imagine why the village was so proud of such doggerel that it was spread far and wide in hopes of luring tourists. A cold wind appealed to no one.

Angus hoped that did not portend a chilly reception.

There was still no response to his knock. Had she peeked out of the window, discerned who stood on her steps, and decided she had no wish to set eyes on him?

Angus's mind wandered in a darker direction. What if she were unwell? Dying?

It was one thing not to lay eyes on her for years. He had made his peace with that. How would he reconcile himself to the knowledge that she no longer walked this earth, that he would never see her likeness again?

Worse, not to have known the precise moment when her soul had fled?

Had he wasted his life in the service of stubbornness and pride?

A chill swept him, along with that cruel, cold wind.

Suddenly the door opened. The very person who had been the subject of his dark speculation stood at the threshold.

Her chestnut hair had streaks of grey. For a moment that gave him a start, but he could only imagine how much he had changed in the intervening years. Certainly, his own hair had only a trace of the red that was his family's distinguishing characteristic.

She was still slender and fit; she probably walked as much as he did. Her height was imposing, a few inches above his own.

He didn't mind that. Indeed, her proportions had kindled not a few thoughts as to how their forms might align, should the occasion present itself.

She was not pleased to see him.

Indeed, the chill in her gaze approached that which had knifed through him at the very thought that she might be ill or dying.

Angus removed his hat and bowed. "Mrs. Steele—"

"Mr. MacDuff," she acknowledged in that frosty, yet dry-as-dust voice known to command nigh-instant obedience from her charges.

No point in hoping for a warmer reception. Nevertheless, he had a piece of information to impart, and he knew it would rouse her in a way that no amount of effort on his part could.

"We are needed," he said.

Confusion swept her features. Her eyes widened. "I-is it Sebastian?"

Angus took her discomposure as an invitation to step

inside, which he did with alacrity. He rather savored the first display of emotion he'd seen in her in years.

Yet it was cruel to allow her to suffer.

"He is well," Angus assured her. "But he seeks our help. I take the liberty of thinking that you will agree we must answer the call."

He handed her Sebastian's missive, which included a private note for her as well.

She read both. "Oh!"

They stood awkwardly just inside the door, for she had not invited him to sit or to make himself comfortable. Angus knew better than to hope for that.

"It is a significant journey," he said. "I would understand if you do not wish to travel such a long way, and in my company."

Her brown eyes narrowed, and the coolness seeped back into them. "Any inconvenience afforded by your company, Mr. MacDuff, is outweighed by my abiding affection for His Grace."

Angus knew Hannah Steele well enough to vouch for that. Affection gained was affection that persevered.

Present company excepted. Then again, she had never truly held him in affection. Perhaps if Hell froze over.

"When do you wish to leave?" she asked.

"When can you be ready?" He could predict her answer.

"Within the hour." She opened the door wider.

And just like that, Angus found himself outside on her stoop once more.

"I must make arrangements," he said, though in truth, he was ready now. "I will fetch you in an hour, if that's satisfactory."

"Quite." She closed the door.

She hadn't asked where they were bound, how long they'd be gone, or what precisely was required of them.

And if the request hadn't come from Sebastian himself,

she would have slammed the door in his face.

He sighed.

***

In the morning, Sebastian put Mrs. Kendall in the baggage coach and packed her off to Horace Busby.

That left no chaperone, presenting him with a moral crisis, especially as he'd spent a much of the night after that closet interlude reeling from the heady experience of being confined with Gwynna Owen in the dark.

As Angus would say, between right and wrong there was no middle ground. Sebastian had a duty to protect her reputation—whatever its state—or at least not degrade it further.

But given a choice between that and subjecting them to Mrs. Kendall's harangues, he'd found it no choice at all.

Mrs. Kendall seemed relieved not to have to travel further into the land of brigands and lawless mobs. Sebastian paid her a generous sum, and her fulsome expressions of gratitude embarrassed and surprised him.

He intended to engage a maid at the first opportunity. There must be no repeat of that intimacy in the closet. It felt *nearly* like a flirtation—and not the safe sort.

Flirtation was a game he knew well. He applied himself diligently to the chore of being society's most eligible and elusive bachelor.

Never did he allocate excessive time to any lady, or give her reason to hope. He allowed no more than three minutes for conversation—else he'd be expected to ask her to dance. With mamas, he had to be quicker. In two minutes, they'd invite him to call the next day.

Consequently, he'd broken no hearts. He sought no intimacy, nor gave it. Any wayward impulses were tossed into an iron-clad box in his brain and imprisoned.

Those strategies eluded him in that closet. Even without a door, there was no getting around the fact they'd been in confined conditions, unchaperoned, in the dark.

Her heady scent—more like a wild essence—crawled up his arms, over his chest, into his nostrils, his mouth, and other cavities he didn't know existed. Sebastian couldn't recall such a thing happening in a woman's presence.

It was like finding a heretofore unknown flower that redefined one's notion of flowers.

Excruciating.

Intoxicating.

Counting proved useless. Finite numbers failed to banish her ineffable presence.

Her night-rail—thank God for that shawl—was a sturdy, serviceable fabric possessing no diaphanous qualities. But he didn't need to see through it to imagine what might lie beneath.

Nevertheless, he had strict boundaries. And although that closet intimacy brought to mind all sorts of boundaries that might be crossed, it was not in him to do so.

Still, her mix of vulnerability and strength drew him. When he'd seen her at the top of the stairs, a step from disaster, his instinct was to protect her—his cursed sense of responsibility for those who depended on him.

Sebastian reminded himself that Gwynna was not part of his life, only someone who wished to be. A pretender, whose claim he would likely disprove.

And all that nonsense about magic? Surely, she didn't think to make him a believer.

Yet today, as their meandering journey into Wales unfolded, he saw that she meant to try. They stopped the carriage often so she could point out landmarks and tell him their legends.

The deeper they got into Wales, the more truth and fiction grew muddled. The land itself seemed to conspire in the telling.

At first, Wales was scrub moors, like Cheshire. Then the moors rolled up into green hills, which swept into artistic crags. Rock became stones, stones became castles, and castles became piles of odd-shaped ruins that might have existed since time began.

Sebastian had seen his share of ruins. England and the Continent had a nigh-endless supply. The Romans left roads, baths, and aqueducts. Medieval kings left castles. Clan barons left ring forts and *chevaux de fries* for defense against cavalry. Unrecorded civilizations built stone circles, their purpose lost in the fog of prehistory.

But nothing had prepared him for Wales's stone and earthen remnants of worlds past. Or its strangely named towns and lilting language, seemingly out of time and place. Ghosts seemed to whisper on the wind, only a breath removed from walking the roads they now traveled.

They crossed a river that emptied into the Irish Sea. Beyond that lay Ireland, and it was no stretch to imagine it and Wales as halves of the same primordial whole.

"The river winds down from Lake Bala in the mountains," Gwynna said. "A sunken town is said to lie beneath the lake. Legend tells of an evil prince, who ruled there and pursued a life of greed and excess. The gods warned him to cease his cruelty, but he persisted."

"Unwisely, I imagine."

She nodded. "He threw a feast to celebrate his grandson's birth and commissioned a renowned harpist to entertain. As the harpist began to play, a bird came and warned him vengeance would soon strike the prince. The bird led the harpist outside and sang him to sleep."

He could guess where this led. "Disaster struck?"

"When the harpist awoke, the palace was gone. A lake had consumed the town. Ever after, the harpist dedicated his music to that which had saved him."

"He dedicated himself to the bird?"

Gwynna made an impatient sound. "*Good* saved him. Evil received its due."

"I pity the prince's guests," Sebastian said. "They died through no fault of their own."

"Those who consort with evil deserve their fate."

"One can take tea with blackguards without endorsing their crimes." In his diplomacy work, he'd broken bread with many such men. "Some guests were simply in the wrong place at the wrong time. What you see as vengeance may only be the unjust hand of fate."

Gwynna's chin rose. "I'd have to be persuaded."

She had a stubborn streak. That bothered Sebastian: What if proof of her parentage was not to be had? Would she give up her quest? Was she, in fact, persuadable?

Diligence would be required.

Perhaps wine!

That annoying voice again. Sebastian tossed it into his brain's iron box.

Over the miles, more stories tumbled out. She told of an evil king known for his drunkenness, cruelty, and other acts she assured him were too terrible to describe.

"Prophecy said a creature would punish the king. The beast's hair, teeth, and eyes would be yellow. The terrified king shut himself in his palace. But one day, the beast appeared outside the castle gates and called out his name."

"Ah. The king's curiosity proved fatal?"

"He peeked through the keyhole at the beast and instantly fell down, writhing in agony.."

It struck Sebastian that the yellow beast might stand for something else—something powerful enough to fell peasants and kings alike. The plague?

Regrettably, he was intimately acquainted with that scourge. He tried not to think of that, and to focus on the stories. He found they reminded him of his mother's tales.

Faylinn's often had a moral, too. Sometimes, evil won. As a child, that confused him. What was she trying to teach him? That evil might prevail, regardless?

She told of princesses married off by their fathers to keep peace or gain power. Of castles built for no reason other than to stake a claim on land so a warring brother could not. Of crowns stolen from their rightful owners, heads separated from shoulders in the process.

Pixies and sprites often meddled in human affairs.

Unexpectedly, he felt a lump in his throat. How long had it been since he'd had enchantment in his own life? Faylinn's stories—like her—were but distant memories.

Instead, he'd contrived his own narrative built on lies—all for Elizabeth.

He recalled the precise moment when he decided she would be his. At sixteen, she'd broken her leg jumping from the rail of a pen used for training horses. He and Drew—he'd again invited Drew to Summerlin—carried her into his house, where a doctor decreed she must stay.

Mrs. Miller moved in to attend to her charge. Sir Bertram and Lady Throckmorton visited daily. Sebastian and Drew became Elizabeth's loyal attendants, fetching whatever she desired.

Drew tried to charm her. He told her he might join the Royal Navy, engage Napoleon's fleet, serve under Admiral Nelson. Elizabeth admired his patriotism.

And he found reasons to touch her. Adjusting her pillows, Drew's hand brushed her cheek. He'd smile enigmatically, his dark gaze filled with promise.

Her blushes spoke volumes. Sebastian wondered how she would react if he did such things. Yet when he had sordid fantasies, Elizabeth didn't figure in them.

Soon she would make her come-out. Men would court her. He would be among them, for he didn't like her dancing with someone else, or sharing intimacies with someone like Drew.

Angus, distracted by their guests during Elizabeth's convalescence, nevertheless noticed his distress. Angus assured him that even though Drew made her blush, Elizabeth could judge character well enough.

Sebastian wondered why Angus hadn't married. Perhaps someone had broken his heart.

Did hearts break? He wasn't happy about Drew's attentions to Elizabeth, but he didn't think his heart was broken. Love would come, and he would know when it summoned him. In the meantime, he would go out into the world and live a full life. And then, return to Elizabeth.

Things had worked out differently than he envisioned But Elizabeth was his.

As he had wanted.

***

Chapter Six

She had not changed.

Angus studied Mrs. Steele's rigid profile as she sat across from him, staring out the carriage window. The years had been kind—or had simply not dared to disturb her countenance, as forbidding as the Herodotus statue in Sebastian's library.

He found the threads of gray in her hair becoming. He liked to think of aging not as a step on the path toward death, but as a process of acquiring experience, seasoning, and significance.

Life ought to be savored, the years celebrated.

Angus had always lived a disciplined life. He did not indulge in transitory pleasures, but adhered to the pillars of right living: abstinence, asceticism, moral rigor, frugality, and temperance. By such tools was chaos defeated.

Meaning inhered in whether a man had done right by others and by his mortal soul.

Angus knew he had an old soul. He suspected this was its last go-round, that after this life there would be no more chances to improve it.

Lately, though, he found himself wondering whether devotion to duty and discipline had led him to miss certain exquisite pleasures that themselves might feed the soul.

Perhaps it was only his recent brush with mortality that gave rise to such thoughts. Studying Hannah Steele's stiff profile did nothing to banish them.

She was still thin, almost girlish. Angus wished she had not swathed herself in high-necked black bombazine, as if she were in mourning. He would have welcomed the opportunity to scrutinize more of that lithe form than was presently available for inspection.

Was this the manner in which she always attired herself, or was it entirely due to his presence? She could not have known that covering herself from head to toe was insufficient to dispel the masculine thoughts she undoubtedly sought to defend against.

Indeed, it only gave rise to the notion of uncovering her—button by button, sleeve by sleeve, layer by layer.

Providing the circumstances were right, which they weren't. Had never been, in fact.

Likely, they'd go to their respective graves with this thing between them unspoken, unanswered, unrequited.

Sometimes, discipline had its drawbacks.

But there was that one time, when he'd seen rather more of her than either of them intended. To be sure, she had been in the arms of another man.

Such thoughts that scene had inspired in him over the years!

Her attention shifted from the window to him. "Will you tell me what has happened?"

Though his eyes wished to focus on her mouth—still pink and impossibly evocative—Angus forced himself to meet her gaze.

"I don't know the whole. The young lady apparently needs guidance. I sense that the duke" — he didn't often use Sebastian's given name in public, even in the confines of a carriage —"does not know what to do with her. She believes they are related."

Mrs. Steele frowned. "A fortune-hunter?"

Angus shook his head. "His Grace's skill in avoiding that breed of predatory female is rather legendary."

"Who is she?"

"Gwynna Owen. From an island off North Wales."

"Is that where we are bound?"

"Not so far as that. We are directed to the old duke's

castle in Cheshire. Apparently it is a pile of stones with an inadequate staff. He wishes to put the place in readiness."

"Readiness for what?"

"I believe he expects to bring the young lady there, and that she needs to be taken in hand. I imagine you will know immediately what is to be done." He hesitated. "There is no one to match your instincts in that regard."

A blush stole over her features.

Angus found it entrancing that a woman of her years was capable of blushing. He'd stated no more than truth: Hannah had turned any number of young ladies into paragons. She had done so with compassion—a quality she did not, however, display to everyone.

Him, for instance.

He wished to reach across the space between their seats and touch her hand, but she would not welcome that. It surprised him to think of touching her. Such instincts did not come naturally to him, for which he was thankful.

Certainly, he was too old to play the fool.

When they reached the inn, Angus carried her trunk up to her room. He wished to make sure there was no inconvenience to disturb her. Not that she'd complain. Though she could be stiff and uncompromising—in truth, she seemed to adapt to life's bumps.

Why else had she changed her name so many times? Angus wished he knew the reasons, but she was as private and closed as any locked door.

"Thank you," she said primly when he set her trunk on the floor.

Angus turned to go, then thought better of it. He didn't know how long this venture of theirs would last, but this awkwardness would grow intolerable over an extended period of time.

Already, the tension had given him a headache.

"I wish to say, Mrs. Steele," he began, "that I am grateful to you for responding to his summons with such alacrity, especially as you can't wish to spend time in my presence. I hope we can dispel this unease between us."

Her lips pursed in disapproval.

"If there is a grievance you care to air, please do so," he continued. "I cannot think that after all these years you still nurture—"

"An abject loathing of you, Mr. MacDuff? That would be unworthy of me, would it not?"

"Hannah," he began.

"Please leave." Her voice left no room for debate.

This was going to be much tougher than he imagined.

***

"From here to Anglesey is not far, but the tides in the strait will not be favorable yet," Gwynna said. "In the meantime, we'll see Conwy Castle."

"Another castle," the duke murmured. "Must be five or six by now."

"We saw those from the road. We'll walk on top of this one."

Conwy was Gwynna's favorite castle. Built by Edward I, it shot skyward atop a massive rock, the better to intimidate challengers to his claim on the land.

As a child, she loved climbing the round tower's steps with her grandfather. They'd walk along the battlements, cast their eyes to the craggy hills, and imagine Welsh archers charging down from them.

Sometimes she envisioned herself among them. Welsh women had fought alongside men for centuries. But though women in her culture weren't weak, like all women, they were vulnerable.

Gwynna understood from an early age that no father would protect her; no mother would ease her path to womanhood. She resolved to find her own strength.

What she lacked in physical stature, she made up for in quickness and stamina. In good weather, she could climb Mount Snowdon in a half day. She managed her grandfather's sheep herd until illness forced him to sell. Her archery skills surpassed those of most men.

But her accomplishments didn't extend to the feminine arts. She eschewed her cousin Rhianna's gently used dresses in favor of breeches. One graceless attempt at a simple country dance left her determined not to repeat it.

Instead, Gwynna consumed books. In *Robinson Crusoe* she found a kindred spirit who saved himself after a shipwreck, using only what sea and land provided. In Mary Wollstonecraft she discovered a like-minded woman who felt the rich were morally obliged to help the poor.

She read about two sea-roving female pirates as swashbuckling as their male counterparts. Rumor held that one eventually became a nun, but Gwynna preferred to imagine her still sailing toward grand adventures.

Often, she read until dusk, perched on a hill above Moelfre Harbor. On fine days, fluffy clouds reflected on the water in shimmering white ripples, forming an ethereal path between lands seen and unseen. Past, present, and future felt like part of the same, unbroken wave.

But there were disturbing ripples. Her grandfather gave her no understanding of those who aimed to defile. When Evans began to stalk her, Gwynna hadn't known what he was about.

He penned notes to her. The first invoked Satan, and his descent into damnation. Evans said she faced the same fate because she was born out of wedlock.

No one had ever condemned her for that. Harsh dogma had no place on Anglesey. Most islanders were dissenters who'd broken with the Anglicans; no bishop was closer than Bangor, on the mainland.

But Evans wasn't a native islander. He arrived a few years ago without family or history, as if he'd washed up on the beach like so much flotsam. But his resonant baritone could command a room; he was soon holding forth in meeting houses and barns.

When he visited her grandfather, he read aloud in that sonorous voice—often, from John Milton's "Paradise Lost" with its doomsday horrors.

A theme emerged: Woman—Eve—was to blame for the world's woes and thus must subject herself to Adam. Some of the lines were uncomfortably explicit. He didn't read those aloud, but saved them for his notes:

"Her bosom smelling sweet…forth flourished thick the clustering vine…up stood the cornie reed."

"With conjugal caresses, from his lip not words alone pleased her….To the nuptial bower I lead her."

There was no mistaking those words. Gwynna kept her dagger close when he was near.

Evans was far from the righteous man he pretended to be. He paid farmers to siphon off crops he sold on the black market in defiance of the Corn Laws. Underpaid miners worked for his smuggling ring to help feed their families.

People resented him, but his illicit operations helped them survive, so they tolerated his hypocrisy.

On the day her grandfather died, Evans came for her. Marrying him, he said, would redeem her sin of bastardy.

She refused. He tried force. Her dagger saved her.

In the days that followed, as Gwynna sorted through her grandfather's few possessions, she wondered if Evans would return. He didn't show himself.

So she set off to find her father—and found someone else entirely.

Who was this duke, really? He professed to seek truth, but kept his own marriage secret. He wielded those grand airs like a weapon.

Oh, but his words were a marvel. Thanks to her tutor's books, words lived deep in her. Apparently, they'd bided their time, only waiting for the right audience—the Duke of Claremont, for whom debate was a blood sport requiring precision—more rapier than broadsword.

As if on cue, the man emerged from the round tower.

Today, his cravat was understated, but no less elegant. The pantaloons and jacket were perfectly cut. The man radiated the authority and wealth of his class.

Yet a Spartan air hovered about his robust shoulders, suggesting substance beneath the show, as if the finery was separate from the man himself—a costume, perhaps.

He joined her at a gap in the battlements that afforded a view across the river to the hills.

"You'll find this worth the climb, Englishman."

"Compelling," he acknowledged. "Those woods beyond the river might hide revolutionaries. Standing on these walls, one has the sense of a bloody battle looming."

"That's it exactly."

A smile played about his mouth. "You'd like that."

She shot him an answering smile. They regarded one another in an extended silence that suddenly felt awkward.

"I imagine dukes are from the cradle trained," Gwynna said, aiming for distraction. "Was all that magnificence instilled from birth?"

He frowned. "I suppose there are some unfortunates who learn before they utter their first syllable that they are destined for a dukedom."

At her puzzled expression, he arched a brow. "Did you think I *wanted* to be a duke?"

"But the money, the title, the property—you did not wish for those?"

Silver cooled his gaze. "You do realize that people had to die? That was not my wish."

She flushed. "I formed the impression there was no love lost between you and William."

"There were two others between the title and me. One was my father. His death I mourned deeply. He died with my mother in a carriage accident when I was seven."

Oh. He had been orphaned, too.

"My father's older cousin, Hubert, also stood to inherit," he continued. "But Hubert died in a naval battle shortly after my parents were killed. So, no, I was not trained for this, nor wished it."

She touched his sleeve. "I assumed much. I'm sorry."

He stepped back, beyond her reach.

"But…is it so great a burden to be a duke?" Gwynna persisted. "You wear it well."

He lifted a brow. "I do, don't I?"

"And it's your choice to dress as you do, to wield that quizzing glass—"

"Yes, it's what I live for—to be shallow and obscenely privileged."

His sardonic tone gave her pause. Did he disdain the very image at which he excelled?

"What does your wife think?" she ventured.

Silence. Then: "I don't know."

"But…shouldn't she have a say in your choices?"

Something flared in his gaze. "She is the reason for them."

The set of his jaw told her she would hear no more. His secrets were closed to her.

But he continued to study her. Almost imperceptibly, his gaze swept her from head to toe. "I sense you value this place for more than its view."

Would a shallow and obscenely privileged man have detected that?

Gwynna nodded. "The rivers, the woods, the hills—they're the essence of Wales, not just now, but through time—vibrant, alive, enduring."

He frowned. "It's but landscape. Passive."

"It's anything but passive. It's all who came before, all who come after."

Willing him to understand, Gwynna moved closer. "It is my home," she said softly. "My *heart*."

The duke's mouth pulled in a tight line.

Then he walked away.

***

Bracing sea breezes tingled Sebastian's skin, burned his lungs, whipped that salty tang through and through him. His senses roused, as if from a long sleep.

Crossing the strait proved as harrowing as navigating heavy seas in a gale. The ferry bucked up and down, side to side, merciless and wild, like an unbroken stallion. One might be forgiven for thinking survival unlikely.

Gwynna explained that tides in the serpentine strait between the mainland and Anglesey flowed in opposing directions from either end, producing strong currents in the middle. "Dozens of ships have wrecked over the years."

"I've little doubt," he muttered. His stomach lurched.

"Two sank here exactly a hundred years apart," she added with a mischievous grin. "Each had one survivor, with the same name: Hugh Williams."

"You'll not persuade me to believe in ghosts." He paused. "Still, I hope no one by that name is on our ferry."

She smiled her approval. "Perhaps you're learning to see with new eyes, Englishman."

Sebastian hoped not. He was wedded to the usual ways of seeing. A year ago he'd made clear-eyed choices. Not once had he doubted them.

Why, then, had Gwynna's words atop that castle—*my home, my heart*—gutted him?

Elizabeth was his home. And if he had a heart, she was surely that, too.

Yet Sebastian knew that if he looked into the mirror, he'd see a home he did not yet have, a heart grievously lacking. The core of him felt empty and hollow.

Worse, his brain lurched in unwanted directions. Atop that castle, he found himself noticing Gwynna's slender waist, gently curved hips, and slim ankles that peeked below the hem of her frock.

Now, he couldn't wrench his gaze from her as she stood on the ferry deck. Her eyes sparkled with pure joy as they approached her island.

No one in his world revealed unadulterated emotion. Calibration ruled. He himself was an excellent calibrator.

But Gwynna set off a jumble of impulses that bumped and bucked like that blasted ferry.

Among them: an utterly foreign need to be...claimed.

Not because he had wealth and a title. Not because he had perfected the artful dodging of ostrich feathers. Not because he knew calligraphy or could ferret out important men's weaknesses. Especially not because he possessed exceptional fashion sense.

He wanted to be claimed simply as Sebastian Traherne, whose parents possessed neither airs nor title, only love in abundance.

Hell. Surely he was not still that forlorn orphan boy, yearning in futility for the unconditional love of those forever beyond his reach.

Alas, as the wind blew and the ferry reared, the sharp taste of yearning overtook him.

Sebastian forced his brain to mundane matters. He'd chosen not to put his coach and team through the ferry ordeal. They were on the mainland with his coachman. Now he needed to hire a conveyance.

But as they disembarked, he realized he wasn't sure of her plans. "Do you return to your grandfather's house?"

A shadow crossed Gwynna's features. "I am reluctant to stay there alone."

Because of that man of God who was anything but.

"We'll stay at an inn," Sebastian said. "I'll engage a maid for you. In the morning, we'll go together to your grandfather's house."

"I do not need a maid."

"I've already risked scandal by sending Mrs. Kendall home. Proprieties—"

"Only you have ever regarded them."

Her defiance kicked his pulse up. They said nothing more until they arrived in Beaumaris, site of yet another castle, its ancient gray walls reflected in a murky moat.

"It's in better condition than the others," he observed.

"Because it's unfinished. That didn't stop Edward from staking the heads of Welsh warriors atop the walls."

Her tone suggested she'd have been happy to battle the evil Edward. Not with that rusty dagger, he hoped. Perhaps with bow and arrow. Could she really shoot?

"You Welsh prefer war, it seems." He handed the carriage reins to the inn's ostler.

"We love peace," she corrected. "But we crave sovereignty."

He slanted her a gaze. "And yet, here you are, part of our little British kingdom."

"Because Edward connived to have his son born on Welsh soil so he could proclaim him Prince of Wales. But the last true Welsh prince was the Knight of Glyn."

"Who?"

"Owen Glendower, as you English know him."

Ah. The "Owen" she spoke of that first night was an actual historical figure. Sebastian tried to recall what he'd learned in school. The man had been a Welsh Tudor cousin with a notable military career in England. But in his later years, he led a Welsh revolt against English rule.

What stood out in that history class—for every fourteen-year-old boy in it—was a 1402 battle, after which Owen allowed Welsh women to mutilate the private parts of English soldiers.

That was her hero. Estimable fellow.

Was Gwynna acquainted with that bit of legend? Did she keep her dagger at the ready for carving her initials on an Englishman's most valued possessions?

"You look as if you've just taken a mouthful of rotten fish," she said.

"Your prince was a tyrant. Mysteriously vanished at the end. Seems he lacked the courage to stand and fight."

"No one knows what became of him, just as no one

knows what became of Arthur."

"King Arthur? That fellow who may or may not have existed?"

"Oh, he existed, Englishman," she said. "I could show you the cave in which legend says he is but resting with his knights for when he's needed. You'll see his red dragon insignia throughout Wales. On Anglesey, we tend to favor Owen's standard—a rampant lion."

He scoffed. "A raging lion. Why am I not surprised?"

"Owen was a visionary," she insisted. "He would have—"

"Murdered all English," he interjected. "I've studied history, too, madam. Your Knight of Glyn was a brute who cut a swath of death and destruction wherever he went."

"I am proud to be descended from him." Abruptly, Gwynna reached under her skirts and pulled the dagger from a sheath strapped to her leg.

Sebastian half-expected her to stab him with it. Instead, she held it out for his inspection.

"This is his dagger," she said. "It's four centuries old. Passed down through our family."

He briefly registered the hilt's embedded red stones and indentations where others had been. But he was still contemplating that fleeting glimpse of her bare calf.

Weren't women supposed to wear stockings?

"Put aside any notion of fighting on this trip," he said finally, his tone stern. "We may be on opposite sides of this business, but I will protect you."

She eyed him strangely. Her bottom lip quivered.

Then she burst into tears.

***

Crying was for missish females. She wasn't that. Yet when the duke promised to protect her, she turned into a watering pot. To add to her discomfort, Rhys Gareth, a friend of her grandfather's, was on duty at the inn.

"Where is it ye've been, Gwynna?" His gaze shifted to

the duke. "Who's this?"

"Perhaps you'll enlighten me as to the reason for your interest," the duke said coolly.

Rhys ignored him. "Why are you with this Englishman, and in need of a room?"

"*Two* rooms," the duke corrected, his gaze hard.

"Your grandfather would be deeply sorrowed," Rhys said mournfully.

The duke turned to her. "Is there reason not to take offense at his insinuations? I'll happily rearrange his features, although he is decades older than my usual sparring partners."

"Rhys is a family friend," Gwynna assured him. Then she spoke to Rhys in Welsh: "This man is of good character. That is the truth."

"There's truth, and there's what my eyes are telling me," he said, also in Welsh. "Why'd you cut your hair?"

She ignored the last. "He is helping me search for my mother's marriage documents."

"You don't need a piece of paper to prove your worth. That's just Evans's talk." He lowered his voice. "A man came by, asking about him. Might be the law."

That surprised her. Had Evans's illicit schemes gained the Crown's attention?

"Might have been just a tourist," Rhys added. "I told him some island stories. Mayhap he'll spread the word. We could use the money." He studied her. "Are ye well?"

Beside her, the duke shifted impatiently. "Am I to kill him or no?"

Gwynna couldn't help but laugh.

"I suppose that must be taken as no." The duke returned his attention to Rhys. "Miss Owen will require the services of a maid."

"I will not," But she couldn't muster her earlier defiance. Something in her had softened.

In Cheshire, when the duke had pledged to keep her

safe, she hadn't known what that meant. Today, he'd been unequivocal—*I will protect you.* That overwhelmed her.

Rhys was silent as he led them upstairs. He shot her a troubled look before he left them.

The duke insisted on inspecting her room. "No lock," he said frowning at the door.

"Locks aren't needed here," Gwynna said.

"I'll have your doubting innkeeper send up a maid."

"I will turn her away."

He gave her a fulminating look. "You're impossible."

"Because I disagree with you?"

His mouth curved. "No one does. Title, and all that."

Goodness. A self-deprecating sense of humor.

The duke studied the furniture. "I'll move that chest to the door. When I leave, you need only slide it a few inches more to prevent anyone from entering."

As he slid the chest across the room, Gwynna forced her gaze away from his easy display of strength. She glanced at the tiny window. Its worn curtains reminded her of her grandfather's house.

To her dismay, tears again threatened.

He was studying her.

"I don't usually cry," she said apologetically. "It's just that no one has ever done this for me."

"No one's moved furniture for you?"

Gwynna managed a smile. "Taken care of me."

"What of your grandfather?"

She hesitated. "He struggled. My mother's death, then my grandmother's—I think he simply lost heart."

The duke scowled. "Whatever his sorrow, how could he neglect a child?"

"Grief changes the heart. I didn't fill the void."

His gaze softened. Amber warmed those hazel depths.

"I don't want pity," she insisted. "I don't want to cry either. 'Tis weak."

'No, not pity." The duke stepped closer. His hands

hovered above her shoulders, as if to comfort her.

Gwynna swayed toward him. But he let his hands fall to his sides.

"If tears are weak, all of us share that weakness," he said gruffly. "'Tis human."

"Not you."

His mouth quirked upward. "I'm not human?"

"Sometimes I feel tongue-tied around you."

He looked surprised. "But words pour out of you, in vast quantities."

"In truth, I'm not used to such," she said. "My grandfather did not like discourse. Perhaps that's why I find our debates stimulating."

The duke eyed her thoughtfully. "Stimulating."

An awkward silence settled around them.

He took a step away from her. "You need only slide the chest an inch or so. I'll wait outside until you do."

When he left, Gwynna closed the door and eyed the chest. It had taken him little effort to move, yet it symbolized much—that this was a man to be relied on.

She leaned into the chest and pushed. "It's done," she called through the door.

After a moment, she sensed he was gone.

***

His brain had turned to cotton wool. Worse, ravenous cotton wool predators clawed at him.

Discipline got him out of Gwynna's room. Alas, it was slinking off in search of more rewarding experiences.

Lying in the inn's surprisingly comfortable bed, Sebastian tried for logic. The fact that Gwynna stirred his blood was no reason to entertain improper thoughts.

They hadn't begun as improper. She was sorrowful. He wanted to comfort her. But he *almost* touched her. *Almost* put his hands on her shoulders.

Thank God, he'd stopped himself. She might have misconstrued the gesture.

Celibacy was a dangerous state. He avoided situations in which it might be tested. He did not train his gaze on other men's wandering wives or mistresses. His conduct was exemplary, because of Elizabeth.

It was for her sake that he spread the story she cried off their engagement. No one must know they were wed until she recovered and decided whether to remain married or to have their union dissolved. Drew would quietly take care of it to protect her from scandal.

Thus, Sebastian threw himself into the role of foppish bachelor. No one thought him possessed of anything beyond overweening self-interest—much less a wife.

But Gwynna Owen disturbed him. She was the antithesis of his plan—the fly in the ointment, the moth in the woolens, the this and the that of ruination.

Each time he got a fix on her, she showed him something unexpected.

At first, she was "dagger-wielding Welshwoman out for Traherne fortune." As their journey progressed, he reworked that into "purveyor of fantastical Welsh legends" and "descendant of bloodthirsty rebel tyrant."

Tonight, she became "orphan raised by neglectful relative," then "vulnerable young woman who should not be left to cry herself to sleep alone."

Yet here he was, safely away. Discipline prevailed.

Touching his watch, Sebastian felt calmer. As the years faded his parents, this token of their love reassured him that the past hadn't been a distant dream. In some essential way, the watch preserved them.

But it was an enigma. Even the London watchmakers couldn't make sense of the case's mysterious designs, forged by some gifted, unknown craftsman.

That the watch was wholly inaccurate mattered not, for it did what nothing else could.

It connected Sebastian to all that had gone before, and that which would never be again.

Chapter Seven

Desolation had claimed the white clapboard cottage. The daybed on which her grandfather spent his final days stood stark and empty. He'd taken to sleeping there because the room let in more light than his small bedroom.

How ironic that he shunned darkness at the end, after years of retreating into it.

"I've already looked for documents," Gwynna told the duke. "There's nothing here."

"With your permission, I'll search again." He wandered into her grandfather's room.

He seemed remote today. Perhaps he regretted that awkwardness in her room last night and sought distance. Her childhood home surely underscored the gap between them, for it must be the very opposite of his.

All the duke would find in her grandfather's tiny closet were simple trinkets, meaningless to him. The rock collection they gathered when she was a little girl. The gnarled walking stick he used on hikes. The miniature of Megan she'd studied to glean hints of the lovely woman with the flaming red hair.

Gwynna went to her room, set her dagger and pouch on a shelf, and reached under the bed, where she kept her bow and the quiver her grandfather had made for her.

Staring at the worn planking she'd scrubbed many times, she let herself absorb the cottage's emptiness and the heavy silence that bled into it whenever she asked about her parents.

"The prodigal has returned," a deep voice growled.

Evans.

Instantly, she rose. "You are not welcome here."

He eyed her reproachfully. "It would wound your grandfather to hear your words. I was his friend. In his hour of need, he sought me out. As you must also."

"This is my house now. I demand that you leave."

"He had hopes for us." Evans's black eyes glinted like coal. "It was his dying wish that you erase the stain on your soul by uniting with me in that holiest of states, that of sacred matrimony. You must not fight God's will."

"I heard no such wish. And you know nothing of God's will."

Evans snaked an arm around her. "Your soul will pay for such blasphemy."

Gwynna pushed him away. "Look to your own soul. It's black as night."

"Thou art willful," he snarled. "I will punish you for your sins of pride and blasphemy."

"I will fight you to the death," she vowed.

"I hope not," drawled another voice. "Alas, I have not brought my mourning cloak."

The duke was propped against the doorframe, watching them with idle curiosity.

But Gwynna had seen this languid pose before. This time, she wasn't fooled.

With elaborate condescension, the duke pulled out his quizzing glass and stifled a yawn.

Had he a pistol tucked away somewhere? Not that he needed one—he held the size advantage. Moreover, Evans was given to rages; the duke was nothing if not controlled.

Her money was on the duke, with or without a pistol.

Perhaps Evans thought so, too, for he stepped away from her and formed his features into a benign mask. "I am January Evans. A man of God, and peace." He gave a perfunctory bow.

When the duke didn't respond, Evans frowned. "Miss Owen and I have a longstanding acquaintance. But I do not know you, sir."

"Sebastian Traherne." The duke moved away from the door frame with all of the languid grace such elegance required. "Lately afflicted with a cumbersome title."

Evans scowled. "Titles hold no sway with me."

"Quite right," the duke murmured.

"Leave Evans," Gwynna said. "You are poisonous."

"It is thou, Daughter of Sin, who poisons the air with thy blasphemy." His voice rose. "Repent, or I cannot answer for thy soul. Listen to the words of thy salvation!"

"It appears she would rather not," the duke observed mildly.

Though his bored expression hadn't changed, his pose—arms limber at his sides, his body poised with an easy, fluid grace—suggested he held himself at the ready.

Evans eyed him with suspicion. "Gwynna's spiritual salvation is my dearest goal. I am forced to wonder, however, about your presence here."

The duke merely arched a brow.

"Owing to her base birth, Gwynna's reputation is beyond repair," Evans added. "Some would assume the worst about your presence here alone with such a woman."

"Those people would insult a young lady connected to my family," the duke said, in a voice of deadly calm. "That would be unwise."

Gwynna blinked. Was he publicly acknowledging a familial connection?

"Regrettably, I do not carry my excellent dueling pistols with me." The duke's gaze flicked over Evans. "Yet I imagine we could make do."

It was a moment before Evans found his tongue. "Devout men do not fight duels. The fact that Gwynna and I are old acquaintances leads me to speak freely to her."

"*About* her, rather," the duke corrected.

Silence.

"Perhaps I was too blunt," Evans said at last. "I cannot

answer for the thoughts of others, but as to Gwynna's birth, I will pray that the gossip be stilled."

"Indeed," the duke said, "that must be your fondest wish."

Evans's lip curled. "Since you claim to be kin, I must inform you that her grandfather wished her future to be joined with mine."

"I suspect her grandfather's wish was to see her happy. She looks quite the opposite in your presence." The duke brushed an invisible speck of dirt off his sleeve. When his gaze returned to Evans, it glittered with ice.

The air in the cottage stilled. Neither man moved.

Finally, Evans muttered something and stalked from the cottage.

The duke crossed the room to her, all pretense at languor gone. "Did he harm you?"

Gwynna marveled at his transformation. "No."

His gaze softened. "You've had a hard time of it, haven't you?"

She stepped forward and buried her face in his chest.

After a moment's hesitation, he patted her back gingerly. His coat's sturdy twill felt reassuring against her cheek. His broad chest felt as if it could take any burden.

"I would be happy to call him out—kill him, that sort of thing," he offered.

She looked up, managed a smile. "You would dirty that exquisite coat of yours."

"Oh, I'd remove it first," he said lightly.

Gwynna stared at him. Five days ago, he'd been a stranger. But now...

When he shifted slightly, she took a step back. He motioned for her to sit, and took a chair opposite her. Then he opened his hand. "Are these from him?"

He'd found Evans's notes.

Embarrassed, Gwynna looked away. "I saved them as proof, if it came to that, of his intent."

The duke read one aloud: "'With all perfections, so enflame my sense with ardor to enjoy thee, fairer now than ever.'" His gaze darkened. "Good God."

She flushed. "They're not even his words. They're—"

"Milton. He loved torment. Fallen angels, sinful Eve, doltish Adam—the list is long."

He read another: "'From about her shot darts of desire.'" He looked at her. "This isn't benign affection. He wants to possess you. And his kind doesn't take rejection."

Bracing his forearms on his thighs, the duke leaned forward. "Did you tell anyone?"

She shook her head. "My grandfather was too ill."

"Was there no one else?"

"Crossing Evans isn't easily done. Evans runs illicit enterprises men need to survive. He profits off their woes."

"And this is tolerated? I thought you Welsh were a rebellious lot."

She hesitated. "I've hoped someone might step forward to lead a revolt against him. The will to fight still exists. It lies in everyone—even you, I imagine."

His brows rose. "I'd *never* do my tailor the disservice of taking these clothes into battle."

"And yet, you came to my defense that night—"

"Accidentally."

"—and repeatedly since."

"Don't make me out a hero," he snapped. "I am far from that."

His curt tone took her aback. Did his usual cool reserve mask a less civilized side?

"Is this why you want my money? To fight him?"

Gwynna sighed. "If men had honest work that paid fair wages, they wouldn't need him. But I'll not ask you for funds. You have no reason to care about our island."

The tension in his shoulders eased. He leveled a gaze at her. "What did that man do to you?"

"The day my grandfather died, Evans tried to force

himself on me. I fought him off with my dagger. He bears the scars still. It's the reason I'm never without my knife."

He hitched in a breath. "Is that why you left home?"

"Partly. But it wasn't until I found my mother's note that I resolved to find William."

The duke frowned. "What note?"

Gwynna fished Megan's note from her pouch and handed it to him.

He read it once, twice. "Why didn't you show this to me earlier?"

"It's unsigned. Anyone could have written the name Claremont there. It's no proof."

The duke stared at her. "It's more than we had."

We.

He pulled a paper from his waistcoat. "Since we're disclosing notes, I found this in William's desk at the castle. Do you recognize the handwriting?"

The words, written in an elaborate script, read: *She had a child—Gwynna Owen.*

Stunned, she tried to make sense of the words. "No. Who could have written to William about me?"

"It, too, is unsigned. But the ink isn't faded, so it's not old. Perhaps this explains why William tried to become your guardian at the end."

"So he didn't know about me until he got this note?"

"I'm unwilling to draw conclusions." The duke rose. "Let's search the island, see what records are to be had."

Gwynna blinked. "You…wish to see this through?"

"What a poor estimation you have of my character. Did you think I would abandon you to your blackguard?" He pulled out the quizzing glass. "Egad. I believe I must take offense."

Then he…winked.

"Get the rest of your things," he ordered. "You're not staying here while he's around."

"I have my dagger," Gwynna protested.

"Which is the veriest pinstick to a man like that."

"It did damage before."

"And now he's warier." The duke took her elbow.

"Wait." She retrieved her bow, arrows, and quiver from under the bed.

And left the empty cottage without a backward look.

***

Gywnna hadn't visited the tomb since she set off to find her father, and instead found this puzzle of a man now walking beside her.

It had been a long, fruitless day. Island marriages sometimes found their way into family Bibles, but with the Anglicans gone, no official repository of records existed.

The duke was perplexed. In his world, titles and lineage mattered. Such events were scrupulously recorded.

They searched old churches and ruins but found no hint of her mother's marriage, just as she'd found nothing when she searched on her own.

When Gwynna suggested they stop for the day, the duke readily agreed. He looked intrigued when she described the ancient burial mound.

They left the carriage in Beaumaris and walked a mile through a grove of trees, lush with the season. A mist fell—not unusual for island afternoons—although the darkening sky portended something stronger.

Gwynna loved rain. It symbolized continuity, since it fell the same across time and cultures. One could believe, as her grandfather had, that lost loved ones weren't forever gone, but waiting elsewhere—perhaps under this very rain.

The mound felt like a gateway to those worlds. She wanted the duke to see it, though he'd likely reject any suggestion that this world, and that beyond, intersect.

Like a sleeping giant awakening, the ancient barrow took shape as they crossed the field. Once, it was the center of a civilization. Every stone, every carving, held significance. Now, it was slowly being reclaimed by time.

Had people spoken the old language still heard today? Or was their tongue lost to unrecorded secrets of the past?

A ring of erect stones once defined the barrow. Most had fallen, and the henge ditch was now little more than a depression in the earth, easily crossed.

Tall stones supporting a capstone framed the tomb entrance. Gwynna touched her dagger to the sentry stone to show respect. The duke shot her a curious look.

"I often come here at dawn, " she said. "Spirits are closer then. My mother is here."

He looked surprised. "The tomb's still used?"

"Rarely. But if someone wishes to spend eternity here, none will gainsay it."

He ran his hand over the smooth outer stones.

"At sunrise on the summer solstice, the sun aligns with the inner passage," she said. "Light hits a carved spiral that conforms to the sun's positions over a year."

"So there was purpose here."

Gwynna nodded. "We think the ancients held ceremonies, burials, even sacrifices. A decade ago, a vicar from Somerset—an amateur scholar—found bones he judged to be several thousand years old."

"I'd like to see inside, if that's permitted."

His interest pleased her. Entering the dark chamber, they made their way to the center's solitary standing stone. Enough light filtered in to reveal its serpentine markings.

"I've seen others like this," he said. "Newgrange in Ireland has similar carvings."

Gwynna eyed him curiously. "How did you come to be there? Were you on holiday?"

"I did diplomatic work during the war."

"Ireland must have posed challenges."

His low laugh rumbled off the stones. "The Act of Union was as unpopular there as here. But the Irish came to support the war. Wellington's Dublin-born, after all."

Diplomatic work. Wellington. Ireland. Serious

business for a frivolous aristocrat—if he was that. She had doubts. "Where else have you traveled?"

"Vienna was my last posting. Where is your mother buried?"

It seemed he didn't wish to discuss his work.

"My grandfather followed the practice of our ancestors," Gwynna said. "She was cremated and her ashes scattered over the grounds of the tomb."

"Not inside?"

"I doubt she'd have wished to be where sun shines only one morning a year."

The duke was silent for a moment. "It's a loss that you did not know her. I am sorry."

It was a pain they shared. "Your mother's name—Faylinn—is unusual. Does it have a special meaning?"

"She claimed it meant fairy kingdom." He hesitated. "It suited her. She seemed magical to me."

A sense of loss—his, and hers—settled over them. For several minutes they absorbed the tomb's stillness and the primitive scents of dirt and rock and ancient bones.

Civilizations faded, yet something remained. Gwynna had imagined an invisible thread connecting her and her mother across the years. Sadly, it always lay beyond reach.

As the duke shifted, she realized the low ceiling made it impossible for him to stand fully upright. It was time to leave anyway. Soon, it would be dark.

When they returned to the tomb entrance, rain was gusting in sheets outside.

By tacit agreement, they sat—Gwynna on a rock to the right of the opening, the duke on a wide slab to the left.

Watching the downpour, she thought of the ancients in this very place, inventing stories to explain the forces that brought such rain.

A story might help pass the time.

"Not far from here is a sheep pasture, where fairies danced on moonlit nights," she began.

The duke's gaze slid to her. "Oh?"

Gwynna bit back a smile. He'd taken the bait. "A farmer used to spy on them. A fairy whose dancing was very spirited caught his fancy. One night, he captured her."

"What does one do with a captured fairy?"

"Marry her, of course," she said. "But with fairies there's always a hitch. She agreed, but only if he could guess her name. Each moonlit night, he returned to the glade. One night, he overheard the fairies mourning the loss of their Penelope. That's how he learned her name."

The duke stretched out his long legs across the tomb opening. "Did she marry him?"

"Yes, but with another condition: He must never strike her with iron, or she'd leave him."

"Ah," he said. "I see where this is leading."

"Years passed," Gwynna said. "They had a happy life and children. The farm prospered. Alas, one day he threw a bridle at a pony and it accidentally struck his wife."

"Made of iron, no doubt."

Gwynna nodded. "She vanished."

He sighed. "None of your tales have a happy ending."

"Not so. The fairy couldn't forget her love for her husband and children. One night, the husband was awakened by a strong wind and a tapping on the bedroom window. He recognized the voice of his wife in the wind."

"What did she say?"

"That she couldn't return, but had conjured a patch of earth in the midst of a small lake. Ever after, she sat there and conversed with her family as they stood on the shore."

Crossing his arms over his chest, the duke frowned. "Even so, the children had no mother to read them stories at night, nor the husband a wife to embrace."

"She was with them in the only way possible. The tiny island's still there. I'll show you."

"I should like that." His voice held an odd, gruff note.

"I'm sorry," she said quickly. "The story must have

reminded you of your mother."

"Loss exists whether one is reminded or not. Isn't that what this trip is about—finding that which is missing?"

A lump rose in Gwynna's throat. "The odds are better with you involved. Thank you."

"I can't promise results. We got nowhere today." He glanced at the entrance. "The rain isn't letting up. Do you wish to make a run for it?"

"Aren't you worried about your boots, Englishman?" she teased.

"No, about you. You're shivering."

It was true. Rain had not only hastened the darkness, it chilled the air inside the tomb.

When he extended his hand, she stared at it blankly.

Gently, he pulled her over to his slab, positioning her to his right, so he was between her and the rain blowing in. He removed his coat and placed it over her shoulders.

"You need it," Gwynna protested. "You're closer to the outside."

The duke crossed his arms, leaned back against the stone wall. The matter was settled, it seemed.

Gwynna studied his profile. Strength lay in every angle of that firm jaw, regal nose, and high cheekbones, and in his wide shoulders and muscled arms.

It wasn't just the natural vigor of a man in his prime. The strength of his character threatened to emerge at every turn, no matter that he was at pains to hide it.

She'd been wrong about him. He was no preening dandy, no shallow aristocrat.

Only pretending to be.

Why?

As if he felt her gaze, the duke glanced at her. "Did you change your mind? Do you wish to leave?"

"No," Gwynna said. "I am…content."

Content to huddle in their earthen cocoon as the rain echoed the thundering of her pulse.

***

This was torture.

Thank God the woman next to him was finally asleep.

Why had he ever thought her to be a boy? Up close—*too* close—her body was soft and womanly.

Affection for Elizabeth lived deep in his bones. But Gwynna's supple form, nestled against his, stirred a yearning to gather her in.

Even as Sebastian told himself it was only to protect her, he recognized other, less noble, instincts.

The celibacy problem, again.

Fortunately, he was a man to whom words meant everything. *Duty, devotion, discipline, denial*—those were the ones he lived by. Angus had made sure of that.

His thoughts about Gwynna were undutiful, however. They spiraled into a heady brew as rain and darkness wove something intimate around them.

The model of asceticism who raised him would have muttered a Scottish curse and swept such thoughts aside. Sebastian didn't have Scottish curses at the ready. What he did have were sobering images that, one long year later, lived on in vivid, horrifying detail.

"Tis the plague. I can offer you no hope."

The words sent Elizabeth into a paroxysm of grief and left Sebastian staring furiously at the dour doctor who consigned her parents to their fate in such a stark fashion.

Sir Bertram had escorted Elizabeth and her mother to join him in Vienna. It was meant to be a celebration of their betrothal as his diplomatic work was ending.

But Vienna's carefree ebullience spiraled into death and illness. Elizabeth nursed her parents day and night, but by the time death took them, she was gravely ill herself.

Her parents were as dear to Sebastian as his own, and Angus. His grief was profound.

He vowed that death would not take Elizabeth. He fought for her life, allowing no one near her, certainly not that unfeeling quack. He alone bathed her feverish skin, washed her soaked clothing, dressed her in clean, dry bedclothes.

No man had touched her so intimately. It was improper for him to do so.

Sebastian didn't care. He simply wanted her to live.

Gradually, as the days became weeks and she began to improve, he knew those intimacies required that he give her the protection of his name immediately.

Elizabeth was shy about such things. During her Season, when he courted her, she had difficulty meeting his gaze, as if this new stage of their relationship was strange. When she accepted his proposal, it was with a profusion of blushes.

It was odd for him, too, to think of her as the woman who would bear their children, and of the intimacies they would share. But Sebastian never doubted they would wed, or wished otherwise.

When Elizabeth at last awoke, she seemed to understand the need for a quick ceremony. But the woman he'd known had vanished, lost to grief and the ravages of illness. Her vibrancy and health were gone.

The cleric was from the chapel at the British embassy. Doubtless he was there in the event Drew's men needed to unburden their guilt at what they'd done in his service.

Working for Drew was like that.

Drew himself produced the license. For once, Sebastian was grateful to the man. He'd been too preoccupied with Elizabeth's health.

On their wedding day, she was propped up in bed, too weak to walk. Her skin was deathly pale, her brown hair dull and lifeless against the pillow.

The cleric seemed just as exhausted, probably from presiding at so many plague deathbeds. He didn't look askance at the bride or the faintness of the vows she spoke to bind her to Sebastian for eternity.

Eternity. Gwynna had some peculiar notions about that state. She seemed to think that death wasn't an end, that spirits floated here and there like old friends.

But Sebastian knew all too well that life was fragile. Loved ones could be ripped away in an instant. He had prayed that Elizabeth would not be among them.

His prayers were answered.

On her first morning as a married woman, she rallied. The next day, she was strong enough to be mortified that he'd had such intimate care of her person. That's when he broached the subject of their ceremony, such as it was.

Sebastian worried that she hadn't been fully in her right mind when she spoke her vows, that she might one day regret being wed in such a slap-dash fashion.

Thus, his wedding gift to her was time.

When she was well, they could wed in proper style in London. But if by then she discovered the state of her heart had changed, he would free her from her vows.

He vowed to wait as long as it took for her to recover.

Society accepted his story that Elizabeth had ended their betrothal amid grief over her parents' deaths. His bachelor charade kept all but the most determined matchmakers at bay.

Alas, when he inherited the dukedom, they returned in droves. Title and wealth obscured his ostentatious lack of character, so he ramped up the role to wretched excess. Narcissism proved the perfect cover.

Sebastian never doubted it was the right course.

Until now.

Until he ended up on a rock slab in this musty tomb with Gwynna sleeping against him. His shoulder, his arm, his chest, his thigh—each place her body touched was aflame, as if she doused him with coal oil and tossed in one of those dangerous sulfur matches.

And though darkness engulfed them, her delicate features—so at odds with that obstinate tilt of her chin—

were engraved on his brain.

Tragedy had burned a vein of steel into her spine. She'd taken a difficult journey with low odds of success, fueled by a fierce passion that didn't easily admit defeat.

Likely she would be just as fierce in her lovemaking.

An unworthy thought, formed before he could stop it.

Thoughts weren't harmless. They led into corrosive canyons of doubt—where the way out condensed into the very thing that had seemed unthinkable and wrong.

Silken strands of Gwynna's hair brushed his jawline.

And even though it was only a trick of the dark, and perhaps the legacy of her fairy tales, something seductive wrapped around him like a siren's song. It filled his senses with a pungent bouquet of past and present, passion and pain, legend and truth.

He'd thought himself dead to all that.

One. Two. Three. Counting summoned discipline to bolster his mental fortress. Denial jumped in to help.

A tricky word, denial.

There was the denial that separated fact from fiction: *That is not black; it's white.*

There was the self-delusional kind: *This is not true* (despite evidence to the contrary).

Finally, there was prohibition, the simplest kind: *No, you may not.*

Regrettably, all forms of the word applied now. Gwynna was *not* the woman to whom he was wed. He was *not* drawn to her. He could *not* act on his attraction to her.

Four. Five. Six. At last, the "D" words rallied round: Duty, devotion, discipline, denial.

One more showed up uninvited: despair. Despair that he was drawn to her, against every principle he held dear.

Gwynna stirred his blood as no woman had.

She was nothing like Elizabeth.

She was...more.

***

Strong arms gathered her in. A robust heart pulsed under her palm. Despite the chill, Gwynna was enveloped in warmth.

The warmth felt decidedly masculine: It had corded legs and arms, a solid chest.

Her eyes shot open. She was sprawled over the Duke of Claremont, her legs tangled with his. The dark outside the tomb had bled into leaden gray, the presage of dawn.

They had slept the night here.

Gingerly, she tried to extricate herself without waking him. But his right arm was heavy on her shoulder, his left locked around her middle. She could go nowhere.

His coat covered her. His shirt, open at the neck, exposed a triangle of flesh. Her eyes moved upward to his jaw, roughened with a night's growth. His blond hair fell haphazardly across his cheek.

Truly, the man resembled nothing so much as a slumbering Greek god. Gwynna's gaze lingered on his wide, sensual mouth before shifting upward to his eyes.

They were open.

Instantly, she recoiled. "I-I thought you were asleep."

"Yes." His sleepy rumble caused his chest to rise under her palm.

"You look dreadful."

He frowned.

"Tired, rather," she hastened to add. "As if you hadn't slept. That rock is no kind of pillow. Whereas I've been cushioned against your…against you. I slept quite soundly, and warm, too, since I had your coat and your arms—"

Gwynna broke off, horrified at her babbling.

Awareness bloomed in his eyes.

One arm slipped from her waist, the other from her shoulders. Unfurling his long limbs, the duke eased himself into a sitting position.

His elbow made a cracking sound. He rubbed the back of his neck and grimaced. The man had paid a price for serving as her pillow.

"You must have a cramp or two," Gwynna ventured.

"The moment we return to Beaumaris," the duke growled, "you'll have a maid."

He rose abruptly, and his head hit the top of the tomb. With a muttered curse, he lurched outside.

She hurried after him. "I don't hold with your English proprieties. It matters not that we passed a night together."

He turned, so swiftly she nearly crashed into him.

"It matters to me. I've dishonored you. And there's no remedy." Rather than anger, his gaze now held anguish. Did he think he'd broken his marriage vows?

"You but sheltered us from the storm," she protested.

"The damage is done." With that, he stalked toward the grove of trees, leaving her to follow.

***

Now they must talk to rocks.

Sebastian stood near the circle of tall stones while Gwynna addressed them as if they were a council of elders. She wore her breeches and a loose-fitting shirt.

"Before Teuth, I humbly ask for strength," she said.

He wouldn't mind some of that strength himself. Yesterday had turned into a horrific night, which bled into today, and somehow it had all become one continuous, unrelenting wave of awareness of Gwynna Owen.

When Sebastian opened his eyes this morning to find her blue eyes only inches from his, her body sprawled atop him, he hadn't immediately recoiled. That came later.

His arms had been wrapped around her, cocooning her next to his heart, as if that was where she belonged.

But she belonged miles away. *Oceans* away.

Some place where his exalted principles—duty, discipline, et cetera—weren't in mortal jeopardy.

She might disregard the fact she had slept in his arms, but Sebastian couldn't.

Nor could he make amends. He couldn't offer

marriage, and if he tried to give her money for passing the night with him, she'd run him through with that dagger.

At least they had a chaperone, of sorts. He paid the innkeeper a fortune to allow his grumpy housekeeper to accompany them on this last, fruitless day of searching.

But when Gwynna insisted they stop here, the housekeeper refused to budge; they left her in the carriage and trudged up a long hill to the circle of stones. Each stood a dozen feet high and about eight feet in breadth.

Facing them, Gwynna spoke in Welsh, then English. "This sacrifice, O Teuth, I humbly make in the name of Megan Glendower Owen."

She held out the dagger and—to Sebastian's alarm—loosened the top of her shirt to expose one shoulder and an area of flesh just below it.

Then she put the blade to her heart.

He jumped forward, batted the knife to the ground. "Killing yourself solves nothing."

Gwynna stared at him. Her mouth curved.

Ah. He blew out a breath. "You weren't, er, sacrificing yourself."

Her smile broadened. "No."

"Damnation, Gwynna. You stand there chanting that Welsh madness like some heathen priestess. Then you point that blade at yourself—what the devil am I to think?"

"That's the first time you've used my given name. I shall call you Sebastian henceforth."

Instinct told him to run far and fast from the intimacy of given names. Still, they had slept the night together; standing on formality seemed silly. "Explain this ritual."

"You wish to learn about my ways?"

"Only if you put your shirt to rights," he muttered.

She flushed. Sebastian bent to retrieve the dagger while she fumbled with her shirt.

Her shirt! Given names! He gritted his teeth.

"My rituals may seem strange to you, but the old ways

connect me to the past," she said.

"How do you know they're the old ways?" he challenged. "Haven't they been lost to pre-history? Likely they were invented by more recent folk."

Her chin rose. "That doesn't rob them of meaning."

"What was the meaning of that bit with the dagger?"

"I asked Teuth to help me find the truth about my parents. Putting the blade to my heart is a loyalty pledge."

"Who the devil is Teuth?"

"A supreme being—Duvv to some," she said. "We have many such beings."

"If there are many, how can one be supreme?"

"They are part of the same whole—good, not evil."

"The world cannot be divided so clearly."

"My world can."

In truth, Sebastian understood, somewhat.

"When my parents died," he said, "I decided God could not cause such tragedy and also be good. But that's a child's view. Good and evil exist together. Sometimes a thing is not one or the other, but both, or in between."

"I'm not a child, nor naïve, Sebastian."

Hearing his name on her lips was an excellent example of good and evil occurring at the same time, he thought. The intimacy beguiled and alarmed him.

Mostly beguiled!

Gwynna pressed his arm. "Have you never believed in magic?"

Sebastian stepped back, beyond her reach. "You conflate religion and fairy tales. Or paganism and—Hell, I don't know anymore. It's all just nonsense."

Instead of taking offense, she eyed him with compassion. "Did no one tell you stories?"

"My mother. But I no longer believe in fairy tales."

"Everyone needs magic," she said softly. "One day, you will find yours."

Sebastian fervently hoped not.

Chapter Eight

Hannah climbed into the carriage, refused Angus's assistance. When he sat opposite her, she looked away.

Had it not been for the fact that Sebastian needed them, she'd have been content never to lay eyes on Angus MacDuff again in this lifetime.

May Heaven forgive her for that small lie.

Watching the countryside through the carriage window, Hannah found herself contemplating the subject of lies, big and small. In this way, she passed nearly an hour in silence. She nearly jumped when he spoke.

"How is your husband?"

"Gone to his eternal reward, like all of them," she said crisply.

He smiled at that. "Must be quite a few by now."

"Four."

"One day you must tell me why you killed them."

"I didn't kill them," she said. "One can't kill what never existed."

"But you haven't taken a new one yet."

"No. I've had this name for several years. I'll probably be buried with it. "

"So that's the end, then?"

"The end of your prying questions, I hope," Hannah retorted.

He regarded her. "Perhaps you might tell me why you also killed what was between us."

Her face warmed. "There was nothing between us."

"Friendship, I thought," he said. "Now, only hostility. I don't know why you carry such anger after all these years.

You cannot believe I ever meant you ill."

Blood rushed to her head. He had never spoken to her thus.

Hannah forced her gaze to the passing scenery. There *had* been a burgeoning friendship years ago. Until she had made a fool of herself with Sebastian's footman.

After Elizabeth's injury, Hannah moved into Sebastian's house. But she had time on her hands.

Peter was handsome, and well aware of it. Idleness blossomed into lingering looks, then purposeful touches, then passionate interludes.

She'd been besotted—and incautious. One dreadful afternoon, Angus opened the door to the butler's pantry. They had not taken the precaution of locking it.

Angus, who held his staff to the same high standards he exemplified, sent the footman packing and gifted her with a single, eloquent look.

Ever after, Hannah could scarcely meet his gaze. She knew he thought her a loose woman, unfit to guide a young lady like Elizabeth.

Deep down, she knew she was unfit. It was a lesson she learned at Miss Abernathy's School for Young Ladies, where her parents sent her to train as a schoolteacher.

For a year, Hannah worked to make them proud. In one afternoon, her efforts were ruined. A teacher—Cyrus Cheltingham, nearly as old as her father—cornered her in an empty schoolroom.

At first, she was frightened. Then, curious—her base nature, coming to the fore.

Unfortunately, Miss Abernathy herself entered the room at a most inopportune moment.

Hannah was deemed to have tempted Cyrus beyond his power to resist. She had to withdraw from school, whereupon she discovered the difficulty of finding suitable work as an unmarried young woman without references.

From that time on, she styled herself a widow. She

arranged her hair severely and wore only black, in mourning for her departed, entirely fictitious husband.

As Hannah Miller, she found work as companion to an elderly woman she met at a market near Oxford, not far from where Hannah grew up in Chipping Norton. The poor lady was not long for this world—and, as she learned at the funeral, an acquaintance of Sir Bertram and Lady Throckmorton. They engaged her to teach Elizabeth.

Ensconced at Summerlin after Elizabeth's injury, Hannah found herself curious about the serious-minded man who ran the household.

Although Angus never claimed to be more than Sebastian's major domo, he treated him as a son. The lad blossomed under his gentle discipline and affection.

After the closet interlude, any hope of friendship with Angus ceased. Yet he never told the Throckmortons about the incident. Hannah was as certain of that as she was her own name. The name that was not, in fact, her own.

Not two years after that episode, Cyrus found her and called at Sir Bertram's house. The family had gone out, and Hannah received him alone. He threatened to tell Sir Bertram of her school disgrace if she did not allow him to pick up where they'd left off when she was sixteen.

She refused him. He began to follow her, often when she was with Elizabeth. Fearing she'd put her charge in danger, Hannah quit her post, changed names, and moved.

Each time, he found her. Each time, Hannah left her position, invented another deceased husband, and found work elsewhere.

Oddly, each time Angus also found her. He'd present himself at her door, assuring her of Sebastian's interest in her welfare and offering employment, should she need it.

She didn't welcome his visits. He was a vivid reminder of her flawed behavior.

The last time Hannah changed her name, Cyrus had not discovered her. Perhaps, as he was decades older, he had fallen on hard times or ill health. She dared to hope.

Finally, Hannah began to feel easy. When the young miss who had been her last charge completed her come-out, Hannah moved back to the Cotswolds. Though her parents had died, she still loved the area.

Stow-on-the-Wold, a little market town, reminded her of childhood, before the world got its tentacles in her, before her options narrowed, before her base nature was exposed. The thatched cottages and quiet dusty lanes felt a world away from Cyrus's ugliness.

She lived comfortably—for to her surprise, Sebastian settled a pension on her, though she'd never worked for him. Perhaps his fondness for Elizabeth was the cause. She even wondered whether that might be Angus's doing.

Strangely, after she moved to the Cotswolds, Angus had not called upon her.

In truth, that disappointed. Hannah had come to expect his visit each time she moved. There was always a period of suspense, when she wondered if he would find her. When he did, it felt as if her world had righted itself.

But after months passed without him calling in Stow, she knew she'd been forgotten. It was bound to happen.

When he appeared with that note from Sebastian, joy had filled her. She was not forgotten, after all.

Now they were traveling alone together. Hannah's thoughts were in a muddle. The fear that lived in her during those years when Cyrus hounded her had receded.

Instead, a new dread leapt across the years.

It had to do with Angus MacDuff and the friendship she'd never had.

And desperately needed.

***

Why did she persist in dressing as if she were one of those dead queens the Egyptians swathed in yards of cloth, with the aim of preserving them for all time?

Angus knew without doubt—the image forever burned

in his brain—that Hannah Miller-Smith-Peabody-Steele was far lovelier without her clothes than in them.

If anything, she was lovelier now than ever.

Young women were alluring in the way of a chick or kitten—possessed of a downy appeal that came without effort or awareness. Each was a blank slate, filled with possibility, but possessed of no special distinction.

Life had yet to write upon a young woman's soul.

Hannah's soul had been written upon. Angus longed to know her secrets.

She had abandoned her usual tight, unforgiving bun in favor of a looser chignon. Some strands had escaped to grace her cheek. He fought an urge to touch them.

He ought to have made a better effort at friendship years ago. But he'd had the raising of Sebastian. There hadn't been room for anything else.

That had the ring of an excuse. He ought to examine that question—rigorously, during the devotional time he set aside for readings and prayers. Often, that led to truth.

But perhaps he didn't wish to find truth. Perhaps he didn't wish to discover that he had wasted the years that passed with Hannah always somewhere else. That he had done nothing to change the trajectory of those years.

He had chosen the Cotswolds for his recuperation to be near her. He hoped some divine hand would cause their paths to cross during his walks. It had not.

Thus, Angus resolved to face the end of hope. He would not approach her this time. He'd had enough of wishing she would set aside her displeasure.

When Sebastian's letter came, hope dawned anew.

But hope required that a man act. Otherwise, it was a fleeting dream, always out of reach.

"I am glad you decided to come," Angus said.

Her gaze shifted from the window to him. "I could scarcely refuse His Grace."

"I'm curious about those husbands of yours. I know

you made them up, but did you never wish to marry?"

She flushed. "Certainly not."

"Why not?"

"It's none of your concern," she snapped. "Is this how you intend to spend our journey, Mr. MacDuff? Asking me impertinent, prying questions?"

"No, only—"

"I hope not." She fixed her attention on the window.

Served him right. He did not know how to speak to women. He'd always been direct and blunt-spoken. Women did not like that.

"Mrs. Steele," he said.

She ignored him. But her shoulders grew more rigid, so Angus knew she had heard.

"There was a time, long ago, that I saw more of you than you would wish," he said quietly. "I never thought to apologize. I should have."

"Dear Lord," she said faintly. One hand went to her forehead. The other fisted in her lap.

Angus did not take those as good signs.

"I was torn between thinking I ought to apologize and thinking it would spare you embarrassment if I didn't speak of it."

"Having endured a debate so difficult that you remember it even now, you surely cannot wish to revisit the subject." She addressed the window, not him.

Angus reached over and touched her hand.

She jumped. Now she did turn to him.

"Pray, spare me this discussion, Mr. MacDuff. It can only cause both of us discomfort."

"Perhaps that is sufficient reason to speak of it," Angus said. "To put it to rest."

She closed her eyes, but said nothing.

Again, not a hopeful sign.

Angus resolved to see it through. "The footman—"

"Peter," she said sharply. "His name was Peter."

He had forgotten that. The fact that she remembered gave him pause. The man had meant something to her, then. "I cannot apologize for turning him off. If he was worthy, he'd have returned to you."

Her eyes shot open.

"Who are you to decide who is worthy?" she demanded. "Who are you to decide the test, the proof, the sign? Who are you to judge, Angus MacDuff?"

At least she'd spoken his name. That was something.

"I was in charge of the household and the people in it," he said. "Their welfare was my concern. Sebastian's. Elizabeth's. Yours. It was my duty."

She leaned forward, her gaze steely. "My welfare was—is—none of your concern. You are a meddling, interfering old goat. And I don't care about your precious sense of duty."

Angus supposed she meant to insult him. But he found himself riveted by the passion that blazed in her eyes. It was far better than the cold looks she'd given him these intervening years.

"I am not as old as all that," he said.

She tilted her head assessingly. "How old?"

"I am fifty-five, Mrs. Steele." He regarded her steadily. "Not dead yet."

Her mouth opened, then formed itself into a wholly unexpected smile. A reserved one, but a smile nevertheless.

My God, Angus thought.

"You're nine years older than I." She sighed. "And sometimes I feel quite old."

He held her gaze. "May I say, Mrs. Steele, that you have never been more beautiful. At any age."

And then, because he had acquired some wisdom with his years, Angus sat back against the squabs, crossed his arms, and closed his eyes once more.

Now he was perfectly content to let the miles go by.

***

Sebastian tried to keep Anglesey at bay. He failed.

As much as he told himself it was an island like any other, Anglesey seemed to exist in a netherworld where the fantastical marched with the ordinary, the past alongside the present.

That was but underscored when they visited Moelfre, a village perched above a small, pretty harbor, Gwynna introduced him to her cousin, Rhianna Griffith, whose shop stocked colorful flags, mementos, teas, folk remedies, and books, including the *Malleus Maleficarum.*

Though his Latin instruction had been ages ago, Sebastian easily translated the title: *Hammer of Witches.* Long ago, it gave authorities a path to persecute heretics.

Perhaps she had it in her shop as a warning against intolerance. There was no indication she had even a passing familiarity with witchcraft. She was young and friendly, with dark red hair and a pink complexion—nothing like the fanciful depictions of witches as old hags.

He didn't believe in witches. That the word came to mind, simply because of a book on a shelf, was a measure of how Anglesey, and Gwynna, altered his perceptions.

The extraordinary—witches, fairies, ancient tombs— felt commonplace, while the commonplace—beaches, gulls, and the like—seemed extraordinary.

Colors were brighter. Air, saltier. Hills, greener.

Something akin to wonder had seeped into him. With it came burning questions.

Was it possible that his life had not been on the right path? That the orderly existence he had fashioned for himself would lead in orderly fashion to a mummified expanse of years that would never end soon enough?

As Gwynna led them along the coastal path west of Moelfre, Sebastian couldn't wrench his gaze from her.

Angus would say thoughts were the same as deeds. But the man invented opportunities for penance, whereas Sebastian saw temptation as harmless if strictly controlled.

Thus, it was a simple mental trick to appreciate Anglesey as a lovely place, and Gwynna as a lovely woman, and decide neither would disturb his orderly life.

Now he felt at peace.

Somewhat.

Gwynna pointed out some odd-shaped stones, including one said to return if carried away.

Contemplating that whimsy, Sebastian found himself noticing how the sunlight burnished her hair red-gold, how breeches hugged her legs as she clambered over the rocks.

"That is the lifesaving station." She pointed to a large boathouse. "My grandfather was a volunteer. To the east is a bay that swallows up the beach very suddenly at high tide. People who walked out too far are stranded. My grandfather saved many unwary couples."

"It's always couples?"

"Often. Perhaps they're too occupied with one another to take care. I suppose that happens."

Sebastian waited for a heartbeat, hoping the impulse to know more fled.

It didn't.

"Is there no one"—he cleared his throat—"who made you forget to watch for the tide?"

Was that a blush spreading across her cheeks? "No. I've wondered what it's like to be in love as my mother was. To have a grand passion."

"Nothing in my interactions with William persuaded me he was capable of grand passion, much less an ounce of tender feelings," Sebastian said.

Her blue eyes flashed. "That doesn't mean he didn't have them. You English may have trouble with passion, but it's in the very air we Welsh breathe."

"Passion is but the failure of discipline," he insisted. "Emotions must be governed, or risk a flood."

Gwynna gave him an arch look. "You think passion dooms the world? Don't you know that only pairs survived the Biblical flood?"

"They had to pair up or face death," he pointed out.

She made an exasperated sound. "Is there no poetry in you, Englishman?"

"Oh, Burns is there until kingdom come," Sebastian groused. Angus had insisted he ingest everything the poet had written. They even had memorizing contests.

The path wound to the edge of a cliff that jutted into the sea, with water on three sides. Offshore, sea lions and gulls basked on a tiny island in such vast numbers they nearly obscured it. Farther out was a large sailing vessel, so distant it appeared as only a thin line.

Fluffy, white clouds reflected off the water in silvery ripples narrowing to the point of a V at the far horizon, where the cerulean sky faded to a band of pale blue-gray.

No painter could render this view. It had to be seen.

Had William had come upon this very sight?

If so, had it spoken to his shriveled soul? Had Gwynna's mother awakened his senses, as if from a deep sleep? Had he, too, begun to question his life's course?

"I've always loved this spot," Gwynna said. "It's as if we're at the end of the world and the only ones alive to see it." She opened her arms wide, as if to embrace the whole.

When he didn't respond, she frowned. "Are you immune to this beauty?"

Sebastian was not immune to the beauty before him. Or to the view.

Something in him began to splinter.

Pieces of him seemed to fly off toward that far horizon, shattering all hope of order.

The decision he'd made would worsen the disruption.

"Let's sit for a moment," he said.

Eyeing him warily, Gwynna sat on a wide, flat rock. When he remained standing, she patted the slab. "Here. You tower over me otherwise."

It was hardly big enough for one. But he sat, trying to

ignore the instant, side-by-side intimacy. Her thigh pressed against his. Sebastian drew in a deep breath of sea air.

Treacherously, it gave him her scent—earthy and full of bite.

"We've found no proof your mother married my cousin. Only the cryptic notes—one, purportedly from your mother, the other sent anonymously to William."

Her chin rose.

"Nonetheless, I can't ignore them," he said. "Absent records, they carry significance. I will instruct my solicitors to prepare documents recognizing you as William's legitimate daughter."

Her startled gasp made his pulse skitter wildly.

"You'll have an allowance." He kept his tone precise, formal. "I'll set Busby to it when we return to Cheshire."

Then he eyed her sternly. "There's one condition— several, actually. None negotiable."

Her gaze narrowed.

"You'll not return to the island until I decide what to do about Evans. In the meantime, you'll learn skills required of a duke's daughter. You'll submit to a new wardrobe, be presented in Town—"

"Good God."

"—and learn proper language for a young lady—which that, emphatically, is not."

"I am not a proper young lady."

"You will be."

Gwynna looked bewildered. "I don't understand. If you mean to be generous, why not—"

"Simply hand you money and have done?"

She flushed—not like her cousin's pink complexion, more akin to blush carnations or Flanders poppies.

Hell. He was debating shades of pink. What was this madness?

"I don't fit in your world. I don't desire to."

Desire was all he heard. He forced his brain to retrieve

whatever she'd said before that. Ah. There it was—she didn't fit.

"You need not change, only learn new skills."

"Why?"

"You're in danger here. The only way I can keep you safe is to give you the means for a different life."

Her jaw hardened. "I don't want to change my life."

"Did you think I'd simply give you money and my blessing and send you on your way?" Sebastian demanded. "That was never an option. You are my responsibility."

"I don't wish to be."

He glowered. "I don't put my family in harm's way. Use that fine mind of yours and—"

"Fine mind?" She looked startled.

"Other than its fantastical tales," he grumbled.

She was silent for a moment. "What if I don't agree?"

"After I've dealt with Evans, you're free to return and finance a bloody revolution if you like."

Silence. Then: "If you mean to set me up with that horrid Mrs. Kendall, I won't have it."

Victory was at hand. "I have someone else in mind. You'll meet her soon."

"I haven't said I'll do it."

"Don't make me carry you off like some marauding pirate," Sebastian warned.

She grinned. "Swashbuckling isn't your style, Englishman."

It could be! that annoying inner voice taunted. Sebastian grimaced.

"I'll need to bring my longbow," she said.

He frowned. "What the devil for?"

"I feel naked without it."

That was the very last image he needed stuck in his brain.

Chapter Nine

Leaving Anglesey, agreeing to learn useless skills—it had happened so quickly.

Sebastian would acknowledge her as William's legitimate daughter. It was what Gwynna had wanted. Apparently, an allowance came with that. But the rest—learning how to go on in his world—that was beyond her.

Moreover, she couldn't let go of hope that proof of her parents' marriage existed, that their love was so deep and consuming it had been formally sealed.

Sebastian, meanwhile, looked as if he had second thoughts. During the whole of the return trip to Cheshire, he scarcely said a word.

Staring at the large, silent figure across from her, Gwynna wondered if she'd made a mistake in agreeing to this. Yet if anyone could be relied on, it was this man.

He'd given her a chance to learn more about William and his family. She couldn't turn that down.

But when at last the carriage rolled to a stop before the old castle, panic swept her. What if her feet tripped her up on the dance floor? What if she had nothing to say to those lofty aristocrats?

"Come," Sebastian said, offering his hand. "There's someone I wish you to meet."

"The paragon who is to turn me into a proper lady?"

His brows rose. "You may like her."

Gwynna grabbed her bow and marched past him into the castle. She wouldn't like anyone who tried to turn her into someone she was not.

***

God, how he had missed the man.

Sebastian clasped Angus's shoulder. "You look better than when last I saw you."

"I am fit," he said stiffly. "Have been for some time."

"Don't take umbrage. I sent you to rusticate because it would kill me if anything happened to you."

The twitch of an eyebrow was Angus's only acknowledgment of the sentiment. "I was damned near dying of boredom when your letter came."

"You see the fix I'm in," Sebastian said. "The castle's a pile of stones."

"I'll grant it's rough," Angus said. "Your Mr. Rowland could use help. Is that why you summoned us?"

"In part," Sebastian replied. "Is she here? Mrs.....I've lost track of her latest name."

"Steele," said a dry voice. "The name I shall likely leave this world with."

She stood at the study doorway, looking much as he remembered. Dark, severe frock, hair pulled back, perhaps looser than she used to wear it.

How had he noticed such a detail as her hair when he was only a youth? Likely because Hannah Miller—Steele, that is—was almost always at Elizabeth's side.

Elizabeth had been inconsolable when Hannah left her post—to tend to a family member, as best he recalled.

Sebastian went to her immediately. "Would you care for sherry, Mrs. Steele?" He didn't bother to ask Angus. The man had no use for aught but good Scot's whisky.

"No, thank you, Your Grace," she said primly.

"You've known me since I was a lad," he said. "Can you not use my given name?"

Mrs. Steele eyed him in alarm. "Indeed not."

He did not miss the smile that tugged at the edges of Angus's mouth at her firm response.

When Sebastian gestured for her to sit, she did so,

stiffly. Angus remained standing.

"I need your help," Sebastian told Angus. "The castle's a horror. Rowland's to keep his post as long as he wishes, but I want you to put the place to rights."

Angus's brows rose. "Not sure I have that many years left on my plate."

"I don't require you to see it through, only to set things in motion," Sebastian said. "There are a few workmen about, but they'll grow old here before anything is accomplished. Hire a large, competent staff, carpenters, craftsmen, stone carvers—whatever is needed."

He turned to Mrs. Steele. "I fear your task is more complex. I need you to bring Gwynna Owen up to snuff."

"That's the young lady with the bow and arrows?"

"And a knife besides. She won't part with them, so don't try. It's the rest of her I wish you to take in hand. It may be that you can even help her find a husband."

Mrs. Steele blinked. Even Angus looked startled.

"There are more genteel ladies to take on such a task," she said.

"Gwynna wouldn't respect those," he said. "I need someone whose understanding is more...down to earth."

Mrs. Steele flushed. "Your Grace—"

"If you attempted 'Sebastian' once, I'd be grateful. I can't pretend to be other than the raw clay Angus lifted from the abyss. With Elizabeth's caring, and yours."

Her eyes softened. "Elizabeth was already a caring girl. I simply attended her." Her expression grew troubled. "I've had no letter from her in quite some time. I wrote after her parents' deaths, but got no response."

Sebastian saw the unasked question in her eyes. It was no secret they planned to marry. But he couldn't tell her the whole. Even Angus wasn't aware they'd wed.

"Elizabeth is recovering from her own illness. I will give her your regards." He paused. "About Miss Owen, I will be frank. You won't be able to turn her into a paragon.

I only wish you to smooth out the jagged edges."

She frowned. "What edges?"

"She's given to dressing in breeches and wielding ancient weaponry, along with the odd Welsh ritual. It's her heritage and runs deep. I don't want her to change, only learn how to go on in our world."

Angus regarded him thoughtfully, waiting for the rest. The man knew him too well.

"I intend to acknowledge her as William's legitimate daughter," Sebastian said.

This statement was met with stunned silence.

"He married her mother in Wales, on the island of Anglesey. Then he seems to have abandoned her. Her mother died when she was born. Gwynna was left to the care of her grandfather."

Angus's gaze narrowed. "Have you proof of the marriage?"

"Mr. MacDuff," Mrs. Steele warned softly.

Now that was interesting. Angus was not a man one admonished. But Mrs. Steele, in her gentle but firm fashion, had just done so. And Angus hadn't batted an eye.

"Others will have the same thought," Sebastian acknowledged. "In truth, she does not wish to be here. But she's in danger on that island. I intend to give her the tools to protect herself and enter society, if she chooses. She'll have the privileges and rank of a duke's daughter."

He eyed Angus. "She's my responsibility. I intend to make amends for William's lapse."

The other man gave a barely perceptible nod. "There'll be speculation."

"Anyone who indulges in such will answer to me," Sebastian said. "I expect she'll have plenty of respectable suitors, when the time comes."

"Does she *wish* a husband?" Mrs. Steele asked.

He sighed. "At the moment, probably not."

"Some women are content in the unmarried state."

"I hope you can make a persuasive case to her," Sebastian said. "After all, you've had—" He broke off, realizing he wasn't certain of the figure.

"Four. Four husbands." She eyed him sternly. "That was personal indeed, Your Grace. One never knows what transpires in another person's wedded state."

Yes, she was just the person for Gwynna, he thought. "Forgive me, madam. You are right to call me to account."

It was then he noticed Angus. The man's gaze was riveted on her.

Mrs. Steele folded her hands in her lap.

The room fell silent.

"You'll meet Gwynna at supper," Sebastian said. "It will be informal. We have no serviceable dining room, only a table off a makeshift kitchen. But it looks out on the moor, so it is not without merit. I hope you'll find your own room tolerable. So few are in this moldy place."

"I am sure it will be quite acceptable." Mrs. Steele rose and left the room.

Angus turned to leave as well.

"A word, Angus, if you don't mind," Sebastian said.

The man looked as if he wished nothing more than to follow Mrs. Steele, but he halted.

"There's nothing untoward about this," Sebastian said. "Gwynna is a member of my family, most likely. I mean to do right by her."

Angus's gaze sharpened. "Most likely? Then you don't have proof."

"What matters is that she's safe," Sebastian said.

He wasn't about to answer the question in the man's eyes, so he simply turned it around. "Do you not think Mrs. Steele looks well?"

"She does."

"And after all these years." Sebastian kept his expression a careful blank.

Angus merely regarded him silently.

146

Sebastian tried again. "I've always thought her kind."

That brought a sharp elevation of those reddish brows. "Sometimes."

Ah. There was a story to be had, if Sebastian did not miss his guess.

Unfortunately, Angus's stony features told him he wasn't about to hear it.

***

Gwynna had no idea how to talk to the two strangers at the table. How would she fare at a fancy London dinner with a larger group of strangers judging her?

Mrs. Steele—the name conjured a harsh, disciplinary matron—was ensconced in a black dress with a high neck and long sleeves. She might have been in mourning.

Something in her eyes gave Gwynna hope she wasn't humorless or mournful. A spark here and there, directed at Sebastian or Mr. MacDuff when they didn't see.

Mr. MacDuff intrigued her as well. Scottish culture wasn't far removed from Welsh, although the reputed loquaciousness of his countrymen was absent. He seemed reserved, but his eyes, too, told another story.

Gwynna thought he held the duke in affection. It wasn't so much his words that revealed him, as the way the corners of his eyes crinkled slightly when Sebastian spoke. He seemed to weigh not only what was said, but also what might be unspoken.

She wondered about their history. It was almost as if there was a familial connection.

Gwynna also sensed something between Mr. MacDuff and Mrs. Steele.

They did not speak to one another. Indeed, they might well be enemies. Mrs. Steele granted Mr. MacDuff nary a favorable glance, nor a kind word. Still, her gaze did light on him fleetingly, when his attention was not on her.

Did everyone at this table have secrets? Sebastian had a secret marriage. Mrs. Steele might have a secret fondness for Mr. MacDuff, who looked to be guarding a few secrets himself.

Gwynna would need to guard herself as well, for the society people Sebastian wanted her to meet would never accept her as she was. The prospect was daunting.

But she'd made a bargain, and a Welshwoman did not go back on her word. Accordingly, Gwynna addressed Mrs. Steele: "I am looking forward to our lessons."

"Lessons are what I gave my charges when I was their governess," Mrs. Steele said. "You are not a child, and I am no longer a governess. You've had ample education, I'm told. There will not be lessons."

That surprised Gwynna. "None in, er, fan fluttering? Is that not an essential skill?"

Mrs. Steele allowed a small smile. "I never learned. My life has not been poorer for it."

Gwynna eyed Sebastian. "If I am not to learn fans and the like, how will I fit in?"

"You won't. Indeed, I suspect you will stand out."

"I'd rather hide in a corner and pretend I am home where I belong," she said.

"Everyone wishes that at some time or other." This, surprisingly, from Mr. MacDuff.

"I don't wish to sound ungrateful, but home is all I can think of," Gwynna said.

He nodded. "Home's inside you, wherever you are."

Sebastian watched him with an odd expression. Mr. MacDuff saw, because he noticed everything, although he kept his gaze on Gwynna.

"I see that home in you, lass," he said softly. "'Tis strong and sure as the windsong from the mountains. Like fairy whispers in the breeze, it will never leave you. It's in your heart."

Gwynna stared at him. He *did* see.

Mr. MacDuff's gaze was steady and warm. "Tell us about home, Gwynna."

Suddenly, she forgot about her strangeness, about her fear of failing, about hiding in corners, about the fashionable people who would judge her.

And told this kindred spirit of her home.

"The ancients came from across the sea," Gwynna began. "We don't know where or why. But they found our land, and decided to stay."

***

Sebastian's brain was reeling. Sleep eluded him. This was Angus's doing.

When you least expected it, Angus turned uncanny, peered right into your soul, saw the need and drew it painfully to the fore as if he'd stuck a knife in your gut and extracted it slowly.

He'd done it to Gwynna at supper, gotten her to spin her tales of spirits and tombs and ancients—none of it proven, of course, since it had never been written down.

Yet proof was beside the point. The longing, the passion, love of country—it was all there, honest and authentic. Belief lived deep in her and wouldn't be denied.

Without even glancing his way, Angus had done the same to him. In that exchange with Gwynna, he articulated the one thing that had driven Sebastian since the death of his parents, that thing he'd sought but never found.

Home.

Not a place to live. A place that lived *in* him. A place he didn't yet have.

Home. Unshakeable, life-giving. Each breath, each heartbeat in the service of that one true home. Gwynna's home was all of that to her.

Angus had been Sebastian's foundation as a child. But the man *knew*, damn it, that the foundation had to be claimed anew when that child became an adult.

Elizabeth was Sebastian's home. But he didn't have her. She was absent.

Sick, his brain retorted. She was sick. Did he not recall?

Yes, he recalled every agonizing moment of that terrible time in Vienna. Marrying her had been necessary, and right.

Why, then, had he not told Angus what he had done?

Yet somehow, Angus always sensed truth.

Even now—months without seeing him—Angus picked out the errant threads, spun them together into one dazzling, heartbreaking message: Something was missing.

Sebastian must find it.

Elizabeth. Years of travel, the rootless diplomacy—he hadn't minded, because he knew he'd come home to her.

With a heavy sign, he turned over in his threadbare excuse for a bed in this ramshackle excuse for a castle. At least there was a breeze blowing in from the window.

Fairy whispers in the breeze.

Blasted fairies.

Never around when one needed them.

***

"I thought to take my bow out this morning," Gwynna told Sebastian over breakfast.

He frowned. "I'm riding out with Busby to meet the tenants. I cannot accompany you."

"Mrs. Steele has agreed to come," she said.

"You need a male companion. Take one of the footmen."

"I will accompany them," Mr. MacDuff said.

Sebastian regarded him closely, but nodded.

A short time later, the three of them were walking across the moor, Gwynna carrying her bow, Mrs. Steele at her side, Mr. MacDuff a few paces behind them.

"I suppose I won't be allowed to shoot in town," Gwynna said. "The duke won't wish it."

Mrs. Steele eyed her in surprise. "Why would he not wish you to enjoy your pursuits?"

"I must change my ways to be a duke's daughter."

"You already are a duke's daughter. That was settled

before you were born."

"I'll be viewed as an oddity," Gwynna said.

"An Original, more like. Had I your mettle, my life might have been different."

"How so?" she ventured.

"I might have stayed to fight my battles instead of running from them."

She didn't elaborate. Gwynna didn't want to pry, so she turned to a new topic. "How do you know the duke?"

"His property marched with that of Sir Bertram Throckmorton. He was friends with Sir Bertram's daughter, Elizabeth. I was her governess. He took instruction with us now and then."

"Sebastian told me about his parents. He didn't say who raised him after they died." Gwynna glanced back at Mr. MacDuff. "It was Mr. MacDuff, wasn't it?"

"Yes. He's like a father to His Grace. Deep affection abides between them."

They walked for another ten minutes. "Could you teach me archery?" Mrs. Steele asked suddenly.

"Why…yes, if you wish," Gwynna said. "Let's stop here. That big oak is a fine target."

They waited for Mr. MacDuff, who carried a blanket. After he spread it out on the grass, Gwynna took an arrow from her quiver and demonstrated.

"Hold the arrow here, where my fingers are," she told her. "Turn the fletchings—the feathers—away from the bow so there's no impediment when you release the string. Now bring bow and arrow up together, as one."

Mrs. Steele frowned. "I'm not sure I can remember all of that."

"It soon becomes second nature," Gwynna said. "See how I have the arrow nearly parallel to the ground? Now sight the target along the shaft. Draw the string, hold for a moment, then release."

When Gwynna's arrow hit the tree, Mrs. Steele

clapped her hands.

Gwynna handed her the bow and an arrow. "Keep your feet shoulder's width apart. Turn your side to the target—yes, that's it."

She helped Mrs. Steele nock the arrow and anchor her string hand at the notch of her jaw. "Let a half-breath out. When you're ready, release the string."

As the arrow flew, Mrs. Steele toppled to the ground.

Instantly, Gwynna went to her. "Are you hurt?"

Her eyes crinkled in amusement. "Only my pride."

"I ought to have said it's important to continue the backward rotation of your string arm," Gwynna said. "You were too forward. It put you off balance."

But Mrs. Steele was not paying attention, for Mr. MacDuff had rushed over.

Their gazes held.

Gwynna decided it was a perfect time to retrieve her arrow from the tree.

***

"Are you injured?" Angus knelt down.

She shook her head. "Merely embarrassed. In truth, it was quite exhilarating."

"Yes. I saw that on your face," he said.

She frowned. "I'm sure I never intended you to."

"What, exactly, was exhilarating?"

To his surprise, she answered readily: "The tension and strength of the string. The power of the bow. And when I let the arrow fly—my goodness! I've no words."

Angus found that he, too, lacked words, for different reasons—chiefly, that she was nearly prone on the grass. He had never seen her in such a pose.

"You got nowhere near the target," he pointed out.

Her sour look lasted only a moment before dissolving into something more charitable. "Truly, the fact that the arrow went anywhere is a victory."

"That was not the only victory," he said softly.

"What do you mean?"

"That perhaps you have not had enough exhilarating experiences. That you are due a great many more."

She drew herself to a sitting position and brushed at her skirts. "That sounds highly improper, Mr. MacDuff."

"I never claimed to be all that proper, Mrs. Steele."

"You have," she declared. "All that rectitude, that righteousness, that rigidity—if those aren't the trappings of a person sitting in judgment as to what's proper, I don't know what is."

He arched a quizzical brow.

"Do not pretend to misunderstand, sir. When all of that nonsense with, er, the footman—"

"Peter?"

"I thought you didn't remember his name," she said.

"Not until you reminded me the other day." Angus regarded her. "Oddly, it seems you have now forgotten."

She huffed. "Why are we speaking of this?"

"You brought it up."

"Only by way of noting that you condemned my behavior—"

"I did not," Angus assured her.

She eyed him in exasperation. "You thought my...closet behavior vile and repugnant."

"Neither word was in my thoughts."

She blinked. "What then?"

"I suspect the word I had in mind was 'naughty.' Not even close to vile or repugnant."

"But you turned Peter off," she pointed out.

"Because he dishonored you."

"In what way?" she demanded. "It was my choice—"

"Women should not be made love to in a closet."

Her mouth opened, then closed again.

Angus caught her hand. When she did not pull away, he ran his index finger lightly over her palm. "The man took advantage of you."

She looked away. "I was a willing participant."

"I wondered if that was so," Angus said. "You cannot imagine how that notion affected me."

"I can." She reclaimed her hand. "Anything undisciplined—against the rules, not to say wild or free—is anathema to you."

Undisciplined. Wild. Free. Quite a heady lot of words to contemplate.

"What fascinates me," Angus said finally, "is that you are both disciplined and free."

"I have never been free," she said bitterly.

He hesitated. "What happened to you, Mrs. Steele?"

"This discussion is too personal. I have no wish to give you additional reasons to hold me in disregard."

"I could never hold you in disregard," he said softly.

"Would you care to try again, Mrs. Steele?" It was Miss Owen, back from retrieving her arrows and, from the look of it, ready to shoot dozens more.

Mrs. Steele's gaze held his. Angus read the plea there well enough. She needed to collect herself. He allowed himself to hope that was not due to her archery mishap, but to their conversation. And perhaps that tiny confession he had added at the end.

"My apologies, ladies," he said. "His Grace tasked me with having Miss Owen on hand to look at some documents. It slipped my mind. We must return now."

The look Hannah gave him was worth that lie.

Angus extended a hand to help her up.

Did she hold it a moment longer than necessary before releasing it? Impossible to tell.

He was such an old fool.

***

Gwynna burst into his study. "I was teaching Mrs. Steele archery when Mr. MacDuff recalled you wished to show me papers. You might've let me know beforehand."

How odd, Sebastian thought. He'd have bet that Angus

had not told a lie in the entirety of his worthy life. Until now.

"Well?" she demanded. "Where are the documents?"

As it happened, he and Busby had been working on papers that pertained to her. Sebastian slid them to the edge of his desk. Gwynna plopped in a chair to read them.

"Mrs. Steele has taken to archery?" Sebastian asked.

"She fell her on first shot," Gwynna said.

"Is she hurt?" Perhaps Angus saw something that made him call a halt for her safety.

"She was smiling when I left her to retrieve the arrows. But now that I think on it, she looked unsettled by the time I returned."

Had something happened between Angus and Mrs. Steele? This grew more interesting by the moment.

"I don't understand these figures," Gwynna said.

Busby looked alarmed. "What don't you understand, Lady Gwynna?"

She stared at him. "Lady Gwynna?"

"It's the address for a duke's daughter," Sebastian said. "Your family name will be Traherne."

Her chin rose. "I prefer Owen."

He frowned. "Wasn't Owen your ancestor's given name? How does it survive as a surname?"

"It's the old way. Children were known as 'ap'—son of—their father's given name. Over time, ap was dropped. Dafydd ap Owen, for example, became David Owen. It was the same for women; often they didn't change their names upon marriage. I certainly won't abandon mine."

Sebastian knew a useless battle when he saw one. "Those of our rank don't use surnames, in any case. You will be known as Lady Gwynna."

She looked stricken. "This is only the beginning of the compromises, isn't it? I'll end up being someone else."

"You'll be financially independent and can choose your path," he insisted.

Sebastian was pleased with his plan. An heiress would

have suitors. The bothersome uneasiness he felt in her presence would disappear.

Gwynna glanced at the papers again. Then she gasped. "Ten thousand pounds? It's too much!"

"You were left to poverty and your hermit of a grandfather. I mean to set that to rights."

"I don't feel sorry for myself, nor should you," she protested. "I won't accept this."

Sebastian shot her a dark look. Neither of them noticed when Busby fled the study.

"There's no proof I'm entitled to this." The forlorn note in her voice tugged at him.

"You are. I'll hardly notice the expense. William was wealthy beyond reason. Even after I pour a king's ransom into this castle, commission the finest *modistes* for your wardrobe—I'll still have a bloody fortune."

"Spend it on your clothes. Your tailor can name another horse for you."

"We made a bargain," he growled.

This was all William's fault. His gaze shifted to the portrait on the wall. Someone had finally dusted the thing. A red speck he hadn't noticed adorned his cousin's lapel.

Gwynna rose. "That's him, isn't it?"

Hell. Why hadn't it occurred to him to show her the painting before now? She hadn't known William—obviously, she'd want to see his likeness.

"Yes, although I remember him as more dour."

Gwynna walked over to the wall, but the painting was hung too high for her to see it in detail. Still, she stared at it for a long time. "I don't resemble him."

"No. The beauty must have come from your mother."

She turned in surprise.

"What I meant," Sebastian quickly added, "is that William didn't have red hair or—"

"Megan's hair was fire-red, like a sunset."

Like hers.

"William's complexion was sallow," he said. "Not ivory, like yours."

Egad. *Ivory?* Gwynna hadn't just brought chaos to his life—she'd spawned extravagant adjectives.

She moved toward him.

Sebastian stepped behind the protection of his desk.

"This arrangement with you is...unsettling," she said, her expression grave. "But I made a bargain. I'll keep to it."

Inwardly, Sebastian breathed a sigh of relief. "Then direct your thoughts to packing. With Angus's workmen everywhere, we can't stay here. We leave tomorrow."

Panic swept her *ivory* features. "For London?"

"No. The country home where I grew up—Summerlin."

Her brow cleared. "Mrs. Steele told me about your childhood friend Elizabeth. I should like to meet her if she still lives nearby."

"She doesn't," Sebastian said. This wasn't the time to tell her that Elizabeth was his wife. Gwynna would want to know the hows and whys and wherefores.

He wasn't up to it.

Shine a light there, and the whole thing might fall apart.

***

Chapter Ten

Sebastian had given her the impression his house was a simple country home.

It was not.

They drove through iron gates and up a long stone drive lined by graceful poplars, beyond which lay a lush expanse of green as far as one could see. A second set of gates led to another drive, edged by stone pillars.

Between the pillars stood green bushes, sheared into precise shapes. Oblong dark shrubs resembled an egg standing on end. Light green bushes were round. The pattern was this: two dark bushes, one light, two dark, and so on.

Beyond the bushes lay geometrical beds of flowers grouped by color. Short, yellow flowers were interspersed with taller upright blooms, also yellow. Beyond those were purple flowers. Plantings on each side of the drive mirrored the other.

At last, the carriage rolled to a stop at the house—a wholly inadequate word for the stately edifice. A boxwood hedge, its top and sides sheared at right angles, prefaced the stone entry.

Eight wide stone steps rose to a landing; ten more led up to the imposing front door, bracketed by square planters holding identical spiral shrubs.

Floor-to-ceiling windows lined the front of the house. Atop the dormered roof rose a cupola, perhaps thirty feet tall. There were at least ten chimneys, each with four caps, signaling the presence of perhaps forty fireplaces.

"This is where you grew up?" Gwynna asked faintly.

Sebastian nodded. "The landscaping is my own design."

"Oh."

His sandy brows arched. "You don't like it?"

"It's very...orderly."

"The back is less so," he said. "There's a gazebo on the edge of the lake. My mother used to tell me stories there when the weather was fine."

A footman opened the carriage door. Nearly a dozen servants waited to greet them.

When he introduced her as William's daughter, no one reacted with surprise.

Gwynna was in something of a daze as she entered the house. Here, too, her expectations were confounded. With that severely formal landscaping, she guessed Sebastian's immense home would be cold and formal. It was anything but.

Light streamed in those big windows, flooded the foyer, and highlighted a graceful curved staircase. Bright yellow walls were capped by wide white moldings at the ceiling. Thickly woven carpets in shades of rust and gray felt cozy under her shoes.

On the walls hung large landscape paintings, along with several portraits of a couple, his parents, she guessed.

The man wore a broad smile; the painter had captured a gleam in his eyes. The woman's eyes were more mysterious, a mix of colors, like Sebastian's.

The foyer opened into other airy rooms. Order abounded here, too. No clutter or artifacts obscured the furniture surfaces. Yet despite the order, Sebastian's house was inviting, filled with light and a sense of...rightness.

How he must have loathed William's castle, shrouded in cobwebs and centuries of dirt!

"It's lovely." Gwynna smiled. "No gargoyles."

"A few ghosts, perhaps." His eyes held a tinge of sadness.

His housekeeper led her up that curved staircase and down a long hall to her bedchamber.

The windows in her room afforded a lovely view of the back gardens and a white gazebo open on all sides, with benches inside for sitting. Its airy, carved scrollwork swept up into an arched canopy, giving it the look of a whimsical, delicate birdcage.

Sheer, wispy hangings floated like spun silk around the carved posts of the bed that was to be hers. Pillows in yellow and lavender nestled against the headboard.

Gwynna had never slept in such a bed. This was a room for a princess.

What was she doing here?

***

They ate a light supper at one end of the large dining table Sebastian's mother had loved.

Gwynna ran her hands over the swirls in the grain of the wood. "It's yew."

"My mother commissioned it." He remembered the day the servants brought it into the house. Faylinn had been thrilled—unaccountably so, he thought at the time. He'd have been all of six, beyond any hope of appreciating wood, or its grain.

Now he wished he'd paid more attention to the table, and the joy his mother found in it.

"Some consider yew sacred," Gwynna said. "It was planted in cemeteries because it was thought to help souls find the afterlife."

Had his mother believed such a thing? Unexpectedly, a shaft of pain tore through him.

After all these years?

He felt Angus's gaze. When Sebastian was a child, Angus had a trick of pretending not to look at him, all the while watching his every movement. Sebastian would make rude, silly gestures, trying to make him smile at something he pretended not to see.

As the years passed, he ferreted out most of Angus's tricks. Peripheral vision was no longer a mystery. Even so, the man still had a knack of noticing things.

Like now. Those green eyes lingered on him, the message unspoken: *Good memories help ease the pain.*

Angus turned his attention to Mrs. Steele.

"I saw that," Gwynna whispered.

Sebastian frowned. "What?"

"You and Mr. MacDuff. That silent communication." She hesitated. "He loves you."

Under the table, she reached for his hand.

Instantly, Sebastian pulled his away.

"Why do you do that?" she murmured.

"You can't simply touch people. It's not fitting."

Touching was dangerous. It invited reciprocation. He might be tempted to stroke her palm or sketch lazy spirals over it with his fingertip.

Fortunately, he had chores to keep his thoughts from wandering in that direction—estates to manage, solicitors to reproach, papers to sign, horses to ride, foxes to hunt.

God knows, the gardener would be lost if Sebastian didn't tell him which flora to plant. Cook craved his guidance on menus. Angus would be bereft if Sebastian failed to help him inflict those sausage-wrapped eggs on the household.

None of that was true.

Nothing in his life was true.

He was living a lie, had been for a year. And he'd added new lies, such as the one where he pretended he wasn't drawn to Gwynna.

It would only get worse, for he had set them on a course that would throw them together. He could only pray that she proved a quick learner. And that someone—not just anyone, mind you, but a man worthy of her—would sweep her away into marital bliss.

Sitting at his mother's dining table, trying not to think

about Gwynna's touch, Sebastian suddenly understood—with cruel and devastating clarity—that a fault line had opened in him. A fissure widening the gap between false and true, wrong and right.

He'd been trying to straddle it.

It could not be done.

Sebastian knew who he was, what he stood for, what he lived by.

Middle ground did not exist.

He'd never betray the woman who was his own, true heart. He knew Gwynna hadn't intended to spark such thoughts, only to comfort. She wouldn't respect a man who betrayed his principles. Nor should that man respect himself.

Oddly, everyone at the table was staring at him. Were they expecting him to affirm, here and now, his commitment to truth, justice, and right-living?

Ah. They weren't staring at him.

Their eyes were riveted on the dining room door behind him. Someone had come in.

Sebastian turned.

Elizabeth.

Thank God.

***

The woman stood in the doorway, trembling. Then she collapsed into Sebastian's arms.

She was so pale that the veins at her wrist stood out as if someone had drawn purple lines there. Her brown hair hung limp against her pallid skin. Her lashes fluttered shut.

They spoke her name—Elizabeth. This must be Sebastian's childhood friend. From the way Sebastian held her, she was dear to him indeed.

Anguish swept his features. "There, there," he murmured. "I'll take care of you."

Oh.

Truth dawned: This was the woman he loved, who had

been ill for so long. *His wife.*

He carried her into the parlor and laid her gently on the sofa. Servants moved about with water and smelling salts. Gwynna stood out of the way, not knowing what to do.

"I'll send for a doctor," Mr. MacDuff said.

"No," Elizabeth's voice was faint, but firm. "It's but a temporary weakness." Slowly, she pulled herself into a sitting position.

Sebastian stared at her in bewilderment. "When did you leave the clinic?"

"A few hours ago."

"They simply allowed you to leave?" he demanded.

"I wasn't a prisoner, Sebastian." She managed a wan smile. "The gig they use for errands was unattended. I wanted to come home. So I did."

"You traveled here in a *gig*? It's nearly five miles."

"Not so far," Elizabeth countered. Though weak, she had spirit.

Gwynna was glad. He deserved a wife with spirit.

"I went first to my parents' house," Elizabeth said. "I thought to stay there. It's the first time I've been there since their deaths. I was...unprepared."

Sebastian's arms went around her. "You're safe now."

For one unworthy moment, Gwynna found herself envying the woman in his arms.

How inappropriate. Elizabeth was his *wife*.

And she was only Gwynna Owen of Anglesey, who emphatically did not belong here.

***

Elizabeth wouldn't let him summon a physician. But with Mrs. Steele's careful nursing, she was stronger. Today was the first time in two days she'd left her room.

It was Gwynna who persuaded her to come down for breakfast. She had befriended Elizabeth, spent hours at her bedside, told her stories with all that magic nonsense.

Elizabeth seemed to relish her company. Perhaps

Gwynna's robust good health cheered her, or perhaps she simply enjoyed being with someone nearer her age. Most of the patients in her clinic were elderly.

"You must eat," Gwynna admonished. "You're in a fair way of disappearing inside that frock. Should you like to see the garden after breakfast? The sun's out. We ought not ignore it."

The Welsh approach to illness had merit; by midday Gwynna had Elizabeth sitting outside on the terrace.

Sebastian joined them, amazed at her transformation. Gone was the vacant, remote look she'd worn at the clinic.

He had penned a forceful letter to her doctors demanding an explanation for the lapse that enabled her to steal off in that gig. Strangely, no one from the clinic had sent him so much as a note to report her absence. If he didn't hear from them soon, he would drive there himself.

For now, he simply rejoiced that she was here in his home—*their* home.

Watching her grow ever more vibrant, he found himself entertaining the idea of a conversation about their future. Did she wish to formalize their vows with a grand wedding, or prefer a simple marriage announcement?

Or did she regret the marriage and wish it annulled?

***

Gwynna had persuaded Elizabeth to take a turn in the garden. She'd also coaxed Mrs. Steele into another archery lesson. Mr. MacDuff elected not to join them.

"I'm not one for crowds," he said.

"There are three of us," Gwynna protested. "Hardly a crowd."

His gaze slid to Mrs. Steele, but he said no more.

For Mrs. Steele's target, Gwynna chose a large maple at the edge of the lake. This time, she did not fall. Her arrow even traveled most of the way to the tree.

"You're making progress," Gwynna said. "You only need to bring the bow up higher."

Elizabeth, she was pleased to see, had decided to stroll on her own and was studying flowers near the gazebo some distance from them.

Gwynna helped Mrs. Steele position the bow. This time, the arrow glanced off the tree. Gwynna clapped her hands in delight.

Mrs. Steele smiled shyly.

It was a shame Mr. MacDuff was not here to witness the excitement in her eyes.

After a half hour, Mrs. Steele's arm was fatigued. She returned to the house for water.

Gwynna went to retrieve her arrows, glad of the excuse to explore the garden, which was less regimented than the front of the estate. Here, flowers and shrubs were arrayed in a serendipitous fashion, as if they had been idly dropped there by a divine hand.

Colorful rhododendrons and dahlias intermingled with trumpet-shaped bluebells and wildflowers. Pink foxgloves, their faces turned up instead of down, grew happily with more conventional yellow ones.

She wondered if the grounds of Sebastian's estate said something essential about him. The man who commissioned that precisely sculpted topiary in the front kept his imperfections hidden. The man who permitted wildflowers to grow with abandon didn't need to.

Over in the gazebo, Elizabeth wore a faraway look as she sat under the arched canopy. Perhaps she was thinking of her childhood, and times spent in that very spot.

Gwynna glanced toward the house to see whether Mrs. Steele was returning, then back at Elizabeth.

That's when she saw a man approaching the gazebo.

He wore dark trousers and waistcoat; his hair was black as well. A white neck-cloth provided the only relief to the deep midnight of the man.

From a distance, he briefly registered her presence, then returned his focus to Elizabeth.

Elizabeth waved him a greeting.

Were they friends? The man's tense, wary bearing suggested menace. Arrogance, too.

As the stranger strode toward Elizabeth, Gwynna's suspicions grew. What purpose could he have toward a woman still recovering from illness? Was he a doctor?

No. His demeanor wasn't that of someone devoted to helping others. He reminded her of Evans—invested in his own power and little else.

Gwynna saw Elizabeth flinch as he spoke to her.

Ought she to fetch Sebastian? Her instincts told her not to leave Elizabeth.

Bracing his hand on the latticework of the gazebo's side support, the man bent over her.

Elizabeth shook her head violently. She cried out.

Gwynna was too far away to run to her defense.

No matter. She knew what to do.

***

"Sebastian and I are happy," Elizabeth insisted.

"You were meant to be with me." His tone was light, but his gaze held a heavier message.

She eyed him uncertainly. Drew Maitland was no longer a youth, or the young blood who'd courted her half-heartedly. He had done so for form's sake, since Drew would never wish for the inconvenience of a wife.

And although he had been kind enough to visit her at the clinic, he was not a kind man. Darkness lived in him, which made his friendship as dangerous as his enmity.

When she was younger, Elizabeth found Drew intriguing and exotic. He'd been to places she would never go, done things she wouldn't think of doing.

But she never got used to his furtiveness. He slipped in and out of rooms, as if he did not wish to be seen.

Once, when she was recovering at Summerlin after breaking her leg, she'd awakened to find Drew standing over her, studying her, as if he knew her secrets.

Her memory was vague, but she recalled his presence at the bedside ceremony in Vienna. He'd made it possible for them to wed when she was too weak to rise.

Being indebted to Drew made her uncomfortable. Only a strong woman could take on Drew Maitland, and Elizabeth did not feel strong.

Coming home was the first step to regaining her strength. She needed to face her parents' empty house. Face the past, then the future.

Yet here was Drew, getting in her way, looming over her. Instinctively, Elizabeth shrank from him. "Why are you here?"

"I have business with Sebastian."

"You'll find him inside," she said coolly.

Drew shot her a murky smile. "In due time. What will you do about the marriage?"

Elizabeth had listened in stunned silence this morning as Sebastian explained he kept their marriage secret in the event she wanted an annulment when she recovered.

It was a lot to absorb. He did not press her to decide.

"We haven't discussed it," she said. Beyond those bare details, anyway.

Drew's gaze swept her from head to toe. "What else have you *not* done?"

The wicked man. She knew what he meant. Her mother had explained what happens in the marriage bed. Her parents had been deeply in love and shared a strong physical union.

Her parents.

Suddenly, the sob of grief she'd been stifling this past year would no longer be denied.

"Go away!" Elizabeth cried. How dare he bring to the fore this terrifying grief?

She put a hand to her face, blocking him from her view. He seemed taken aback, then bent to wipe her tears with his linen handkerchief.

Suddenly, a *whoosh* rent the air. Followed by a *thunk*, and an odd reverberation.

Instantly, Drew recoiled.

An arrow had lodged in the gazebo between two spread fingers of Drew's right hand.

"Step away from her." Gwynna advanced, another arrow aimed.

Drew stood motionless and, by his expression, thoroughly flummoxed.

With exquisite care, he eased his fingers away from the still-quivering arrow shaft and slowly backed away from the gazebo. He held his hands up in surrender.

"Now I'm an easier target," he snarled. "Perhaps you won't miss next time."

"I didn't miss," Gwynna said.

As comprehension dawned on him, Elizabeth began to laugh.

"Best take yourself off, Drew, while you are able," she said. "Don't shoot him, Gwynna. You've already dealt a mortal wound to his pride."

She kept her arrow trained.

"So it's true." Drew's mouth curved into a thin smile. "Claremont has brought us a warrior. England could use your services, madam."

Gwynna's gaze was steel. "England can go to Hell."

***

Summerlin's library was Sebastian's favorite room. Floor-to-ceiling windows afforded a magnificent view of the back gardens and lake.

Faylinn had loved the gazebo. She'd sit and read or write notes, or simply stare out at the garden with a wistful air. The cause of her melancholy lay beyond a boy's ken.

Why did so much of his mother lie beyond his reach?

Elizabeth was in the gazebo now, enjoying the air. Every day, she was regaining her strength.

Sebastian was watching her just as Drew Maitland

came into view. He registered Drew's intimidating pose as he bent over Elizabeth.

When he saw her cry out, Sebastian tore open the door. He sprinted outside as Gwynna let that arrow fly.

The arrow had lodged between Drew's fingers as he braced himself on a piece of wood scrollwork.

Drew's stunned expression had transformed into one of sly gratification, as if he'd been gifted with a perfectly seasoned Christmas goose.

Sebastian turned to Elizabeth. "Are you well?"

Her eyes sparkled. "Quite. Truly, this is the most excitement I've seen in months."

He shot Gwynna a quizzical look, but her attention was locked on Drew. She held her bow and arrow at her side, but at the ready.

Sebastian clamped a heavy hand on Drew's shoulder. "Explain, Maitland."

Drew shrugged. "You've been avoiding me so I decided to beard the lion in his den."

"Yet you did not come directly to me, but intruded on the ladies." Sebastian propelled Drew toward the house. "Never the direct path—always the oblique."

In the library, Drew helped himself to his brandy.

Glass in hand, he regarded Sebastian with the dead stare that usually made babbling fools out of those unfortunate enough to find themselves in his sights.

But Sebastian knew this game. He merely returned a bland gaze and waited for the man to show his hand.

"I called at the clinic." Drew drained the glass. "When I learned Elizabeth was no longer there, it seemed logical she'd be here. I wanted to see if she was well."

"That from a man who possesses not an ounce of concern for anyone other than himself."

Drew's mouth thinned. "That's harsh."

"Well-earned. You upset Elizabeth."

"What upset her was my asking what she intended to

do about the marriage," Drew said. "Thus, I believe her distress might be laid at your door."

"Our marriage is none of your concern."

Sebastian glanced out the windows. Elizabeth and Gwynna were strolling toward the house, arm in arm—relaxed and easy in one another's presence.

A placid scene, with no hint that one of them had nearly killed the man now drinking his brandy.

Drew splashed more brandy into his glass. "You wouldn't have had a wedding if not for me. Another man in your position might consider himself in my debt."

"Not a position I care to embrace at the moment."

"Your Miss Owen is quite the archer." Drew's bored tone was a giveaway. He was never bored, for his brain was always actively scheming. He wanted something.

"It's odd that you know her name," Sebastian said. "I'm not aware you'd been introduced. Perhaps if you had, she wouldn't have tried to kill you."

Drew's laugh held little mirth. "If she'd wished to kill me, I'd be dead. No, that was a warning shot, precisely placed. Don't tell me you haven't noticed her talents?"

"You haven't said how you know her identity."

Drew shrugged. "I found myself on holiday—"

"The devil doesn't take holidays."

"Amusing," Drew allowed. "Lovely place, her island. An innkeeper bored me to tears with its folklore. Given Miss Owen's barbaric heritage, it's no surprise she has lethal skills."

Yes, well, it was a surprise to him.

To be sure, Gwynna was inordinately fond of that relic of a dagger. But a dagger was for self defense—or, in close combat, the *coup de grâce*. Archery was for attack—in the right hands, deadly accurate.

That confounded him. Silenced by one man, stalked by another, she nevertheless possessed the skill to fight.

Did she not know her own strength?

"She is William's daughter. Stay away from her."

Drew eyed him in surprise. "You're acknowledging her as his by-blow?"

"No. As William's legitimate daughter from his marriage to Megan Glendower Owen."

Drew's gaze sharpened. "Have you proof?"

"All the proof I need."

The other man studied him. "Need is a powerful thing. It leads to all manner of foolish deeds."

Perfect. Drew, who saw everyone's vulnerabilities, now had him contemplating all the implications of "need" as it might apply to him and Gwynna.

Drew set his glass on a table. "As it happens, I have need of you."

"I no longer work for the Crown."

"The Crown disagrees. It wishes you and Miss Owen to perform a service for England."

"I feel safe in saying Miss Owen has no interest in performing any service for England." Sebastian pulled out his watch. "Time for you to leave, Maitland."

"You've heard of the Black Legion?"

The name jogged a memory. From one of his history classes? More recent, Sebastian thought.

Now he had it. "Some moldy French military unit that tried to invade England twenty years ago. Failed miserably, as I recall."

"At Fishguard, southwestern Wales," Drew said. "The invaders were convicts and ne'er-do-wells under the command of an Irish-American rogue."

He glanced at his watch. "Five seconds to explain why I should care."

Drew allowed a thin smile. "The Welsh were outnumbered, but the French were drunk. They mistook some women in red cloaks for British reinforcements and surrendered."

"You've left out the most important part," Gwynna

said from the doorway.

Drew swept her a bow. "It's a pleasure, Miss Owen. I am Andrew Maitland."

She eyed him coldly. "You made Elizabeth cry."

"Elizabeth is one of my oldest friends," Drew said smoothly. "I'd never cause her distress. But pray, what did I omit from my account of the Fishguard invasion?"

"You gave no credit to the Welsh women. One by herself captured a dozen invaders with her pitchfork. Other women joined her. *That's* why the French surrendered."

Drew eyed her in amusement. "Were they Amazons?"

Her eyes glinted ice-blue shards. "No. Strong Welsh women out to save their land. A word of warning, Mr. Maitland: Never stand in the way of Welsh and their land."

"Nor an archer with an eagle eye," he murmured.

The man was enjoying himself, Sebastian thought darkly. "Get to the point, Maitland."

"We have word that a new invasion is planned. The site is the island of Anglesey."

Gwynna gasped.

"Do not believe him," Sebastian warned. "Drew has only a passing familiarity with the truth. And as the world knows, the war is over."

"There are French mercenaries and the like who see profit in the fact that Wales is inadequately defended," Drew said. "The locals don't want British regulars there, and we've none to spare anyway. The invaders would establish a base, then press into Cheshire and points east."

He glanced at Sebastian. "That's your seat, is it not, Claremont?"

"If you think I'd lift a finger to defend my decrepit castle, you haven't seen it."

"It pleases Claremont to play obstructionist," Drew told Gwynna. "But you must wish to prevent a French invasion on Welsh soil."

"*British* soil," Sebastian corrected.

Gwynna stared at Drew in bewilderment. "I don't understand what you think I could do."

"Help raise a militia of locals," Drew said.

"That's the Crown's job," Sebastian snapped.

"Actually, it's the lord lieutenant's. That's you, Claremont. Lord Sidmouth has authorized you to oversee formation of a militia."

"Why Anglesey?" Gwynna persisted. "Wouldn't the French pick a closer site, like Fishguard?"

"Since that worked so well before," Sebastian muttered.

"There's precedent for an Anglesey invasion," Drew said. "The Romans did it."

"Two millennia ago, therefore not relevant," Sebastian declared. "Besides, the French aren't students of history or they wouldn't keep having the same revolution over and over again."

Drew moved to Gwynna's side. "Your support is key. The Welsh won't join a militia without the involvement of one of their own. Your ancestor is revered."

She blinked. "How do you know my history?"

"Enough," Sebastian growled. "I won't allow this."

"She'll be safe," Drew assured him. "You'll be with her."

He shook his head. "Elizabeth needs me here."

"You are right to stay with your wife," Gwynna said.

Sebastian eyed her in surprise. "You know?"

"Perhaps I ought not to have mentioned it. But I suspect Mr. Maitland already knows."

Drew turned to Sebastian. "While Elizabeth ponders matrimonial questions, it wouldn't be helpful for word to get around that she's wed. Think of the scandal if she decides she wishes to be free."

"I was wondering what you'd done with the real Drew," Sebastian snapped. "Making an ill woman the pawn in your game? That's the Andrew Maitland I know."

Gwynna eyed him in distaste. "Why should we trust you?"

"Regrettably, no one does," Drew acknowledged. "That's beside the point. You may decide that protecting your homeland is what matters. Sebastian may decide that what matters is protecting the secrecy of his marriage and giving his bride time to know her mind."

With a snarl, Sebastian started toward him.

"There's something I neglected to mention," Drew said. "The reason we suspect an invasion at Anglesey is we've learned one of the islanders is complicit. He made an offer to the French through his smuggling channels."

Gwynna looked bewildered. "A traitor, on Anglesey? Who?"

Sebastian sighed. He knew where this was leading.

Drew's face was a careful blank. "He goes by the name of January Evans."

She stared at him. "Evans is plotting with the French?"

"This strains all credulity," Sebastian snarled.

"We have suspicions, but we must catch him in the act," Drew said.

"He violates the Corn Laws," Gwynna said. "Is that not enough?"

Drew shrugged. "It is an unfortunate result of the laws that they promote conditions in which profiteers thrive. But we believe Evans's activities have caused sufficient resentment among locals that they'll see a militia as a way to unite against his practices."

"An organized militia." Gwynna looked thoughtful. "Yes, that might serve."

"No," Sebastian growled.

Drew glanced at her. "You need time to consider. I will call tomorrow." He left them.

Sebastian turned to Gwynna. "He's a ruthless liar."

"He knew about me and Evans, about my heritage—"

"It's his skill to make it seem so. Note that he didn't

mention how we'd catch Evans. Or the danger."

"I don't care about that," she said.

"You ought to. And by the way: Drew is a high-ranking government official. Did you consider the consequences when you launched that arrow at him?

Gwynna grinned. "Not for a moment."

"If you had killed him—"

"The first shot is always a warning. Unless it's war."

To his alarm, her expression grew rapt. "His plan is very...swashbuckling. We'd end Evans's reign, expose a traitor, save my homeland. How can I refuse?"

"By remembering that the man who spun that *swashbuckling* image is a cold-hearted deceiver who will do anything for the Crown."

She looked at him, her expression troubled. "I said I'd come to London and learn your ways. But this feels more like who I am. I'm not meant for drawing rooms."

Indeed, that would be a waste. He understood that now. She was destined for more. Still, he clung to hope. "You don't have to fit in—"

"I know. And I know that Mr. Maitland is clever, making it seem as if I am crucial to his plan. I don't flatter myself that I can do all that he says, but..."

Gwynna captured his hand. "Somehow I must try."

Sebastian couldn't pull away. The conviction in those blue eyes had him mesmerized.

"Don't you see?" Gwynna's voice thrummed with excitement. "I was *born* to do this."

Chapter Eleven

In the afternoon, Elizabeth walked to her parents' home, accompanied by Sebastian, Gwynna, Mrs. Steele, and Mr. MacDuff.

Perhaps it was the company, but with the sun shining, the day didn't seem as oppressive as when she'd driven the gig here. Yet nothing would ever be the same again.

She needed to make peace with that. And with Sebastian.

An eternity ago, they had been the best of friends. Now the air between them was strained. Today he seemed preoccupied, even troubled.

Elizabeth knew the year must have been hard on him.

They needed to settle things.

She wasn't accustomed to making decisions. During her convalescence, they'd been made for her. It was time she took the reins of her life, even if she didn't know how.

If only she could be like Gwynna. Her new friend did not lack for courage. Facing down Drew with that bow and arrow, she'd been formidable indeed.

Drew deserved the scare. The man was always trying to intimidate. As much as Elizabeth had been drawn to him over the years, she had been a little afraid of him, too.

Gwynna didn't seem to know fear. Yet from the details Elizabeth had gleaned, her life had not been easy.

Sebastian's decision to acknowledge her as William's daughter was more proof, as if Elizabeth needed any, of his generosity. He didn't shirk responsibilities, though they must sit heavy on his shoulders with the added duties of the dukedom.

Elizabeth loved him dearly. There could be no more devoted husband.

But something was off.

After touring the house and grounds, they sat side by side on the old swing her father had hung from the ancient tree behind their house. It had been wide enough for two when they were children, but Sebastian had grown into a sizable specimen of masculinity.

With their bodies wedged together, Elizabeth was very aware of his proportions. For a moment, she allowed herself to absorb the physical presence of the man.

They would be intimate.

Doubtless Sebastian would be skilled in the art of lovemaking. He would teach her what she needed to know.

He'd make a fine husband. He *was* a fine husband.

But he treated her as if she were made of glass.

Perhaps that was to be expected; she'd been ill for so long. Still, she didn't want to be seen as fragile. She wanted to embrace life—and her husband. Even if it meant venturing into uncharted waters.

"I remember little of the ceremony," Elizabeth said. "There wasn't an 'after,' was there?"

Sebastian looked perplexed. "After?"

She took a deep breath. "We didn't have…relations, did we? I hope I would have remembered that."

His mouth curved. "I hope you would have, too."

"So, no?" she prodded.

"No."

Yet another example of the difficulties she had caused. "I will try to make amends."

He covered her hand with his. "You owe me nothing. All I wish is for you to get better."

"I *am* better," she insisted. "You must not treat me as if I were frail."

He looked wary. "I won't risk harming you."

Elizabeth mustered her courage. "You might put your arm around me. I can survive that."

Sebastian stared at her.

"Pray, don't make me ask again," she said, mortified.

"You never have to ask," he murmured. "But this swing is meant for smaller folk. We're so wedged that if I move any part of me we'll both end up on the ground."

"We could double up." It was a scandalous notion. But she'd spent the last year shut away from the world. Now she wished to taste it in full measure.

Elizabeth eased herself off the swing and faced him. How did one go about sitting on a man's lap? Should she heave herself at him? What if she missed and took a spill?

Sebastian's features were a careful blank.

"You might help," she complained.

"Turn around."

She did. His arms went around her waist from behind, and lifted her onto his lap.

"I can't see your face," she protested.

Sebastian shifted her sideways, cradling her lightly across his chest. "Better?"

This was a daring arrangement, indeed.

"It's a bit shocking," Elizabeth confessed. "But I wish to get accustomed to it. Otherwise, I will never be a properly married woman."

"Are married women proper?" His voice held a teasing note.

"My parents were not very proper, at least according to my mother. My ears are still burning from the things she tried to educate me about."

Sebastian's arms slid more snugly around her; they felt solid and strong and secure.

Elizabeth looked up into the face she loved, the sand-colored hair that fell over his high forehead, the mouth that curved into an easy smile. His lips were full and sensual, his eyes alight with mischief. He would teach her much.

"I was accustomed to us being one way, and now we're another," she said shyly.

Sebastian nodded, and Elizabeth knew he understood. They had been friends, but now would be lovers. It was only natural for the change to seem awkward at first.

"We'll find our way." He brushed a kiss across her cheek.

Elizabeth hesitated. "Has…there been anyone else? Not ever, just since we've been married? Not that I would blame you."

He stilled. "No. How could you think it?"

She rested her face in the curve of his neck. "I don't. But I had to ask."

"Whatever you wish to do—a formal wedding or simply a quiet announcement—I am ready," he said. "But if your feelings are altered, I'll have the marriage quietly annulled. Drew arranged things, and he can undo them."

"I don't wish to be beholden to Drew."

He laughed. "No one does. But I will make him do our bidding, if it comes to that."

Elizabeth smiled. She liked Sebastian's arms around her. How would it feel to have his hands on her, in all of the forbidden places?

She caught his hand and moved it lower on her hip.

He made a sound low in his throat that thrilled her.

"I won't press you for an answer now," he said softly. "But we seem to be approaching a point where decisions might be necessary."

With that, he began to rock them slowly in the swing. With his arms locked around her, their bodies moved as one, in perfect accord.

This was where she belonged, Elizabeth thought.

Wasn't it?

How did one know?

How?

**

Angus was tired. The presence of young people in their prime made him feel his age.

Miss Owen, tiny as she was, fairly brimmed with life. Apparently, she was an archer of rare skill—according to Elizabeth's account of The Incident At The Gazebo.

Now Elizabeth and Sebastian were out on the swing, looking like two lovebirds. Miss Owen had darted off somewhere.

That left him alone with Hannah, who was studying a landscape on Sir Bertram's dining room wall with a degree of concentration that seemed suspicious.

Perhaps she was only pretending to regard the thing as if it was a Turner masterpiece—perhaps because she didn't know what to do here, alone with him.

Angus had a few ideas about that, but as they would probably frighten her senseless, he kept those to himself.

Or not. He was weary of thinking about her and never progressing beyond mere thought.

Did one progress at his age? What did one do with recalcitrant women when one no longer had youth and vitality on one's side?

One did not stand motionless like furniture. Life was too short.

And so, Angus fixed his gaze on Hannah, until he was quite certain she felt his scrutiny.

Finally, she looked over at him, her irritation plain.

But perhaps that slight flush came not from irritation, but something more interesting.

Hard to tell from here.

He crossed the room and stood before her. "Mrs. Steele."

"Mr. MacDuff," she acknowledged primly.

"I am obliged to tell you something important that I have lately learned."

She frowned. "What is that, Mr. MacDuff?"

"It's this: Eventually, one runs out of time." He

regarded her steadily, and was pleased to see her flush deepen.

The notion that he was the cause, that perhaps she wasn't as indifferent as she pretended, made the blood rise in his ancient veins. It warmed him beyond all measure, and the warmth spiraled into a reckless flame.

Hannah was slightly taller, but Angus had no trouble sliding his hand around the nape of her neck and brushing that still-lovely, full mouth with his.

She gasped.

Did that breathless sound mean she was insulted? Repulsed?

Charmed? Captivated?

Either way, Angus suspected he would find out in a moment or two.

***

Hannah could scarcely breathe. Angus MacDuff's mouth was settling in for rather more than a brief touch of their lips.

She didn't push him away. Was that because of shock? Or because she was—Heavens!— enjoying his kiss?

How very *daring*.

Women alone in the world did not put themselves into situations where they could be kissed. Thus, she had not been kissed in a very long time.

Mr. MacDuff had never seemed a passionate man, although lately she had detected something lurking in those green eyes that made her wonder.

In her younger days, she had been subjected to wet and sloppy kisses, often involving intrusive tongues. Those made one feel ill.

This kiss was not wet or sloppy. This was cool and dry and…tender.

Angus MacDuff kissed her as if she were some rare, priceless treasure.

At length, he pulled back to look at her.

"I-I may faint," Hannah managed. Indeed, she felt quite dizzy.

Whatever was the man thinking?

"Whatever were you thinking, Mr. MacDuff?" she demanded.

He tilted his head. "I don't believe I was thinking. But I suspect you were. Do you think you could think less?"

"Dear Lord." She fanned herself. "I *am* going to faint."

"You are not. Don't forget: You shot arrows today."

Hannah stared at him. "What is that to anything?"

His mouth—the same mouth that had just caressed hers—curved. "Only that you are strong, and occasionally willing to escape that brittle shell of yours."

She glared at him. "I believe you just insulted me."

"On the contrary," he said softly. "I am filled with admiration for you."

Hannah turned away. "I rather think you are filled with images of when you found me with the footman. But I am older and wiser. I don't wish to continue in this vein."

His hand lightly touched the curve of her shoulder, and he turned her around to face him.

"It's true," he confessed. "I am filled with images of you with that cursed footman. I will not claim otherwise."

She stared at her feet. "I'm not that woman, Mr. MacDuff."

"Hannah."

She would not look at him. She would *not*.

But he touched her chin and brought her face up. His eyes, quite a nice velvety green, held…longing.

Longing. For her? For the woman she had been, rather. Not the woman she was now.

"Stop," she said.

He released her.

Hannah's spirits plummeted.

"Mr. MacDuff," she whispered. Embarrassingly, there was a catch in her throat.

Strange as it seemed, his eyes bloomed with something that looked very like desire.

Why? She was nobody, really.

He caught her hand and brought it to his lips. Then he turned it over and kissed her palm.

"I'm also filled with admiration for the person who has persevered against obstacles she chooses to keep private, who has been a loving guide to those in her charge, and who possesses more heart than she lets on—perhaps more than she knows."

Hannah inhaled sharply.

"And if I cannot know all of her secrets," he added, "I pledge to take great care of those she chooses to share."

He released her and stepped away.

Hannah's pulse launched into a dizzying, dazzling, *daring* little dance.

***

In archery, consistency was key. Each step flowed into the next as one fluid motion, a seamless whole.

As her grandfather retreated into darkness, Gwynna pushed herself to achieve ever more difficult shots. But lately, she wondered whether she had used archery as an excuse for her own retreat from the world.

Had she been too passive, too willing to shirk her legacy? Too reluctant to face who she was?

She'd been shooting all afternoon. The visit to Elizabeth's parents' home made her restless to do more than watch Mr. MacDuff and Mrs. Steele ignore whatever was between them, or Sebastian and Elizabeth find their way back to each other.

Sebastian was different here. Those windows admitted all the light that old gray castle did not.

Light loved him. It burnished the gold in his hair, limned his features with a painter's keen eye. His high forehead evoked a Roman emperor preparing to storm the enemy's stronghold. His sensuous mouth conjured a dashing lord on a different sort of conquest.

What the light loved best, however, were Sebastian's eyes. A wealth of colors lurked there— bronze and moss and silver, depending on his mood.

Often, that gaze was guarded. Not so, at Summerlin. Here, he had no need to conceal himself. When he spoke to Elizabeth, his love for her warmed those hazel depths.

Gwynna nocked another arrow. Light had found her, too, in a way. Certain truths were trying to slip into the open. She wasn't foolish enough to think Mr. Maitland needed her. But *something* did. Something called to her.

His offer rekindled a longing for adventure her books had inspired. But he'd also invoked her heritage—the burden shadowing her, no matter how far she ran from it.

One couldn't escape fate. She was her mother's daughter, Owen's kin. Somehow, she had gone awry.

Now she had to write her life's story anew, with authenticity. Yet the path forward was hazy. Unlike archery, Gwynna didn't know the steps.

But each story began with a word, a sentence, a page.

And she did know this: The woman she aimed to be would not ruminate about a man wed to someone else, especially as that someone else was a friend.

With that, she found her first sentence: She would return home and form a militia. And the second: She would embrace who she was, and who she could be.

"I've never seen a woman with such skill. Or a man."

Gwynna turned. Mr. Maitland stood behind her.

"Welsh are archers," she said coolly. "'Tis not an uncommon skill."

"I've always assumed the stories were myths," he said. "Shoeless archers condensing from the mist unleashing a torrent of arrows far exceeding the speed of any crossbow."

"Some of that isn't true."

He arched a brow. "Which part?"

"They weren't shoeless."

His mouth pulled appreciatively. "And the rest?"

"A skilled longbow archer can shoot more than a dozen arrows a minute with precision, from several hundred yards. One must practice, of course."

"Given your gazebo strike, I'm forced to conclude that you practice rigorously."

Gwynna narrowed her gaze. "In truth, I'm out of practice. I could have missed the space between your fingers and hit your black heart instead."

He laughed. "I'm not often accused of having a heart."

"Why are you here? This morning you said you'd give us time to consider." Gwynna brought her bow up, trained her arrow on a small branch of a large oak.

"I've prepared a note with information for Sebastian."

Gwynna drew the bowstring.

"He loves her, you know," he said, as she let the arrow fly.

It sailed wide.

She glared at him. "I'm persuaded you know nothing of love."

"I do wallow in the baser emotions," he acknowledged. "It's why the Crown values me."

"Are you in love with Elizabeth?"

Surprise swept his features, then vanished behind that cool mask. "Sebastian and I have often been in competition. I wanted her because he did."

"Do you often try to take other men's wives?"

"'Borrow' is more accurate."

"You won't draw Sebastian away from her," Gwynna said. "He's loyal."

"Like a faithful dog," he agreed.

Gwynna nocked another arrow, this time facing him. Her target was an elm behind him. But she sighted the arrow path mere inches above his right shoulder.

He didn't flinch. "I see I've touched a sore spot. You want him for yourself."

Stillness settled over her. Gwynna drew the string.

"In that case, my plan offers the perfect opportunity. The two of you together, trying to catch a traitor, settling scores with your Mr. Evans, discovering true passion—"

Her arrow whizzed by his head, two inches above his shoulder, before striking the elm.

He turned to study the tree. "That was…stimulating. England is fortunate to have you on its side."

"I am not on England's side. Or yours."

"Pity." He held out a sealed missive. "This is for Sebastian, in the event you agree to my plan. But you must promise not to give it to him until you get to Wales."

Gwynna eyed it suspiciously. "Why don't you give it to him yourself?"

"Perhaps because I value my life," he said lightly.

"What if I give it to him now?"

"The plan will be ruined. He won't take on your Mr. Evans. You'd regret that."

"Do you know everyone's weakness?" she bit out.

He shrugged. "People reveal themselves, Miss Owen. I merely notice when they do."

Gwynna snatched the note from him. "One day, someone will figure out *your* weakness."

He merely bowed. Then he was gone.

***

Elizabeth stepped into the silent, dark corridor and moved toward Sebastian's chamber.

She was resolved to be a proper wife.

Today, in that swing, she had glimpsed what the future might hold: passion, intimacy. She wanted that.

She was on the cusp of re-establishing her life.

Who would she be? Not the person she was. Someone stronger, willing to take chances.

Her hand stilled on Sebastian's door. He was her husband, her dear friend. He had taken care of her parents and saved her life. He had sacrificed much over this year.

She loved him.

For a year she had been lost.

Now, she was found.

***

The knock on the door was barely audible, but Sebastian came instantly awake. He reached for his dressing gown and went to the door.

Elizabeth stood at the threshold, her face pale.

Alarm filled him. "Elizabeth! What is wrong?"

She stepped into the room. "I—that is, could you close the door?"

He closed the door and quickly lit a candle.

Elizabeth stood very still in the middle of the room. Her hair was loose, and the night-rail too thin for warmth. It was more in the nature of a chemise, and a revealing one at that. The neckline was low, with soft gathering. It lacked sleeves, and her shoulders were quite exposed.

Sebastian put a steadying hand under her elbow. "Come to the fire. Are you ill?"

She gave a shaky laugh. "It's only that I've never done this before."

"Done what?"

Her face flushed. Was she feverish? Ought he to summon a doctor?

"Tell me what is amiss," he urged.

Elizabeth took a deep breath, then met his gaze squarely. "I wish to seduce you."

He blinked.

"Or, you could seduce me," she added with a crooked smile. Her hands twisted in the fabric. "You know more about such things than I do."

He struggled to comprehend. "You wish to…"

"Do what married people do," she said firmly.

Sebastian steered her toward a chair. She perched on the edge. "I wish to resume my life."

"I see." But he didn't.

Elizabeth didn't look away from his scrutiny. "I-I thought we could…lie together."

Cold panic seized him. "I'm not sure this is the time."

"How can there be a better time?"

Sebastian hesitated.

"Do you not wish to?" Her voice wobbled.

He bent and kissed the top of her head. "My heart. Do not cry."

She rose from the chair into his arms. "Make love to me, Sebastian. Please."

As her trembling form pressed his, he was aware of every curve under that thin fabric.

This felt strange.

Sebastian told himself it was because he wasn't accustomed to touching her like this. There was bound to be strangeness at first.

Still, he hesitated. Warring forces pulled at him. What if this was an impulse she'd regret? Shouldn't he protect her from that? Yet who was he to deny her voice?

What he couldn't deny were his instincts, which rebelled.

As he stood there, motionless, Elizabeth slipped her finger under one shoulder of her chemise, slid the fabric down her arm. She did the same with the other shoulder.

The silky confection pooled at her feet. She was naked—and trembling.

Instantly, Sebastian brought her into the circle of his arms, enveloped her in his warmth. But she continued to shake, even as her arms slipped around his neck.

"Show me how to do this," she whispered.

Sebastian stared at the woman whose features he knew so well, whose sweet, generous nature had warmed his heart as nothing else. Who waited for his kiss.

He lowered his mouth to hers. His arms slid around her waist and, after a pause, over her bare back. Her soft, smooth skin was everything a woman's flesh could be.

It had been a long time since Sebastian had held a naked woman in his arms. He had locked that part of him away in a recess of his brain.

Unfortunately, his brain now insisted on talking to him. It nattered on about those rebelling instincts. About how this wasn't quite right.

"Elizabeth," he murmured. "Is this truly what you wish?"

She took his hand and placed it on her bare breast.

His traitorous hand, unencumbered by self-doubt, closed over that soft roundness. Sebastian spoke something—he knew not what—as she slid her hands between the edges of his dressing gown.

Her fingertips feathered across his chest.

Under his palm, her nipple pebbled, straining for him.

Elizabeth was his wife, and she wanted him.

Sebastian swept her off her feet. He carried her to the bed and laid her down with exquisite care. He would take his time. She was fragile.

"Please, Sebastian," Elizabeth urged. "Quickly."

Quickly?

His cursed brain chose that moment to find its way to Shakespeare. *If it were done when 'tis done, then t'were well it were done quickly.*

One did not make love and think of Macbeth and murder.

Sebastian brushed his fingertip over her cheek.

"We have been through too much together to be less than honest," he said softly. "Does this not feel…forced?"

She buried her face in his chest and sobbed.

His heart felt nigh to breaking as he wrapped his arms around her. "Don't cry, my love. Whatever is wrong, I will fix it."

Sebastian rocked her in his arms. He loved her. She loved him. They had an eternity to get this right.

Even so, this shook him to his core.

When at last there were no more tears, Elizabeth eased herself into a sitting position and pulled the sheet up to her neck.

"I don't know what to do." Her eyes were bleak. "My parents' house is sad and empty. I don't seem to belong here in your bed. I need to start a new life, but I don't know how."

He stroked her hair. She was hurting. He was, too.

But he wouldn't flinch from truth.

"Do you not wish to be married?" he asked gently.

Her watery gaze met his. "We should be together. I've always known that."

"Is 'should' sufficient?"

"Perhaps if we give it time."

"I've pledged that you may take all the time you need to decide." Sebastian hesitated, wondering at the odd thought that tugged at him. "Is there someone else?"

She was silent for a moment.

"There was a young doctor at the clinic who seemed to pay me special attention," she said. "I wondered if he was fond of me. That made me feel...unsettled."

Sebastian stared at her, his heart in his throat.

"Then I saw he treated all the female patients as if they were special. So it was nothing, really. Still, it worried me to think that I could be attracted to someone who wasn't you."

Now his heart truly did break.

He took a deep breath. "By coming to me tonight, did you hope to discover whether that would banish all thoughts of anyone else?"

Elizabeth shook her head. "It's always been you. But when you describe it that way, it gives me pause. I fear my behavior has been unworthy."

Sebastian pulled her close. "You could never be unworthy."

"I thought the answer would be clear." Her voice

caught. "It's not."

Ah, but it was to him. His brain, ever poetic when that was least wanted, gave him Burns.

Fare thee well, thou first and fairest!
Fare thee well, thou best and dearest!
Thine be like a joy and treasure,
Peace. enjoyment, love, and pleasure!
A fond kiss, and then we sever;
A farewell, alas, forever!

But this wasn't farewell, nor forever.

Forever changed, perhaps.

Elizabeth pressed his hand against her heart. "I will be your wife. I made a promise."

He managed a smile. "You were half-dead when you made it. I'll not hold you to it."

A tear rolled down her cheek. "I owe you my life."

He shook his head. "'Tis I who owe you mine."

Elizabeth sighed, and his heart shattered anew on that soft, delicate sound.

They stayed with their arms around one another for a long time. Finally, he fetched her chemise. She slid her arms through.

Covered, once more.

Sebastian lifted her into his arms and carried her to her room.

***

Chapter Twelve

Angus had a strict morning routine. First came reading. It might be Scripture or philosophy or poetry; the point was to start the day in someone's head other than his own.

A man's thoughts got tangled if they did not have something else to fix upon. And sometimes, no matter what he did, they got stuck.

Today, they were stuck on the puzzle of Hannah Steele. Or Miller, as he still thought of her, for it was the first name by which he knew her.

He couldn't explain her hold on him. That closet episode ought to be no more than a bawdy memory he could revisit sometimes, dust off the cobwebs, then forget.

But he'd never forgotten her.

Perhaps it was her courage that captivated him. Hannah kept her sufferings and secrets to herself. She had developed a stiff backbone and steely armor.

Angus respected that. Still, her eyes gave her away. They could be hard and unyielding, but sometimes he saw a young and winsome lass looking out at him.

Yet he wasn't in thrall to a younger version of her. Hannah had become a woman of substance, whom he vastly preferred to that impulsive chit in the pantry.

Under that armor, he suspected she still had dreams.

What had happened to smother them?

Angus burned to know.

He burned for her.

The door to his sitting room opened.

It wasn't the woman he burned for, miraculously come to entice him from his devotions.

Sebastian stood there, as forlorn as when Angus first saw him sitting on that school bench with a small bag of possessions, so inconsequential after the loss of what really mattered.

He'd grown into a fine man. It gave Angus no small thrill to have had a hand in that.

Nevertheless, Angus saw that sadness had come upon him in no small dose. This sorrow ran to his soul.

Circles ringed Sebastian's bloodshot eyes. He was dressed carelessly, his neck-cloth askew, no waistcoat, his shirt open at the top—remarkable, indeed.

Sebastian dropped into a chair. "I don't suppose you can fix things, as you used to, before I grew up."

"I fixed nothing," Angus said. "You made yourself what you are."

"A made-up person." His tone was bitter. "It's been a burden. The cost has been dear."

"Some burdens are thrust upon us," Angus said. "Others we choose."

He didn't know why Sebastian had chosen to wear that frivolous diplomatic persona long past its usefulness.

"I've always admired your discipline," Sebastian said. "Thank you for giving me that."

"Discipline can be a false god. Gets in the way of life."

Alarm filled those red-rimmed eyes. "I've never heard you talk this way. Is something wrong? Your health?"

"Not another word," Angus growled. "I'm fifty-five. Not a hundred, nor dying."

Sebastian shook his head. "You're so damned private. You give nothing away."

"A man's entitled to hold some things close."

"I'm painfully aware of that." Sebastian sighed. "It's been my life for the last year."

"It's Elizabeth that's the trouble, isn't it?"

Sebastian gave a rough laugh. "How do you know everything?"

"Anyone can see what's written on your face. What happened?"

"She came to my room last night."

"Not certain I need to hear this."

"Nothing happened. It didn't seem...right." Sebastian shook his head. "I don't understand. It's always been her. I thought the rest would come in time."

"The rest?"

"The wanting, the passion. But the love between us is more...familial." He rubbed his eyes. "I can't make love to my sister."

"Is it Miss Owen who's in your mind, then?"

He looked startled. "Gwynna? God, no. She's fierce and determined and..."

"Full of passion?" Angus offered.

Sebastian's brows drew together. "It's not like that."

The denial hovered there. Angus was content to let it do battle with extended silence.

"I was betrothed once," he said finally.

Sebastian made an incredulous sound. "Impossible. Who would put up with you?"

"A fair question," Angus conceded.

"I want the whole."

"Perhaps the half, if you're lucky," Angus retorted. "When I was young, I thought to serve the church. I'd be a vicar, or some such."

"You'd have made a fine one."

"Not sure about that," Angus said. "Anyway, her family and mine were close. It was assumed that we would marry. I liked her well enough, so we agreed on it."

"What happened?"

"One night, we went to a church event. A supper. St. Stephen's Day, I think it was. A man from the next parish came up to her, introduced himself. He was intent on her, whereas I was merely complacent. If I'd cared more, I might have made more of an effort."

Sebastian eyed him in astonishment. "She was the love of your life, and you let her go?"

"That's the point—she wasn't," Angus said. "We'd have made it work, but neither of us cared enough to fight for it. In the end, we didn't mind how things turned out."

"If that was supposed to be a piece of wise advice, it missed the mark."

Angus smiled. "Here's the question: Have I missed something by not having a wife I didn't care to fight for? Perhaps. But it's not a hole in my heart."

Sebastian rose abruptly. "I wasn't like you. I *fought* for Elizabeth. I nursed her in Vienna. I even married her to give her my name in the event it was discovered how intimately I took care of her."

He slanted Angus a gaze. "I might have neglected to mention that."

"I see. So all this nonsense this year—"

"What nonsense?"

"The folderols, the sartorial silliness. The altitudinous neck-cloths. The quizzing glass. The parties where you allowed those young ladies to think you had an available heart before carelessly flitting away without remorse —"

"Hell. Was it as bad as all that?"

"I wouldn't know," Angus said. "I have not been in London for some time."

"Merely followed my flitting folderols."

"Even in the country, talk reaches me."

"You are such a fraud," Sebastian muttered.

Angus studied him. "You were explaining why you went to such extremes."

"Elizabeth wasn't well when we wed. I wasn't sure she knew she'd said vows. I decided to keep the marriage a secret until she was well. Then, if she had regrets, I'd arrange an annulment. The masquerade was to throw everyone off. No one guessed I was married."

"You were protecting her. How…responsible." As the

person who helped instill that ramrod sense of responsibility, Angus felt a tinge of guilt. "What happens next?"

"I've interrupted your devotions in hopes you have the answer."

Angus regarded him with compassion. "You lost your parents young. Their deaths left a void, and you thought Elizabeth would be the filling of it. But it sounds as if you now believe she belongs in a different place in your heart."

"What's between Elizabeth and me is real affection," Sebastian insisted.

"Is that enough for you, lad? Affection?"

"More than enough, I thought. But everything was off. It's been a year since we were ourselves with one another. Perhaps the prolonged absence is the problem."

"Absence can bring out the truth," Angus said. "I learned that recently from a woman."

Sebastian gave him a sidelong glance. "Not certain I need to hear this."

"I've long been content," Angus said. "I was spared a life sentence with a woman toward whom I felt affection, but little else. It's possible my contentment also derived from refusing to want what I did not, or could not, have."

"That's sensible. Why wish for what you can't have?"

"Well, you don't wish for it," Angus said. "But when one is always striving to forget that which is unattainable, sometimes that very thing can become an obsession."

Sebastian frowned. "It's difficult to imagine you with obsessions."

"Haven't been many. Perhaps only one. But the more one is aware of an obsession, the less it retreats." Angus sighed. "Indeed, it demands to carry the day."

"Can't you refuse to allow it to do so?"

"Spoken like a man who has never endured one."

Sebastian laughed. "What did you do about yours?"

"An opportunity came that allowed me to stop fighting

it and gain courage to act. I have you to thank for that."

"Me?"

Angus smiled. "I suppose it's fitting that the person dearest to me was the instrument."

"This obsession is a person, I assume. And now you're acting on it, er, her?"

When Angus started to respond, Sebastian waved him off. "Never mind. Happy to be spared details."

"It might be more than obsession," Angus confessed. "It might be a grand passion."

Sebastian stared at him in wonder. "Have you fallen in love?"

That took Angus aback. Had he?

If obsession was rooted in the need to possess, and possession rooted in the drive for that without which one could not be whole—then love and obsession were not dissimilar. Perhaps they varied only in degree.

"It is a question worth asking," he conceded. "But as to your situation, I'm afraid I have no useful advice. Unless it's this: Pain can lead to discovery. Same with the unfamiliar. Don't turn away from either."

Sebastian smiled wearily. "I knew you had it in you. I'll leave you to your obsession."

If only, Angus thought wistfully.

* * *

A whirlwind of activity followed Sebastian's abrupt announcement that they would go to Wales, form a militia, and catch a traitor.

Mr. Maitland's ledger, cash, and badges were swiftly loaded into the coach.

Mr. MacDuff and Mrs. Steele would stay at Summerlin and help Elizabeth put her parents' house in order. Gwynna wondered whether Sebastian was aware of the undercurrents there.

But his mind was elsewhere. As he and Elizabeth bid one another goodbye, Elizabeth was near tears. Sebastian looked similarly stricken.

In the carriage, he made no effort at conversation.

When, rather than going directly to the castle, they detoured to Mr. Busby's village, Gwynna eyed him in dismay. "I don't want her."

"We need a chaperone."

"No one cares about that, least of all—"

"*I* care." His forbidding expression silenced her.

After ascertaining Mrs. Kendall was available—when was she not?—arrangements were made. They would fetch her at first light. She'd be allowed one bandbox, since the coach was packed with militia accoutrements. Mr. Busby could barely suppress his glee.

When they finally reached the castle, Sebastian strode past Gwynna to his study. She hurried after him.

"Whatever is amiss? If you don't wish to do this, why accept Mr. Maitland's proposal?"

He scowled. "Is there no pleasing you? Are you not thrilled at the chance to avoid London, save Wales from the bumbling French, and put an end to the evil Evans?"

"I am not glad of anything that puts you in such a mood," she retorted. "I'd have pleasanter conversation with a dragon."

"You like dragons."

"Not if they snap at me. Or act as if I have the plague."

His features hardened. "You are not to speak of the plague."

Something was terribly wrong.

Sebastian poured a glass of brandy, thrust it at her, poured another glass, raised it. "Here's to luck. We'll need it since we know only the barest part of Drew's scheme."

That's when Gwynna remembered Mr. Maitland's note, tucked in her skirt pocket. They weren't in Wales, but it must be important. Should she give it to him now?

Perhaps after he recovered his temper. "If you doubt his plan, why did you agree to it?"

"Less fraught with consequences than killing Maitland outright."

"You don't mean that."

He eyed her darkly. "Tell me how this makes sense: Rather than solve diplomatic crises where the fate of nations hang in the balance—something for which I have a modest talent—I chose to try to persuade hostile Welshmen to arm and protect the union they despise."

"Sebastian—"

"Rather than the comforts of home, I chose this crumbling pile of stones and the company of Mrs. Kendall." He tossed back his brandy. "Looking forward to that, I must say."

His gaze drifted to William's portrait.

"Rather than address the urgent question of whether my wife chooses to remain in the wedded state, I chose to detour to Wales—though the answer is now painfully clear to both of us." He poured more brandy.

Gwynna didn't understand that last, but his marriage was his own affair. Still, his pain was heartbreaking.

She placed her hand on his shoulder, gave it a reassuring shake.

His gaze locked with hers. Down deep, under the misery, glinted flecks of amber, as if he was reaching for something beyond pain.

Hope, maybe.

"Rather than spurn my unproven parentage, you chose to acknowledge me as part of your family," Gwynna said softly. "Rather than ignore the man who stalks me, you pledged to stop him. That is a man I am proud to know."

He stared at her.

"To be sure, you're saddling me with Mrs. Kendall. But I know your wretched sense of propriety dictates it. And though I disagree, I respect you all the more."

Sebastian went still. After a moment, he took a long, shuddering breath. "I may have lost my bearings."

He took out his watch, ran his thumb over the case. After a moment, he seemed calmer.

"It's beautiful," Gwynna said.

"My father's wedding present from Faylinn. The markings have puzzled me. The case top design is simple, but the back is complex. It's as if the watch has a story to tell, if one could but ferret it out."

He held it out, and she studied it closely for the first time. The top bore a raised circle with three lines inside it.

Gwynna eyed it in astonishment. "It's the Awen."

"What?"

"A Welsh symbol. It stands for the muse—inspiration behind art, poetry, and the like."

Sebastian frowned. "How do you derive that from three lines and a circle?"

She traced the design with her finger. "The lines are in perfect proportion, meeting at the top. They're for harmony, balance, and truth. Arthur himself is believed to have embraced the Awen."

His brows knit. "My father was English. Not Welsh, nor a mythological king."

Gwynna turned the watch over. Entwined leaves formed the back design, but the pattern was unusual. Instead of leafy curves, points shot out at odd angles.

It was as if another figure was hiding amid the leaves. Suddenly, she saw it.

"Dear Lord,." Gwynna whispered. "It's a dragon."

***

His precious keepsake, carried to keep his parents with him always, was not what it seemed. Indeed, it appeared to be adorned with Welsh symbols.

Impossible. Yet, every other pillar of his foundation had shifted, so why not this?

"My father cherished this watch," Sebastian said. "I've treasured it because it connects me to them. Now, suddenly, it's a mystery."

"Perhaps one of the craftsmen on Anglesey will recognize the work," Gwynna said. "All is not lost. We'll solve the puzzle."

All is not lost.

Yet it felt that way. Elizabeth, his parents, the watch. All lost.

Sebastian inhaled for a count of five, then a long breath out, as his mother had taught him for the night terrors. But it was no use. Emotion swamped him.

His treasure had lost its meaning.

He called for Rowland. Again, more loudly. Finally the man appeared, slightly out of breath. "Your Grace?"

"You served the late duke for years." He spoke calmly, as if his world hadn't upended.

"Thirty," Rowland said proudly.

"Did you ever meet my father—Gerald?"

Rowland nodded. "He was a breath of fresh air."

Yes, Gerald was light to William's dark. But how had a Welsh watch found its way to him? "Did he and William travel together? Say, to Wales?"

"No, Your Grace."

Sebastian's spirits sank.

"I do recall a time Mr. Traherne called on the duke— marquess, as he was styled then—after returning from holiday," Rowland said. "It was a difficult visit. Voices were raised."

Instantly, the man looked horrified. "Forgive me. I've spoken out of turn."

"Not at all," Sebastian said. "As their only living relative, in truth I yearn to learn what I can about their interaction." Not for nothing had he excelled in diplomacy.

Rowland inclined his head, but said nothing.

"My father was lost to me at a young age," Sebastian added. "All I have are memories, and those end when I was seven." Shameless play for pity, that.

Rowland looked stricken. "Indeed, Your Grace. I lost

my own father when I was but a lad. Difficult as it is to say, I can no longer recall his voice."

The man's pain resonated. The mind preserved only a poor imitation of what time had stolen. Lost forever were the particulars—the undercurrent of amusement embedded in the living Gerald's speech.

Sebastian swallowed hard. Soon they would both be watering pots. "Is there anything else you recall about that exchange between them?"

"His Grace could, upon *rare* occasions, give rein to his displeasure," Rowland said.

"I'm sure it was *very* rare," he murmured, though he knew William wouldn't have hesitated to launch a tirade.

"One remembers only the good times," Rowland said.

Gwynna stepped forward. "But that particular time they had words?"

Rowland nodded. "As painful as it is to say…"

Sebastian's jaw was a fair way toward grinding his teeth to bits. This was torture.

Gwynna smiled encouragingly. "It was a dispute?"

"Yes. Over…" Again, Rowland trailed off.

"Money?" Gwynna ventured.

He recoiled. "Certainly not."

"A woman?"

Sebastian nearly laughed. William and Gerald fighting over a woman? Preposterous.

"Yes," Rowland said.

"What woman?" Gwynna asked.

Rowland hesitated. Sebastian had had enough. "Gerald and William had words over a woman and you cannot remember more than that? Good God, man—"

"It's natural to forget," Gwynna said smoothly. "It can't have been a pleasant memory."

Rowland nodded mournfully.

"Did you hear her name?" she asked. "Anything that might shed light on who she was?"

"His Grace called her a witch."

Sebastian sighed. William undoubtedly thought the entire female species to be witches.

Gwynna touched Rowland's sleeve, which caused the poor man to freeze. "Do you know where Gerald had traveled? Did anyone say where the…witch was?"

"I don't think so," Rowland said. "Directly after that, ah, discussion, His Grace—that is, his lordship then—ordered a coach readied within the hour. A great deal of running about and packing followed. We scarcely got him out the door by the time the hour stuck."

"Out the door to…?" she prompted gently.

Sebastian eyed her in wonder. She might have been waiting out a recalcitrant sheepdog.

"To the north. Or west. There was talk of sea breezes, so perhaps the coast. He left in a rare taking—*rare*, you understand—but I do believe he came to like the place."

Sebastian frowned. "What place?"

"His Grace went back for several summers," Rowland said. "I can't for the life of me think where it was. It was so long ago. Will that be all, Your Grace?"

"Yes," Sebastian said. "Thank you."

After Rowland left, they stared at one another.

"Wales," Gwynna whispered. "Anglesey. It must be."

"But why, if William tore there in a rage, would he return to Wales again and again?"

"I can think of a very good reason, Englishman. Megan Glendower Owen."

Chapter Thirteen

Mr. MacDuff was a handsome man, for his age.

For *any* age.

Hannah watched him as he spoke with Elizabeth in her parents' garden. They spent the morning at the house, making a list of needed repairs.

It had been largely unoccupied for over a year, save for a few servants. Still, it was in good condition—likely the duke's doing, for her father had made him a trustee.

For each repair, Mr. MacDuff explained to Elizabeth whether it was essential or could wait. The kitchen stove's flue, for instance, had cracks and a soot buildup.

"If flame finds a crack, it can catch the house on fire," Mr. MacDuff said. "The chimney's too old and narrow to be fixed. Probably ought to seal it off, move the stove to the outside wall, and build a new chimney."

"That sounds frightfully expensive," Elizabeth said.

Mr. MacDuff nodded. "A greater expense, yes. But you need a stove, and if this one can't be used without risking a fire, there's little choice."

Elizabeth was quiet on the return to Summerlin. She seemed preoccupied, as if trying to find her bearings.

Hannah knew what that was like. She'd spent most of her adult life moving from one place to another.

She was no longer young and foolish. Yet Mr. MacDuff made her feel like a schoolgirl, full of blushes.

When those flinty green eyes softened to fine velvet, something came to life inside her.

His eyes held none of the callow eagerness of youth. They held maturity. Patience. Knowledge. Sensuality.

Expertise.

The direction of her thoughts alarmed her. No matter that he had kissed her and made it plain he wished for more, a woman her age had no business engaging in dalliances.

Still, she studied Mr. MacDuff surreptitiously. He was trim and fit. His hair was no longer vivid red, but she had gray threads, too. His looked very distinguished.

Thank heavens for Elizabeth's presence. There was no need to dwell on Mr. MacDuff's attributes, when Elizabeth needed tending to.

But after they reached Summerlin, Elizabeth suddenly retreated to her room, leaving Hannah and Mr. MacDuff standing quite alone in the massive foyer.

"Would you care to take a turn in the garden?" He extended his arm.

Hannah wondered what his flesh looked like under the fabric.

"Heavens, no!" That was aimed at her, not him.

He looked taken aback. "Would you prefer to sit by the fire? Take tea? Read?"

That green gaze warmed her more than any fire. Hannah could not formulate a response.

"You look unwell." Mr. MacDuff touched her elbow, steered her into the parlor and to the divan. "Was the walk too much?"

"Not at all." Hannah folded her hands in her lap. Her gaze fixed on the wall.

Mr. MacDuff was not one to rush to fill a silence. They sat awkwardly for some time.

"I have never been married," Hannah said suddenly.

"You said you made up those husbands, so I suspected as much."

She turned to him. "Because I am not the sort of woman men marry?"

"Because you are not a woman to easily give your heart—even once, not to mention four times," Mr. MacDuff said. "The notion defies credulity."

Hannah eyed him indignantly. "How do you know? I might be just the sort of woman to fall in love time and time again. Indiscriminately, even. Constantly."

A corner of his mouth curved upward. "Is that so?"

She looked away.

"Will you tell me about the man who led you to such a state?"

She scoffed. "It is just like a man to assume the reason I am unwed is another man. As if I had no free will, nor sense enough to make my own decisions."

His silence infuriated her.

"You are toying with me, Mr. MacDuff."

"I didn't know you could be toyed with, Mrs. Steele."

Hannah glared at him. "Very well. If you must know, there was a man who set me on this path. There. I've said it, and I will say no more. Do you feel vindicated?"

He shook his head. "Only sad."

"I don't want your pity." She rose abruptly.

Mr. MacDuff rose as well. "Not pity. Never that."

His eyes held compassion. To Hannah's dismay, hers grew moist.

"There is nothing you can say that will change my opinion of you," he assured her.

"Which is what?" The words were out before she could stop them.

"I'm not sure you wish to know."

Hannah flinched. "I understand very well who I am, Mr. MacDuff." A dried-up, useless prune of a woman, bereft of youth, hair streaked with gray.

"I've never been able to get you out of my mind," he said. "Not from the very first moment I saw you. As I was telling Sebastian, you've been something of an obsession."

"You spoke to him about me?" She was horrified.

He seemed not to notice. "Nevertheless, I know that you are not one to be drawn to a man just because he is drawn to you."

Well.

"More than mere attraction is needed to bring two people together," he added.

Though that was not nothing, Hannah thought.

"You have my deepest admiration," he said.

Which was more than she'd received from any man.

Ever.

"I confess I have never been more attracted to any woman," he said. "Painfully so."

"Painfully?" she croaked out.

He stilled. "I did not intend to insult you."

She took a steadying breath. "I did not take offense."

Mr. MacDuff caught her hand. "I find that at this point in my life, honesty is essential."

Hannah could not disagree. If he told her what he wanted from her, she might protect herself.

"I respect your intellect, your strength, your character, that prickly armor you wear against the world," he said. "I could add all measure of compliments, Mrs. Steele, and they would all be true, but I know that you are not a woman to be swayed by compliments."

Such words! Hannah fanned herself with her free hand. "I believe I will just sit again."

"Are you ill?" Concern filled that green gaze.

Lovely eyes, really.

"Perhaps." Indeed, she felt quite weak.

"I will fetch some hartshorn," he said quickly.

Hannah caught his arm. "Do not go anywhere, you wretched man."

She had never asked any man for anything. She was too wary, too…shriveled. "Mr. MacDuff?"

"Yes?" He sounded quite bewildered.

Courage.

"It would be quite all right," she said in a small voice, "if you kissed me."

Hannah met his gaze straight on.

He touched his palm to her forehead. "Are you ill?"

She pushed his hand aside. Brought her mouth to his.

For one long, awkward moment, they sat with lips touching, yet frozen.

Then Mr. MacDuff moved his mouth over hers.

Joy spiraled through her.

Hannah reached for him. He pulled her gently against his chest.

His embrace grew stronger, his kiss longer.

Something inside her turned to liquid. It flowed in and around that perfect, lovely kiss.

No.

***

"This is wrong," she said. "Terribly, horribly wrong."

Angus pulled back. Her eyes looked wild, panicky.

Hadn't she wanted that kiss? Did she not initiate it?

"I am confused," he said.

"I am too old for this, Mr. MacDuff." She sounded a little breathless.

"Could you bring yourself to use my given name?" Angus asked.

She edged away. "That would be scandalous—intimate, even."

"And yet, we did just share a kiss," he pointed out. "Was that so terrible?"

Her eyes widened. "No. That was…lovely."

Thank God. "Are you afraid?"

"It's…I'm not a girl anymore, Mr. MacDuff. I gave up foolish notions a long time ago."

"Because of that man."

"That was ages ago," she snapped. "One does get over these things."

He tilted his head. "Does one?"

"I am decades beyond that. *Decades.*"

"Who was he?" To Angus's ears, he sounded calm. It

was the same tone he'd used with Sebastian long ago, to soothe him when he awoke from the nightmares.

But inside, he was not calm. He was seething over whatever had happened to her.

"A teacher. At my school. I was studying to be a teacher myself. I was sixteen. Naïve." She eyed him warily, as if to gauge his reaction.

Angus tucked her hand into his.

"I would find myself alone with him in a classroom. I thought it was a coincidence. Then I realized he arranged it. At first, I was flattered such a respected man would seek me out. Too late, I understood."

Angus wanted to weep for that innocent girl. But he only nodded.

"The headmistress found us together." She hesitated. "Unlike that time you found me in the closet, I wasn't willing. I suppose I ought to be grateful she intervened."

He felt the blood rush to his head.

"I had to withdraw from school. He was important, and I was no one. I never told my parents what happened. I was too ashamed."

Angus eyed her helplessly. "I am sorry."

"That wasn't the end. He came after me. For years."

A tight, hard rage rose in him. "That's why you left positions, changed your name. Each time, he found you."

She nodded.

"Tell me where to find the man," Angus said. "I will kill him for you."

She stared at him. "Oh, my. You dear man."

He leveled a gaze at her. "I am not dear, Hannah. I am filled with hatred for the man who did this. I will find him and make him pay. It will be my mission for the rest of my days."

"You quite take my breath away, Mr. MacDuff."

"Angus," he growled.

"Angus," she repeated softly.

That breathless tone would have done him in, save for the anger that braced him. There was right, and there was wrong. About some things, there was no in-between.

"I don't need you to fight my battles," Hannah said. "Besides, that was a very long time ago."

"When was the last time you changed your name?"

"Two years ago. The last time he found me."

"Not so long ago, then."

"He is old by now, perhaps even dead. The fact that he hasn't found me again—"

"His name."

She took a deep breath. "Cyrus Cheltingham."

"And the school?'

"I don't know if it still exists."

"The name of the school," he said evenly.

"Miss Abernathy's Academy for Young Women. Not far from here—near Oxford."

The wheels in Angus's brain were turning. He would check the death records of every town where she had lived. And he would go to the school itself.

"Mr. MacDuff—Angus."

He returned his attention to her. "Yes?"

"This strangeness between us—"

"Strangeness?"

She flushed. "Perhaps that is the wrong word. The thing that afflicted us a moment ago."

He arched a brow. "Desire? Is that what you are speaking of, Mrs. Steele?"

She looked mortified, but nodded. "Part of me feels too old for this."

"And the other part?"

She looked away. "You make me feel girlish."

The deep blush that swept her features almost made him forget his rage at the man who caused her to flee for much of her life.

Angus touched her chin, gently brought her face

around. "You are not too old, nor too young, Hannah. You are the perfect age."

Her gaze searched his. "I know little of desire. I don't understand why I have inspired it."

"Were you not listening before?"

"I heard your words. But I have not trusted any man's words in a very long time."

"You don't trust me?"

She considered that. "I do. You are trustworthy and upright, if somewhat judgmental."

He frowned.

"It's that the woman you describe, that admirable, strong woman—I don't recognize her as me."

"Admirable, strong, *desirable* woman."

She blushed anew. "I do not know what to do with desire, Angus."

"We will remedy that."

"I don't wish to rush into anything."

He suppressed a sigh. "I never thought otherwise."

***

Perhaps Mrs. Kendall would be a tolerable companion were she not so didactic. When she began a diatribe about posture only minutes into their journey, Gwynna turned to her with a polite smile.

"I have many imperfections, ma'am," she acknowledged. "They might be easier for you to tolerate if you weren't so intent on pointing them out."

With that, Gwynna sat back against the squabs. She was determined not to look at Sebastian. He would think her manners deplorable. And perhaps they were.

Mrs. Kendall burst into tears.

Gwynna eyed her in alarm. "Pray, forgive me, ma'am! I spoke too harshly."

The widow only sobbed more loudly.

Sebastian thrust a handkerchief at Gwynna—the message clear: She caused the problem and must right it.

Gwynna felt terrible. She had intended to set limits, not insult her. "Mrs. Kendall—"

"My husband was a poet," Mrs. Kendall said.

"That is…unusual and…worthy," Gwynna managed.

"It was *not* worthy," Mrs. Kendall snapped. " Byron's peculiarities are tolerated because he is brilliant. Those with lesser gifts are derided. And penniless, I might add."

Gwynna searched her brain for something positive to say. "Did your husband write poems to you?"

She nodded glumly. "Long, perfectly awful poems."

Sebastian's brows rose in an unspoken challenge. Clearly, he thought she could salvage nothing from this.

"We were always poor," Mrs. Kendall said. "No children, so there weren't hungry mouths to feed. But one morning, he woke up dead. Rather, he didn't wake up."

"I am sorry," Gwynna murmured.

"I had to take lodging with my sister and Horace. It's been ten long years. I'm faulted for marrying a penniless husband, and thus viewed as inferior. Horace is so very full of himself, just because he serves a duke."

She eyed Sebastian. "I beg your pardon, Your Grace."

Looking pained, he waved a dismissive hand.

A tear ran down her cheek. "I read *La Belle Assemblée* and *Gazette* accounts of the parties. I tried to learn the correct way of doing things."

"And did imparting that correct way to others make you feel less…inferior?" Gwynna ventured.

The widow gave her a rueful smile. "You begin to see why Horace cannot abide me."

She fell silent. Gwynna began to relax. Then she remembered Mr. Maitland's note.

What was she thinking, to hold onto such a secret? The sooner they knew what Mr. Maitland was about, the better. It was duplicitous to keep that from Sebastian.

His hat was angled low over his eyes. Was he asleep, or pretending to be?

Fishing the letter from her skirt pocket, Gwynna placed it on his knee. "Mr. Maitland asked me to give this to you when we reached Wales."

Sebastian tipped his hat up, frowned. "You've had it since Summerlin? Why didn't you give it to me earlier?"

"Mr. Maitland said that if you read it you might not undertake this trip," she confessed. "But here it is, well before Wales, so no harm is done."

Warily, he broke the seal.

As he read, disbelief swept his features.

Then something far, far worse.

She'd made a mistake. But whether the mistake was in not giving it to him earlier or in handing it over now, Gwynna couldn't guess.

Sebastian read the missive a second time.

Then he looked at her.

His eyes were murderous.

***

Sebastian couldn't speak. It might be days before he could form a single syllable.

There is no gentle way to frame this, Drew had written, *so I won't bother.*

My dear Sebastian, your observation skills failed you in Vienna. Doubtless it was due to all that illness, death, and dying around you. Were I capable of tender emotions, and burdened with your wretched sense of responsibility, perhaps I'd understand. Alas, such sensibilities have never plagued me, so I can only conclude that you lost your mind a little.

Did that man of the cloth look shabby about the edges? Those holy robes frayed and filthy? Surely a man of your sartorial tastes would have discerned it. But no: You were mired in grief and desperation at seeing Elizabeth ill and her family borne off by the plague.

Still: How is it possible that you failed to see what must have been obvious to even the most novice of our colleagues? That the man of the church, he of the shabby cloth, was anything but. That you, Sebastian, have not spent this year living with a secret marriage. That Elizabeth is not, in fact, your wife.

She knows by now. I have sent her a note, couched in a kinder vein. (Perhaps you may discern that I, too, hold Elizabeth in affection, to the extent that I am able.)

You did not serve her well. That musty clinic drained her. (Yes, I visited. How distressing to see her so cossetted, so robbed of any need to think, and do, for herself.)

By now you'll have figured out that I left that gig for her. Arranged for a discharge order to be in place by the time the staff discovered her absence.

You know me well enough not to doubt the effectiveness of my methods. The proof was in the woman I saw at Summerlin: Elizabeth, becoming herself once more. You, too, have seen the color return to her features, the strength of character bloom in her eyes.

She is stronger than you think, tougher than you know. She wouldn't have taken the gig were she not ready. I only gave her the opportunity.

Rage, sorrow, disbelief, despair.

But truth, as sharp as any blade, cut through those: Elizabeth *was* better at Summerlin. She was trying to forge a new life; she never would have done so in that clinic.

Even though the place was reputed to be excellent— he'd researched the matter thoroughly—he ought to have seen what had been readily apparent to Drew.

You will have come to your senses by now, agreed that I did what is best for her. And I've made sacrifices. The first was forcing myself to take time to devise a plan for her release, rather than ripping her away from that place instantly.

Another sacrifice was my note to her. I wished to make you out a fool, dear boy, but I did not. (You cannot know what it cost me to refrain from shredding your character, which would have grieved her. Yes, I believe I may love her a little. Not, anything on the order of True Love, which is doubtless what you felt for her.)

Did he?

Finally: She must be left to discover her own path, without your influence or mine. That is my biggest sacrifice, as the need to manipulate runs deep. It is why—in all modesty—I am superb at my work. (Notwithstanding my failure to draw you back to the peace talks.)

I have faith in Angus and in Mrs. Steele (this is her current name, yes?) to help Elizabeth bloom as she's meant to. They won't interfere overmuch, as they're too consumed with one another. The fact that you haven't noticed this confirms that you have lost your way, dear boy.

Angus and Mrs. Steele? Was *she* his obsession?

Drew was right: He'd lost all powers of observation over this year—lost his way, lost himself.

Still, I have faith in you, else I would not have set you on this mission. I have even greater faith in Miss Owen. As to the mission itself, perhaps you have guessed that it is not exactly as I described to you both. More on that later, at another place down the road.

Miss Owen has undoubtedly had an attack of conscience and delivered this missive to you prematurely. (Sometimes my ability to judge character astonishes even me.) Thus, you have the rest of the journey to reflect on the wisdom of my judgment (and the flaws in yours).

Yours,

Andrew Maitland.

Postscript: The next time we meet, I trust that you will have exorcised the urge to kill me. Perhaps you'll also be good enough not to point Miss Owen in my direction. She and I have no longstanding acquaintance to call upon, and I suspect she will never be a merciful opponent. The thought of that arrow, so close to my flesh, keeps me awake at night. Indeed, those thoughts lead to contemplation of Miss Owen's other undiscovered skills.

Her passion is what makes her dangerous, is it not? Perhaps one day you will be in a position to enlighten me.

"Is it bad news?" Gwynna asked.

There was no area of his life Drew had not manipulated. The fact he had a point or two worth considering was irrelevant. Rage wasn't tempered by facts.

But the man miscalculated. When next they met, Sebastian intended to call him to account with whatever weapon he had—even if it was only Gwynna's dagger.

Gwynna.

Drew's insinuations in that postscript resonated.

Being with Elizabeth had pushed thoughts of Gwynna aside for a time. Now they roared back.

How often had he compared the two? Each time, Gwynna emerged as more vibrant and alluring. Luckily, he'd broken no marriage vows.

Vows he hadn't taken, it turned out.

Part of him wished to turn the carriage around and return to Elizabeth. Another part understood that she must find her own truth.

How he hated it when Drew was right.

Guilt and sorrow swamped him. Despite his best effort, he had failed Elizabeth, perhaps even delayed her recovery by keeping her in that clinic too long. But he had no intention of turning to Gwynna. Indeed, he resolved to keep her firmly at a distance.

She was looking at him, waiting for a response.

What to say? That he had a wife when he began reading but ended with none?

That if he ever recovered from his shock, he might begin to think of Gwynna in all the forbidden ways that had taunted him since the day they met?

Hell, no. That would never happen.

Chapter Fourteen

"Good morning, Mr. MacDuff."

Angus rose as she entered the breakfast room. "And to you, Mrs. Steele."

She seated herself at the table, looking well rested, which was more than he could say for himself. He'd spent last night tossing and turning and thinking of her.

Today her frock wasn't as severe as usual—pink and yellow flower designs on a dark green background.

Her mood seemed lighter. Had clearing the air about that evil teacher lifted a weight from her?

Angus fought an urge to tell her how that green color brought out her doe-like brown eyes. How the pink and yellow flowers gave her a fresh, dewy look, how—

"Do you have any hobbies?" she asked.

He blinked. "Hobbies?"

"Interests you pursue when you aren't running things here."

"I don't run things now. Sebastian wishes me to spend my time in useless relaxation. Why do you wish to know about my interests?"

Blushing a most becoming shade of pink, she looked quickly around to make sure there were no servants about. "We have had rather intimate contact."

"Not that intimate."

"In my view it has been so," she said sternly. "There have been kisses."

Angus regarded her. "Yes."

"It is important to learn about a person with whom one has been, or might be, on intimate terms."

"That is why you wish to know about my hobbies?"

She frowned. "I have already said so. Are you trying to be annoying?"

"I pray."

"What?"

"In my free time I pray," Angus said.

She looked startled. "I suppose that is commendable."

"Or meditate."

"That can be very improving, I'm sure. What do you meditate about?"

"Life. Death. You."

"Me?" She looked startled. "Surely there is nothing about me to inspire—"

"Your eyes. Your hair. The way your face turns pink if you are caught by surprise or confused, as you are now."

"If I am, it is because you are trying to confuse me," she retorted. Her blush deepened.

"Would it be more honest of me to say that you are never out of my thoughts?"

Her little gasp sent his pulse racing. "How...strange."

"Obsessions are strange," Angus agreed. "This is something of a learning experience."

"Obsession?" She stared at him.

"I fear so."

Her gaze grew wary. "You can be very disarming, Mr. MacDuff."

"Evidently not disarming enough."

She smiled at that.

"You have a nice smile," Angus said. "I would like to see it more."

Instantly, it disappeared.

"Do you really pray?" she asked.

"Yes," Angus said. "I am a creature of habit."

She considered that. "I have always admired your discipline, Mr. MacDuff."

"I have less of it these days."

Their gazes locked. She was the first to look away.

"You were a disciplined, yet compassionate, father to Sebastian," she said.

Angus sighed. "It would have been better if he'd had his real father."

"Yes, but you helped him find his way."

"When he was young, perhaps. He needs to find his own way now."

"I suppose we all do." She studied him. "Have you never been married, Mr. MacDuff?"

"I came close once."

Interest sparked in those brown eyes. "What happened—if it is not impertinent to ask?"

"She met someone else," Angus said.

"Oh! I am sorry."

"It was for the best," he said. "There was no fire."

She looked puzzled. "Fire?"

"Rhymes with desire."

Her face went scarlet. "You are impertinent, Mr. MacDuff."

"And you are the most fascinating woman I know, Mrs. Steele."

A prolonged silence followed, and Angus wondered if he had gone too far.

"We have known one another a long time, without really knowing one another," she said at last. "I was convinced that you condemned my behavior in that dreadful closet."

"Is that why you slammed the door in my face so many times over the years?" he asked. "Because you thought I disapproved of you?"

"When one feels disapproved of, one tends to return disapproval," she confessed.

"Perhaps you were also embarrassed. Between disapproval and embarrassment, you persuaded yourself that you loathed me."

"I was certain that I did."

"Do you still?" he could not resist asking.

Her brown eyes were measuring. "No woman can like being exposed in such a fashion. But I put myself in that very vulnerable position. I can't remember now why."

"Passion?" he offered.

She took a deep breath. "I thought so at the time. Later, I felt silly and purged all such thoughts. Happily, they have stayed vanquished."

"All of them?"

She looked away.

"I told no one about that incident," he said.

"You have always been discreet, Mr. MacDuff."

Her hands pressed flat on the table, her reddened fingers betraying her effort to maintain her composure.

"And yet, I have the strongest urge to be indiscreet," Angus murmured. "Reckless, even."

His reckless urge involved sweeping the dishes to the floor and lifting her onto the table. If she knew his thoughts, she would certainly flee.

So they were back at hobbies. "Do you have hobbies, madam?"

She looked relieved at the change of topic. "Not until recently. Work takes one's time."

"Don't forget the frequent moving and starting over. That is time-consuming as well."

"Yes," she agreed. "But I haven't had to lately. With the pension the duke provides, I don't need to work. Perhaps I've become lazy."

Angus smiled. "You must have cultivated a few hobbies, then. Tell me about them."

"I knit landscapes."

His brows rose. "I didn't know one could knit landscapes."

"One can knit anything. It's a textile art. Living in the Cotswolds, I've done a great deal of walking. There's a beautiful rise above Chipping Campden I decided to knit."

"What a coincidence," Angus said, hoping it sounded so. "I've been on…holiday there."

She looked surprised. "Do you know that hill above town? It is a gradual climb at first, then suddenly you are looking down at the fields and the villages."

Angus knew it only too well, having ascended the hill endlessly in his quest to regain his health, the health that was as fine now as it had ever been.

What would have happened if he had run into her? It had been a faint hope, but in his heart Angus had known he couldn't rely on fate to send Mrs. Steele into his path.

Fate must be seized, and if not, forever regretted.

"I thought it the loveliest place," she continued. "So I resolved to keep it with me the next time I move. I worked the image in yarn. Knitting can't convey verisimilitude, but I fancy that it captures the essence."

The next time I move. Angus's brain stuck there. He'd not allow her to slip away again.

"I would like to see your art," he murmured.

She flushed. "I haven't shown it to a soul, but I do like that landscape and its wildflowers. I love colors—"

"But you've never worn them," Angus said, mystified. "Only black or brown."

"Protective coloration, Mr. MacDuff. The aim is to recede and not draw notice."

"I noticed you," he said softly. "For years and years."

Her brow furrowed. "But I've worn only dreary bombazine."

"There's a noticing that transcends bombazine."

Had Angus not been attuned to her every breath, he might have missed her tiny gasp. It sent a bolt of heat into him that would've scared her senseless.

He rose and pulled her to her feet.

"Did this conversation satisfy your curiosity about me?" Angus spoke close to her ear. With only a slight adjustment in position, he could have kissed her.

Instead he simply smiled. Her eyes grew wide.

"I will tell you anything you wish to know about me, Hannah. I will leave it to you to decide when you know enough." He brought her hand to his lips, then released it..

With a polite bow, he left the room.

***

To a child, life was simple. People were here; then they weren't. One could do nothing.

But a man had the means to safeguard loved ones. If there was a health scare, like Angus's fainting spell, doctors were summoned, restorative holidays ordered. If the girl he'd grown up with, the woman he wanted as his companion through life, was lost in grief and illness, a man moved heaven and earth to save her.

Those lost before he had power to keep them safe were preserved in memory. But if a memory was false—as with a trinket that refused to conform to the history he'd given it—what happened to those beloved people?

They slipped away, elusive as that duplicitous artifact—or a sham clergyman.

Sublime melodrama!

For once, Sebastian didn't try to silence that voice. Thus, it erupted in operatic frenzy:

Write sonnets to love and loss! Byron will be envious!

No, he wouldn't. The man was a self-absorbed prick.

Sebastian refused to meet Gwynna's gaze. Pondering whether life still had meaning brought too much pleasure.

It gave rise to others: Imagining the myriad ways to repay Drew for his hubris and deceit. Anticipating the pitfalls that awaited as they drove deeper into Wales.

Here came his old friend denial—uninvited, as usual.

Fact: He wasn't married. His life hadn't ended, even though it felt that way.

Self-delusion: Thinking he could control the universe.

Prohibition: Elizabeth must find her own way, et

cetera, et cetera. He wasn't to intervene.

Now he looked at Gwynna. Speech was beyond him; he sent her a silent message: *Do not worry. I shall recover.*

That blue gaze lanced him with her response: *Enough wallowing.*

***

Sebastian sat as rigid as a statue, shoulders immobile, one hand on his thigh, the other clutching Mr. Maitland's letter as if it were a death sentence.

Gwynna resolved to draw him out, but the ferry soon commanded everyone's attention. When the boat began to bump and roll, he went to see to his team—they'd brought the coach with the militia supplies, as well as his great horse. Then a terrified Mrs. Kendall began to wail.

Digging into her pouch, Gwynna found a small bag she'd put there weeks ago. "Try this. My cousin Rhianna is a healer. It's one of her remedies."

The mugwort was intended to ward off house flies, but it calmed her. By the time they reached the Beaumaris inn, Mrs. Kendall was tranquil indeed. Gwynna sat with her until she fell into an easy sleep.

She found Sebastian outside, organizing the militia paraphernalia.

His dark mood hadn't abated. Anger carved deep lines in his forehead. His jaw was set. He looked ready to erupt, like a tea kettle left too long on the fire.

"I should have given you the letter straightaway," Gwynna said. "I'm sorry."

He busied himself with the militia supplies. "Drew's a masterful judge of character. You did what he expected."

"Still, there was trust between us, and I betrayed it."

"The betrayal was Drew's."

"Would you like to walk down to the strait?" she ventured. "There's a fine view. It may clear your head."

"My head is clear," he growled. "Damnably clear."

But he didn't resist when she took his arm and drew

him toward the road.

In silence as thick as Sebastian's black mood, they followed it down to the water. At the water's edge was a bench; by tacit agreement, they sat.

Boats bobbed on the blue-green strait, far more serene viewed from here than on the crossing. On the mainland beyond, wych elm and ancient spreading yew greened the low hills that rose into mountains.

Sebastian crossed his arms over his chest and stretched out his long legs. Some of the tension seemed to leave him. Perhaps he was ready to talk.

"How will you persuade men to enlist?" she asked.

He kept his gaze on the view. "Sign-up bonus and a month's stipend."

Gwynna frowned. "They will need money for more than a month if we are to pry them from Evans's clutches. Is Mr. Maitland unwilling to make a longer commitment?"

"Drew's methods"—the name was snarled—"are thorough. If Evans is involved in an invasion plot, he'll be exposed and quickly imprisoned."

"What if we don't catch him in treason? How do we stop him? Will the Crown look the other way if our farmers evaded the Corn Laws and sold crops locally?"

"Drew admitted the laws' unintended consequences. He'd likely agree."

"I'd trust nothing less than a signature in his own blood," Gwynna declared.

Sebastian laughed.

"That's the first time I've seen you smile since you read his note." She hesitated. "May I know what was in it? I have a right to know his plan."

His smile vanished. "He gave no details. We'll recruit in places men gather, pubs and the like. But my words will have little sway. You're the one they'll listen to."

She eyed him in alarm. "I'm not used to speaking in public, to a group. I don't have the skill."

He glanced at her. "A great number of words are tumbling around in that brain. I've not noticed any shyness when you deploy them."

"That's because you listen," Gwynna said. "My grandfather didn't; neither did Evans. Owen would have taken them on, but I retreated into silence."

"It's not the same. Your Owen was a warrior."

Gwynna's chin rose. "I'm not afraid to fight."

Sebastian eyed her sternly. "You won't be fighting."

That remained to be seen. "Mr. Maitland must have faith in us to entrust us with this mission."

His mouth pulled into a bitter line. "Drew has faith in no one. There'll be surprises. We'll have to stay on guard."

"Against what?" Gwynna demanded. "Was there a clue in his note? It must've held something disagreeable to put you in such a temper."

The fight seemed to leave him. "Drew informed me the man who performed our wedding ceremony was not a cleric. Elizabeth and I aren't married."

Gwynna gasped. "But…how?"

His gaze shifted to the water. "After Waterloo, Sir Bertram brought his wife and Elizabeth to Vienna to celebrate. With the crowds and heat, many people grew ill. Her parents died. Doctors said it was plague."

You are not to speak of the plague. Now his words made sense.

"Elizabeth herself grew deathly ill. I…tended her, slept at her bedside," Sebastian said.

Of course. He'd have done nothing less.

"I decided to give her the protection of my name to spare her embarrassment or scandal. She was so weak we said vows at her bedside. Drew arranged it."

"Why would he stage a false ceremony?"

"Complications arose in the peace talks. I'd had success with the parties. I think he reasoned that if Elizabeth had my name, and the best doctors that came with it, I'd feel easy leaving her to return to the talks."

"He made the mistake of thinking you were like him."

Sebastian shrugged. "I had paid for the best doctors all along. But after they failed her parents, I wouldn't allow them near her. I'd never have abandoned her for diplomatic nonsense with Nesselrode or Metternich. When she was able, I took her home to England."

He gave a heavy sigh. "I wasn't sure she'd wish to stay married once she recovered."

Wonder filled Gwynna. "That's why you put on a show of being a shallow, er…"

Sebastian eyed her darkly. "Peacock?"

"You pretended to be a frivolous fribble so no one would think you married." Gwynna stared at him. "You're nothing like the image you present to the world."

"Oh, I *am* shallow," he insisted. "I could care less about militias and plots by Frenchmen who don't understand that they've lost the war and Napoleon will die on Saint Helena."

"Then why take this on? Is it because Mr. Maitland threatened to disclose the marriage?"

He shook his head. "An empty threat. Drew has a soft spot for Elizabeth, likely the only one he has. He would not cause her harm—and knows I'd kill him if he did."

"Then, why?"

The sun's waning rays illuminated a flash of amber in his eyes. "Your tormenter."

That took her aback. "But…Elizabeth needs you more than I do."

"Drew tells me—and the damned thing is, he's right— she needs neither of us. She's well enough now to find her own way."

"Yet you seem so well-suited."

Sebastian's gaze softened. "Elizabeth is dear to me. Our connection is longstanding. But both of us now understand that it is not that sort of connection."

Regret deepened the lines in his forehead. His ragged, weary sigh made Gwynna's heart ache for him.

"That must be painful," she said.

"Angus tells me pain leads to discovery." He shot her a rueful glance. "I'm hoping for a more useful discovery than the fact that Drew made fools of us."

Gwynna took his hand. His fingers closed over hers.

"I wonder if the reason Mr. Maitland didn't procure a real clergyman was that he didn't want you and Elizabeth to marry," she said.

"He didn't want ours becoming a *real* marriage. As long as she was ill, there was no danger of that. When she left that clinic, the situation grew more…urgent."

"Oh." His meaning sank in. "Does he wish to marry her now?"

Sebastian scoffed. "No. He simply doesn't want anyone else to have her."

Gwynna supposed that was the way of such men. But Sebastian was cut from a different cloth. Character was not a cloak he took on and off when it suited him.

"Whatever his motives, *you* are the reason Elizabeth is alive," she declared. "You took care of her—heroically."

He made a disparaging sound. "Did that herb you gave Mrs. Kendall affect you as well?"

"Strength lives in you, Sebastian," Gwynna insisted. "You try to hide it, but it's there for all with eyes to see."

Abruptly, he rose. "Come. There's work to be done."

He offered his arm. Gwynna took it, savoring the strength that was so much more than muscle and bone.

How wrong she'd been about that man on the moor.

She slid her hand down and laced her fingers with his.

He didn't pull away until they reached the inn.

Chapter Fifteen

Hannah studied her reflection in the mirror. Her room at Summerlin was the nicest she'd ever slept in, nearly large enough to hold her little cottage in Stow-on-the-Wold.

A handsome quilt lay folded at the foot of the four-poster bed. Its center design was a golden harp, laid over green applique that formed rolling hills. The airy bed hangings fluttered in the breeze from the windows.

Despite the room's serenity, Hannah's thoughts were a jumble. She found herself imagining Mr. MacDuff's lips on hers, his hands caressing her no-longer-young body.

Why would he wish to? She had wrinkles. Gray in her hair. A pinched look about her face. Her flesh would never regain its youthful tautness.

Only now, did she grasp the effect of Cyrus's actions. Dismissed and dishonored, she'd felt unworthy—a feeling that escalated when Mr. MacDuff discovered her in that closet. She turned her embarrassment into loathing of him.

Hannah no longer loathed Mr. MacDuff. Far from it.

Could she trust her thoughts? Were they simply girlish hopes that had not seen fit to die? What accounted for this odd mix of sentiment and danger in his presence?

You are not one to be drawn to a man just because he is drawn to you.

Yet for the first time, Hannah dared to think of herself with worthy man. Her gaze drifted to that four-poster bed. It was spacious enough for two.

Heavens.

Today, she and Elizabeth were walking to her parents' home. It would take her mind off Mr. MacDuff.

You are strong, and willing to escape that brittle shell of yours now and then.

Was she? The very thought sent a thrill through her.

***

Save for a word or two about the fine weather, Elizabeth was quiet until they reached Throckmorton manor. As they stood on the porch, she regarded Hannah with a flush of embarrassment.

"May I ask you some questions, Hannah, about marriage? Please forgive the intrusion. It's just that you have been married. I thought I was, but it seems I'm not."

Hannah eyed her in alarm. "Perhaps we should sit."

Elizabeth sank into a rattan chair on the porch. Hannah took another chair. "I am confused. You believed you were married, but you are not?"

"Sebastian and I married—we thought—in Vienna a year ago."

"Oh! Well, you always were the best of friends. It was expected, was it not?"

"We planned to marry, but when my parents died in Vienna, and I grew ill, Sebastian thought it best to wed quickly so there would be no awkwardness about the fact that he took care of me so…intimately."

"I see."

"He didn't wish to announce our marriage until I recovered." Elizabeth looked away. "I have not been myself for a very long time, it seems."

Hannah patted her arm. "You are stronger every day."

"I owe Sebastian my life." Elizabeth's eyes filled with tears. "He has done so much for me. He found that clinic, paid the bills, managed my parents' estate."

"Yet you are not truly married?"

She shook her head. "The minister in Vienna was one of Drew's men, not a clergyman. I've had a note from Drew confessing the whole. The marriage isn't valid."

Hannah was astonished. "But…why?"

"Whatever the reason, it appears I am free."

"Do you wish to be?" Hannah asked.

Elizabeth was hesitated. "There's always been great affection between Sebastian and me. That's why I want to ask you—that is, I went to his room several nights ago."

Hannah blinked.

"You are shocked. But I believed us married, and I was tired of being treated as if I were fragile."

"And now, you find you are unmarried but in the, er, condition of a married woman," Hannah ventured. "That complicates things, does it not?"

"That's just it. Nothing happened. We could not...go through with it."

Elizabeth caught her hand. "My mother spoke frankly about the delights of the marriage bed. I want what my parents had. Does passion come with time?"

"I do not know."

"But you've had four husbands. Forgive me, but...was there not pleasure? There must be couples who don't feel passion when they marry, but find it with time. Am I wrong?"

Hannah took a deep breath. "Why could you and His Grace not go through with, er, it?"

"Sebastian said it felt forced, artificial. He was right."

Nothing felt forced with Angus, Hannah realized. An inexorable force pulled her to him.

"The truth is I haven't been married four times, nor even once. I took those names, pretended to be a widow, because it was the only way I could protect myself."

Elizabeth eyed her in dismay. "Are you in danger?"

"I am quite safe now. But though I've never been married, I know a little about passion," Hannah said. "Only a little, perhaps, but I am learning more every day."

"Every day?" Elizabeth looked intrigued.

Hannah knew her face must be red. Still, Elizabeth had asked, and she owed it to her to try.

"I think passion can develop, but I don't believe true passion feels forced," Hannah said. It felt more like a storm, ready to break overhead, with no shelter in sight.

"Sebastian is my dear friend." Elizabeth sighed. "But I don't think friendship is reason to marry."

"I suppose you must trust your instincts."

She gave a ragged laugh. "I don't know if I have instincts. I do know that Sebastian shouldn't be saddled with a passionless wife."

"I've come to think that passionless women simply haven't been found by the right man." Hannah envisioned a pair of green eyes that held a naughty promise.

A storm was coming, one that might shake the rafters.

Did she have the courage to face it?

***

"All clever, supple, healthy young fellows who have a mind to try a soldier's life and immediately receive the highest bounty given," the recruitment handbill read.

Sebastian didn't care about "supple." They'd take anyone who could move. The dozen or so Welshmen were lean and sinewy from a lifetime of working the land, mines, or sea. Some were older than the usual soldier fodder, but that hardly mattered.

The Beaumaris pub was their first recruiting effort. The gimlet-eyed men in the tap room didn't disguise their skepticism as Gwynna showed them the militia badges.

"Small, ain't it?" One man eyed the badge as if it were week-old fish.

"Regulation size," Sebastian assured him.

"Where do ye wear it?" another demanded.

"Regulars wear them on the chest," Sebastian said.

"The Scots have plaids on their uniforms." This from Rhys, the disapproving innkeeper.

"And feathers," put in another.

Sebastian nodded. "Kilts, too. Can't see Welshmen taking to kilts."

Laughter. No, the Welsh would not be wearing kilts.

After that, they listened more politely. They were still dubious, even when he promised them an enlistment bonus of two guineas on the spot, and five for the month.

"Trust English to pay?" grumbled one. "I'd sooner sink the milk cow in Llyn Barfog."

He'd have to ask Gwynna about that story.

Other than badges, they'd have nothing to make them look like a fighting force—no hats, uniforms, or gloves.

The miners in the group were receptive; their jobs hung by a thread. Parys Mountain produced such quantities of cheap copper ore that it gutted the Cornwall market, leaving unemployed Cornish miners willing to work for any wage. If Welsh mine owners turned to them, Anglesey men would be out of work.

Sebastian was acutely aware of the gulf between him and these men. They struggled to survive; he need not labor at anything more taxing than the architecture of his neck-cloth.

Gwynna kept to the sidelines during his remarks. Her reluctance to address a group of people she'd known all her life could be laid at her grandfather's door, he thought.

She'd been robbed her of the natural confidence that ought to have been hers. When she left Anglesey to seek her father, she left that fettered existence—and bloomed.

Now she moved among the men, showing them the paraphernalia, speaking to a few of them individually.

Some shot her curious looks, as if they wondered why she'd thrown her lot in with an Englishman—and why, beyond the money, they should.

What they needed was inspiration. But not from him. Only Gwynna could provide that. Yet she hung back.

Suddenly, the men took it out of her hands.

Two of them lifted her onto a table. Gwynna made a startled protest, but when they began to chant her name, she couldn't contain a smile. They gathered around her.

She glanced over at Sebastian, her cheeks flushed. On another woman, that might have signaled embarrassment, or even anger at such treatment.

Gwynna's features radiated pure joy.

Sebastian's breath caught.

She turned to the men, speaking hesitantly at first. Her voice grew stronger as she told of the men in Cheshire who marched at night, preparing to face a shared foe.

"They had strength in unity," she said. "That's why the militia makes us stronger. It will protect Anglesey, but also help us defy the mine owners and Evans."

"Where will ye be, Gwynna, when we're thumbing our noses at them?" demanded one.

"Are you accusing me of cowardice, Dylan?"

"Nay, lass. But we've nothing to bargain with. If we lose our jobs—"

"The mine owners said they'd take care of us," another man interjected.

"They won't." This, from a man in the back.

"Their promises are as empty as our pantries," Gwynna said. "That's why we need a militia."

Her gaze roamed the room. "You have doubts, since it's English making the offer. But Sebastian is a man of his word. If you enlist now, he'll pay a signing bonus tonight."

"What would we be enlisting for?" demanded a man. "The war's done."

Sebastian stepped forward. "Wales is vulnerable to mercenaries who don't care about country or wars. They seek to profit off an easier economy than the Continent's."

"If they come after our jobs, we'll dump them in the bay," a man growled.

More grumbling, much of it in Welsh. Gwynna answered in the same language.

Sebastian knew she'd be honest. She'd promise no money beyond the first month, or glorify the militia as a call to patriotism.

As for Evans, Sebastian had seen enough of him to know he'd be angry when word of the militia got to him. Fortunately, anger made men do stupid things.

Surprisingly, his own rage and shock at Drew's treachery had faded.

In their stead was a vast emptiness.

He'd prided himself on his diplomatic skills, tailored his approach to each man's weakness, preyed on their vanity. But while that was the game, it was a hollow one.

Nothing about Gwynna was hollow. Belief lived in her for all to see. She made others believe.

Made *him* believe.

Sebastian tried to clear his head. Gwynna couldn't be his rescuer. She couldn't be the person who restored meaning to his life after all that had been lost.

A man saved himself, Angus would say. But first, he had to know himself.

He had banked every fire waiting for Elizabeth to heal, lost whatever ballast tethered people to the truest version of themselves. He wouldn't dodge that hard truth.

Alas, Sebastian now knew another hard truth: The woman standing on that table importuning her countrymen was the most exciting he'd ever known.

And lo, a fire stirred.

He wanted to deny it. Instead, he closed his eyes and allowed it to consume him.

An image of brilliant blue eyes, wild red hair, a defiant chin, and a petite frame that belied its strength burned into his brain.

A dangerous, disrupting, *disastrous* flame seized him. Trying to banish it, he sought refuge in pain at the emptiness that ate at him.

Suddenly, Gwynna was tugging on his sleeve. Her fingers tore at the hair shirt he was meticulously stitching, scrambled his alliterative thoughts, sent his well-earned pain elsewhere.

He opened his eyes, forced himself to meet her gaze.

Hers sparkled with triumph.

She had signed up every man in the room.

***

After Beaumaris, they shifted their base to Moelfre, the picturesque village where her cousin Rhianna had a shop. Mrs. Kendall offered to help her and spent much of her time there.

Sebastian exercised Captain in the mornings, and Gwynna practiced archery. In the afternoons they recruited at farms and village squares, and at night, the pubs.

In two weeks, they recruited six dozen men. But even as their efforts flourished, Sebastian remained silent and withdrawn.

Gwynna suspected he was mourning the loss of his marriage. About sorrow, one could do little. It had to work its will. Still, his mood left a tightness in her chest.

At the same time, her awareness of him sharpened.

She admired the ease with which he hefted the militia gear, the breadth of his shoulders, the flexed muscles of his arms. When wind bedeviled his hair, she suppressed an urge to brush her fingers through it and set it aright.

Yet there was breathtakingly more to Sebastian than looks. She yearned to plumb the core of him, those deeper parts he held back. But cool silver inhabited that hazel gaze of late, a clear refusal to be plumbed.

She longed to see the other colors that lurked in those changeable depths—the moss that conjured a shady walk in the forest, the amber flecks that chased that icy chill.

Today, as he drove them past fields fenced by rocks dug up over centuries, Sebastian made little effort at conversation—until they passed a lake.

"At the Beaumaris pub, a man spoke of a milk cow and a lake," he said. "I'd like to hear the story."

Gywnna glanced at him. "You've been such poor company, Englishman, I've a mind to make you beg."

"Not in the mood to beg." Was that a scowl? Or the hint of a smile?

"Very well. A poor farmer lived near Llyn Barfog—the Bearded Lake, as it's known. The farmer owned only a few thin cows that didn't give milk. One day, he came across a white cow grazing at the lake and took it home."

"His fortunes took a turn?" Definitely, a smile.

"Indeed. The cow produced extraordinary milk and butter. It mixed with the farmer's herd, and new cows were born. They, too, produced fine milk. He grew rich."

"There'll be a twist."

"The white cow grew old and gave less milk, so the farmer decided to fatten her for slaughter. He was greedy for the price such a big carcass would bring. He took the cow to the lake to kill her, but suddenly couldn't move his arms. Then a cry came from the lake."

Sebastian lifted a brow. "The lake protested?"

How she had missed that brow raising—and the teasing note it came with. "The lake fairies called the cow. It walked into the water, along with the entire herd. Only one cow remained. It changed from white to black and became the black cattle we have here today."

"What of the farmer?"

"He went every day to the lake and begged the fairies to return the cattle," Gwynna said. "They merely laughed. One day, he drowned himself in despair."

Sebastian grimaced. "Fairies in your tales are cruel."

"The farmer was greedy. He deserved his fate."

He was silent for a moment. "The lakes in your stories—I sense they signify more than mere geography."

"Legends suggest they're gateways to other worlds. It's comforting to believe there's intersection between the world that surrounds us and the world we cannot see. That unseen others walk with us, even if they're out of reach."

"Sometimes I think you are part fairy yourself," he murmured.

Gwynna laughed. "I hope not. Fairies are notoriously temperamental."

"Perhaps the magic makes up for their difficult natures." The warmth in his tone sent a shaft of *something* through her.

Flustered, she looked away. That's when she saw where they were. "Goodness. It's the lake."

He frowned. "The lake with the cows or the one with drowned town?"

"Neither. It's where the fairy conjured the tiny island so she could sit and talk to her husband and children. Remember? I promised to show you."

Sebastian squinted. "Not much of a lake."

"More pond than lake," she conceded. Rushes had overwhelmed the spit of land in the middle. Still, it wasn't difficult to envision the fairy keeping her vigil for her human family.

"Legend says the fairy's descendants still live here," Gwynna said. "Her name was Penelope, remember? Some say that over the years, 'Penelope' became 'Pelling.' The Pellings are a very old Anglesey family."

That seemed to give him pause. "Pelling, you say?"

"They live nearby. Would you like to meet them?"

"Not if you mean to introduce me as the Englishman who wishes to meet the fairy folk."

"As the Englishman seeking to discover who fashioned his watch. The Pellings are artists. They may recognize the craftsmanship. Are you game?"

He hesitated. "You have a way of making the impossible seem possible."

His wistful tone brought her up short. She hadn't meant to hold out false hope. The watch meant much to him. What if the Pellings couldn't solve its mysteries?

And yet, from that tiny island overrun with rushes, she felt a welcoming breeze.

***

Gwynna led them to a circle of thatched-roof cottages that belonged to another century.

The story of the captured fairy who became a wife and mother would not leave him. How Sebastian wished he'd heard Faylinn's voice on the wind, like that farmer.

Even years after the loss of his parents, the force of it still ambushed him. A woman's voice might remind him of his mother; a man's friendly face could summon Gerald's smile.

The sorrow doesn't end.

Sebastian wanted to send those thoughts elsewhere, but Gwynna had conjured fairies and watchmakers and lost souls, and they lingered still.

The cottages sat on a narrow lane of ancient gray stone that was curiously empty.

"Evensong," Gwynna explained. "Though the Anglicans are long gone, people still gather at that hour at the foot of Castle Hill. We'll go there."

"Another of Edward's castles?"

"Earlier. Built by a Norman invader. There's a story, but I fear you are tired of them."

"You have a storyteller's gift," he heard himself confess. "I'll gladly hear another."

Gwynna flushed at the compliment and started toward the hill. "This castle dates to William the Conqueror. Robert of Rhuddlan built it on orders of the Earl of Chester to fortify the lands William claimed."

She glanced at him. "The earl's title would have come to you if the Crown hadn't stolen it."

"How do you know that?"

"After I found my mother's note, I researched the Claremont title. It was created to console a later Earl of Chester after his title went to the royal heir, where it remains today."

They reached a clearing, where more than a dozen people were milling about. Some children were laughing as they raced each other up the steep hill to the castle.

Gwynna shot him a mischievous smile. "Now it gets complicated, so pay attention."

"Always." Indeed, Sebastian found it impossible to look away from her.

"As Robert was building his castle, Griffith, the grandson of a Welsh king, was consolidating power on Anglesey. At first, he and Robert were aligned. But Griffith was battling a cousin for power, unaware the cousin had formed a secret alliance with Robert's people."

"Ah. Ample potential for betrayal."

"The cousin went so far as to enlist Norman archers, with their ridiculous crossbows—"

"Why ridiculous?"

She scoffed. "A skilled longbow archer shoots faster than any crossbow, with greater accuracy. Griffith killed his cousin and became king. The Earl of Chester invited him to discuss an alliance, but imprisoned him instead. Griffith escaped and returned to plunder this very castle."

It was the usual Welsh saga of betrayal and bloody battles. But judging by that mischievous glint in Gwynna's eye, there was more.

"The name of the Welsh cousin Griffith fought and killed was Traherne." She grinned. "Consider that you may have Welsh blood, Englishman."

He blinked. "There's not an ounce of Welsh blood in my veins. Nothing in my family history suggests it."

"And you trust that? History is written by victors. They portray events as they wish."

She had a point. But Welsh blood? Ambrose and his ilk wouldn't have allowed it.

"Let's find the Pellings and show them your watch." Gwynna walked over to a woman holding a baby.

Sebastian took in the peaceful scene. She belonged here, not in London. Whatever came from Drew's scheme, he would defeat her tormenter. She deserved that peace.

Oddly, when Gwynna returned to him, she looked unsettled. "It's Taliesin we need to see. He didn't come for evensong, so he must be in his cottage."

"Unusual name," he observed. "What does it mean?"

She stared at him intently, then looked away. "Wizard. 'He of the shining brow'. It signifies wisdom."

Gwynn began to retrace their steps to the village. "Long ago, a prophet by that name predicted the Celts would defeat the Saxons and retain their Welsh homeland: 'Their Lord they shall praise, their language they shall keep, their land they shall lose—except wild Wales'."

She was walking quickly—as if she wanted to flee.

"What English don't understand is that we'll always be Wild Wales," she said. "They keep trying to bring us under their thumb."

Sebastian stepped up his pace. "Tell me more about Taliesin. Is he old and wizened? Does he speak in rhyme? Chant spells? That's the sort of thing wizards do, isn't it?"

"He speaks Cymraeg—Welsh—and your language," Her voice was devoid of warmth.

After that, he kept silent. Something was amiss.

Gwynna halted before a cottage at the center of the circle of thatched-roof houses. A young woman answered the door, and they spoke in Welsh.

As they entered, Sebastian looked around in wonder.

Parchments hung on the walls. They contained text— and much, much more. Intricate, embellished designs consumed the space around the words.

In Ireland, he'd seen Medieval texts the monks had embellished with ornate motifs and religious iconography. Those used block lettering; these were penned in flowing strokes, much like the calligraphy he'd studied in Vienna.

Unlike those Medieval texts, the language on these parchments wasn't Latin. It looked to be Welsh. And the embellishment wasn't gold, as the Gospel artists favored, but a deep red that made the words look as if they were adorned in blood.

Undeniably Welsh.

Sebastian wanted to study the work more closely, but the young woman showed them into a parlor, where a white-haired man sat in a chair smoking a pipe.

His frame was bent, in the way of elders whose spines had rebelled with age. A faded brown shawl was draped around his thin shoulders.

When he extended a gnarled hand to Gwynna, she bobbed him a curtsy. But she looked uneasy. Was this man a threat to her? What had she risked by bringing him here?

"Taliesin, I have brought Sebastian Traherne."

The man studied Sebastian for a long, silent minute.

Puzzled, Sebastian looked at Gwynna. She refused to meet his gaze.

He returned his attention to Taliesin, sharpened his focus.

That's when Sebastian's heart nearly stopped.

Taliesin had Faylinn's eyes.

***

Chapter Sixteen

Gwynna saw the moment Sebastian made the connection. She hadn't made it herself until she talked with one of Taliesin's granddaughters in the glade.

From the first, Sebastian's eyes had struck her as unusual. They niggled at a memory she couldn't place—until she came face to face with the distinctive eyes that ran in the Pelling family.

What set them apart was their changeability. That moss-tinged silver could deepen to forest green; those ochre flecks could suddenly blaze, chasing the chill.

Was he distantly related to the Pellings?

Taliesin pointed to the chairs on either side of his and bade them sit.

With a slow, disbelieving shake of his head, Sebastian lowered himself into a chair.

"Why did you come?" Taliesin demanded.

When Sebastian didn't speak, she rushed to fill the silence. "Sebastian—in truth, he has an English title—"

"Which we will not regard," Taliesin said.

"—possesses a watch we hope you can identify," she finished quickly.

"Can the man not speak for himself?" Taliesin turned to Sebastian. "I will see the watch."

Wordlessly, Sebastian took the watch from his waistcoat and handed it to him.

Taliesin ran his thumb over the gold case. He traced the three lines that formed the Awen on the front, then turned the case over and studied the entwined leaves.

"There's a dragon, but it is hidden," Gwynna said,

uncertain as to the state of Taliesin's ancient eyes.

Taliesin opened the watch case. "That was the intent."

An odd response, Gwynna thought. But her attention was quickly claimed by the watch interior, which she'd never seen. Tiny jewels twinkled at the quarter positions.

"The diamonds are an unnecessary embellishment." Taliesin snapped the cover shut.

Sebastian frowned. "Do you know who made it?"

"The craftsmanship is extraordinary," Taliesin said. "It cannot be duplicated."

His gaze shifted to the wall, where a quilt hung, its center design a beautifully stitched golden Welsh harp.

Taliesin stared at it for a long time.

Sebastian watched him intently. "You made it."

Taliesin shot him a wistful smile. "My hands were younger. Now they are twisted and stiff. As I say, it could not be duplicated today."

"How did it come from your hands to mine?"

Taliesin's gaze measured him. "The watch was a wedding present for my daughter. I wished her to remember her Welsh heritage, to treasure it always."

For a moment, he seemed to struggle for words. "I did not know that 'always' could be so short. The very blink of an eye, in fact."

The sorrowful words hung there, suspended in the heavy silence that followed.

Sebastian went still. "Your daughter's name?"

Taliesin sighed. "If you haven't guessed, my lad, you've none of her blood."

Sebastian closed his eyes. "Dear God."

At that, Taliesin seemed pleased. "So you *have* a drop of her after all."

"Faylinn." Sebastian spoke the name so softly, Gwynna almost didn't hear.

His *mother*.

"You named her for a fairy kingdom," he said slowly.

"Aye, and there be some say it's an English word for all that," Taliesin said. "From the first, I sensed her fate would take her away to England. As it happens, it was love did that. I suppose there are worse reasons."

Abruptly, Sebastian rose. "Why did you not make yourself known?" he demanded. "I was but seven when she died. Why did you not come?"

"I suppose that's every orphan's cry." Taliesin pulled the shawl more tightly around his shoulders. Strangely, he was looking at her, not Sebastian.

Sebastian strode to the window, his large frame obliterating the waning light.

Gwynna went to him, but when she touched his shoulder, he angrily shrugged it off.

He turned to Taliesin. "I want the rest."

Taliesin studied him. "I see more of her in you now. She did have an obstinate streak."

Sebastian uttered a low growl and crossed the room to tower over the man.

Fearing for Taliesin's safety, Gwynna tried to catch Sebastian's arm. But when he turned, she realized she'd misjudged.

His eyes held no vengeance, no anger, no unforgiving ice. Only a searing flame of anguish.

Sebastian knelt down, his face even with Taliesin's.

"Both of us lost her," he said gently. "But you knew her longer. I beg you: Tell me about Faylinn—the girl, the daughter, the woman. I want all of her."

The two men stared at one another. Sebastian extended his hand.

Suddenly, Taliesin's features crumpled. "She wanted diamond chips at the quarters. Said they were like his smile. She was right. A brighter smile I never saw, save hers."

He clasped Sebastian's hand.

"The watch was meant to call her home." Taliesin's paper-thin voice was barely a whisper. "It brought you instead."

Gwynna covered her mouth, afraid she would cry out at the pain she saw in both men.

But Sebastian didn't flinch. His firm jaw and steadfast gaze conveyed what words could not: Strength. Willingness to share the older man's burden.

He placed his hand on Taliesin's shoulder, bracing him.

In that moment, truth swamped her.

This.

This was Sebastian Traherne, without pretense or pose. Not a lofty duke, nor a man with secrets. Not closed off, nor shallow.

Open and giving. Possessed of the humility and courage to reach across generations, across cultures, across grief and pain.

To take care of his own.

***

Sebastian was silent on the return to Moelfre. How was he supposed to reorder his life to fit this new reality?

Not that he hadn't been fascinated to hear Taliesin's stories of Faylinn and how she met Gerald when he'd taken himself on a Welsh walking tour. They only whetted his appetite. He couldn't wait to hear more.

As he suspected, William had dashed off to Wales in a rage—likely after that argument Rowland had overheard—to confront Faylinn's family and break what was, by then, unbreakable—for if Sebastian was correct in his math, Faylinn was already with child.

There's not an ounce of Welsh blood in my veins. Hell. Had he sounded as disdainful as William or Ambrose about preserving his bloodline?

It was simply that one side of his family had always been a blank. Faylinn never filled in the missing pieces, and Sebastian never imagined them to be Welsh.

Had she been ashamed of her heritage? Surely not.

Gerald had far more reason. One did not brag about being related to the likes of Ambrose and William.

Sebastian ran his thumb over the watch, its meaning changed again. Now it was a precious work of the heart—Taliesin's—and the key that unlocked his own past.

Once, he read a story about a man who inadvertently drinks a magic potion while wandering in the mountains. He falls asleep, and awakens in the belief he has only napped. In reality, it is two decades later. His wife has died, and his children are grown.

Like that man, Sebastian had frozen his life with his carefully controlled charade. But the world had gone on around him: Gwynna fought off an assailant, buried her grandfather, embarked on a mission to find William. Angus nursed an obsession. Elizabeth began to recover.

Rigorous control had deprived him of life itself. He left no room for the forces that came at one unawares, buffeting and tossing and bucking like that wild ferry.

Chaos had been his enemy. Today, it became his friend. It brought him family, answered a need for completion Sebastian hadn't known he possessed.

By the time they reached the inn, he was reeling.

Gwynna hurried after him into the parlor where they took supper. "I didn't know, Sebastian."

Sebastian whirled on her. "You had no idea I was related to a blasted family of fairies? You, who have spun one fanciful legend after another for days? Not credible, Gwynna Owen."

Her mouth twitched. "They're not fairies."

"Right," he growled. "And there's no farmers wooing sprites dancing under the moon, no King Arthur waiting in a cave to save Wales from English tyranny, no Owen similarly biding his time. I'm to believe that the purveyor of such lore failed to notice my very Pelling eyes?"

"I didn't make the connection until today. Likely, I was blinded by your ducal splendor."

Sebastian arched a brow. Truly, there was nothing to compare with ducal brow arching.

"There," she said accusingly. "Do you practice that hauteur in the mirror each night?"

"No, I'm busy devising elaborate methods of tying a neck-cloth around my neck. Sketching new designs, ruining yard after yard of linen to achieve more altitudinous heights."

Which was, sadly, the truth. All in the service of his masquerade, but still.

Gwynna shot him a pitying look as servants carried in an assortment of dishes. Of Mrs. Kendall, there was no sign. Truly, she was the worst chaperone ever.

"You can't believe the Pellings are fairies," she said, when the servants left.

"A sane man would not," he grumbled. "But I left that state behind about the time you introduced me to my wizard grandfather."

"He is not—"

"And what about that Traherne nonsense?" he demanded. "Is there yet another branch of the family you're keeping from me?"

She fiddled with her fork. "I invented that to torment you a little. I didn't know you had actual Welsh relatives. You're a diplomat. Have you never shaded the truth?"

"Only when necessary."

That brought her chin up. "Pretending not to be married was—"

"A necessary lie—I thought. But Drew's lie curdled everything." He sighed. "I suspect there's a lesson there."

Gwynna placed her hand over his.

Sebastian wanted to pull away. Couldn't.

"The only lesson I see is that one ought never trust Mr. Maitland," she said. "Still, he wouldn't have given us these resources if he meant to play us false."

"What resources?" he challenged. "Badges, a ledger, a

few guineas—there's little enough underpinning this. Besides, Drew's had his share of disasters. A submersible boat that failed. A flying balloon that crashed in flames. He's drawn to risk."

She blinked. "A flying balloon? How does it work?"

Sebastian wasn't in the mood for physics. "A burner heats the gas. The gas expands, makes the balloon rise."

"I should love to fly. What a grand adventure!"

"You would have died," he said mercilessly. "The gas in that balloon was hydrogen. It exploded. Everyone aboard was killed."

"Oh, no! Mr. Maitland must have been distraught."

"God, no. He viewed it as simply a setback on the road to a better flying apparatus that will give England the advantage if—*when*—we go to war with France again."

"Nothing so dreadful will happen to us," she insisted. "And if the militia stops Evans, it will be worth any risk."

Such conviction in those blue eyes—did she not grasp her own power?

"Let's not delude ourselves," Sebastian said grimly. "Those men's loyalty comes down to you."

Her gaze faltered. Doubting herself again.

But she fought it. And determination won out. She squared her shoulders and abruptly rose.

"Then let loyalty begin with me," she declared. "I give you my pledge as an Owen: I will fight by your side, and I will die in the fight, if need be."

Sebastian half-expected her to whip out that dagger and perform a blood oath.

He was riveted.

"You won't be fighting," he insisted. "I'll risk no lives on Drew's schemes."

She didn't reply. But enough steel lurked in that blue gaze to make him wonder what new chaos awaited.

***

"Would you care to take a basket lunch down to the

stream? 'Tis a fine day."

That Scottish burr made it more so, Hannah thought. The idea of taking the air with him made her pulse flutter.

Angus already had a basket packed. It seemed he was always two steps ahead of her. At one time, that would have annoyed her. Now, she felt flattered.

They walked to a small stream less than a mile from the house. She carried the blanket, and they spread it out on a rise near the stream's edge. The sun was out, and the air filled with the scent of wildflowers.

Angus unpacked a bottle of wine, two glasses, and an assortment of food, including something shaped like an egg but far larger and with a coating of some sort.

"Is that an egg?" she asked.

"An embellished one, if you will," he said. "It's a Scottish dish. The egg is boiled, wrapped in meat and breadcrumbs, then fried. I've brought sauces for dipping."

He poured out a glass of wine for her.

Hannah eyed it dubiously. "I ought not."

"As you wish." Angus set the glass before her and poured another for himself.

When he raised his in a silent toast, Hannah decided it would be churlish to refuse. She lifted her glass as well, and took a sip.

A *frisson* of excitement swept her. Was it the wine? That green velvet gaze? If Angus knew her thoughts, he would think her a brazen woman.

But she was simply Hannah Steele, shriveled on the vine. And this was simply an ordinary picnic on a lovely afternoon with an amiable companion. It ought not send her into a dizzying flurry of anticipation.

She tried to fill the silence. "Do you have siblings, Mr. MacDuff?"

"A brother. Four years older. He was transported to Botany Bay some years ago."

"I am sorry." She was curious as to how this very

upright man could have a relative who turned to crime.

"We grew up hard. After our parents died, we were farmed out to relatives. None had money. They resented the burden. That's no excuse for what Robbie did."

"What did he do?" Hannah asked, before she could stop herself.

"Ran off to London to make his fortune, took to waylaying toffs near the gentlemen's clubs. After too many arrests, he was sent away."

Hannah was filled with new respect for him. Angus had grown up in the same difficult conditions as his brother but had avoided the temptation of easy money.

"I don't suppose we will meet again in this lifetime," he said. "I've made my peace with it. We're each responsible for the choices we made. Still, I wish his had gone another way."

A new silence stretched between them. Hannah took another sip of wine and watched the ripples in the stream shimmer in the sunlight.

When she shifted her attention to Angus, he was studying her. His eyes were captivating. It wasn't just the vivid green color, which made her think of lush fields of clover, but the way they seemed to *embrace* her.

That sensual gleam—yes, there it was—conjured mysteries, knowledge, experience. It made her wish to know all his secrets, erotic and otherwise.

Erotic? At her age?

Hannah drank more wine. "This…is foreign to me."

He frowned. "The wine? I prefer whisky but thought you wouldn't."

"This picnic. The wine. The stream. It's picturesque and…leisurely. There's been no room in my life for such." She gave a shaky laugh. "Nor have there been gentlemen to offer it."

He added wine to her glass. "I'm glad to be the first."

The first man to respect her, the first to genuinely want

her company and conversation. Perhaps he wished for more than conversation, but he didn't press the matter.

Moreover, he was honest. There was nothing devious about Angus MacDuff. The truth of the man was there for all to see.

Fine brows framed eyes that missed nothing. Gray tempered the red in his hair, suggesting wisdom earned over a sober, purposeful life. His still-firm jaw radiated strength.

Angus was an oak that had survived storms and refused to be dislodged.

Warmth filled her. Something long buried rose to the surface: Girlish dreams.

Hope.

Hannah closed her eyes and tried to stop such foolish thoughts.

"Mrs. Steele."

Her eyes shot open.

"You are not to do that again," he said sternly.

"Do what?"

"Doubt yourself."

She sighed. "One does not easily abandon habits of a lifetime."

"No," he agreed.

"Nor should one," she insisted, a shade defiantly. "They are the reason for my survival."

She drained her wineglass. When she looked over at Angus, his gaze held hers.

"The day is pleasant, and I hope you find the company so," he said. "I won't push you into anything. I am simply enjoying spending time with someone I deeply admire. After so many years of receiving your disapprobation, I am content with its absence."

Deeply admire.

And there it was, that sensual gleam.

Her gaze narrowed. "You are content to sit and contemplate the scenery, Mr. MacDuff?"

"If that is what you wish."

They regarded one another in silence.

"It is, and it isn't," Hannah said finally. "I, too, find the scenery, and your company, pleasant." She hesitated. "But if I had the courage, I would seek…more."

His gaze was unreadable. He didn't move a muscle.

"You might make things easier," she admonished.

"That would require knowing your thoughts, madam. Perhaps you might abandon riddles for clarity and save us both from making a mistake."

Hannah looked away. "Speaking plainly requires more courage than I have."

"I cannot help you there." Angus eased himself back on the blanket, put his hands behind his head, and closed his eyes.

Wretched, wretched man.

But he was right. She must find her own courage.

Deeply admire.

Angus MacDuff did not waste words, or prevaricate.

Difficult as it was to think of any man admiring her— much less this exceedingly principled Scot—Hannah concluded she had no choice but to take him at his word. That meant he would not turn her away, nor make her feel like a foolish woman with girlish dreams.

With a deep breath, Hannah reached for his hand.

As their fingers met, his closed lightly around hers.

Why should the mere joining of fingers set her pulse racing? She wanted to draw closer to him.

Instead, her spine stiffened. But a stiff spine was hard to maintain when one's hand was entwined with that of a reclining person. It was as if her appendage were a flag, flying off at an odd angle from her body.

"Mr. MacDuff," she began.

"Angus." That low voice made her quiver inside.

He'd been honest; she would, too. The wine helped.

"I do not know how to say this, Angus, without

seeming quite wanton—" She broke off and nibbled at her bottom lip.

His eyes opened. "I could never think you wanton."

"Oh, but you did, that time when you found me with Peter," she said. "And I was, perhaps, but I was silly and young then. I am neither now."

Angus propped himself on one elbow. "What wanton thing would you be wishing, Hannah?"

"I like...being close to you."

"I do not think that is wanton," he said gravely.

She closed her eyes in mortification. "I am decades past girlhood, yet I am overcome with girlish foolery when I am with you."

"You are yourself," he said. "Like all of us, a mix of impulses, some silly, some not."

"You will not persuade me you have had a silly moment in your life, Angus MacDuff."

Their fingers were still entwined, and now his thumb stroked her palm in light circles.

"I've never felt silly, although you made me feel foolish at times. All those doors shut in my face. I don't know why I kept showing up on your doorstep."

"I am glad you did," Hannah said.

The ensuing silence was so thick, it might have served as another picnic blanket.

"May we return to the subject of wantonness?" he said at last. "What did you have in mind?"

Hannah felt her face flame. "That I might lie there next to you. Shocking, is it not?"

"Very."

"You are making sport of me."

"No." He paused. "But just so I don't misunderstand, perhaps you could show me what you envisioned."

Hannah eased herself down on the blanket next to him. She felt awkward. It was a bold step.

But something was not quite right.

"When I was young, I had a stuffed toy goose that I slept with at night," she said.

He was silent for a beat. "Oh?"

"I kept my arms around it all night long," Hannah added. "It was ever so cozy."

"You could put your arms around me," he offered. "Pretend I'm that goose."

She turned toward him. Their faces were inches apart. "I could never pretend you are aught but yourself, Angus."

"Show me."

She eyed him in alarm. "What?"

That green gaze grew stern. "You are deliberately being obtuse, Mrs. Steele. I demand that you throw your arms around me as if I were simply myself and not a stuffed goose."

Hannah could not help but laugh.

It was no very great thing, after all, to rest her arm lightly on his torso and snug her body closer so that she was nestled in the crook of his arm.

Angus's arm firmed around her shoulder.

His warmth was exquisite.

"Is that acceptable, then?" he murmured. "Not wanton?"

"More than acceptable. If you want the truth—"

"Always."

"It's not quite wanton enough."

"Mrs. Steele," he said softly, "I do not know where you are taking this but I cannot wait to find out."

"Not far," she said firmly.

"Show me."

Hannah didn't take well to commands. But this was more in the nature of a dare. She rose on one elbow. "I do think you look best from this view."

"Dear God, woman. Why is that?"

Hannah brought her mouth near his. "Because you cannot walk away from me."

His arms slid around her. "You are not a woman I can walk away from."

"You have," she said. "Repeatedly."

"Only to save myself."

"Well," she said softly. "There's no saving you now."

Hannah kissed him, hesitantly at first—and then not.

It seemed she did have courage after all.

***

She would kill him; of that Angus was certain.

Her mouth, capable of such tart retorts, was sweeter than anything on earth as it met his. Nor did she mute that innate firmness—her lips pressed his with bracing valor.

He tried to live in this sublime moment, this delicious present. But, damn his eternal soul, he wasn't meant for ephemeral pleasures. He would not allow Hannah Steele to be ephemeral. Need for her consumed him.

Angus had tried not to rush his fences. He didn't wish to frighten her. She'd been knocked about by life and had put up a sturdy defense. It was breathtaking that she still had it in her to explore. She was stronger than she knew.

Which made it all the more remarkable that she was kissing him as if she wanted him.

"Hannah," he whispered.

A plea. A bargaining of his immortal soul, if that's what it came to.

She pulled back to look at him. Her gaze was thick with a passion that surely must have surprised her. Her lips were parted and full, as if they yearned to touch his again, as if they could not be satisfied until they did.

Good, he thought. Good.

Angus moved his hands up her arms and over her shoulders, until at last they framed her face. He drank in her loveliness, and if he died this very moment he would be grateful for this last, best sight.

And yet. He wanted the impossible.

Thus, he hesitated. A man ought not to hesitate in such

a circumstance. But he had always been cursed with an inconvenient clarity.

Confusion swept her features. "Is something wrong?"

"I must be truthful."

Her eyes widened. "You don't wish to continue?"

He kissed her forehead. "That is very far from truth."

"What then?" Her voice quavered. Angus hated that he caused that.

"This—between us—is as important to me as life itself." He tried to smile, as if that would render his words harmless. "I know that sounds alarming. It may make you uncomfortable. God forbid, it should make you flee."

She tilted her head. "Do I look as if I wish to flee?"

"Not now. But later, you might have regrets."

"Why?"

"Because I will want to make you mine. For as long as God grants us this earth."

Hannah blinked in astonishment.

Angus sighed. "So if you think you might walk away later, 'tis best to do so now. I could face a future without you, but it would be the bleakest sort of existence."

Shock filled her lovely brown eyes.

Yet he pressed on, for life was short and truth was all. "If you are but toying with me—"

Hannah looked horrified. "Do you think I am in the habit of kissing men just for the thrill of it?"

Oh, now she had done it.

"A thrill, was it?" he asked softly.

She blushed deep pink. "Quite the biggest thrill of my life, Angus. No one has ever made me feel so…special."

Their gazes held.

"Dare I hope you might one day return my feelings?" It was the wrong thing to say. He ought not push her.

To her credit, she did not look away. "You've put me through quite a lot these past few days."

To say nothing of the years of agony she'd put him

through. But that had been his choice, not hers.

"You have upended my life, and so very late in the day," Hannah continued. "I have been content knitting landscapes in the Cotswolds, for goodness sake."

"Forgive me, but that sounds rather lame."

"Perhaps to a man of your consequence."

"Consequence?"

"You are a worthy man, Angus. No worthy man has been interested in me. It is a heady experience. And then this—" she made a motion that encompassed them both— "*this* has caused me to do things I have never done."

"Never?" Surely she could not mean that.

She eyed him in exasperation. "Most of the kisses I've known are ones I tried to avoid—men who thought they had the right to touch me, when I never gave them encouragement or tried to attract their notice. Well, I did encourage Peter—my one futile attempt at passion."

His fingertip brushed her cheek. "I am sorry."

"It was my lot to attract the attention of pigs."

"I should have been there to slay them for you." He meant it.

She beamed.

"I understand." Angus did his best to suppress a sigh. "You have shunned men, and now I have brought this obsession of mine to you, and you do not wish to have it."

Hannah touched his face. "But I do, Angus. You are helping me discover who I am."

That gutted him. His spirits sank into the abyss. He would get no commitment from her, not yet, maybe never.

Worse, he could do nothing. Persuasion, seduction, reason—these were not the tools to arrive at love. That could only come from within her.

He was merely the means for her self-discovery. Not that he begrudged her that; he simply knew his limitations.

Angus sat up, eased her gently away. He put the wine bottle into the basket and began to pack up the food.

"We are leaving?" Hannah eyed him in confusion.

"I can think of no reason to stay. Can you?"

"But—"

"What do you want, Hannah?" He tried not to sound harsh, but heard the bitterness in his tone. "Kisses? Practice so you can discover the side of you that's been there all along?"

Tears came to her eyes. Angus felt bad for it, but there was nothing to be done.

Silently, she helped him put the food away.

He folded the blanket and handed it to her to carry.

"When you know who you are, come and find me," he said.

Chapter Seventeen

She was down on the beach in breeches, drilling that ragged militia. The men responded as if she were their captain—marching and chanting cadences like regular soldiers, albeit without proper uniforms. The men disdained those paltry badges and refused to wear them.

Sebastian respected them for that. They'd take the Crown's money, but not look ridiculous doing it.

Over the month, nearly ninety men had enlisted. He'd come to know many—even that Beaumaris innkeeper, not a bad fellow, it turned out. They drilled late in the day, after their fishing or farm work. Miners were the largest group; they'd been locked out by the owners two weeks ago and needed every penny.

Whether they could fend off an invasion was to be seen. They had succeeded in drawing Evans's attention. He often watched the drills from a hill near his cottage.

He'd soon show his hand. If invasion was in the offing, arrangements would already be in motion. Time was closing in on him.

Sebastian still had doubts about Drew's scheme, but working with the militia was better than being at Summerlin and watching Elizabeth discover how fortunate she was not to be wed.

The sting had worn off. Or nearly so.

Friendship had always been the heart of their relationship. They weren't suited for more. The night she came to his room, he felt tenderness and compassion.

What he hadn't felt was passion.

Had he forgotten how to stir that sort of fire?

Alas, he had such thoughts—but not about Elizabeth.

Even now, Sebastian couldn't tear his gaze from the woman drilling her troops on the beach.

She was under his protection, but beyond reach. Besides, he had a new family to learn. Faylinn had been Taliesin's only child, but she had cousins and aunts and uncles. By now, he'd met most of them.

Instead of viewing the Englishman with suspicion, they welcomed him. They shared stories—some in Welsh, when they forgot he didn't know the language.

Among them: The Yellow Beast. (He did know that one.) Glendower's Chimney, the mountain fissure by which Owen Glendower escaped King Henry IV's soldiers, who feared to follow him to certain death.

Gwynna's precious Owen hadn't died, of course. None of the figures in Welsh legends did. They simply joined the great mass of absent souls infusing the air, waiting to be summoned for wisdom or inspiration.

Try as he might to resist, those stories captivated him as did Anglesey. He found himself returning again and again to that bend in the coastal path just west of Moelfre.

Standing atop that cliff, watching clouds drift out to infinity, he could almost believe that people did not vanish into nothingness, but lived on in earth and sea and sky—and perhaps some mysterious realm beyond human ken.

No wonder Gwynna loved Anglesey. It returned the favor. Its beauty echoed hers, its legends lived in her. Her passion and fire was visible even to the casual observer.

Which he no longer was.

She disturbed him in some fundamental way.

Her hair, longer now, curled around her face in untamed abandon. Her eyes could twinkle in amusement, often at his expense, or sharpen with merciless intent, as when she trained her arrow on Drew.

Gwynna's mind was equally alluring. Despite limited schooling, she had consumed great quantities of literature, philosophy, and commentary.

At one supper, she brought up Mary Wollstonecraft, which led to discussion of her daughter, also Mary. She'd taken up with Percy Shelley and was said to be writing an allegory of the human condition featuring a monster.

The subject roused Mrs. Kendall, as it involved a poet behaving badly. Mrs. Kendall insisted the failure of Shelley's marriage—he abandoned his pregnant wife for Mary—was undoubtedly aided by the interference of his wife's sister, who opposed breastfeeding.

And so it went throughout that week and the next and the next. Sebastian never tired of engaging Gwynna, though he tried to steer clear of talk about breastfeeding.

One night, Sebastian broached a subject that had been niggling at him since he'd met his maternal grandfather.

"That anonymous note I found in William's desk with your name—the script is similar to Taliesin's," he said.

Gwynna looked startled. "How would he know William was my father?"

"We know they met when William tried to part Faylinn and Gerald. And we've surmised from Rowland, that William returned to Anglesey repeatedly, likely because of Megan. I imagine little escapes Taliesin."

"But why would Taliesin have waited until just a few months ago to write to William?"

"Taliesin keeps his own counsel. He wouldn't have interfered in your grandfather's decision to keep your paternity a secret. But your grandfather was dying, and perhaps he sought to set things right."

She looked pensive, but said nothing more. He took refuge in their routine. Each night, he escorted the two women to their room across from his at the Moelfre inn. It was the last he saw of her until morning.

Ah, but she invaded his dreams, and it was no use pretending her intellect was the cause. His dreams were acutely—*painfully*—amorous.

He couldn't allow such impulses purchase during waking hours. Instead, he focused on how to prevent Evans from ever harming Gwynna again.

She had faith that Drew's plan would free the island from his tyranny. But they couldn't count on that. Sebastian had yet to come up with an alternative. She scrambled his thoughts.

As he watched Gwynna marshal her troops on the beach below, his brain simply refused to work.

She had one hand on her hip, the other on her bow, as if ready to lead the charge. The reticence that plagued her when they began this mission was receding.

Gwynna Owen was coming into her own.

It wasn't just her easy command of the militia, or the way she challenged herself in archery—choosing difficult targets and adverse light conditions, like nighttime.

Confidence sat on her shoulders, begging her to take notice. If she ever went to London, she'd be proclaimed an Original—that rare woman who was only ever herself, without need to make herself over to please a man.

Guilt plagued him. He had disdained the ladies of his set. But economics required they find husbands; they adorned themselves in superficial finery to catch the male eye. Who was he—a man who played the peacock past all absurdity—to proclaim them shallow?

Hell. Epiphanies abounded.

Here was another: The boy Elizabeth lifted from despair had taken into manhood his conviction they belonged together—without a second thought.

He had fought for her life in Vienna, but she deserved someone who would fight for her love. She would chart her own course.

It was time he did.

Angus would say that one had to leave home to find it, to wallow in the depths to scale the heights. Had the man never found himself at a crossroads, where longing made a muddle out of discipline, where lofty principles faded into the fog of confusion?

Where what he wanted was that which was least likely to come to him?

He felt humbler than when he'd met Gwynna on the moor that night. His ambitions were smaller—perhaps no bigger than this spit of land off north Wales.

She was walking up the steep hill toward him. Naturally, she disdained the easy switchback. Each step that brought her closer left him more unsettled.

An Original, without doubt.

Who disdained the easy path.

***

Evans stepped into her path midway up the hill.

"I know what you're up to," he growled. "The Crown isn't paying those men to defend Wales. It's to take profits from me."

Gwynna forced herself to stand her ground. "You overstate your importance. The Crown doesn't care if a blackguard profits off men who can't make ends meet."

Evans stepped closer. His hulking frame dwarfed hers. "It pleases you to see me as a villain, but I've always had your welfare in mind."

At the hilltop, Sebastian stood regarding them with a deepening frown. Gwynna refused to let him distract her.

"You pretended to be my grandfather's friend, but it was me you were after," she declared. "That's villainous."

"Your fault. You and your feminine wiles—"

She gave a rough laugh. "I have no wiles, feminine or otherwise."

"You parade around in revealing clothes—"

"These are boys' breeches," she protested.

"—and act surprised when a man takes you up on what you're offering."

That was too much. Gwynna balled her hand into a fist and punched his chest, hard.

He barely noticed. Instead, he eyed her mournfully. "I had a wife. She died in childbirth, with my babe."

Was this a new ploy to gain sympathy?

"Punishment for her sins," he added. "Emma had a blemish on her soul."

"Whether a woman dies in childbirth has nothing to do with her soul."

Evans's dark eyes glittered. "I came to Anglesey to start over. When I met you, I knew you were the vessel. You will fill the place that Emma and the babe left."

The vessel.

Almost, she felt compassion for him. He'd suffered a grievous loss. But that did not excuse his actions.

"You dishonored their memory by assaulting me," Gwynna said softly. "And I will *never* be your vessel."

Outrage suffused his features.. A thick vein in his neck pulsed. He looked a moment away from striking her.

Her chin rose defiantly. She refused to back down.

A heavy hand clamped down on her shoulder.

"Enough!"

Sebastian's voice, guttural and grim.

He put his other hand at her back and propelled her up the hill.

***

"You didn't need to intervene," she grumbled.

Sebastian pushed her ahead of him, gave her no chance to retreat. "You were goading him. You'd have tipped our hand."

Not the real reason for his temper. Didn't she see what danger she put herself in?

As they gained the hilltop, his brain remained fixed on the image of her taunting an oaf twice her size. "You are to stay away from him."

"Don't give me orders."

For a moment they glared at one another. Then she arched a brow—a perfect mockery of his gesture, including

265

the narrowed gaze that finished it.

Sebastian's anger slid into grudging appreciation. Her sudden smile left him floundering.

"I've thought about an invasion site," she said, changing the subject and throwing him off balance yet again. "It's likely Red Wharf Bay."

He didn't want to discuss practicalities. He wanted her to stop tempting dangerous bullies and creating chaos.

"At high tide, the beach vanishes, but the water's deep. Boats can come up nearly to the road. Invaders could make land swiftly, before being noticed. It's ideal."

Sebastian barely heard her words. A new truth had landed like a boulder: He could protect Gwynna now, but after their mission, she'd follow that foolish courage wherever it led—beyond his reach.

"If we hurry, we can see the bay before dark," she said. "It's low tide, so you'll see the entire beach. But Evans mustn't know we suspect the site. Your carriage would attract notice."

Might as well pretend this invasion business was real. "We'll take Captain, then."

By the time they reached the inn, the ominous clouds overhead matched his mood.

Captain easily took their combined weight, as he had that night on the moor and the morning he fetched Gwynna from her dawn outing.

This time, she needed no coaching to hold onto him. Her arms slipped around his middle, and her legs snugged under his thighs. Her breasts pressed into his back.

That's when yet another truth hit him:

His defenses were disintegrating.

***

The beach curved in the shape of a giant horseshoe. Fog rolled in, and with it, a mist hinting at approaching rain. The air held an unmistakable salty tang.

Dismounting, Sebastian turned to assist Gwynna.

When she slid down into his arms, his hands went to her waist to steady her.

Stayed there.

Sebastian took a healthy step back, as the wind lifted her hair. He longed to run his fingers through it.

"The smugglers work the caves at the west end." Gwynna pointed toward a massive rock formation in the distance nearly engulfed by fog. "Here, at the east end, is where the water rises to the road at high tide. It's less used, since it belongs to the witches."

Her saucy look dared him not to ask for that story.

They had no time for that. Dark would soon be upon them. Already, the mist had turned to rain. He strode to the water for a better look at the beach. She fell into step with him.

"Long ago, a small boat washed up here," she began. "It had no oars or rudder. The people in it were nigh to starving, without food or water."

"Criminals," Sebastian said absently. The beach was an immense swath of sand. When the tide swallowed it, the invaders would indeed have a gift.

"Yes, that's how criminals were dealt with then—put to sea, with little hope of survival. Islanders tried to stop them from disembarking. We weren't always hospitable to strangers."

Sebastian thought of Vienna, welcoming the tourists celebrating the peace—until plague broke out. Then came talk of shoring up the ancient walls to keep out the hordes.

"Two men jumped out of the boat," Gwynna went on. "One hit the beach with a stick, and fresh water sprang up. That's when people decided they were witches."

"Ah. Demonizing starving foreigners."

She nodded. "Sadly."

"You don't believe in witches?"

"Of course not. Anyway, these folk settled in cottages near Llanddona and lived by smuggling. The men wore black cravats with black flies knotted in. When crossed, they unleashed them. Ever after, people gave the east end a wide berth."

A gust of wind whipped sand around them. They ought not linger. Still, curiosity seized him. "How is it you don't believe in witches, but do believe in ancient spirits?"

"Witches are fiction. People were branded as such for political or religious reasons. The ancients were real—we see their stones and monuments. They left no written history, so we are free to invent one. And perhaps that's fiction, too, but Welsh have never lacked for imagination."

If only he could control his.

"Let's assume this is the invasion site, due to road access and emptiness due to the, er, witches," he said. "An invasion plan will have alternate sites. Any ideas?"

Gwynna pointed west, to the high bluffs that formed the enormous rock. "Smugglers favor the caves at Castell Mawr. It's a logical fallback."

"Castle Rock?"

She nodded approvingly. "You're a quick study, Englishman."

Her sudden smile put the moon to shame, just as her eyes outshone the stars.

What was wrong with him? There was no moon, no stars. Only fog, rain, and swiftly descending darkness.

Sebastian took her arm. "Come. The night has turned on us." He couldn't wait to see her safely back to her room with Mrs. Kendall.

The wind lashed them as they made their way to Captain. Just as he pulled Gwynna up on the horse behind him, the rain unleashed a fury.

Even a few yards was miserable going. Behind him, he felt Gwynna shivering. He turned so she could hear him over the tempest. "Where can we take shelter?"

She pointed toward Castle Rock, its top nearly swallowed by the stormy heavens.

When they reached the stone monolith, Sebastian was relieved to see a cave opening. Looping Captain's reins around a scrub tree at the entrance, he pulled Gwynna into the blackness inside.

"Stay close to me. I'll try to keep you warm."

"The only thing that will warm me is a hot bath," came her disembodied voice.

Gwynna, naked in a tin tub. Not an image he needed.

They fumbled along the walls of the cave until they reached a spot where Sebastian could almost stand. Thick, oppressive darkness surrounded them.

"Thank you." Her voice came from a point near his upper arm.

"What for? You pointed us to this shelter."

Her hand found his. "For giving me the means to bring Evans to justice."

"We haven't accomplished it yet," he cautioned.

"And for everything you've done since I disrupted your life—" That catch in her voice nearly undid him. "I don't blame you for resenting what I've put you through."

A whiff of dirt and moss infused the cave's still air with earthy pungency. A dripping sound came from somewhere. Absent sight, other senses were magnified—the touch of her hand, her soft breaths that echoed the thunderous beating of his heart.

"You see me as an enemy, don't you?" Gwynna said, misinterpreting his silence.

"No."

She hesitated. "Perhaps we're friends, then? Like you and Elizabeth?"

Her fingers twined with his.

A sudden wave of desire hit him.

That figured. Miserable night. Tight space. Gwynna.

Each time he found himself trapped with her—the closet, that tomb—he'd beaten desire down. He'd thought himself married, and Angus had not raised a man capable of infidelity.

Circumstances had changed, but not his resolve. She was under his protection. Boundaries were in place.

"Are we?" she prodded. "Friends?"

Sebastian hated talking to her in the dark, because his mind filled in the rest. He knew that those breeches, wet like his clothes, clung to her legs.

Men ought not be reminded that they have...parts.

He needed to get past this.

"We're friends," he said. "Now I want a story."

***

"Cuchulinn was a great hero," Gwynna began. "Like Odysseus, he traveled to many lands. One was the land of the fairies."

"Must it be about fairies?"

She ignored that. "He fell in love with a beautiful fairy named Fand. When he returned home, he couldn't forget her. His wife was consumed with jealousy."

"He had a wife? Not much of a hero, was he?"

"Most heroes have flaws. It makes them interesting. The Druids gave him a potion, which banished memory of Fand. He had other adventures but never saw her again."

"Don't you know any happy tales?" he groused.

"Cuchulinn's unfaithfulness causes his wife pain and costs him the fairy he loved. How would it be if he were rewarded for his infidelity?"

"He *was* rewarded, by losing all memory of what he'd lost," Sebastian insisted.

Why did he feel so strongly about a silly story?

Then it hit her.

"That tale wasn't aimed at you," Gwynna said. "I know you have a wife—*had*, rather, since now you don't—who is—*was*—Elizabeth, who was—*is*—an estimable person. And you've never been other than honorable. In fact, I wondered—"

"Gwynna," he growled. "Stop."

Thank goodness he interrupted her before she said something unwise: *I wondered what it would take to crack that ironclad discipline of yours, to cause you to look at me even once as a real woman, not as a responsibility.*

Undercurrents churned between them. Had they always been there? She caught the intoxicating scents of damp leather and something ineffably masculine.

Gwynna gripped his hand more tightly—for balance, she told herself.

"I have another story," she said. "You'll like it more."

His chin tipped down. "Only if the ending's better."

Now that her eyes were used to the dark, she could discern that firm jaw. It epitomized the man—strong, like the rock sheltering them. Capable of weathering the storm, and then some.

Could he guess her thoughts?

"Near Anglesey is a peninsula that juts into Cardigan Bay," she said quickly. "Land once filled in the bay across to Saint David's Head. It was ruled by a drunkard prince who didn't keep his sea wall in repair. The land flooded. All that was left were fairies."

Sebastian gave a longsuffering sigh. That broad chest rose, disrupting her senses.

"The land where fairies live cannot be destroyed, so it wasn't really gone." It was her grandfather's favorite story. She could almost hear his voice.

That stopped her. She had held on to her anger at him. But he hadn't meant to hurt her. His pain over Megan's loss had simply been too great to talk about her.

Instead, he'd given her what he could: these stories.

Her anger dissolved. And with it, a heavy weight.

"Is something wrong?" Sebastian's low rumble felt as intimate as a caress.

"My grandfather loved this story." Her voice broke. "And it will live as long as I have breath."

His arm firmed around her shoulder. "Then I'll gladly

hear the rest."

Gwynna took a deep, steadying breath. "Sailors spoke of seeing green isles rising out of the mists, but when they sailed closer, they saw only the bay. The fairy land was invisible because of a magic herb that grew there."

"If none saw the land, why did they suspect it was there?"

"Strangers began appearing on the peninsula. Small, silent folk who paid for their wares in silver pennies."

"Ah."

"One man decided that if he could find the herb, he'd see the invisible land," she said. "He went to Saint David's Head and searched, to no avail. Then he accidentally stepped on a small patch of land. The sea vanished. Fields, towns, and roads of the lost land appeared."

"I can guess the next: He ran to tell others," Sebastian said. "Speaking as one who shares a kinship with fairies, that's when trouble comes."

"The Pellings are *not* fairies. But you're correct: When he returned with others, the land was gone. No mortal has seen it since."

He was silent for a moment. "I wonder why your culture is so steeped in magic."

"We've had to fight for our land and our ways," Gwynna said. "Magic gives hope to the powerless."

"You aren't powerless," he said gruffly. "You're the strongest woman I know."

That startled her. "I felt powerless when Evans was stalking me. Part of me wondered whether it was my fault, whether I'd done something to draw his attentions."

"Men like that manipulate their victims, make them doubt their own perceptions."

"I should have stood up to him sooner."

"We all have things we wish we'd done sooner, or later, or never. We can't undo the past. I've come to think what matters is doing what seems right at the time."

She pondered that. "I've never be able to speak about Evans to anyone. I'm glad we're friends."

He shifted. "I don't know what we are. It's damned confusing."

Right. They were from different worlds. They weren't true friends, merely comrades in arms, temporarily bound by circumstances.

Yet Sebastian could have ended their connection at any time, for excellent reasons—Elizabeth, Mr. Maitland's scheme, the family he hadn't known existed.

But he was here with her in the cave, his clothes as sodden and muddy as hers.

"I'm glad you didn't take me to London," Gwynna said. "I'd never have passed muster. Other women display themselves to advantage. I ought to learn. I don't know how to draw someone like—"

She caught herself.

"Like…?"

Her pulse lurched. "Like…you."

She felt him stiffen.

"You and I don't see each other that way," he said.

A reckless impulse seized her. "Maybe I'm beginning to see you that way."

"Damnation, Gwynna," he growled. "That closet, the tomb, and now this cave. It's too much. *You* are too much. Why can't I be rid of you?"

"Perhaps you aren't trying very hard." To Gwynna's dismay, her voice wobbled.

"Apologies," he said quickly. "That was harsh."

"What a way you have with words," she retorted. "You must've been a horrid diplomat."

He hitched in a breath. "When you are near, I can't seem to find the right words."

"Therefore, you choose brutal ones. How nice that I bring that out in you."

"You bring out something in me," he muttered. "It's

driving me mad."

His words hovered there. They seeped into her and settled in a place that belonged only to him.

In it were their differences, trivial and consequential. His pretense, her stubbornness. The letter she'd withheld. His watch. Her dagger.

His pledge to protect her. The care he took with those he loved. His loyalty.

Suddenly, Gwynna understood what he'd left unsaid.

"You feel it too, don't you?" she asked softly. "This, between us."

Silence.

That's when she realized her mistake. "It's Elizabeth, isn't it? I'm sorry. Your heart is broken, and I've been talking of trivial matters—"

"My heart isn't broken," Sebastian said. "I tried to make our friendship into something it wasn't. Loath as I am to admit it—Drew did the right thing."

"Oh."

"That doesn't mean," he added quickly, "that I have any desire or intention of forming an arrangement with anyone else or…with you."

Well. That was clear as could be.

"Besides, you disrupt things," he groused.

Yes. He prized order. She'd brought upheaval.

But: Sebastian's heart wasn't broken. If it could be had, she wouldn't shy from the fight.

She rose on her toes, kissed the corner of his mouth.

Sebastian froze. "That is *exactly* what I mean."

***

The touch of her mouth jolted him. *Inflamed* him.

Magic, fairies, spirits—Sebastian prayed for one and all to steal Gwynna away.

None came—not a surprise, since he didn't believe in them.

As her lips pressed the corner of his, she slipped. His

arms went out—*only to steady her!*—and pulled her tightly against his chest.

Sebastian's senses bolted awake.

Frolicked, as it were.

Her wet shirt—why could she not wear something protective, like armor?—did nothing to blunt the exquisite pressure of her breasts. Her nipples could not be bothered to discipline themselves, and pebbled provocatively.

Her arms locked around his neck.

Sebastian barked out a word, possibly her name.

She took no notice, so perhaps he hadn't managed anything. He tried to shift so an iota of separation existed between them. But Gwynna hitched herself higher, and his hands found themselves under her thighs, bracing her.

"Gwynna." It crawled out of his throat, animal-like.

The most feminine part of her was excruciatingly close to the corresponding part of him that was responding with embarrassing alacrity.

Then she pressed her mouth full against his.

His brain weighed eons of celibacy against this one, determined kiss.

And laughed.

Heat swirled through him. It summoned a devilish twin—need.

One kiss. He could withstand that.

But this kiss had the force and power of a lightning bolt. Had solid stone not been behind him, he'd have been rocked back on his heels.

Her mouth was closed, her lips relentless. Sharp and fierce as the woman herself, the kiss stabbed him with battle force. He'd have bruises. Blood would be spilled.

Doubt mounted a feeble protest. Gwynna's murderous kiss burned through it.

Surely, most men made it into the next life without being kissed like this.

Sebastian's lungs forgot to breathe. His heart forgot to

beat. For all he knew, the world forgot to spin. Gwynna kissed him to the very ends of the earth and back.

His brain envisioned him tearing at her clothes and impaling her with raging, uncontrollable lust—as if she were some Covent Garden harlot.

"Gwynna," he rasped.

She lifted her head to look at him. He could just make out that killer instinct in her eyes.

"Was that not a proper kiss?"

Sebastian managed a ragged laugh. "There's no word in the English language for that kiss."

"I'm certain there's a Welsh word."

"An obscene one, I'll wager."

"I did it wrong?" Uncertainty crept into her voice.

Dark though it was, his brain filled in the shadows. Her unruly red hair, yearning for his fingers. Her flushed cheeks, begging for his caress. Her mouth, longing for his.

Fantasies all, from his forbidden dreams.

But as their gazes locked across the scant inch between their faces, Sebastian saw the truth blazing in her eyes: She did want those things.

Gwynna wanted *him*.

It was no small wanting. She did nothing by halves.

Even as Sebastian fought to hold on to those ridiculous principles of duty and responsibility—*hadn't he already lost that battle?*—an abiding heat snaked through his veins and kindled something far beyond simple desire.

As if a meddling fairy tossed magic dust over him.

What blossomed was a rare flower, invisible to mere mortals. A magic herb, unveiling an unseen land.

His heart leapt up, finally summoned to account.

Gwynna. *She* was the magic.

"You didn't do it wrong," he murmured. "But let's try this."

Chapter Eighteen

Sebastian's mouth brushed hers, ever so lightly.

Again.

So gently, it might have been a butterfly's wings.

Again and again, his mouth caressed hers. All the while, he supported her, his hands under her thighs, taking her weight as if it were nothing.

Such strength. Such tenderness. She *had* gone about it wrong.

Her kiss was hard, violent. His were the opposite. They hinted of mysteries to be unveiled, promises to be fulfilled.

Sebastian treated her like a treasure deserving of exquisite care. He feathered kisses over her cheek and along her jaw, his mouth coaxing—demanding nothing, tempting all.

Each kiss stoked a heat that flowed ever deeper, like molten lava seeking its limits. When his breath warmed the hollow of her ear, she gave an involuntary shudder.

He made a sound low in his throat.

Now his mouth did bruise hers. Their tongues tangled in delicious combat. Gwynna met him with equal force— this sensual violence felt right.

Gwynna cinched her legs around his torso.

Another growl. Hers? His?

This was not the man who insisted on chaperones, who kept distance between them. This man wanted her—wet clothing, inept kisses, and all.

Impatience swept her. His hands supported her, but she wanted them free, leading her through this storm.

As if he read her thoughts, he shifted her across his

body. Cradling her, he lowered them to the cave floor.

"Gwynna." His voice was ragged, full of need.

Regret.

He took a shuddering breath. "This, with us, is—"

"Too much." Gwynna spoke the words before he could. "*I'm* too much, as you said. Always pushing, never knowing proper boundaries."

Sebastian shook his head. "You are unlike any woman I've ever known. But this cave is the wrong place for...whatever this is."

"I want the wild, uncontrollable part of you," she said. "I glimpsed it just now, and I want more."

"There's nothing wild about me."

Gwynna moved to face him, straddling his thighs. "Make love to me, Sebastian. No one has."

"All the more reason not—"

"Shhh." She put a fingertip to his lips. "Do you hear that sound?"

Sebastian stared at her, his gaze thick. "Fairies dancing in a glade?"

"No." Gwynna caught his hand and placed it over her breast. "It's my heart."

***

Damp, dark, rocky—so many reasons this place, this time were wrong.

But his principles had fled to some other realm where they had a prayer of justifying their worth. If he had a working brain, he might find them. But here, with his hand over Gwynna's breast, the only functioning part of him was well south of that.

His brain mounted a last, feeble objection. Sebastian flung it into that other realm, where it would think twice before trying that again.

Gwynna was his. Damned if he wouldn't take her.

With that, he tumbled into a chasm prowled by wild beasts in their natural habitat. Here, men did not devise tricks to keep temptation at bay. Desire was not denied.

In this foreign land, the control he'd cherished since the day his parents had betrayed him by dying—*and yes, he was still a little angry about that*—held no sway.

Neither did that artificial world he constructed to keep the world at bay. He'd thought it sufficient.

Until Gwynna entered his life.

Until Elizabeth fled that clinic.

Until Angus developed an obsession.

Until his watch sprouted dragons.

Until the chaos led him here, to this cave, with the most desirable woman he'd ever known straddling his lap.

The beast in him was a heartbeat away from carrying the fair damsel off to its lair for wild, insatiable congress.

But she deserved more than this miserable cave.

And he, it seemed, was still a prisoner of his own conscience.

***

He lifted her off his lap. "I've pledged to protect you."

"Is it a burden to carry all that righteousness on your shoulders?" Gwynna demanded, stung.

"Yes, unfortunately."

She placed her hand on his chest. "I want the deep-down truth of you—the part you keep from the world. There's poetry in you, Englishman. Don't hide it."

Sebastian rose. "The only poetry in me is Burns. Thanks to Angus, he's lived in my head for years."

"Prove it."

"I need to see if the rain has stopped."

Gwynna caught his arm. "One poem."

He glared at her. She glared back.

"'O then, the heart alarming, and all resistless charming, in love's delightful fetters she chains the willing soul.' The words, half-growled. "There. Done."

Gwynna stared at him in wonder. "Who is it about?"

"A woman named Chloris. Other women dress in

showy fashions and jewels, but Chloris outshines them, for she is unpretentious and only ever herself."

He paused. "I expect she dons breeches now and then."

With that, he moved toward the cave entrance. She had no choice but to follow.

The rain had indeed stopped. Gwynna watched as Sebastian untied the horse. The air felt heavy and strange.

"This…awkwardness is my fault," she ventured.

His attention fixed on the horse. "Awkwardness—is that what you're calling it?"

"More like desperate longing that won't be denied, no matter how determined you are to pretend otherwise."

Sebastian mounted and pulled her up behind him.

By the time they reached the inn, the silence was nigh unbearable. After settling the horse, he walked her to her room and waited, as usual, for her to go inside.

As if they hadn't had that intimacy in the cave.

As if they hadn't been on the verge of…something.

"I shouldn't have kissed you," Gwynna said. "It's made things strange between us."

He looked pained. "I don't suppose you would consider not having this conversation."

"You wish to pretend everything is as it was before?"

Sebastian shook his head. "I'm done with pretending. I don't know what this is between us. I have no answer."

Her chin rose. "That's answer enough, I suppose."

Gwynna slipped inside her room, careful to not wake Mrs. Kendall.

***

Sebastian stared at the door. She was safely inside—had been for five minutes. He'd counted every second.

Time to retreat to his room for another night of fruitless dreams.

His clothes were wet; he needed to shed them. Gwynna would be doing the same. He closed his eyes against that image.

There *was* a wildness in him. In the cave, he'd barely tamed it. Before control clamped down, the beast had tasted freedom. It wanted more.

Fortunately, her door was closed. Even so, if Mrs. Kendall hadn't been in the room, he might have broken it down.

Angus had failed to mention a few things about obsession: How it could cause a man to contemplate the violent removal of any obstacle between him and the object of his desire. How desire, long suppressed, could explode with the force of a planetary collision.

How magic, once found, became the lodestar.

Honor reminded him of his responsibility to protect her from men in whom beasts lurked. It pointed out that she was an innocent, that he was depraved for wanting her.

All true.

But his vision clouded, as if William's grotesque gargoyles, mocking and evil, had gathered round in anticipation of bringing him into their dark fold.

Couldn't they see he was impervious to temptation? He wasn't some depraved beast out to ruin innocents, even those so unwise as to ask—*demand*—to be made love to.

Sebastian backed away from her door.

Fool that he was, he kept his gaze there, willed it to open. Willed her to hear his plea.

And because Gwynna Owen was as fey as one of those dancing fairies…

She did.

He stared in disbelief as the door opened.

She wore a night-rail of thin lawn. She didn't look surprised to see him standing there after bidding her goodnight long minutes ago.

"Sebastian." Her voice was hushed, throaty, as if they shared a secret.

His duty was clear: Return her to the safety of her room. Lock the door to keep her there.

She tilted her head, looked him a challenge. Those clear blue eyes saw past the pretense, past the falseness.

Demanded only truth.

Sebastian closed the distance between them, reached behind her for the door. Gently, so as not to disturb Mrs. Kendall, he closed it.

Then he lifted Gwynna into his arms and carried her to his room.

***

Gwynna had learned to distinguish the man from the image. As layers of that façade had fallen away, his true character emerged. It was sterling, like fine silver.

But she craved the tarnish, the shadows and flaws. Just as her dagger's pitted scars spoke of battles endured, Sebastian's wounds were testament to trials survived.

It took that to steal her heart.

He closed the door of his room, sealing them inside. As he laid her on his bed, his gaze held doubt, regret, a tinge of despair.

But need, most of all. Slivers of moonlight slipped through the window, illuminating that fire.

Gwynna rose on her knees and faced him. "I'm not afraid, Englishman."

"Some would say that's foolish."

"They have not seen your eyes." She brushed a lock of golden hair off his forehead.

For a moment he froze—struggling, perhaps, to adhere to some civilized version of himself. Then his arms slid around her, and he drew her against his chest.

Scents of rain and earth clung to him, remnants of the storm and cave.

When she shivered, he pulled back to look at her.

"My shirt's wet. I've given you a chill."

"Take it off."

He hesitated. "Is this—with me—what you want?"

"We Welsh throw ourselves into the breach when the

cause is right, Englishman." Not that he was a cause, exactly. More like her destiny.

Were his hands unsteady as he fumbled with that damp shirt? Finally, with a muttered curse, he pulled it over his head.

Gwynna's breath caught. She had tended her grandfather, but he'd been shrunken and frail. Sebastian was a man in his prime. Her eyes drank in his sculpted curves, the solid expanse of shoulders, the firm flesh that disappeared into the fabric of his trousers.

"You are beautiful," she said softly. "I want to see all of you."

He glowered. "I haven't seen any of you."

"I am wearing *one* article of clothing. It can be removed in the blink of an eye. But you are a work of art. I want to savor every inch."

His gaze thickened. "Gwynna."

No one had ever said her name thus, as if she were the beginning and end of all wanting.

"Tell me what to do," she whispered.

A gleam of amusement flickered in his eyes. "I wouldn't dare."

His hand slid around her nape, all amusement gone as he brought her face to his. Just as their lips met, Gwynna couldn't stop a breathless sigh of surrender.

Sebastian swept her down to the bed. His forearms bracketed her, taking his weight, protective of her even in this.

But his bruising kiss held all the wildness she craved. Gwynna arched into him, pitting her need against his. If this was a taking, she intended to be an equal partner.

When he lifted her into the curve of his body, she melded to him like a magnet finding true north.

When his hand slid over her abdomen, she covered it with hers, relishing the weight of his palm, claiming it.

Her hands swept over his back. "Take off the rest."

"Night–rail," he parried. "The blink of an eye, you said."

Gwynna's fingers shook as she worked the buttons. Sebastian made no move to help her. Perhaps he wanted to be sure she came to this freely.

But as he watched her, his expression grew fierce.

Fierce thrilled her. Fierce was the antithesis of reason. Fierce wrecked control.

She tossed her gown aside, as her mother must have done in the face of the fire in her lover's eyes.

"God, help me," Sebastian growled. "I cannot save you from this."

"I don't want to be saved," Gwynna retorted. "I want to go down in flames."

***

Alas, so did he.

The pieces of him that had been fracturing as Gwynna reordered his world had reconstituted themselves into a new, unrecognizable whole.

Sebastian wanted to protect her, but the animal inside craved Gwynna Owen unto death.

And if the choice was between death at her hands and the life he'd known—it was no choice at all. Whoever he was, whatever he had become, was hers.

Somehow, she got those damp breeches off him, reduced their world to shared nakedness.

Then her clear blue eyes impaled him. "I will take what comes."

Impossible to reconcile these base cravings with the person he thought he was. More than order, more than discipline, more than honor—he needed to claim her.

Sebastian bore her down into the bed and allowed himself to live again.

***

His body was a revelation, so much larger and more

powerful than hers. Gwynna wanted to explore every inch, especially that part pressing against her with hard, unbridled urgency.

But when her hands slipped between their bodies, Sebastian stopped her. He drew in a ragged breath.

"I've not been with a woman in a long time. If you touch me, things may go awry. I wish to last for you."

Whatever that meant.

"If you don't, er, last, I suppose there's always the next time," Gwynna said.

His gaze faltered. "Dear God. You mean to kill me."

"To the battle joined," she whispered in his ear.

With a low growl, Sebastian pinned her arms above her. Then he brought their lips together in a kiss that was both weapon and plea.

Gwynna hooked her leg around him, yoking them even closer. Tension rippled across his shoulders.

That powerful body pressed her down, let her feel his strength. And even though his size dwarfed hers, they felt like a perfect fit.

His chest was hard in the places she was soft, the hairs coarse where she was smooth. His hands, twice the size of hers, skimmed along her flesh with exquisite gentleness, discovering her slowly, as if he were a harpist finding chords meant for her alone.

Sebastian trailed kisses along her neck, over the rise of her breasts. When his mouth closed over her nipple, Gwynna gasped at the excruciating pleasure.

Slowly, tantalizingly, he pleasured her. His kiss found the place on her abdomen his hand had warmed earlier. Then he went lower still. His lips brushed over her sex.

Perhaps a true lady would be embarrassed. Gwynna was never so glad not to be that.

Each place Sebastian touched conjured a craving for a joining—not just with his flesh, but with that deeper part he hid from the world.

Gwynna yearned to discover how to pleasure him, but when Sebastian stoked her intimate folds and teased a finger at her opening, she ceded the fight.

Her body found the rhythm, as if she'd known it all along. She couldn't muster a shred of shame.

Instead, she dug her fingers into Sebastian's shoulders and gave herself over to this glorious, perfect death at his hands. Her incoherent whimpers pleaded for more.

And when the heat he stoked exploded into blissful release, it stole her breath, sapped her strength, robbed her of all sovereignty. She lost herself to his power.

His victory. But it felt like hers.

She would never be the same.

But she would take revenge.

Her hands slid over his powerful shoulders to his buttocks, and the soft vulnerability underneath.

Those globes intrigued her. She wanted to learn them, but first she wanted to explore the hardness that pulsed with such potency.

Her hand closed around him.

His shaft, so very large, was silken and smooth. When she stroked him down to the root, he shuddered.

Good, she thought. *Good.*

Her searching gaze met his. She read reluctance—did he still fear to hurt her?

"I want what you're keeping," she insisted. "I want what you're holding back."

Instinct had her angling her body upward, to take the tip of him.

"Gwynna," he growled.

And drove into the very heart of her.

***

Lethargy settled over her, the aftermath of a well-fought battle. The room was still dark. If she had slept, it hadn't been for long. Gwynna glanced over at Sebastian.

His sculpted features were hard, unforgiving stone.

"There are sheaths and the like," he said in a ragged voice. "I ought to have protected you—"

"No second-guessing, Englishman."

He turned to her. "You might conceive a child. What was I thinking?"

"Neither of us was thinking. I am glad of it."

Sebastian studied her intently. "Did I hurt you?"

"There was a moment or two," she acknowledged. "You are...quite substantial. But I have no regrets. The opposite, in fact. Is it unseemly to say so?"

He took a deep breath. "Gwynna, this, between us, it's not—"

"Stop." She wanted to halt the hurtful words. "I know I have no claim on you."

"Don't say that—"

"I'll speak when I wish." His rejection stung.

"That I don't doubt." Sebastian caught her hand, brought it to his lips. "You have every claim on me. Did you think this meant nothing?"

"Is that not the way of men of your world? To engage in dalliances?"

He scowled. "This is no dalliance. It's possession."

Oh, worse. Was she something to own, like that watch?

"I am not your possession," Gwynna snapped, her heart in tatters.

"No," he agreed darkly. "It's the other way around."

His fingertip brushed her cheek. His eyes softened to velvet. And the fire in that hazel gaze called to every foolish dream and hope she dared not nurture.

Sebastian brought their lips together in a kiss so perfect and true that Gwynna knew this is what she had sought for a lifetime, and for all the previous lifetimes.

It couldn't last. They were from different worlds. A king did not love a dragon.

Nevertheless, Gwynna snaked a leg around him, pulled him into an intimate embrace.

"We shouldn't," he warned. "You must recover."

"I am quite recovered." *I will never recover.*

If she couldn't win the war, she would at least win this night.

"This time will be better," he murmured, as their lips met.

"Not possible," she whispered.

But it was.

Chapter Nineteen

When you know who you are, come and find me.

The words repeated in Hannah's brain. How would she know? Who was ever ready for the possibility of heartbreak?

Yet the force that drew her to Angus overwhelmed. Was mere sensuality? No, this was beyond *mere*.

But he had laid down that ultimatum. And today, he hadn't sought her out.

She had glimpsed him in the kitchen, perhaps doing whatever he did to those eggs to make them so excessive. In the garden, trimming a rose bush. Sitting in the gazebo with a book.

This was his home, of course. She was the interloper, the one who had made everything between them strange by her inability to…to what?

Trust?

Men had always wanted something from her, gave nothing in return. How did one overcome such experiences? She'd spent years simply trying to survive. She had become rigid and fearful, unwilling to change. There'd been no reason to.

Until now.

"Mrs. Steele?" Elizabeth stood at the door of her sitting room. "Am I disturbing you?"

Hannah put away her knitting. "Not at all, dear."

Elizabeth took the chair next to her. "I must move back into my parents' house. Staying here will just make it more difficult for Sebastian. And for me."

That was so, Hannah realized. But the notion of

Elizabeth rattling around in her parents' house with only a few servants seemed sad.

"Until I figure out what to do next, I must put the house to rights. Face whatever it is I've been afraid to face." Elizabeth sighed. "Loneliness, I suppose. Sorrow."

Hannah reached for her hand. "You are very brave, dear." Braver than she was, it seemed.

Elizabeth smiled. "I'm not brave, but I must face facts. My parents are gone. I can't change that. Sebastian and I were not right for one another, though I'll always be grateful he saw me through my illness. I hope we remain friends. But I must press forward, wherever it leads."

"Is there anything I can do?" Hannah asked.

Elizabeth regarded her shyly. "Would you consider becoming my companion?"

That took her aback. "Come and live with you?"

"Yes," Elizabeth said. "You'll be handsomely paid and I would love your company."

Hannah did not know what to say.

"You need not answer now," Elizabeth said. "Whatever you decide, I'll still be forever grateful that you were my governess."

"As will I, dear."

Elizabeth rose. "I intend to move in the next day or so. I need some new things, though. May I impose on you to come shopping with me in the village?"

"It's no imposition," Hannah said. "I need some items myself."

Her spirits rose. Shopping would be just the thing.

***

Angus had done everything possible to draw notice, simply by putting himself in plain sight. The garden, the kitchen, the gazebo—like some lovesick whelp, he had staged himself in places where Hannah might see him.

The idea was to remind her of his presence, but from far enough away so that any encounter would require effort on her part. She'd have to enter the kitchen, stand next to the rosebushes, march herself out to the gazebo.

She did not. So much for staging.

It was silly anyway. Angus prided himself on being forthright. Yesterday he had put his cards on the table, without subterfuge.

But she had left them there.

Angus had successfully avoided the breakfast room this morning when he knew Hannah was there, but he could scarcely avoid her at dinner.

He waited politely in the parlor for the ladies, glad they had taken themselves off today doing whatever ladies did in the village. How anyone could spend hours shopping was beyond him. Staring at frocks and ribbons and furbelows—nothing was more boring, or useless, or—

"Good evening, Mr. MacDuff," said a voice in the doorway.

Hers.

Angus turned, and was nearly struck senseless.

No bombazine. Not even a spring floral.

A long, pale gold gown graced her lithe form. The airy fabric flowed from a band just under her bodice down to a flared hem trimmed in a scallop of gold lace.

An especially interesting lace overlay began at the side of the gown and swept around to the front in a graceful diagonal. It fluttered loose, as if it would drift open with a slight breeze.

Or touch.

The gown's low neckline didn't plunge dramatically but ran severely straight across—a delicious irony, for it nevertheless exposed the rise of her breasts.

Moreover, the cut was wide, the fabric barely gracing her shoulders, making it appear as if the gown was on the verge of sliding down her arms.

One could only hope.

And the sleeves! Her arms had always been covered,

but these sleeves descended only eight or nine inches down her upper arms, leaving a tantalizing swath of skin available for his inspection.

Angus swept her a deep bow, and was pleased to see a flush spread across her cheeks. Her eyes sparkled with…something.

Surely, he misread the signs. He would have expected Hannah to flinch from the frank appreciation she must see in his eyes.

Instead, her eyes held some odd bit of business that—if he hadn't known better—might be taken as invitation.

Angus allowed his gaze to rove from those flushed cheeks down to that mischievously severe bodice and provocative lace overlay.

When he returned to her face, he saw no censure or reprimand at his boldness. Only that becoming blush.

What was this? he wondered.

Another voice greeted him—Elizabeth's. Was she in the room? Angus couldn't bring himself to notice. All he saw was Hannah in that mesmerizing gold gown.

"…shopping today…dressmaker's…lady who ordered it found herself unexpectedly increasing…fit Hannah perfectly…….she thought the neckline daring, but I said…"

Angus's brain refused to work. He could not rip his eyes away from Hannah.

And still she did not turn away from his scrutiny.

He would die of pleasure before soup was served.

Dinner. He was supposed to take them into dinner.

He murmured something nonsensical, somehow got them both to chairs.

Once or twice, he thought Hannah swallowed hard, as if she, too, was a bit at sea. But she found her courage and smiled at him.

What had changed? Had she come to some decision?

When the ladies rose, Elizabeth murmured something and disappeared, leaving Angus and Hannah to adjourn to the parlor.

She took sherry. Angus went straight for that new whisky from Islay, where the peat made for interesting alchemy.

He silently raised his glass to her. Hannah blushed.

Then she took a large gulp of sherry, and he began to wonder. "Are you well?"

"I am," she said, rather forcefully. Her glass tipped at an angle.

Angus took it from her hand and set it on the table.

"I wasn't finished," she said tartly.

Ah, there was the Hannah he knew.

Their gazes held.

"I believe I am an inch or two taller than you," she said.

He sipped his whisky. "Yes."

"Do you mind?" she asked.

"No. I'm enjoying the view. Do *you* mind?"

Hannah shook her head, then took a deep breath, which made the neckline of her gown rise, and then fall, then rise again. Angus tried to steer his eyes to her face.

She hesitated. "I have thought about you constantly."

He stilled. "As often as that?"

"More," she whispered.

Angus moved closer and inhaled some faint, arousing scent. Vanilla? No, vanilla was for cooking. It had never aroused him. Cinnamon? That, too, belonged in food.

Jasmine. That was it.

It was as if a sea breeze had dipped into a tropical garden, sampled the flowers, and carried their essence here for the sole purpose of beguiling an unsuspecting Scot.

But the important point was that she was thinking of him—*constantly*.

"What can be more often than constantly?" he asked.

"You are being provocative," she retorted.

"Mrs. Steele," he said softly, "*you* are provocative. Indeed, you are more provocative tonight than you have ever been."

Her flush deepened. "Do you...like my gown?"

"I have never admired anything more," Angus said, "save the person wearing it."

"Oh." She looked flustered.

"You're different somehow. It's more than the dress."

Her gaze fixed on the fireplace. "Elizabeth has asked me to live with her as her companion. She means to return to her parents' home."

That sudden, unwelcome news required more whisky. Hannah tucked away with Elizabeth. She would be close by, but he wanted her here, under this roof. With him.

"What have you decided?" he asked carefully.

"That I will support her in whatever way I can."

"I see," Angus said, his hopes plummeted.

"I don't think you do." Hannah faced him. "As much as I love Elizabeth, I am not ready to grow into old age as her companion."

Angus scarcely dared to breathe. "How would you like to grow into old age?"

"I'm not sure. I'm mindful of your words—that you don't wish to help me discover myself."

Was it only yesterday he'd spoken so intemperately?

"I am willing, as long as you don't mean to walk away after you...discover." Angus caught her hands. "Look at me, Hannah. Tell me what you see."

Her gaze moved from his face, down to his feet, and back. "You are fit. Your eyes are a very nice green. I like the gray in your hair. It's reassuring, even comforting."

Angus did not wish to be comforting.

"Anything else?" he growled.

"Strength," she said softly. "Honor. Good."

"I'm not good," he said. "I feel very wicked at this moment. Do you know why?'

Mutely, she shook her head.

"You *do* know." He slid his hands up her arms, over

skin laid bare by those sleeves. "I want to do all manner of things with that gown. Starting with removing it."

"*Oh.*"

"Walk with me outside." Angus pulled her with him to the terrace doors.

***

The sherry had gone to her head.

Rather, it was that look in Angus's eyes that made her dizzy. No man had ever looked at her that way. As if he wanted her more than life itself.

Hannah put her hand to her breast. Truly, her heart wanted to fly out of it, to him.

That would require abandoning everything she had.

Which was what, exactly? A comfortable position with Elizabeth? Her little cottage in the Cotswolds knitting landscapes? Was that what life was about?

Here, with this man, those seemed the very ghosts of what life could be.

He came up behind her, and Hannah leaned back against him. Instantly, his hands went around her waist.

"I like your hands on me," she said.

Angus was silent for a beat. Then: "Too much sherry, I'm thinking."

"Is a woman not allowed to state what she wants without someone thinking she is drunk, delusional, or disabled?" She pulled his arms forward, around her. Now their bodies were nicely snugged, her back to his front.

"I knew there was a reason to take the night air." Angus's voice sounded uneven. Normally, he was an *even* sort of man.

He toyed with the free edge of that diagonal lace panel on the front of her gown. "Does this go anywhere? Or is it just a tease?"

She laughed. "The latter, I'm afraid."

Hannah turned. "When you look at me, Angus, what do you see?"

"Strength. Honor. Beauty. Same words you had for me, save the beauty part."

"You left out good," she said.

"I am not looking for good at the moment."

Nor was she, it seemed.

What if she disappointed him? She eyed him helplessly. "What is to become of us?"

"What will. Some things lie beyond our control."

"This…between us…I don't know how to control that."

One brow arched rakishly. "Why, in the name of all that is holy, would you wish to?"

Hannah bit her lip. "Part of me wants to see where this leads. Only—"

"The time for 'onlies' was about ten seconds ago." Angus slid his hand around the nape of her neck and brought her face to his.

Hannah sighed against his lips. "It seems I cannot do without you, Mr. MacDuff."

***

A wealth of meaning lay in those words, but for once, Angus didn't want to know more.

Pulling Hannah into his arms, he savored the softness of her body, the gossamer lace of her gown, the warmth that curled in and around him as she filled his senses.

He wanted to give her what she should have had all those years ago, when men with base intentions shut that door and forced her to withdraw into that brittle shell.

"I wish us to marry as soon as possible," he said.

She pulled back. "Is that a requirement?"

"It is."

"Another ultimatum." She pursed her lips in that disapproving Hannah-way that had gutted him so often in the past.

"The truth is, I'd take you on any terms. But I'd be a lesser man for it, and it would erode what is between us. I don't want half measures, Hannah. I want all."

Her eyes searched his.

"I know in my heart that the only way we can be what we're meant to be is with that commitment," Angus said. "I cannot begin to tell you what it would mean to me, what I would give you in return."

She put her hand over his mouth, silencing him.

He had done it, then. Chased her away.

"No half measures," Hannah said softly. "All."

Angus tried to absorb that. "Commitment. Marriage straightaway. Together for the rest of our lives. Is that what you're agreeing to?"

She drew in a shaky breath. "Yes."

He'd detected hesitation. "Is there a 'but'?"

"A small one," she confessed. "I don't want to get married now."

"Hannah," he growled.

"Maybe tomorrow, or the day after. For now, I'd like to start...discovering."

She slipped her arms around his neck.

"That's it," Angus whispered. "I've died and gone to heaven."

Hannah touched her mouth to his.

"Not quite yet," she murmured.

***

Gwynna was gone.

Sebastian had stirred lazily awake, memories of the night tugging at him, only to find a cold, empty spot where she had lain.

She wasn't at breakfast, or anywhere in the inn. He told himself not to worry—this was her island, her village, her people. She was safe.

A deep-seated dread rose in him, nonetheless.

Last night, he had given himself to her in some profound, unalterable way. Her absence gutted him.

He must not lose her. Gwynna was his. He felt it in his

bones.

That knowledge swamped him as he strode through the streets of Moelfre, desperate to lay eyes on a woman in breeches with a shock of red hair and sapphire eyes—likely carrying a dagger capable of inflicting mortal wounds like the one he now suffered.

His blood was indeed flowing through the streets of Anglesey. It flowed out of his heart, his soul, his very being, past that glistening sea and out to infinity without hope of rescue.

Angus drew solace from meditation in times of need, but Sebastian had only those cursed Scottish poems the man had instilled in him. But poetry made one restless. It caused the soul to commence searching and created disquiet. Not what he needed.

Nevertheless, a great number of lines raced to his brain when they were least welcome.

> *O could the Fates but name the price*
> *Would bless me with your charms and you!*
> *With frantic joy I'd pay it thrice,*
> *If human art and power could do!*

It was a lament by a man fated to gain only friendship from his beloved. For melancholy, one could do no better than the Scots, who dispensed despair in equal terms with bliss.

Sebastian tried to reason his despair away. After such prolonged celibacy, proximity with any woman was bound to cause trouble.

Wouldn't a starving man be vulnerable to a feast? Wouldn't he delude himself into thinking that what his eyes beheld was the very thing he most yearned for?

And wouldn't a taste cause him to want more?

Ah. He hadn't discovered some rare magic. Gwynna was a woman, like any other. They'd shared a night, as lovers do. He simply felt it more acutely because…

Alas, his brain objected. It insisted that Gwynna was

not any woman—that there was none like her, that she had waked him from a long, deep sleep.

That because of her, he was finally, agonizingly alive.

And that truth—especially when it wrought such inner turmoil—was not to be ignored.

***

"Your Grace." A smiling Mrs. Kendall presided at the small counter of Rhianna's shop.

Sebastian blinked. When had Mrs. Kendall learned to smile? Why was she here, running this shop? Was everyone trying to upset the natural order?

He tried to tame his pulse, his tone, his deranged soul, long enough to make a credible attempt at calm. Counting was beyond him.

"Mrs. Kendall," he acknowledged.

Where is she? his brain demanded.

Sebastian cleared his throat. Words did not come. Only great, screeching thoughts: *Give me her direction this instant, or I will rip every witch's manual from these shelves until I find the spell that brings her to me!*

"I…" A croak. He tried again. "I don't suppose you have seen—"

"May I offer you some tea? It is a new blend."

I don't want your cursed tea! By all that is holy can you not see that it's Gwynna I crave?

Without waiting for his response, she poured him a cup and thrust it into his hand.

The aroma was strange. *Poisoning me now, are you?*

The voices would not still; his hands shook.

Tea, then. Tea would ground him, scald him, kill him—all preferable to this chaos.

Warily, he took a sip. He couldn't place the taste.

"It's something I give the men who come in," Mrs. Kendall said. "Or rather, their wives."

"I see." But he didn't.

"Rhianna has been teaching me about tea. I've started

blending my own."

Sebastian wondered whether Horace Busby would take to tea like this.

"I may not return to Cheshire," Mrs. Kendall added.

He frowned. "Is that not your home?"

"It's been my home since my husband died. But Horace doesn't want me there. Widows with no income occupy a low place in a household."

Sebastian vaguely remembered her talking about that in the carriage. Tears had been involved. He prayed she would not break down now. It took considerable effort to keep his own wildly unstable emotions in check. If she wept, he'd likely join her.

"Where will you go?" he asked after a moment.

"I don't know." She brightened. "Would you like to purchase something, Your Grace?"

"I have little use for tea, I'm afraid."

"We have other items. The Glendower flag is very popular."

She looked so hopeful that he purchased a flag, a garish banner with alternating red and yellow squares, each bearing a lion poised to attack. He had no idea what he'd do with it.

By the time Sebastian finished his tea, he felt calmer.

Gwynna had run off, but he would find her.

"I am glad you enjoyed the tea," Mrs. Kendall said. "Black currants give it that smoky taste. They're brewed in the water of dandelion roots soaked overnight."

Egad. Sebastian placed the cup on the counter, wishing he'd learned that part earlier.

"It's said to be a remedy for male problems. ."

He frowned.

"Something unfortunate happens to some men as they grow older," Mrs. Kendall said. "The dandelion is said to stimulate production of a substance that helps them to—"

"Thank you, madam," he said quickly. "Do you know

where Miss Owen has got to?"

"As to that, I cannot say. Gwynna was not in the room when I awoke this morning." She gave him a speaking look. "And I awoke at dawn."

Dawn.

There was one place where dawn had special significance. It was a slender reed upon which to pin his hopes, but it would have to do.

Chapter Twenty

The tomb was magical at first light. Gwynna loved to watch the sun's rays peek over the horizon, steal across the fields, skim the entrance rock, and sail on to the new day.

For years, her grandfather brought her here at dawn on her mother's birthday to see how the elm he'd planted in her name had grown. Now it was over thirty feet tall.

Today, although dawn had come and gone, Gwynna was reluctant to leave. Peace lived here, and lately her life held little of that.

Sebastian.

A sixth sense had tugged at her last night as she changed into her night-rail. Somehow, she'd known he would be on the other side of the door.

She embraced her fate, as her parents had embraced theirs. Had they, too, found destiny in the other's eyes?

If so, why had they parted? Perhaps they thought they had time—William to make arrangements, Megan to accustom her father to what they'd done.

But time is both thief and healer. It works its will, heedless of consequences. And sometimes it does not grant more than it already has given.

Self-preservation had driven her from Sebastian's bed this morning. He had awakened a need that shook her to her core. She wanted more of him.

All.

Loving a man who held back would destroy her. Time might ease his pain from the demise of his marriage, but it would stab her with bitterness of what he couldn't give.

Yet if fate granted them only that night, all the more

reason to have seized it. Not to have done so would be tantamount to refusing a ride in one of those hot air balloons if it landed at her feet.

Risk and life were inseparable. If they had conceived a child, it would have what she lacked—a mother's love.

And a father's. Unlike William, Sebastian took care of his own. He would protect his child with the care he gave to all who depended on him.

That brought her up short. He could offer a child far better circumstances. Would he try to take the babe? With his wealth and connections, he would prevail.

Gwynna sank to the ground. Last night had been a grave mistake.

"I thought I might find you here."

A masculine voice—not the one she wished for.

Evans stood a dozen feet away. Anger suffused his features. "You've wrought disaster."

He strode to her. Gwynna scrambled to her feet.

"The farmers you turned into militiamen aren't bringing me their crops," he growled. "This must stop. *You* must be stopped."

Her chin rose. "I've bested you before."

"You think you can fight me?" Evans backed her against her mother's elm.

But anger was his weakness. Likely, he hadn't noticed the dagger sheathed at her waist.

"'Tis a wonder you can stand before any congregation and pretend to be righteous," Gwynna taunted. "No one is fooled. You're a fraud."

His face went florid. He reached for her.

Gywnna's dagger slashed through his shirt, shredding it and exposing the long scar that ran from his right shoulder down his chest. A permanent reminder of how she had defended herself the day her grandfather died.

"A matching scar would provide symmetry," she goaded.

With an angry roar, Evans lunged.

Gwynna ducked under his arm and ran to the tomb. She scrambled up the grassy mound.

"Begone, Evans. The ancients claim this place. They don't favor you."

"No one believes such heathen nonsense."

She flung him a scornful laugh. "*I* do. You'll not win this fight."

A throat cleared.

"I would offer to help, but that appears unnecessary," drawled a masculine voice.

The very one she wished for.

***

Sebastian had spurred Captain through the grove, chased by cold dread. Instinct told him she was in trouble.

He found her standing atop the burial mound, a Welsh princess in full war mode, her dagger pointed down at Evans, whose shirt hung in tatters. The man had no obvious wound, although a long, impressive scar bisected that exposed chest.

He bears the scars still. Sebastian's brain grew thick with rage.

"Good morning, Englishman," Gwynna said. "Evans says we have disrupted his food scheme. He wants the militia disbanded."

Sebastian tried to claw his way through her words, but emotion waylaid reason. Evans had attacked her.

No one had protected her. She'd had to save herself.

"Tell her the truth, Claremont." Evans's dark, glittering gaze met his. "The money won't last. England won't pay Welsh militiamen indefinitely. When it ends, they'll return to me."

Sebastian forced himself to a leisurely dismount. Gwynna was unharmed, he told himself. He had no ready excuse to kill the man. Nor would that serve their plan.

So he forced his eyebrows skyward, arranged all

elements of contempt in their proper places—nose elevated, eyes hooded—and clenched his hands at his side so they wouldn't accidentally find their way around the man's thick neck.

"England can't send regulars to Wales. That's why a militia is needed." He spoke with exaggerated patience, as if Evans had only minimal understanding. "Even if the militia is disbanded, Anglesey won't be abandoned. My family has considerable interest here."

Gwynna eyed him in surprise, as well she might. Sebastian hadn't known he would stake himself to Anglesey's fate until he spoke the words.

"I see where your *interest* lies." Evans's gaze shot from him to Gwynna. "Your predecessor defiled her mother, and you are cut in the same mold."

"My mother and William wed," Gwynna declared. "I know it in my heart."

"Your heart is insufficient evidence," Evans snarled.

Sebastian suffered a moment of guilt—he'd once told her something similar, before he knew to put faith in the conviction he saw in her eyes.

"I have acknowledged Miss Owens as a member of my family," he said coldly. "Any man who says otherwise must reckon with me."

"A reckoning will come—of *my* making." Evans turned to go, a repeat of their confrontation at the cottage. As with most bullies, the man was a coward.

Normally, Sebastian had a wellspring of patience. Hubris, defiance, insult—as a diplomat, those didn't faze him. But world peace did not hang in the balance today.

And he was no longer a patient man when it came to Gwynna. As Evans strode away, Sebastian moved to intercept him.

When he put his hand to Evans's throat, the devil on his shoulder rejoiced. When he slammed the man against a stout oak, a satisfied growl emerged from deep inside. And when he wrenched Evans's arm half out of its socket, Sebastian felt a distinct, unworthy pleasure.

Pain reflected in the man's eyes. Sebastian tried to feel remorse. Couldn't.

But his own hand had gone red from the force he applied to Evans's throat. The man's face had turned blue.

Ah. Not breathing, then.

With an effort, Sebastian summoned discipline, duty, et cetera—had they not yet found something better to do?—and released him.

"Go," he said softly.

The man half-stumbled as he fled across the field.

Gwynna descended the mound. He whirled on her.

"You left this morning without telling me," he growled. "You were in danger here."

Her blue eyes flashed. "This island is my home, and I will not constrict my movements. I never agreed to inform you of my whereabouts. And, as you see, I am unharmed."

"Anything could have happened in this isolated place. It's sheer luck that I came here when I couldn't find you in Moelfre."

"Is it an affront to your masculine pride that there was no need to ride to my rescue?"

Sebastian took a slow, measured breath. "Is that who you think I am? A bully like Evans, who needs validation at every turn? Who must rescue damsels in distress to shore up his pride?"

Gwynna flushed. "No."

That, at least, was gratifying. But she seemed determined to resist his effort to prevent those he cared for from coming to harm—ever, ever, ever.

Sebastian could no longer pretend she wasn't on that list, perhaps at the very top. Truth was staring at him with those brilliant blue eyes.

"You looked for me?" she asked, shyly.

With the hounds of hell at my heels, conjuring dire,

desolate, desperate images of your lovely, lifeless form—

"When you weren't at the inn, I searched the village," Sebastian said carefully, forcing feral thoughts elsewhere. "I was frantic, if you wish the truth."

No one wants the truth, you idiot.

Gwynna tilted her head. "I always want truth."

He put his hands on her shoulders. "You're under my protection."

Hell. That sounded positively medieval.

Instantly, her dagger was at his throat.

"On the contrary, Englishman." Her voice was a low, sultry growl. "You are under *mine*. You live because I allow it. Never forget that."

Sebastian lifted a brow.

A smile flirted at the edges of that impudent mouth.

The imp.

No, not an imp. A woman—the most arousing he'd ever known.

Yes, he'd been long deprived of female affection. He was the proverbial starving man.

But looking down at Gwynna—cheeks flushed, eyes glittering as she teased that dagger against his throat—Sebastian knew no other woman would satisfy his hunger.

Alas, it would have to be the bloodthirsty one.

***

He put his fingertip on the dagger and carefully redirected it. His gaze dropped to her mouth, but he didn't kiss her. His expression was grave. "Last night was—"

Magical, transporting, breathtaking—so many words rushed at Gwynna.

"Important," he finished. "It is fitting that we marry."

She blinked.

"We'll live at Summerlin. You need never go to London. You'll have your archery, embroidery—"

"I don't do needlework."

Sebastian eyed her warily. "We'll find something

else."

Cold shot through her. "*We* will not."

"You'll have new gowns, ones that suit you, without frills or lace—"

"I have no need for new gowns."

He frowned. "Did you not tell me you wished for more frocks?"

Gwynna's chin rose. "A wish is not a need."

"Fine," he growled. "You'll have only breeches, a closet full of them. Mind you, I would commission a slightly larger size than the pair you have, to leave something to the imagination."

"What else?" she demanded. "What else would you do to change me?"

"I don't wish to change you. Only keep you safe. You'll want for nothing—"

"Can you possibly believe I wish to be locked away in a gilded cage, where nothing can happen to me? That's what you have in mind, is it not?"

Sebastian was silent for a moment. "Probably."

"I belong here. You belong in ballrooms with important people like Mr. Maitland."

He recoiled. "I don't give a damn about important people or ballrooms—"

"What do you give a damn about? Me?"

He looked taken aback. "How could you doubt it?"

"Because you use words like 'important' and 'fitting.' There's not an ounce of feeling in them."

"Do you have better ones?" he challenged.

Gwynna did not want to discuss a future they could not share. She wanted his body joined to hers, the life force surging between them.

And love. She wanted that.

"Here are *my* words," she said softly. "Last night was beyond 'important.' It was all the things I never dared to dream—a new world, and you were its center, its sun. And if I never see its like again, I will go to my grave thanking the heavens for that one, perfect night."

Sebastian stared at her. "But…we'll have every night."

"You feel responsible for me. That's not enough."

He frowned. "It's right that we wed."

"That, of course, is just the sort of proposal every woman dreams of."

"My duty—"

"Even better. Every woman wants to be married out of a sense of duty."

"Damnation, Gwynna. William was the sort to bed a woman and leave her with a child to raise. I'm not."

So he *would* try to take the child. Even that was no reason to wed. "I won't marry a man who offers no hint of feeling."

"I have a morass of feelings," Sebastian protested. "I just haven't made sense of them. We would have a fine life together."

"I have a fine life here."

"Do you?" he challenged. "Do you ever wonder whether you and this island are so entombed by reverence for the past that you miss other possibilities life lays at your doorstep?"

Gwynna narrowed her gaze. "Do *you* ever wonder whether you have spent so long burying emotion behind that ducal façade you're incapable of genuine feeling?"

"I don't bleed emotion at every turn, like you," he insisted. "Plunging full tilt into things—I couldn't live like that. I'm in control of my life."

"You're just playing at life, Englishman. Living in the shallows, never the deep."

He shot her a fulminating look.

Gwynna sighed. "Tonight may deliver us an invasion. We've better use of our time than talking about feelings. Or, in your case, the lack of them."

Even as she flung those words at him, she yearned for

him to close the chasm between them. Why could he not dispense with that nonsense about duty and responsibility?

But that was not Sebastian Traherne.

To her surprise, his gaze softened.

"It's a conquering you want, isn't it?" he murmured.

Yes, she wanted a conquering—his. She wanted him to confess his feelings so she'd never fear she had given her heart to a man who couldn't give his.

Alas, that was not Sebastian Traherne.

***

He'd made a tactical mistake. Gwynna would never submit to a cage, gilded or otherwise. Naturally, she wanted blood spilled at the altar of feelings.

Sebastian had no pattern card for romantic love save his parents. But he recalled how his mother's face would fill with joy when she greeted Gerald. How Gerald had doted on Faylinn, as if she were the center of his world.

A new world, and you were its center, its sun.

Love—was that what Gwynna meant? Her face certainly hadn't filled with joy.

She was right, though: He had suppressed emotions that threatened his comfortable distance from humanity. Now he had no compass, only new, goading thoughts.

She likes swashbuckling! Why not carry her off, like a pirate? He had no intention of trusting that voice.

Besides, his proposal was eminently logical. He had to keep her safe. Otherwise, what happened when they were done with this mission and she simply walked away?

Idiot. She's walking away now.

Gwynna had started for the field beyond the mound.

Yes, he was a morass of confused, foreign feelings. But last night she had come apart in his arms, given him what she'd granted no other man.

He meant to win this war.

***

Large, masculine hands swung Gwynna around, hauled her against a solid chest.

"What are you doing?" she demanded.

"How about we don't name it?" Sebastian tossed his coat on the ground. "Sit."

When she only stared, he pulled her down with him.

And kissed her—gently, belying that display of temper. Like fine silk, his mouth soothed her. He brushed her cheek, then found a sensitive spot under her ear that made her shiver in pleasure.

He was punishing her with sweet torture, reminding her that not even their differences could stop this fire.

And when, at last, Sebastian's mouth found hers, his naked hunger dared her to resist.

Gwynna launched herself at him, half-climbing, half-crawling into his lap. If he'd been a less substantial man, she might have bowled him over.

But his arms secured her as she pressed into him, wanting to crush and be crushed.

With his coat shielding them, the field's prickly hawkweed transformed into a lush bower, grass still redolent from dew, birds deep into their morning songs.

Gwynna held no illusions: He couldn't give her a love that would bridge the boundaries of class and culture, much less his own tangled emotions. And if a child was born, they'd do battle.

Heartbreak would come. But she would face it, as her mother surely had. She wanted him too much not to seize this moment.

Sebastian's hand slipped under her shirt, slid along her bare flesh, then dipped to the flap of her breeches.

"Last night," he said softly, "was…*important*."

His fingers slid under her breeches. Her breath caught.

"It is *fitting* that we marry." The low rumble resonated in his chest as his hands explored her. "You'll have your archery, embroidery—"

"I-I don't…"

"Not to worry." His hand unerringly found the very place that burned for him. "We'll find something else."

As he stroked her intimate folds, he gently taunted her with the very words she had rejected.

"Sometimes," he murmured, "wish and need are one in the same."

His breath was hot against her skin. His heat burned her. His hands stirred magic.

When at last, waves of pleasure swamped her, Gwynna uttered a feral cry.

"As now, perhaps," he whispered.

Helplessly, she clung to him. She knew what he'd done—proven that though his words were prosaic, the passion between them was not.

"I will kill you," she vowed, when she could speak.

"Now, if you like." With a sly smile, Sebastian pulled her atop him.

Even as she fell into the rhythm of his powerful, perfect body, Gwynna knew the truth: Fate would drive them apart, but she was his.

Now, and for all time.

***

In gathering darkness, the militia stood on the cliff at Castle Rock, surveying the beach below. The horizon had all but vanished; whatever lurked offshore remained unseen.

If no invasion occurred tonight, they'd reassemble tomorrow. But conditions were right. The moon was fickle enough to both light the invaders' way and hide them in shadows.

Some of the militia would remain at Castle Rock in the event it became the landing spot. Sebastian and Gwynna would take up positions along the east end, the likelier site because high tide provided access to the road. More militiamen would take cover above the road.

Was it possible this scheme of Drew's might actually bear fruit? Regardless, Sebastian intended to keep Gwynna safe. She was his.

Well, not precisely—despite what had transpired between them in that field this morning.

Fathering a child didn't alarm him. He had sterling examples: Gerald loved without reservation. Angus had taken him to manhood; their loving bond was unbreakable.

What alarmed him was giving Gwynna power to destroy his world, simply by leaving it. She might happily commune with ghosts, but it was beyond him.

Thus, he held back. What did she see in a man who avoided embracing his own emotional truth?

Someone worthy of her, it seemed. But she laid down that marker: *Feelings.*

Mortality would end those. Could he accept the brutal certainty of loss?

"The tide's in," Gwynna said. "It's time."

She slid that leather quiver over her shoulder, held her bow at the ready. He wondered how she could shoot under a moon that declined to show itself with any reliably.

But as he studied her silhouette, Gwynna's position shifted. Her feet moved slightly apart, distributing her weight. She held her body erect, poised. The bow and quiver became a natural extension of that compact frame.

With that, Sebastian's universe reshaped itself. He saw what his tethered vision had obscured.

Gwynna Owen was not the woman who had taken her pleasure in his arms, not the rebel who declared she wouldn't fit into his world, not the belligerent waif he rescued on the moor. Rather, she was all that, but something else besides.

A warrior. Born and bred.

Her journey to find her father had burned confidence into her, strengthened her voice, hardened her resolve.

Power reposed in every inch of her, for all to see. She

was ready to launch herself into the dark universe with every expectation of winning whatever fight came.

Sebastian suspected she was yet unaware that she could command the heavens—and certainly the thunderstruck man determine to protect her at all cost.

Damned if he didn't feel those ancient folk stirring the air, sounding their spirit trumpets as she stood there, prepared to embrace her fate.

She started for the beach.

Behind her, the militiamen didn't move.

When she realized they hadn't followed, Gwynna halted in bewilderment.

"Why aren't they coming?" she asked Sebastian.

Easy one, that.

"They await words from their leader," he said.

She frowned in confusion.

"It's you, Gwynna. They need to hear from you."

Her gaze shifted to the men. They stood at attention, watching her.

"I don't know that to say," she whispered.

"Nonsense. You're Welsh, aren't you? And an Owen besides."

Gwynna blinked. She squared her shoulders, took a deep breath, and addressed them.

"This cause is foreign to you, as it is to me," she said. "Welsh do not aid English."

Some nods.

"Yet if we accomplish this tonight, we rid ourselves of a man who claims to be one of us but who has curdled the very blood that flows in him, and in all Welsh."

More nods.

"Evans is a traitor, not only to England, but to Wales, to Anglesey, to our heritage." Her voice rose. "By his evil acts, he demeans us. Tonight we reclaim our sovereignty."

Gwynna said more words in Welsh. Then she turned to Sebastian. She caught his hand and clasped his shoulder with her other hand, as one might a brother in arms.

Lifting their locked hands skyward, she faced them.

"Fierce the beacon light is flaming, its tongues of fire proclaiming. Chieftains, sundered to your shaming, strongly now unite!"

Gwynna turned and strode toward the beach.

As one, the militia marched forward.

Wind ruffled her hair. A sliver of moon caught its red fire. Her shoulders carried the weight of history as she advanced, bow at the ready.

Sebastian followed, a pace behind.

Because that is what one did in the presence of the last true Princess of Wales.

***

A shard of moon peeked through the clouds, sufficient to illuminate the silhouettes of two longboats. Each appeared to contain about ten men, rowing steadily.

Scarcely an invasion force, Sebastian thought. Perhaps a larger ship waited offshore.

The first boat swept in on the surging tide, the second behind it. The men disembarked.

He and Gwynna were positioned a few dozen yards from the ruins of an ancient boathouse. From this distance, it appeared the invaders carried no obvious weaponry. Perhaps they had small knives or pistols he couldn't make out. Still, this was an odd offensive by any measure.

Would Evans show himself?

"I see him," Gwynna whispered.

There.

Evans lurked on the far side of the boathouse ruins between their hiding place and where the invaders landed. They could just make out his silhouette.

But it was no crime for him to be here. They had to catch him engaging with the invaders.

A tiny gleam of light, too small for a lantern, flickered in his hand. A flint.

Also not a crime.

A man from the first boat saw the signal. He made his way to Evans, who handed him something. The man motioned to the others, who continued up to the road.

Evans retreated to the boathouse, clearly intent on being elsewhere. Sebastian couldn't make a run at him without tipping off the invaders still on the beach.

The chance to catch him in the act was slipping away.

Just then, the moon peeked out from behind a cloud, briefly illuminating the boathouse.

Sebastian heard the *whoosh* of an arrow.

And then it was over.

Dozens of militiamen surrounded the interlopers.

Evans hadn't moved. Had Gywnna killed him?

She was running toward him, her bow raised.

As Sebastian caught up to her, he saw what had rendered Evans immobile: An arrow pinned Evans's shirt sleeve to the boathouse's rotting wood.

She had another arrow trained.

"We have them!" It was Rhys, the innkeeper.

Slowly, she lowered her bow. "Any willing to talk?"

"Most of them. They're frightened out of their wits."

Sebastian frowned. Out of character for mercenaries.

Moreover, Evans looked enraged, not fearful. A man who had committed treason would display a modicum of fear at being caught.

Besides, catching them had been too easy.

"Any of the men French?" Sebastian asked.

Rhys shook his head. "Cornish, seems like."

Cornwall. Where mines fell victim to cheaper Welsh copper. Cornwall, where scores of men were out of work.

This was no invasion.

It was Evans's latest scheme to profit off others' misfortunes. Unemployed Cornish miners were desperate. He'd get a hefty fee from Welsh mine owners to import cheap labor.

As usual, Drew played a deep game. He orchestrated Elizabeth's departure from the clinic, probably to pursue her himself. That meant getting Sebastian out of the way.

Child's play for a master manipulator.

Sensing the pull between him and Gwynna, Drew knew Sebastian wouldn't pass up an opportunity—not to prevent an invasion, for that was bound to be hogwash—but to stop the man who posed a danger to her.

To protect her. *To safeguard her.*

He wanted to kick himself. Usually, he saw the whole chessboard and unerringly predicted an opponent's moves.

But the singular charms of the woman who wielded that arrow with such precision destroyed that skill.

And Sebastian knew, without doubt, she'd also demolished the fortress he constructed around his heart. Then again, it wasn't much of a fortress. A shell, really.

Where did that leave him?

He used to be good at reading people. Now he couldn't even read himself.

Chapter Twenty-One

Gwynna's head was spinning. The invasion hadn't been real. It was another of Evans's moneymaking schemes.

But though he wasn't a traitor, his plot to bring in Cornish workers to take wages from Anglesey men finally exceeded the island's tolerance. The militia gathered his possessions, took him across the strait, and left him there.

Now she and Sebastian were bound for his castle. She wanted to visit William's grave. She hadn't told Sebastian she meant to return to Anglesey, but surely, he expected it.

He had been distant and brooding during their drive. They didn't even have Mrs. Kendall to break the silence. She stayed on the island to help Rhianna.

"I wish we'd caught Evans in treason," Gwynna said. "Banishment only means some other woman will become his next victim."

For the first time in an hour, Sebastian regarded her.

"He's been pressed into the Royal Navy," he said gruffly. "On his way out to sea. No women aboard."

She eyed him in wonder. "How did you arrange it?"

"I'm a damned duke." Spoken as if it were a curse.

Was it only two days ago they made love in that field? Now they seemed like strangers. He hadn't tried to recapture that intimacy or renewed his marriage proposal.

Just as well. She couldn't marry him. What she wanted—his heart—Sebastian was unable to give.

Still, he'd lived up to every promise—stopped Evans, searched for marriage records, secured her inheritance— when no one in his position would have. He'd even wrung pledges from Mr. Maitland not to enforce the Corn Laws on

Anglesey, and from the mine owners to raise wages.

In deeper ways, too, he had wrought a sea change. He treated her as an equal. She'd found her voice, claimed her legacy as an Owen.

Nonetheless, he declined to find his way to the foolish dream she dared to dream.

"Those words you spoke to the militia," he said suddenly. "About flaming lights and chieftains. Where do they come from?"

"A song." She slanted a gaze at him. "There's a story, involving another castle. Do you wish to hear it?"

He eyed her darkly. "If it pleases you."

"Edward built a castle at Harlech, on the mainland, southwest of Anglesey. Owen Glendower captured it from the English in 1404."

"Of course," Sebastian muttered.

"Do you not wish to hear the story?"

Something flickered in that hazel gaze. "I do."

"Later, in the War of the Roses, a Welshman held the castle for the Lancaster side against Edward IV. The song was written to bestir local Welsh, men of Harlech, to revote against Edward. But they lost. It was a slaughter."

"The words are stirring."

"More so in Welsh. It's about fighting for a cause even when that cause is lost."

Sebastian's gaze was hooded. "Why do it, then?"

"Fight isn't defined by victory or defeat. Win or lose, each person decides what cause is worth his life. No one else can gainsay it."

They fell silent for the rest of the journey.

Here, she realized, was another lost cause: A man who stole her heart, but would ever withhold his.

But that was his decision. She could not gainsay it.

***

Horace Busby looked taken aback. "It's difficult. There are several gates that must be unlocked and a heavy stone statue that partly blocks the last gate—"

"See to the matter," Sebastian ordered. He'd never been to the family mausoleum, and suspected it was a crumbling and gloomy place. His own parents were buried at Summerlin. But Gwynna wished to see William's resting place, and it was her due.

An hour later, they trudged toward the imposing stone structure perched on a hill above Claremont Castle.

Centuries ago, it must have seemed a capital notion to plant generations of Trahernes here to lord over the surrounding countryside in perpetuity. But the place had fallen into disrepair. Only the ghost of a path lingered, likely cleared for William's transport months ago.

His cousin must be having himself a grand old time here amid the vines and weeds. Like his crumbling castle, this was a place fit only for lost souls.

Gwynna didn't belong here. She belonged at Summerlin—striding around the lake, shooting at targets—especially Drew, if he ever dared show himself.

Oh, but she'd said no to all that, hadn't she? Because being an Owen meant waging endless battles against all things English. It meant living amid ancient burial mounds and ruins of centuries past. It did not mean marrying an English duke and retreating to his gilded cage.

He had thought of little else on their journey here.

Busby was struggling with the gates, and Sebastian moved to help him. Finally, the last gate swung open and they stepped into the mausoleum.

It wasn't a welcoming sight. Stone gargoyles and cherubs with blank eyes guarded the dead. Some crypts bore inscriptions; most had long since lost legibility.

Presiding over all was William, sufficiently elevated to signify consequence, but not too high for irrelevance.

On the expanse of stone that entombed his casket was carved in imposing letters: "William Edgar Traherne."

Gwynna ran her hands over the words. Sebastian was

so focused on her that he almost missed the smaller inscription chiseled under William's name.

When she turned to him with a stunned expression, Sebastian studied it. Once, the words would have been foreign to him. Now, he recognized them as Welsh.

"What does it say?"

Gwynna read aloud in Welsh, then translated: "The remembrance of thee, thou golden beam, never passed over me without weeping."

Her voice broke. "It's from a poem by Gruffudd Llwyd. A lament for a loved one lost."

"His Grace had a poem carved on his tomb?" That, from Busby. "Not like him at all."

"It was written four hundred years ago about Owen Glendower—'thou delightful eagle,' as he is called," Gwynna said. "It's unbearably sad. I learned it as a child."

Of course. While he was learning benign nursery rhymes, Welsh children were immortalizing a tyrant. But the poem moved her, which mattered.

"I'd like to hear more of it," Sebastian said.

"Longing almost brought me to my grave upon thy account," she recited softly. "Tears ran down my wrinkled cheeks, and watered my face like showers of rain."

Gwynna pressed his arm. "Don't you see? William mourned Megan, even in death."

Indeed, Sebastian saw how it might have been: During that mad dash to Wales to prevent Gerald's marriage, William had met his fate, found love when he least expected it, among people he disdained.

The words confirmed something more: No man whose grief was such that he inscribed them on his tomb—decades after his lover's death—would have abandoned the child of that union.

William hadn't known about Gwynna until he received Taliesin's note, just before his death.

Instead, all he had through the years were memories of

Megan that grew fainter with time, and bitterness over what fate had denied him.

No one saw the grieving man behind the mask.

"I hope he told her." Tears streamed down Gwynna's face. "I hope he didn't save those words of love for his tomb."

***

Hours later, the words still haunted Sebastian.

He hadn't slept. He'd spent the night thinking about *feelings,* and how he'd taken refuge behind his own mask.

His heart had limped along, starved for nourishment, while he held himself apart from anyone not on his short list of intimates.

The hole in his heart was no one's fault but his.

Had Willian confessed his love to Megan? Or had he, too, been plagued by fear of granting her that power?

In the bleak gray before dawn, Sebastian forced himself to examine—with all of the rigor Angus had taught him—what he feared: Love. Losing those he loved.

Hell. Had he not moved beyond the emotional maturity of a grief-stricken seven-year-old?

He had. Angus MacDuff had raised him. Angus did not fear his passions—even if they curdled into obsessions, even if they risked the kind of loss that could not be undone.

Grief was simply the price of love. Only fools or cowards questioned whether love was worth it.

Sebastian decided he was both.

The ice in his soul had thawed, unleashing a flood of feelings. He had to could embrace them. And her.

O could the Fates but name the price
Would bless me with your charms and you!
With frantic joy I'd pay it thrice,
If human art and power could do!

Perhaps Burns's poem wasn't a lament, after all. Perhaps it was a call to arms.

***

This was farewell.

Gwynna had visited her father's tomb at dawn, said an ancient prayer for his spirit, and spilled a drop of her blood on the stones as her pledge of remembrance.

Now she stood in his study in search of a memento to take home.

She placed her bow and quiver on the floor, then threw open the curtains to allow the rising sun to penetrate the shadows. Someone had been cleaning; only a few dust motes floated upward in the light.

William's portrait had been dusted, too. He looked young, in the prime of life.

His bookshelves held familiar classics Gwynna had studied with her tutor—works by Homer, Plato, Aristotle.

Plato had an allegory that seemed eerily akin to her own quest. It told of prisoners who spent their lives chained to a wall in a cave. A fire near the entrance cast shadows of people passing by outside—a distorted reflection of the world beyond.

One day, a prisoner managed to break his bonds and flee. When he saw the sun for the first time, it changed his understanding of the world.

Had she not embarked on her journey from Anglesey, she'd be like those prisoners, studying shadows, never discerning what was real. Much about her parents remained unknown, of course. But the inscription on William's tomb beamed light into the darkness.

Might that poem be here, among his many books?

For a quarter hour, Gwynna searched. Then panic began to set in. Sebastian was an early riser. She had no wish to see him. Leaving him was easier done in stealth.

Her gaze fell on a corner nook, where an upholstered chair stood, its cushions worn. Had William sat there, mourning his bride? Had he, like those cave prisoners, lived only in the shadows of the life he might have had?

She sat in the chair. From this perspective, a shelf lay within easy reach; a red volume stood out. Though tattered and worn, its gold-leaf lettering was legible.

As was the author's name: *Gruffudd Llwyd.*

Gwynna's hands trembled as she opened the book.

It was in Welsh. Surely, William hadn't learned the language. Perhaps Megan read it to him as they sat on Anglesey's beaches, or at that overlook Sebastian loved.

She decided to take it. Sebastian could have little use for poetry in a language he didn't know. As she tucked the book into her pouch, a folded parchment, yellow with age, slipped from its pages.

Carefully, she opened it. Welsh emblems—a leek, daffodil, a fearsome red dragon—embellished the corners.

Except for one corner, which held the seal of the Archbishop of Bangor. And two names: William Edgar Traherne and Megan Glendower Owen.

They had crossed the strait to wed in Bangor in an Anglican parish. The certificate was dated five months before Megan's death—and Gwynna's birth. Her mother had been increasing on her wedding day.

Her quest was over. She ought to be rejoicing.

Yet here, with this document her father saved until his dying day, she was no closer to knowing him.

Time had stolen him.

Gwynna studied his portrait. Absent the dust, his likeness was clearer. His coat held a tiny burst of red near one lapel. She pushed a chair to the wall and stood on it to get a better look.

Over his heart, William wore an insignia—a red lion in profile, forepaws raised mid-attack, on a yellow background.

The Glendower standard.

Why would an English duke honor the man who fought for England but ultimately led the Welsh in revolt against the Crown?

The answer was clear: William, like Owen, belonged to two worlds. But only one claimed his heart.

"Did you think to leave without telling me?"

Sebastian stood in the doorway, his mouth set in a grim line.

There was no point in denying it. Her pouch and travel clothes betrayed her.

He crossed the distance to her in two strides. "I never took you for a coward."

Gwynna stepped down from the chair. "I found their marriage certificate."

He frowned. "Where?"

"In the book with the poem William had inscribed on his tomb. This was tucked in the pages." She handed him the parchment. Sebastian glanced at it.

"Bangor. That's why we found no records on Anglesey." His bloodshot gaze met hers. "As I've already acknowledged you as his legitimate daughter, this changes nothing."

Her chin rose. "It proves they wed—and for love."

"The date is mid-summer. Weren't you born in December? She was with child. That was likely the reason."

That he remembered her birth month surprised her. But why was he being so difficult?

"There's something else," Gwynna insisted. "The insignia William wears in the portrait is the Glendower lion. He honors her heritage, just as he did on his tomb. You know in your heart that I am right."

Sebastian's gaze flicked to the portrait, then to her.

"My heart is an entirely useless organ," he said gruffly. "It ought never wander to islands or beaches or caves in the company of a lady whose skill at inflicting mortal and other sorts of wounds is without parallel."

Gwynna stared at him. "What…other wounds?"

"The kind that ruin a man for all time, I fear."

"Sebastian—"

325

"Damnation, Gwynna. You tried to leave without telling me. I've a mind to call you out. Arrows at twenty paces."

"You'd lose."

"Far preferable to the state in which I find myself."

He did look unlike himself. Fatigue was etched on his features. He wore no waistcoat.

"Where is your watch?" Gwynna asked.

"How the devil should I know?"

Not like him at all.

"Come home with me to Summerlin." His gaze held an odd vulnerability.

"I can't." How could she expose her keening heart to the deafening silence of his?

Yet what fate severs, memory might preserve.

Gwynna rose on her toes and kissed him with all the longing in her undeclared heart, all the secrets she would hold until the stars aligned for them in another lifetime.

With a growl, he swept her off her feet. Carried her to his desk, perched her on the edge.

She tore at his clothes, clawing through the layers that separated them—the doubts, the words that remained unsaid, the barriers physical and symbolic.

Sebastian's mouth crushed hers. His unshaven chin scraped her flesh—sharp proof that, if only for a moment, what they had was real.

Gwynna slid her hands over the breadth of his shoulders, the curves of his chest, the hard ripples of his ribcage—memorizing his flesh before they must part.

He gave a savage grunt of pleasure. His hands went under her, lifting her.

Time had run out for them. This would be no leisurely sensual journey, but a ruthless battle, with one urgent, undeniable end.

Sebastian fumbled with her breeches, as desperate to claim her as Gwynna was to be claimed.

And when finally they were joined, she clung fast, wanting no part of her untouched by the fire.

Her very soul cried out for him. Alas, he would ever withhold his.

***

Gwynna was furious. His fault.

Seeing her standing on that chair, dressed for travel, undid him.

Demons fell upon him, flew him up to the crumbling towers of despair and dashed him down, leaving him in pieces. He wouldn't be whole until Gwynna was his.

Oh, he'd had a plan. His sleepless night had generated a remarkable speech by which he would persuade her. Lovely words, really. Not for nothing had he been first in debate class.

Every word vanished when he saw her ready to flee.

Anger jumped into the breach. Emotion tossed a cloak of obfuscation over all, save his conviction that she must not leave.

Was love the thing that afflicted him? Did love come with raw need and reckless daring?

If so, love seemed perilously close to loss of sanity.

A wedding—yes, he dared to think it—presided over by proper English clergy would be out. Sebastian knew that, just as he knew the balls and routs she would not attend, the manners she would never learn, the social conventions she would refuse to abide.

Why didn't she see that none of that mattered to him?

Worse, after their frantic, feverish interlude in his study—*interlude* surely the wrong word for what had transpired between them—Gwynna had declared her intention to take herself off to Anglesey, on foot and by herself as planned. She would hear none of his objections.

Sebastian's tenuous hold on reason fled.

Recall that she likes swashbuckling!

He snatched up her bow and arrows, tucked them under

his arm. Then he hoisted her over one shoulder and carried her to the carriage—half-expecting to feel the dagger between his ribs.

For a moment she struggled, then went still, as if it was beneath her to fight a man so low as to use his size and strength to dominate her.

In the carriage, she sat as far from him as possible, her profile rigid.

That tight expression, the grim set of her mouth, those brows knit in anger—even those he craved. He wanted to breathe her in to the point of intoxication, hold her until there was nothing between them, bind her to him forever.

Sebastian couldn't even count. A minute was beyond him. He managed thirty seconds, so he recited that over and over, hoping cadence calmed desperation.

Summerlin would settle him. He would persuade her that the world would come to her, on her terms.

And if that failed, if he had to go to her cousin's shop in Moelfre and demand some spell or potion or loathsome tea to persuade her, by God he would do so.

Sebastian thrust aside the gathering dread that Gwynna would be swayed by none of those, only by capitulation in a language he did not understand.

And by that, he did not mean Welsh.

Two long, silent hours later, the carriage rolled to a stop at Summerlin. When he turned to help her exit, she shrugged off his hand, and marched up the steps alone, clutching her bow and arrows.

Not a good sign.

To Sebastian's surprise, Angus was waiting in the foyer, Mrs. Steele at his side.

Close at his side.

Hardly a shred of daylight between them.

Angus cleared his throat. "I obtained a special license."

Sebastian eyed him blankly.

Guilt—a quality embedded in the man's soul—

suffused Angus's features.

"I invoked your name to speed the process," he confessed. "The Archbishop was most gracious."

Sebastian's gaze shifted from Angus to Mrs. Steele and back again.

"We didn't know when you'd return, so it seemed…prudent to hurry things along," Angus added, his face reddening. "Neither of us wished to live in sin."

Mrs. Steele stepped forward. "Mr. MacDuff didn't wish to live in sin. I was quite willing."

Finally, Sebastian's brain was working. He grinned. "I am to wish you happy then?"

Angus's brow cleared. "Yes."

Sebastian enveloped him in an embrace. "You deserve every happiness. I am overjoyed you've found the only woman who can provide it."

"See, Angus?" Hannah said softly. "I told you all would be well."

Sebastian took her hand and brought it to his lips. "Angus is fortunate indeed."

She blushed.

"He can be difficult," Sebastian warned. "Given to poetry and the occasional sermon."

"Indeed." Her eyes sparkled.

For his part, Angus appeared beyond speech. He mopped his brow with a handkerchief.

Surely this was a fine omen, Sebastian thought. He smiled at Gwynna, who had swiftly moved to embrace Hannah. She went to Angus, and hugged him as well.

Only then did she glance at Sebastian.

Daggers glinted in those hard blue eyes.

Chapter Twenty-Two

"I didn't want Elizabeth," Drew said. "I simply didn't want you to have her."

"I should call you out," Sebastian growled. "In fact, consider it done."

Drew was unfazed. "I fixed matters, did I not? Helped Elizabeth flee that musty clinic, informed you both of the facts—"

"In a cowardly manner, by note, and separately." Sebastian scowled. Drew didn't belong in his light-filled library. He was the very embodiment of darkness. A dungeon would be fitting.

"Each of you is the better for it," Drew insisted. "No unfortunate consummation, no being saddled with the wrong partner for the rest of your days—"

"I am the better shot, so you won't want pistols. Broadsword, mace, war hammer, fisticuffs? I'd find the last especially satisfying."

"Damnation, man," Drew protested. "It's not worth ending a friendship over."

"*What* friendship?"

"We have known one another half a lifetime."

"That does not a friendship make," Sebastian said coldly. "Whereas falsifying a wedding ceremony, manipulating Elizabeth's health, letting us labor under the misimpression that we were wed—those make enemies. Lasting ones."

Drew shrugged. "It might have been worth it if Elizabeth and I…" He trailed off.

"If you truly wanted her, there'd have been no 'might'

about it."

"An odd sentiment, coming from you," Drew said. "Don't tell me that Welsh girl—"

"Her name is Gwynna Owen," Sebastian said evenly.

Drew arched a brow. "You should thank me."

Sebastian crossed his arms. "For the lie that England was being invaded by French mercenaries? For the trouble you put us to? You sent us on a fool's errand."

"Now I detect the problem." Drew studied him. "You don't have her yet. That's your fault, not mine. If you can't bring her around in all that time I threw you together—"

"Pistols, or poisoned arrows. I'm indifferent."

"You do realize I am an important person?" Drew drawled. "Lately in charge of the darker aspects of the war effort. If you kill me, Castlereagh will have your head."

Sebastian grabbed Drew by his coat, shoved him to the door. "You're a blackguard without conscience or compassion. Get out, while I'm of a mind to let you live."

"How unlike you to choose violence over words." Drew adjusted his neck-cloth. "If you recover your sanity and wish to return to diplomacy, let me know."

His gaze swept the room—force of habit for a man with so many enemies—and lingered on the windows that afforded a full view of the back garden.

"There, if I am not mistaken—and I rarely am—is Miss Owen," he said. "Looking especially fierce with all those arrows. Can you manage to snag her without my help?"

With that, he stepped deftly out of the room.

Sebastian muttered a curse. He fumbled for his watch, but it was useless. Nothing had meaning without her.

If you truly wanted her, there'd have been no 'might' about it.

His gaze fell on Faylinn's bow, hanging on the wall.

In that moment, the path was clear.

***

Gwynna would rather fight a horde of invaders than

stand in Sebastian's garden practicing archery. He'd brought her here by force, like a Norman usurper.

Except this wasn't about sovereignty or country.

It was about her heart. Or rather, his. And the wall he built around it.

Loss. That was the key.

Welsh knew better than most how grief wrote upon the soul. Losing his parents had caused Sebastian to guard himself against further loss. She didn't fault him for that.

His heart was here, at Summerlin, where light chased dark and nature did his bidding. Yet she sensed Anglesey had worked its way into him.

Who could stare at that endless sea and not believe that invisible threads connected all humanity? That something eternal transcended centuries and civilizations.

That love, once claimed, was the strongest bond of all.

Yet fate could be cruel, dangling possibilities, only to deny them. Like her mother, she loved a man who could never be her life's mate.

But this time, she wouldn't leave in a cowardly way. She would tell him what was in her heart.

Already, Gwynna felt steadier. She nocked an arrow.

"I fancy a duel."

Sebastian stood there, holding a bow.

"My mother's," he said. "She taught me as a child. After she died, I knew archery couldn't bring her back, and that was too sad a thought to confront every time I picked up the bow. So I stopped."

"Perhaps she's here, in her own way," Gwynna said.

He scoffed. "Ready to give me pointers on form?"

"Nothing so literal. But as long as memory survives, I believe she does."

"It's a notion I'd have resisted weeks ago." He held her gaze. "Now I find I want to hold it fast."

He started toward some trees, walking with purpose. Gwynna hurried after him, and they soon emerged into a meadow. A cottage sat on the far edge.

It had a whimsical thatched roof that curved over the windows like eyebrows. Climbing roses stood out against the white mortar and stone, to charming effect.

"My father used to bring me here," Sebastian said. "At night we'd make a fire and cast shadow figures on the walls. I haven't come here in years. I suppose it's time."

"Time?"

He exhaled. "To stop mourning the past. I've let sorrow rule. Allowed no one close."

"Angus and Elizabeth got close."

Sebastian shot her a rueful smile. "They came when I was a child and couldn't fend them off."

He pointed to a large tree a few dozen yards away. "I propose a contest. The target is just below the junction of that lowest bow and the trunk. Whoever makes the worst shot confesses a secret."

"Discovering your secrets intrigues me," she said.

"I've already confessed to an embarrassing one— afraid to care, and all that. Don't make me say it again. Though I will if you wish it."

Oh.

Her hands weren't entirely steady as she sighted the tree, but she managed the shot. When Sebastian's arrow missed, she couldn't stop a grin. "Your secret, please."

"It's this: There's something odd about your parents' marriage certificate. The designs, the artistry, wouldn't be out of place in the Book of Kells."

Gwynna hitched in a breath. "Is…it not genuine?"

"It is. The mystery is how it came to be embellished. The answer must lie in William's actions after he learned of your mother's death."

Sebastian ran a palm over his bow. "What if your grandfather didn't ignore your mother's note asking him to send for Claremont? After all, it was her last wish."

"Even if he wrote to William of Megan's death, he

wouldn't have asked him to come to Anglesey."

"Little as I knew of William, I don't believe he would have read such a letter and done nothing more," Sebastian said. "I would have taken action. I believe he did, too."

"You...would have gone to Anglesey?"

"In the blink of an eye. Suppose William brought the certificate to your grandfather as proof of the marriage. I'm guessing your grandfather turned him away."

Sadly, he would have, she thought.

"Remember those parchments on Taliesin's wall?" he added. "I think he embellished the certificate for William."

Gwynna frowned. "Why? William had insulted Taliesin by trying to keep your parents from marrying."

"If the woman I...loved was lost to me, and I knew Taliesin could transform the proof of that union into a treasure I could hold across all the sad years to come—"

He cleared his throat. "To possess such a treasure, knowing that the true treasure was forever lost, I'd have groveled before God—and certainly before Taliesin."

The emotion in his voice summoned an image of Sebastian kneeling before Taliesin in his cottage that day, quietly pleading to learn about Faylinn. It was not such a stretch to envision William doing the same.

My grandfather caused such pain," she said. "But I can't change the past. Forgiveness is easier."

"I suppose I should ask forgiveness for forcing you to come here." He paused. "Truthfully, I'd do it again."

Her chin rose.

"It's not because you're my prisoner," he said softly. "It's that I'm yours. I love you, Gwynna. I will say it every day of our lives together, if you'll have me."

Not a single thought came into her head.

Sebastian caught her hand, pulled her over to the cottage, threw open the door.

Stunned, Gwynna stood at the threshold. Why had he brought her here?

Sebastian loved her. Nothing else registered.

Her gaze skimmed over the fireplace, a pantry, a bed along one wall, a pair of boots near the door. It was a spare, but appealing room.

Yet something niggled at her.

The fireplace.

A flag was mounted above the mantel.

Red and yellow squares formed the background. On each stood a lion, its forepaws raised for battle.

The Glendower standard.

***

Ten seconds. Twenty.

She stared at the flag for so long, a paralyzing anxiety seized Sebastian. Had he misjudged? Instinct had guided him, but he was new to all that.

When he'd seen Faylinn's bow on his library wall, he thought of the flag he bought from Mrs. Kendall. It was as if Faylinn was showing him how to bring things full circle.

How to let go of the past—no, how to *build* on it.

Damn. She was crying.

"It's meant to honor you," Sebastian said. "It's my pledge. I will face down a bloody revolution with you if it comes to it. And that spot on the coastal walk in Moelfre would be a fine place to build a home. Marry me, Gwynna."

Gwynna turned to him.

"W-we'll make shadow figures on the wall." She spoke into his chest, her voice muffled. "I will tell you stories of Owen and of Arthur and—"

Scarcely daring to breathe, he gently tipped her face up. "That's yes? To marriage—is your answer *yes*?"

That blue diamond gaze pinned him. "It is."

And there, in her eyes, Sebastian saw what must have captured William's shriveled soul.

Love, into infinity.

And yet.

"There's one thing," he said. "It's this feelings

335

business. They've come to matter."

Her gaze didn't falter. "You wish to know mine."

That was the woman he loved. Who faced things squarely, who'd taught him to.

"I mistook your character at first, but that's your doing, since you set out to deceive," Gwynna said. "And perhaps you mistook mine, for I am not so wedded to myth and fanciful tales that I miss what's true and real."

Sebastian arched a brow.

"Rather, I *am,* somewhat," she amended. "But you are not the superficial aristocrat I met on the moor. Your character is inestimable—"

"Dear God," Sebastian muttered.

"You are responsible and dedicated and—"

"Therefore, the most boring man in England," he growled. "The last thing I want is a character reference."

She smiled. "You have my heart. That you give yours moves me beyond words."

"A first."

"Oh, I have many words, Englishman. And I mean for the world to hear them. I shall proclaim my love for you from the top of Castell Mawr."

"Egad," he said. But his pulse raced.

Gwynna pulled out her dagger.

"Here are my words: 'Behold Sebastian Traherne, an Englishman who risks his heart for love. By such daring doth he gain favor with the line of Owen Glendower, the last true Welsh prince. I claim him as mine.'"

"Excessive, I think." But he couldn't suppress a thrill.

She touched the dagger to her heart. "And all the spirits who have ever lived and those yet to come will hear my words until the end of time."

Gwynna pressed her lips to his. "But our love will live long past that, for time itself is but a trick of magic."

Flowery stuff, that Welsh madness.

Ah, but it seized him, then—madness and magic and

fairies dancing on a moonlit night.
And the hole in his heart was no more.

***

Epilogue

Six months later.

I am afraid I have bad news, Mrs. MacDuff."

Hannah looked up from her knitting.

"It's about that man who tormented you," Angus said.

The knitting fell from her lap. "Cyrus has found me?"

"It's rather that I have found him." He ought not to spin this out. But part of him wanted to gauge her reaction.

Oh, he knew she hadn't been drawn to Cyrus beyond that first curiosity. Still, Angus could see how it might have been. In her younger days, she was eager and fetching, before time put that hard shell on her.

That was nothing to how she was now, so lovely in her maturity it made his heart skip a beat.

And that hard shell? To see it soften was a pleasure beyond compare.

She eyed him sternly. "Tell me this instant."

How he loved Hannah's orders. He loved how she came at him with that defiant bent, drawing a line in the sand—knowing that he would step over it, or dare her to.

One of them would have to surrender, and their journey would have twists and turns until it arrived at that ineffable moment when surrender and taking merged.

Obsession had blossomed into a love so beautiful, he might try his hand at poetry. Surely, there was no other way to express what filled him when he looked into her eyes and saw the one person in the world meant for him.

She was still frowning.

"Found him in Oxford. Seems like he ended a stone's

throw from Miss Abernathy's School. I was researching a site for Sebastian's new orphan charity and—"

"Ended? You mean—"

"He's in a graveyard near Christ Church Cathedral." Angus took her hand. "He'll not bother you again. Even if he still walked this earth I would say the same. I would not let anything happen to you, nor any man cause you harm or pain as long as I have breath."

The frown remained. "Only a woman with her eyes blind to the world's realities could believe such a pledge."

Angus pulled her to her feet. "Kiss me. Then tell me what is real."

Hannah's flushed features bespoke surrender. Next time it would be his turn, but for now…

"You put me in mind of a Burns poem, Mrs. MacDuff," he murmured into her ear. "A naughty one."

She looked up at him. "I'll hear it, if you please."

"It's Scots dialect," Angus cautioned. "You wouldn't understand the words."

Her lips pursed. "You'll explain them to me."

"The poem is called 'Nine Inch Will Please a Lady.' It's, ah, metaphor. There's a reference or two to battering rams, if you catch my drift."

Her eyes widened. "Oh, my."

Curse it all. He'd shocked her. He hadn't meant to be coarse.

Hannah's lips curved in a saucy smile.

And he was done.

END

Author's Note:

The Anglesey tomb where Gwynna and Sebastian spent a rainy night is Bryn Celli Ddu, the Mound in the Dark Grove. Unlike some of its tourist-infested kin elsewhere, this place is quietly waiting for you to discover it.

Amble down a country lane, over a footpath, and through a grove of trees into open farmland. See the barrow emerge like a sleeping giant awakening. Cross the sunken henge ditch to the mound. Enter the passage to discover the mysterious spiral-carved pillar at the center. On the summer solstice, the rising sun follows you in.

You'll wonder about the people who lived thousands of years ago. Alas, their story is lost to prehistory.

But perhaps history doesn't have to be written to be felt. Go, then, to Anglesey.

See the bay that swallows the shore at high tide. See the lifesaving station with the great orange boat that rushes out to save those caught unawares. In the Moelfre ice cream parlor, pick up a book on Welsh battles and legends.

Wander along the coastal path and see tiny offshore islands where gulls and seals sun themselves. Contemplate the fluffy white clouds reflecting off sun-dappled waves as far as the eye can see.

You may come to feel that the past never truly vanishes, that we are the product of all who came before. That while their time may end, something yet lives on in that endless horizon.

That love never dies, but ripples outward like those waves—and returns.

Books by Eileen Putman

Historical Romances:

League of Rogues series: Daring English lords who risk all for their country. Hardened and deadly, they have no use for love—until it ensnares them...

King of Hearts

Not for nothing is Gabriel Sinclair known as the King of Hearts. He's never met a woman he couldn't captivate. He shuns hopeless causes and any whiff of permanence.

Widowed Louisa Peabody tolerates no man's touch. She devotes herself to helping women in need, and persuades Gabriel to help her stage a daring rescue. Can she protect herself from that wild, reckless fire in his eyes?

(Read on for an excerpt.)

Regency Romances:

Love in Disguise: Daring masquerades, with love as the prize:

The Perfect Bride
The Dastardly Duke
A Passionate Performance
Reforming Harriet

King of Hearts

Prologue

Spring 1815
London

He wasn't about to traipse all over London looking for virgins.

Not as long as Our Lady of Mercy convent lay cheek by jowl with the Market Street dock, where his newly acquired boat bobbed in waters swollen by high tide. With any luck, he could be on his way before the tide went out.

Like most of the ladies Gabriel Sinclair met, luck danced to his tune. This very night, luck had dealt him a perfect vingt-et-un, while the Earl of Sedbury had gone bust trying to improve on his puny pair of sevens — thereby gifting Gabriel with the earl's trim little yacht. Luck had not given him the courage to sneak into a convent full of sleeping nuns, but Gabriel had found that in the earl's wine.

The gnarled gypsy who had emerged from the midnight shadows as a glum Sedbury was showing him around the boat would have given any man pause. An ageless wisdom inhabited her wrinkled face, and her eyes gleamed with fury.

"Death," she intoned, pointing her bony finger at them. "Death seeks to bring you into his bosom. Bring me a lock of hair from a virgin's head, taken without harm, given without regret. Only then will death loose his grip on your soul."

Sedbury had shooed the woman away. "They haunt the docks," he grumbled. "It's that new prison hulk. Too close by half. Draws the riff-raff." He eyed the yacht wistfully. "Always meant to move her upriver."

They had shared a laugh at the old woman's attempt to scare them. Then a strange light had come into Sedbury's eyes, and the wine had flowed anew, and the gypsy's words became a reckless new bet that sent each man reeling drunkenly into the night in search of a lock of hair from a virgin, one of the scarcest commodities in all London.

The gypsy's curse hadn't bothered Gabriel. He was not afraid of death. In the years since leaving England for Jamaica, he had beaten that black angel more times than he could count. Boredom alone unsettled him, for it left him face to face with a man he did not care to visit long.

Besides, the gypsy had it wrong. Luck, not death, embraced him tonight. Luck had caused him to wander past this convent, thereby showing him the means of winning the new wager and depriving the earl of his London townhouse, the stakes Sedbury had put up in his desperate bid to regain his boat. But desperate men made unwise bets. The earl would never find a virgin at this hour, when chaste women slept peacefully in their own beds.

Gabriel suppressed a yawn. What did he need with Sedbury's house, anyway? He didn't intend to remain in England, though it might be diverting to sample the life he could have had if he'd been dealt a different hand years ago. A boat was all he needed. With it, he could bid the past farewell as sweetly as these sleeping maidens had said their evening prayers.

In the darkened convent bedchamber, he surveyed them. They were young — novitiates, perhaps. A veritable bevy of virgins. And none of them had thought to latch the front door. A trusting group, indeed.

Which would he choose? Gabriel studied their sleeping forms, forever removed from the world of men. He imagined them in the secular world, dressed in fine gowns and jewels, their hair piled high atop their heads and secured with combs of finest ivory. They would fan themselves coyly, each daring him to choose her. Would he select the blonde, the chestnut-haired, or the chit with the riot of auburn curls?

He usually had his pick, for women adored him. They

were all alike: vain and prideful and needy. Even nuns, he suspected, had their vanity.

Gabriel slipped his knife from the slim leather holder he always wore under his waistcoat. He moved quickly past the bed of one young woman whose breathing was shallow and uneven — much too light a sleeper. He passed two others whose nightcaps obscured their hair. At last, he came to a young woman whose single blonde braid lay invitingly on the pillow. She snored so loudly that nothing short of cannon fire would wake her.

He stared at the knife and briefly wondered whether he'd lost his mind. A lock of hair from a virgin's head, taken without harm, given without regret. He didn't believe in the gypsy's words, but he did believe in fate that masqueraded as luck. For the moment, he would be its pawn.

Gingerly, he lifted the braid, feeling its weight, judging its substance. He could certainly take it without harm; he wasn't sure about the regret part. Then again, the girl could hardly regret what she didn't know. He shifted the knife to his right hand and bent over her.

"What are you doing?"

Gabriel froze. Carefully, he turned toward the voice. The girl he had pegged as a light sleeper sat upright, staring at him. "What are you doing to Mary?"

She looked just groggy enough that sleep still had a few tentacles in her. He pitched his voice low, so as not to wake the others. "Blessing her, of course." He was surprised that his words sounded slurred. Perhaps he should have left the cork in that second bottle.

"But —"

"Keep your voice down." He tried for a note of command, but a whisper had its limitations. "It is forbidden to speak," he improvised.

The girl hesitated. "Who are you?"

"Gabriel." Here, of all places, that name should carry weight.

344

Apparently, it did. She stared. "The...angel?"

"Archangel," he recklessly volunteered.

"You do not look like an angel."

Insolent chit. "Appearances can be deceiving." He still held the sleeping girl's braid. If his annoyingly persistent questioner would just look the other way...

"What is that thing in your hand?" Her gaze was riveted on the knife, though the room was dark enough he doubted she could make it out distinctly.

"It's a, er, wand." Did angels carry wands? No, that was fairies. Hell.

The girl stared at him in stunned silence. Suddenly, her eyes widened.

"A knife! You've got a knife!"

"Quiet, brat," he growled. That did not sound very angelic. Well, he might as well have something to show for this night's labors. In one swift movement, he sliced off the sleeping Mary's braid. She never stopped snoring.

"Murderer!" the other girl shrieked.

Even as he dashed down the stairs, Gabriel heard footsteps on the landing.

"Mother Dolores! Help! Come quickly!" The answering screams of the others as they awoke rose in a jarring harmony that would have waked the dead.

When he gained the street, Gabriel looked wildly around. He had not planned for this. Sedbury's carriage was long gone, the traitor. Gabriel had no means of escape except his own two feet, and they were looking strangely blurred at the moment.

Suddenly, his gaze lit on a dray cart and horse standing placidly across the way. No sign of a driver. Once again, luck had intervened. He sprinted across the street, took a moment to tuck the braid safely into his pocket, and grabbed the reins.

But as he flicked them smartly on the horse's rump, a flock of nightgown-clad young women and one fire-breathing dragon of a Mother Superior in a hideous red nightcap streamed into the street. They threw themselves in front of the horse.

"Stop!" shrieked the dragon lady — the worthy Mother Dolores, no doubt. She clutched a chamber pot and waved it wildly at the horse. Like baby chicks following the mother hen, the novitiates raised their arms, too. And just like that, the street was filled with a mob of flailing, screaming females in high-necked night-rails.

Gabriel had a sinking feeling his luck had turned.

The horse did a nervous sideways dance and tried to rear, something no self-respecting dray nag would do. The women ran toward him — didn't they have better sense than to race into the path of a thrashing horse?

He jerked on the reins, forcing the horse to still. The horse shuffled backward, trying to ease the pressure of the bit. Gabriel bent forward just as the nag's tail whipped up and caught the corner of his eye. The searing pain brought tears to his eyes.

"My hair! He cut off my hair!" cried a young woman he took to be Mary, awake at last.

"Quiet, child!" cried Mother Dolores, whose nightcap dipped perilously low over one eye. She turned to Gabriel. "You shall die for this, you scoundrel. They will hang you forthwith, and I shall be among the spectators."

"Now, now," Gabriel warned. His eye hurt like hell, and he was in no mood for vengeful nuns. "You must set a proper example, Mother. Charity and forgiveness and all that."

Mother Dolores stared at him. "What sort of monster are you?"

"He claimed he was an angel," said the girl who had first discovered him.

"I see." Her face was grim. "Matilde, fetch the Watch."

"That is not necessary," Gabriel assured her. "I was on the point of leaving." Shielding his injured eye, he jumped down, squinting as he searched for a path through the sea of women. But their flailing forms pressed against him, forming a human wall.

Imprisoned by virgins. Was there anything more lowering?

"Ladies, step aside," he thundered, trying his best to sound archangelic. "My work here is done. The, er, heavens demand my return." He saw the indecision in their eyes. Almost, he had them. Then the dragon lady intervened.

"Sit on him, girls!" she commanded.

As one, the young women wrestled him to the cobblestones and planted themselves on him.

"Now, angel," she scoffed, waving the chamber pot at him. "Let's see you fly away."

"Alas, 'tis the molting season," Gabriel managed, forcing air through his badly compressed lungs. "My wings have been clipped."

"More than clipped, you heartless villain. Your goose, sir, is cooked!" With that, Mother Dolores brought the chamber pot down on his head.

Yes, virgins were nothing but trouble. He would never go near one again.

Chapter One

"The hanging is at noon," said a gruff masculine voice.

"I do hope Miss Wentworth will be brave." Louisa Peabody tied a black scarf over her hair, obscuring flaxen gold so gleaming it could be seen from a distance. She shrugged into a man's dark jacket several sizes too large. Then she placed a cap over the scarf and checked her appearance in the dingy tack room mirror. "I am afraid this is the best I can do."

The man at her side inspected her dark breeches, boots, and coat. When his gaze reached her head covering, he frowned uncertainly.

"Do not worry, David," she said. "I have tied the scarf

tight. Not a strand of my hair is visible. Besides, I will be inside the carriage."

David Ferguson was a man of considerable size but few words. Although he did not reply, the tension in his jaw was answer enough. Louisa made one last effort to assuage his doubts. "Alice Wentworth has no one, David. All she did was steal a loaf of bread to feed her child. We must help her."

Their gazes met in pain shared and remembered. Then, without a word, David walked out to the carriage.

"Be careful," warned the only other occupant of the stable, a boy of about twelve. Holding the halter of a big black stallion, he regarded Louisa with a mixture of determination and doubt. The weight of nascent masculinity sat uncertainly upon his slender shoulders. "I still say you ought to let me go. Midnight and I could cut through a crowd like a knife through butter."

Louisa shook her head. "Midnight is too high-strung, and he is not yet ready to be ridden again. Besides," she added gently, "you are too young, Sam."

"If you got caught..." His voice, straddling the cusp of manhood, wavered.

"We will not."

"The last time —"

"Was unfortunate. But we learn from our mistakes. Do not worry. David will take care of me." She gave him a quick smile, then followed David out to the carriage.

***

His head was in the noose. Any moment, now, the executioner would release the lever on the scaffold and send him on a permanent trip to the Great Beyond. He supposed he should be filled with despair, but he felt nothing. Only a vast emptiness, far more desolate than the possibility of death.

The crowd was enormous, no doubt due to that nun's embellishments at his brief trial, which had been reported in all the newspapers. "Fallen Angel," the headlines had called him. It wouldn't surprise him if she was out there somewhere, waiting for him to die.

Through his suffocating hood, he could hear the impatient shouts, the jeers. A great clamoring mass of humanity had gathered outside Newgate to watch the life jerked out of him in the gruesome satisfaction of justice.

If there was any real justice in the world, those nuns would pay for their lies. They had made him out to be a rapist and attempted murderer. No wonder his trial had taken less than an hour.

Ah, well. The life of a scoundrel was mercifully short. And the life of a clumsy drunk with the stupidity to invade a convent armed with a knife even shorter.

In truth, many of the details of that night eluded him. He remembered the chamber pot being brought down on his head, then darkness. Still, a blow like that would not account for the gaps in his memory. He'd awoken in pain, chained to a wall in a dark cell crawling with vermin. He must have been beaten, for the darkness and pain entwined in him, leaving shadowy images of a thick beam brought down across his shoulders and many fists and implements applied to his person.

One day they had cleaned him up and brought him to the Old Bailey, where he could not summon enough brainpower even to speak his name or account for the circumstances that brought him there. Only after he saw the head nun — Mother Dolores, she styled herself — and listened to her vivid testimony had shreds of memories returned. Pieces were still missing, for a well-dressed Lord Something-or-other testified about events for which he similarly had no recollection; apparently he tried to steal his lordship's yacht.

Surely, the witnesses had exaggerated. Whatever his crimes, they could not be so heinous as attempted murder, rape, fraudulent taking of his lordship's yacht, and the theft of a cart and horse. He might be a scoundrel, but he was fairly certain he had no taste for crimes such as those.

Justice being what it was, his protestations of innocence mattered not. With no recollection of his actions, he could not supply a convincing alibi; nor could he summon character witnesses, having no memory even of his own name.

So he was here on the scaffold, a mere two days after his trial, wishing he could recall whatever it was he should know to prevent his imminent journey into Hell.

"Save yerself, angel!" jeered a voice.

"Fly away, angel," ridiculed another. "Fly on to heaven."

A chorus of laughter rose from the crowd. He felt the executioner check the ropes that bound his hands. Snug and tight. No way out there. He heard the man speak to the magistrate. He couldn't make out the words, but his imagination easily supplied them:

I'll let him swing long enough to please the crowds, then hand him over to that surgeon who's been after me to give him something for that anatomy class of his. Did you want him to suffer a bit first, my lord? Those nuns seemed awfully upset.

By all means, Executioner, let the bugger suffer. I've seen the way you snap that platform down, and if you do it just right, their necks don't break right away and they hang there reaching with their toes, trying to gain a purchase as the air sucks out of them. The crowd loves that.

Well, he was always one to please the crowds. And this was better than that new treadmill invention he had been threatened with, the cylinder of steps that had to be walked until one dropped. Better to die from hanging than boredom.

He supposed he should say a few words to his Maker, but he doubted anyone up there would hear him. Still, it was worth a shot.

I was looking forward to taking up residence at

Sedbury's townhouse. Might have turned respectable, made something of my life, taken a seat in Parliament.

Sedbury's townhouse? Parliament? Where had those thoughts come from?

Could've turned all those lords against slavery, told them about Jamaica and the plantations.

Jamaica. Another memory teased his brain.

What's that? Yes, I know it's late to make promises. No, I don't mean a word of them. Hell, the last thing I want is a home.

He knew in his bones that last was true. No home, no family. Never again.

More memories seeped from the recesses of his mind. Perhaps his own name would join them. Surely, he was someone. Surely, he knew people who could vouch for him.

Abruptly, the floor beneath him shuddered. No time, then. Apparently there was no one Up There to hear the ramblings of a doomed man. He tried to swallow, but the noose cinched him, closing his throat. *I wouldn't have minded one last chance…*

A cheer went up from the crowd. Bloodthirsty buggers. He had barely formed the thought when his feet left the ground.

Excited shrieks came from somewhere, probably the vicinity of Mother Dolores. The rope cut into his neck, shooting dizzying pain through him. He could not breathe. His hands wanted to claw at the thing that was choking the life out of him. But they were bound, and it was only in his dreams that he grabbed the rope and flung it off, restoring blessed air to his lungs.

Soon he would slip the knot of his human misery.

The cheers of the crowd faded into oblivion. He heard a strange slashing noise. Felt a jerk. The noose released its hold, and he floated heavenward to his final reward.

Heaven was deuced uncomfortable, though. Heaven felt like a man's strong arms pulling him through the air, depositing him unceremoniously on his head on the floor of a carriage. Heaven sounded like a man's confused curse and a woman's urgent admonition as a blanket was flung over him and the vehicle lurched forward with angry shouts in pursuit.

He should have known he would go straight to Hell. How else to describe the sensation of being slammed about, blind to his surroundings save for the pain? His neck felt as if it had been seared by flames. His air-deprived lungs struggled for breath.

Every time he tried to right his bruised body, a booted foot pushed firmly on his posterior and a woman's sharp voice cut through his misery. "Stay down!"

He stayed down. He would not risk the ire of this Mistress of Hell. But he longed to remove the oppressive hood, to take in enough air to banish the dizziness that threatened his mind's thin hold on the events around him. The jostling of the carriage and the burning in his lungs and neck were his only reality.

Was this Heaven or Hell? Maybe there was no difference, after all.

At last, the carriage rolled to a stop, and someone lifted the blanket that covered him. He heard the woman gasp as her hands removed his hood.

"You are not Miss Wentworth!" She turned to the Goliath who suddenly appeared outside the carriage door. "It is a man, David, a man!"

She removed the cap from her head and a black scarf that had hidden hair the color of spun gold. But that was not what rendered him speechless. It was her eyes, which regarded him with a mixture of fury and confusion and which were as deep and bottomless and blue as the sea on a cloudless day. And the tiny birthmark that sat between her upper lip and the tip of her nose.

Hair kissed by the sun. Eyes bluer than blue. A small, tantalizing mark above her lip. If Heaven had angels like this, he had come to the right place.

"Madam," he rasped, his voice all but destroyed by the hangman's noose, "will you marry me?" He gave a wild, mirthless laugh as the world around him faded to black.

***

Louisa stared at the limp form at her feet. "What in the name of all that is holy am I to do?"

David shrugged. "Take him home, I suppose." He climbed back up to his perch and with a flick of the reins sent the team of horses barreling down the road.

Louisa crossed her arms and stared out the window, trying to look anywhere except at the motionless man on the floor. But outside held only trees and grass and the occasional cow. At her feet was the scourge of her sex.

A man. And from the look and sound of him, an insolent, puffed-up, arrogant, shameless example of the breed. Madam, will you marry me? Mad hubris, indeed. Facing death had not humbled him. Doubtless he had deserved his death sentence.

And she, of all people, had saved him.

He lay on his side, filling the floor space between the seats and then some. Louisa curled her legs under her to avoid touching him and then decided that in his current state he would scarcely know if she rested her feet on his back.

His hands were still bound, and his body jostled roughly as the carriage raced over the road. Senseless, he was hardly a danger to her, so she reached down and tried to loosen his stiff bindings. At last she freed his hands, and they flopped limply at his sides. There was nothing harmless about their size, however. They were of a piece with that broad back; his shirt fabric strained across the wide expanse of muscle and bone.

The man they had saved was strong and dangerous. A criminal, likely a killer. Yet even if he had been none of those things, Louisa would have hated him on sight.

***

Gabriel awoke to find the giant towering over him. The man was six and a half feet, if he was an inch. His face bore deep, irregular scars, as if unskilled hands had chipped his features out of stubborn granite. His hair was dark, his chin bearded, and he resembled a savage ogre who feasted on naughty children and wayward princesses in fearsome fables. The man studied him from his impossible height, his face as expressive as stone.

His angel sat in a chair beside a hearth with a blazing fire. Her hands were crossed primly in her lap. She held herself stiffly and regarded him with an icy gaze. That long, golden hair flowed around her like a halo.

"Who are you?" Her voice was as dry and brittle as dead leaves.

He was lying on the floor. Not the way to meet an angel. It put him at a distinct disadvantage, for though he was not as tall as the giant, he could certainly stand as straight. And a man on his feet thought better than a man on his posterior.

Gabriel tried to rise. He struggled to his knees, pushed off from his hands, and tried to heave himself up. But he was weaker than he thought. Like a babe whose reach exceeds his grasp, he fell backward onto the floor.

He ached all over. His neck felt as if it was belted in edged steel. His lungs could not take in enough air. His stomach lurched queasily.

An encroaching blackness clawed at him, narrowing his sight to a pinpoint of light, pulling him into the blessedness of oblivion. And though he fought it, his brain felt fuzzy, as if it was packed in cotton wool.

"Name," he murmured, fighting off the blackness. He had to know her name.

"I am Louisa Peabody," she said crisply.

"Lu-we-sa Pe-body." He tried to say it, but his tongue seemed twisted. He must be hallucinating.

"Who are you?" she demanded.

"King," he managed.

"King?" He heard the note of puzzlement in her tone. "Mr. King?"

"Not mister," he said thickly. "King — Majesty."

He grinned. It was a little joke — bitter as sin, and too much work to explain, even if he could recall the details. Perhaps his joke would drive that chill from her voice.

"You are a king?"

He nodded, pleased that she understood. Too bad her features kept blurring around the edges. His eyes must be crossed, for her nose kept moving around on her face. It would be difficult to rivet her with one of his meaningful stares. Mistresses of Hell were probably impervious to masculine charm anyway.

Frowning, he tried to conjure the elusive memory at the edge of his awareness. He vaguely remembered talking to someone — or something — about mending his ways.

Where was he now? Among the living or the dead?

"The only king we have is old George," she said. "You do not look anything like him."

Mad George in Hell, too? He hadn't heard that the king had cocked up his toes, but then Newgate prisoners led a sheltered existence.

"Not George." His voice slurred. "Gabriel." That much had come back to him. Perhaps, there would be more.

"King Gabriel." She rolled the words around on her tongue. "Pray, what are you king of?"

He heard the derision in her tone. Gabriel looked up at her from his lowly position on the floor. She was studying him, her head tilted to one side, waiting. The firelight caught the lights in her hair and sent their shimmering warmth straight to his gut, a spear of heat that threatened a mortal wound. He tried to say the words that burned in his befogged brain.

"Take you there," he vowed.

A large booted toe nudged him in the ribs. He had forgotten about the giant. Gabriel ignored the man and smiled at her.

Her eyes filled with uncertainty. Good. He had her interest — much better than her contempt. Conquest would be his. Unless she really was an angel.

She turned toward the giant. "You had best fetch the doctor."

No doctor, Gabriel wanted to say. He was better now. He might even be alive. He raised his head, tried to speak. "Island. King of island," he said weakly.

Lu-we-sa Pe-body eyed him in disgust, then rose and left the room. The monster lifted him off the floor as if he were a sack of feathers, carted him up some stairs, and tossed him onto a soft feather bed. As Gabriel sank gratefully into it, letting the darkness take him, the man bent down close to his ear.

"And I," the giant snarled contemptuously, "am Queen Charlotte."

***

"What happened to Alice Wentworth?" Louisa eyed David worriedly.

"'Pears they thought this one" — he jerked his thumb skyward, indicating the upstairs where the stranger slept — "needed killing first."

"But...didn't they publish the list of executions?"

"Aye, and she was on it." He shrugged. "Wasn't until I'd driven us into the thick of things that I got a good look at the prisoner. By then, I'd cut the rope and the mongrel was falling into my arms. Nothing for it but to grab him and get out before the crowd closed in."

David had had all he could do to control the team and speed them away from the angry mob. Louisa hadn't wanted to take the cumbersome carriage, but after the debacle with Midnight at Violet's rescue, David had not wanted her to risk exposure. And so she'd sat helpless and protected inside while the mission went terribly awry. Never again, she vowed, would she abdicate her responsibility.

"Do you think they will proceed with her hanging?"

David shook his head. "Not for a while. Too much confusion after today."

Louisa paced the parlor in frustration. "Let us hope she is safe for now. In the meantime, what is to be done with him?"

David said nothing. There was no need. They both knew that no man had occupied a bed at Peabody Manor since her father moved away to the Continent. And Richard had not lived to do so. The fact that a heinous criminal now slept the sleep of the blameless upstairs was almost incomprehensible.

"I can't have a man here, David," she said in a wobbly voice. "You know that."

"Aye," he said softly. His hand came up, hovered over her trembling shoulders for a moment, then fell to his side without touching her. "We could put him in the dower house, but we couldn't watch him there. Besides, he is ill and can nae do ye harm."

David understood her fears, accepted them. "I will keep ye safe, lass," he added.

Louisa knew he would, as far as it was in his power to do so. But long ago she had learned that the only help for a woman alone in the world was her own two hands — and that was rarely enough. Women could not control their own money, much less their fate. They were married off to benefit the family's coffers, sold like chattel to the highest bidder.

Her father had traded her to a man with a charming smile and a soul as dark as the devil's. She had despised them both for making her an object to be bartered, no better than a whore. But she had survived, and adversity had made her strong. She had put the past behind her and devoted herself to helping women who couldn't help themselves.

There were no men in her life, save David. She was pleased with her carefully constructed world — as long as there was no reminder that it might topple in an instant if some clever male decided to apply himself to the task.

The man upstairs had to go. Besides being a criminal, he had the look of trouble — too charming by half, even fresh from the hangman's noose. A rakish brow bespoke devilish intentions under that tousled red hair. Green eyes glittered with daring and dash and promises never to be fulfilled. A self-mocking mouth hinted of devilish secrets.

Take her to his island, indeed. Nonsense uttered in the heady exultation of escaping a fate he had undoubtedly deserved.

A king, was he?

Aye, king of a thousand hearts he had doubtless broken. Louisa's gaze narrowed. She knew the breed well.

<u>Keep reading!</u>

www.eileenputman.com